LONG J(

Home

MW00806050

LONG JOURNEY
Home

A HOPE SPRINGS NOVEL

SARAH M. EDEN

Copyright © 2018 by Sarah M. Eden

All rights reserved. No part of this book may be reproduced in any form whatsoever without prior written permission of the publisher, except in the case of brief passages embodied in critical reviews and articles. This is a work of fiction. The characters, names, incidents, places, and dialogue are products of the author's imagination and are not to be construed as real.

Interior design by Heather Justesen
Edited by Annette Lyon and Lisa Shepherd

Cover design by Mirror Press, LLC, and Rachael Anderson
Cover image © Sandra Cunningham / Trevillion Images

Published by Mirror Press, LLC

ISBN-13: 978-1-947152-29-8

Dedicated to Josephine, 1857–1860

Chapter One

MARCH 1873

In New York City, only the wealthy could afford to truly live, and only the wealthy could truly afford to die. Maura O'Connor was nearly as poor as possible and was quickly growing as ill. She'd a son to raise with hardly a penny to her name. There was little to spare for doctors or medicines or being too sick to work.

She'd pinched together what money she could to bring in a doctor, desperate for answers she dreaded hearing. Her wheezing, difficult breaths sounded like Jenny's had, and like Mary Elizabeth's and countless other women's she'd worked with for long years in the cotton mill. The cough sounded as theirs had *early on*. She knew where they'd all ended. She needed to know if that was where she was headed.

She sat in the silence of her one-room tenement, waiting to hear her fate. After drawn-out moments listening to her breathe and asking questions about her symptoms, Dr. Dahl sat back in a rickety chair across from her. His expression was not one of relief.

"Is it brown lung?" she asked.

He simply nodded.

"But I've not worked in the factory for months." Her lungs were the reason she'd left. Cleaning houses didn't pay as well, and the work wasn't as steady, but she'd not known what else to do to avoid the same fate as Jenny and Mary Elizabeth.

"Sometimes, Mrs. O'Connor, a person leaves the factories too late, after the damage has been done." He began packing up his instruments. Dr. Dahl was the only man of medicine who frequented the tenements of the poor in this area of the city. He charged little, but that meant he could not afford to spend very much time with each patient.

"Are you quite certain, then? I won't get better?"

He shook his head. "Once the cotton gets into your lungs, it doesn't leave. And so long as it's in there, it takes a toll."

"Will my condition grow worse?" Heavens, she hadn't that luxury.

"Only time will tell you that." He stood. "In a few more weeks, I can listen again."

"I'll not have money enough for another visit so soon." She'd likely need nearly a year to tuck away enough for his admittedly modest fee.

He offered a brief look of sincere empathy. "Once you are able, I'll check on you. But in all honesty, you will likely already know by then."

Her heart stopped a moment. "How will I know?" Did he mean her lungs would be worse? Or that she would be dead?

"If your symptoms have not changed in the next few months, then this is likely where the disease will remain *for a time.*"

"What do you mean by 'for a time'?" A breath wheezed in, then pushed back out with a cough. "Will I grow worse no matter what?"

He hesitated in the doorway. "Nothing can reverse the damage already done. You may live many years with little more than this cough and a bit of tightness in your lungs, or you may deteriorate quickly. I cannot predict the timeline with any certainty, but you *will* eventually grow worse. Nothing can stop that."

She knew she was taking more of his time than her meager payment justified, but she needed answers. "Can it be slowed?"

"To a degree, yes, if you take care of yourself." he said. "Send for me if you grow worse or contract a cold or anything else that impacts your lungs. A bit of medicine to help you through rough patches may grant you more time."

She could afford neither to call the doctor again nor to buy medicine, not when she struggled to put food on the table, or to replace the clothes her son outgrew or the shoes he wore holes through.

"I have a son. He's only fourteen."

The doctor's solemn expression remained unchanged. "Send for me when things change. Proper medical care is your only real chance."

When things change. Her heart dropped to her toes. *When.*

He stepped into the corridor and tipped his hat to someone just out of sight. In the next moment, Maura's neighbor Eliza appeared in the doorway, her little baby, Lydia, in her arms. She watched the doctor walk away before turning back to Maura, concern in her eyes.

"You've had the doctor in?" Eliza eyed her with concern. "What did he say? Good news, I hope." After Eliza had first arrived, Maura had needed time to grow accustomed to the sound of an English accent. Eliza hadn't a truly proper manner of speaking, having come from circumstances as humble as Maura's.

"He offered me a few things I might do to feel better." 'Twas a bit of a stretching of the truth, but she wasn't ready to talk about how little hope he'd left her with. "Come inside."

She closed the door behind her friend and reached immediately for the baby. Eliza set her wee one in Maura's arms.

"Hello there, sweet Lydia." Maura tucked the blanket more securely around the baby. "Have you a smile for your godmother?"

Lydia was too sleepy for anything but a few slow blinks.

Eliza watched Lydia a moment before turning to Maura. "Would I be imposing on you too much if I left her here with you for a spell while I rush to the market?"

"Not imposing at all. And my Aidan'll be home in a bit. You know he loves when little ones come for a visit."

"You've both been so good to us." Sadness touched Eliza's eyes. "I don't know what we would do without you."

Maura shifted Lydia so she rested against her shoulder then set her free arm around her friend's shoulders. "We love you, Eliza. And we love your Lydia. You bring us joy. So don't you ever feel like a burden. Not you, and not Lydia. Not ever."

Eliza's answering smile was a bit tremulous. "Lydia is certainly fond of you."

"Of course she is." Maura stepped away enough to give Eliza room to compose herself. "Lydia and I've known each other from the very beginning." Maura had acted as midwife at Lydia's birth, the fifteenth she'd overseen in this tiny tenement building over the past eight years. "The Widows' Tower," the locals called it. An old, worn-down building, too shabby for even immigrant families in such a poor section of the city, it had become a refuge for destitute widows simply trying to survive. Some came with children, others alone, and in particularly heartbreaking instances, some arrived while carrying a child to be born without a living father.

"Please give Aidan a hug from me," Eliza said. "He's seemed sad lately."

"He has," Maura acknowledged. "But Lydia will lift his spirits, I'm certain."

"I thank you, Maura," Eliza said. "I'll not be long."

"Don't you fret. We'll be grand."

After Eliza slipped out, Maura rocked Lydia, who rested against her shoulder. The little one had grown heavy and lax with sleep. Maura walked from one end of the room to the other, a journey of only ten steps. She gently rubbed Lydia's back. Now five months old, she was finally beginning to sleep well. Poor Eliza had been stretched to her very limit since Lydia's birth. Many a night Maura had walked the floor of Eliza's tiny room above her, trying to keep the colicky newborn quiet and soothed enough for her exhausted mother to get a bit of sleep.

Maura knew what it was to be alone in this world with a child to care for. She remembered clearly the fear that had followed her those first months and years. She saw it daily in the faces of the other women in the tower. 'Twas likely in her eyes again now.

Proper medical care is your only real hope.

She couldn't begin to afford it. She and Aidan both worked, but their combined income only just covered the necessities, and sometimes not even them. She'd not an extra penny to her name.

A cough rattled through her and, with it, a deep, searing pain. She tensed against the urge, trying her utmost not to wake the baby. Her cough had been agonizing these past months.

And it'll not ever go away.

Her goal, then, was simply to not grow worse too quickly. She had to find a means of securing medical care. In the first few years after Grady died, she'd sold everything of value they owned. Anything remaining they needed or couldn't hope to get any money from.

Except . . .

A wave of dread crashed over her. One thing Maura owned would fetch a good price. One precious, treasured item. Heaven help her, how could she part with it?

Careful of Lydia, she crossed to the bureau that acted as clothes press, kitchen cupboard, and linen chest. She pulled open one of the small drawers on the top row.

A quick shifting of rags and cloths revealed the drawstring bag she sought. She clutched it tightly in her free hand, removed it from its safekeeping, and pushed the drawer closed with her hip.

She set Lydia in the make-shift cradle Aidan had helped her fashion from discarded bits of wood two years ago. Nearly all the babies who'd lived in the building since had slept in the tiny bed at one time or another.

Maura moved as quietly as she could to the table and sat. With shaking hands, she tugged at the top of the bag, slowly pulling it open. 'Twasn't a large bag, neither was it full, yet it contained items more precious to her than all the gold in the world. She peered inside. Beside two hinged leather frames and atop a neatly folded handkerchief, lay a simple, thin gold ring.

She carefully pulled it out, holding it tightly between her finger and thumb. The dim light spilling through windows, made dingy by the grime of the city, glinted off the metal. She'd stopped wearing the ring when she'd first begun working in the factory nearly eight years earlier. Too many horrifying, whispered tales had reached her about what happened to hands and fingers when unyielding rings grew entangled in the unforgiving machinery.

That long-ago morning, as she'd slipped off the ring, she'd wept bitter, soul-shaking tears. 'Twas the first time it'd left her finger since the day Grady had put there. He'd been gone for two years by then, but taking off his ring had made his loss agonizingly new again. Made it evermore real.

Sitting at the table in this tiny, cramped little room where she'd raised their son alone for eight of the ten years she'd been a widow, Maura couldn't shake the feeling of inevitable defeat that began trickling over her. This ring was made of gold. It'd fetch a price good enough to see her through likely a couple of years of the doctor visiting and powders to see her health maintained. This, one of her dearest, most treasured possessions, was all she had with which to save her very life. Yet it was also all she had left of her sweetheart.

Another cough surfaced, tearing at her as the previous had. As *all of them* did now.

She set the ring atop the limp drawstring bag. Her eyes wouldn't leave it. How well she remembered the look of pride and affection in Grady's expression when he'd at last managed to scrimp and save enough to buy her that ring. He'd worked so hard and done without for so long.

"I love you, my Maura," he'd said. "I'd give you jewels if I could. I'd give you all the world."

"It must have come very dear." She'd not wanted him to suffer for that offering. He'd worked tirelessly. The money he'd spent on the ring would have seen to many of his own needs, needs he must have neglected to purchase it.

"Knowing you'll wear it and treasure it, and that it'll last a lifetime, and you'll think of me whenever you see it on your hand, makes it a bargain at any price."

"Is that your way of saying you're fond of me?" she'd teased a little. Jests had come easier then.

"*Fond* doesn't come close," he'd answered. "I love you with all my heart, and I will for all my life."

They'd not been married long when he'd left to fight in the war that broke out between the states. His ring and his words had kept him close to her and had given her hope. Years later, word came of his death in battle. His grandest, most tender offering, the ring she had then worn, remained the only tangible connection she had to him.

And here I sit, pondering how much I could sell it for. What else could she possibly do? She had a son. *Their* son. She couldn't leave Aidan an orphan simply because she was too sentimental to do what was necessary for her to stay alive.

For many wealthy people in New York City, seeing a doctor or buying medicine was little more than an inconvenience. But no matter how long the hours she worked, no matter that they never bought anything that wasn't a necessity, she and Aidan would always be poor. She'd lived that truth too long to be fooled into believing anything else.

I am going to die because I am poor. She and so many of her countrymen had fled the same fate, buoyed by the promise of America, only to discover that not much was different here. In Ireland, they'd died of starvation while those with wealth and power looked on in indifference. In America, they died of illness and injury, while those who profited from the very labor that killed them declared their deaths an acceptable cost of doing business.

She ran her finger over the ring. No item in the world meant as much to her as it did. But Aidan was far more important than any object. If she didn't sell it, and she died, he would be all alone.

Grady would have understood. She told herself as much again and again, even as tears of mourning and frustration threatened to pour from her. If he'd known that his death would leave them in this dire situation, he would understand. He wouldn't have begrudged her anything she needed to do to protect their son. He would not have been disappointed in her no matter how much guilt she heaped upon herself.

The door handle turned. Heavens, was it time for Aidan to be home already?

She quickly slipped the ring inside the bag and pulled the strings tight. With fast step, she reached the bureau and set the bag carefully atop it, then turned to greet her son, praying her distress did not show.

He stepped inside, dragging his feet. Without looking up, he shut the door behind him. To her untrained eye, he seemed tall for fourteen. Had Grady been tall at that age? She hadn't met him until he was a man grown. His family were halfway across the continent, unable to offer any help.

Aidan dropped his bag of shoe shining equipment on the table and then slumped into a chair. He'd once been of a sunnier disposition, apt to smile. He'd grown more withdrawn every day since he'd begun shining shoes on the street corners.

"How was your day, lad?" Maura asked.

He shrugged a bit. "Fine."

"You meant to try a different corner. Had you any luck?"

"Another boy was on that corner already. Corners aren't shared. Had to go back to my usual one." Though he had two Irish parents, Aidan sounded almost entirely American. They didn't live in an Irish neighborhood, and he had no extended family nearby. His days were spent on the streets. It was a wonder any bit of Ireland remained in his words and mannerisms at all.

"Lydia is visiting." Maura motioned to the sleeping baby. Being older brother to the children of the Tower always lifted his spirits.

"Where's Mrs. Porter?" he asked.

"At the market."

Aidan nodded. "The Connellys upstairs have the measles. I thought maybe she'd got it."

"Oh, heavens. I hope not."

Posture still slumped and voice low, he said, "With how cramped we all are in this building, the whole Tower'll have it by week's end."

"Not us," Maura assured him. "We've had it already."

"Aren't we lucky?" he muttered.

He was not usually so despondent. He'd been discouraged a lot of late and, as Eliza had noted, his spirits had been a bit low. But today he looked utterly defeated.

Someone knocked at the door. Maura crossed the room and opened it. Tara Upton from the top floor stood on the other side of the threshold.

"Have you a minute, Maura?" she asked.

"Aidan's having a difficult bit just now."

Tara's expression grew more anxious. "I'll be only a moment, I promise."

Maura hesitated. Aidan needed her attention, but so did a lot of other people. Telling herself that she would return to her son as quickly as possible, she nodded.

Her neighbor motioned into the corridor. Apparently, this was to be a private chat.

Maura looked over at her boy. "Keep an eye on the baby for me. I'll be but a moment."

Once in the relative privacy of the corridor, Tara began. "Have you heard if there might be a tenement coming available in the Tower soon? I've a friend at the factory needing a safer place to live. The man who owns the building where she's living now is . . . taking a bit too much notice of her."

An unfortunately too-common problem.

"I haven't heard of anything, but I'll let you know if I do."

Tara appeared dissatisfied with that answer.

"Is she needing something immediately?" Maura guessed.

"I think it'd be best."

"Does she have no family she could turn to?" 'Twould be the best solution.

Tara shook her head. "She came to America alone."

"What about her late husband's family?"

That did not appear to be a satisfactory answer either. "They really tolerated her only while her husband was alive. Now that he's passed, they'd rather forget she'd ever been anything to them."

How well Maura knew that feeling. The letters she'd exchanged with Grady's family out West had stopped after she'd sent word of his death. She'd been forgotten, and Aidan with her. That hurt more than she could bear to think about. She had, until then, felt a part of their family, welcome and wanted.

"I'm afraid for her, Maura." Tara's words pulled her back into the moment. "What can I do?"

So many in the Tower had come to expect Maura to have all the answers. What would they think if they knew she hadn't answers enough to even save her own life?

"Could your friend stay with you for a bit? Something's bound to come available, if not here, then at least somewhere safer than where she is."

Tara thought a moment. "We'd be tight as Dick's hatband, but I think we could manage it."

"Then I suggest you go fetch her," Maura said. "But don't do it alone," she quickly added. "It mightn't be safe."

Tara nodded. "That's wise."

"I wish you luck on your mission of mercy." Maura stepped toward the ajar door.

"Thank you, Maura," Tara said. "I just knew you'd help me sort it."

Maura had been doing the same for the other widows in the Tower for years. Being useful kept the despair at bay. Being part of their lives relieved some of her loneliness. Yet when her own world was crumbling, she faced her crisis more or less alone.

She returned to the warm confines of the room she and Aidan called home. He stood with his back to the door, bent a bit over the bureau. She could just make out the corner of a leather frame, no doubt taken from the drawstring bag she'd left out. She blinked and swallowed and breathed shallow, knowing the photograph he was looking at.

Every inch of that image was burned into her memory. Grady, with hair dark as the midnight sky, eyes as light as that same sky at midday, a face so handsome he'd drawn attention everywhere he went. In the photograph, he wore his Union Army uniform, tattered enough to tell he'd passed through some agonies in the weeks and months before it was taken.

At Aidan's request, she'd brought out the photograph earlier that year, only to discover that her boy, who was quickly becoming a young man, had grown into the very copy of his father. The resemblance had caught her unprepared and hurt too acutely to hide her reaction. She very much feared that Aidan had seen her response and had been disheartened by it. He hadn't asked to see the picture again, though she'd caught him looking at it now and then.

"I hate it here, Da." His whispered confession floated to her. "I hate

10

this city. I hate the noise and the dirty air. There're too many people everywhere, so close I can't even think. I hate shining shoes while my own feet are pinched and blistered. I hate it."

Maura stood like one at a mark. His words, filled with such desperation, were completely unexpected. She knew he'd been feeling low, but his broken words went far beyond mere discouragement.

"I've heard about the West," he continued, still whispering, still speaking to the unmoving, unhearing image of his long-departed father. "There's space, and it's clean and quiet. People have land instead of just a room. Why didn't we go there? Why'd we have to stay here?"

A fist delivered directly to her jaw couldn't have stunned Maura more.

Why hadn't they gone West with Grady's family? Because she hadn't wanted to. Because she'd been so sure that leaving behind her own family members in this city would be too much to endure.

But they were all gone now. Grady's were on the other side of the continent. She and Aidan were alone, and he was miserable, stuck in a city he, she now knew, hated. But she couldn't afford doctor's visits and medicines, so she certainly couldn't afford to find them a new home.

"We should've gone with them," Aidan said. "We shouldn't have stayed here."

Maura's heart silently broke for her boy. Did he realize how often she regretted that very decision, how often she wondered how their lives would be different now if they hadn't stayed in New York all those years ago?

Aidan would be happy.

Grady would still be alive.

And she would not be dying.

We should have gone with them. But it's too late now. We're stuck.

Chapter Two

HOPE SPRINGS, WYOMING TERRITORY

Three times in his life, Ryan Callaghan had experienced a moment of breath-snatching premonition. First on the day his father died, again in the days before the family left Ireland, and once more in the weeks before the invitation to move West came. Not in any of those instances had he known what was coming—his was not the second sight—but had, rather, been filled with a feeling, unshakable and unrelenting, that *something* hovered on his horizon, something of such significance that it would change his whole life. Each time, the feeling had proven correct.

As he lay awake on a cold April morning, he felt it again, undeniable, and unspecific, clutching at him, nagging him. Somewhere, the winds of life had shifted. He felt it as surely as he felt the cot beneath and the quilt atop him. He felt it as real as the nip of cold air on his face. Yet he hadn't the first idea what the coming storm would bring.

He closed his eyes for long moments, trying to shake off his uncertainty. *Please*, he begged the heavens, *let it be a good omen this time*. He'd long-since earned a bit of good fortune.

Ryan rolled off his rickety cot, dressing quickly. He had a lot to accomplish that day. He could not allow an unanticipated jolt of forewarning, especially one so frustratingly vague, to distract him. Whatever was coming his way would come, regardless. He'd do well to be as prepared as he could possibly be.

He climbed down from the low-ceilinged loft where he slept. His sister-in-law, Ennis, stood at the far end of the room pouring oats into a cast-iron pot. Ryan made his way to the near corner and the hanging quilt Ma slept behind. A smile pasted on his face, he drew the blanket back. "A fine good morning to you."

She sat on the edge of her bed, waiting. As always, she'd managed to dress herself up until the point of fastening buttons and tying ribbons. Her hands were a bit twisted. Buttons weren't impossible, but they were a struggle, one that inevitably left her fingers pained the remainder of the day.

Ryan sat beside her and did up the buttons of her dress. "Did you sleep well?"

"Well enough." Hers was a hopeful disposition, but it had grown heavy these past two years.

He hoped, prayed, the vague omen he was wrestling didn't mean he'd soon be losing her. Surely the heavens didn't mean to snatch away the only parent he had left.

"What of you?" she asked. "You don't look terribly rested."

"I've a bit on m' mind," he confessed. He tied the ribbon at her waist, then moved to sit on the floor. "I mean to make my proposal to Mr. Gallen today." He slid her right boot on her foot; she struggled with her shoes as well. "I've practiced m'explanation dozens of times, imagined every argument he might make. I think I've a good chance of convincing him to do business with me." He tied her laces, then took up the other boot. "If he agrees, the other ranch owners will as well, though perhaps not this year. But once they see I grow good-quality hay and can save them ⌐ compared to buying at market, they'll all want to buy it, I'ˡ

"'Twould be a fine thing, Ryan. You'd have ⸱⌐ future."

He tied off the laces then looked up into her w

kept low on account of the rest of the family being not far distant in this tiny house, he reminded her of the best bit of all. "We'd have a home of our own, too."

A wistful smile touched her lips. "That'd be grand, wouldn't it?"

"More than grand, it'd be a godsend."

They lived with Ryan's older brother, James, and his family, an uncomfortable arrangement for everyone. Ma missed having a household of her own and a say in how that household was run. Ennis had lived her entire married life in a home she shared with her mother- and brother-in-law. There was no privacy for any of them. And, though it pained Ryan to acknowledge it, resentment had been growing among them all for years.

Maybe *that* was the premonition he was feeling. A fruitful meeting with Mr. Gallen would certainly change Ryan's future, Ma's, as well. So would a disastrous one. His premonitions never came with enough flavor for him to know if the winds of change meant to be merciful or cruel.

He stood and held his hand out to Ma. She took hold of it. Slowly, carefully, painfully, she rose to her feet. A moment passed before she had herself balanced.

She moved fairly well for one with such extensive rheumatism. The pain and stiffness she'd spoken of for years had begun to manifest itself in the twisting of her hands and feet. But with a bit of help when rising and sitting, she got about. He was grateful for that, yet how much longer until she couldn't move around on her own at all?

He walked at her side around the hanging quilt. The house had but one bedroom, now used by Ennis and James. Ma had a corner. James's wee one had another. Ryan slept in the narrow loft. They were beyond snug, packed in nearly as tight as in the steerage section of the ship that had brought the family to America. And with an addition to James's family soon to arrive, they'd only grow more so.

"Where would you like to sit?" he asked Ma.

"Set me down at the table. We'll see if Ennis has something for me to."

His sister-in-law was bent over the fire, stirring the pot she'd earlier

14

poured the oats into. Her little one, Ryan's niece, sat on the floor nearby, fully occupied with her whittled horse.

"Good morning, Ennis," he said as he took hold of Ma's arm and steadied her as she lowered herself onto a chair at the table.

"Good morning," she answered, tapping the spoon against the side of the pot. "Did you sleep well?"

"Well enough," he said. "And Ma looks quite bright eyed, so I'd wager she passed a fine night." He knew perfectly well she hadn't, but he had quickly learned after Ennis and James had married, that any complaints about one's sleep were taken as a complaint about the accommodations, which always seemed to prick at Ennis. Early on, Ryan had assumed it was a matter of wounded pride. He'd come to suspect, though, it was more a matter of doubt: in herself, in her place, in her ability. 'Twas a difficult thing living under the watchful eye of one's mother-in-law, no matter how good a soul that mother-in-law was. "Is your husband out making trouble, then?"

Ennis turned toward them both, eying him with weary confusion. "You know perfectly well he's milking the cow."

Four years she'd been in this family, but Ryan still hadn't sorted her sense of humor. He'd heard her laugh—James had a knack for amusing his wife—but she never seemed to find Ryan the least bit entertaining. Ma no longer even tried teasing or jesting with Ennis. Laughter had always filled every house Ryan ever lived in. That had been a defining feature of their family: laughter, happiness, joy in each other's company. Now they were mostly uncomfortable, James included.

"I'm passing the mercantile today." He spoke to both women. "Can I fetch anything?"

"I'm running a touch low on sugar," Ennis said. "Let me gather a few coins."

"Keep your coins, Ennis. I eat the food in this house. I can contribute to the pantry."

She looked at him. The aloofness that usually marked her expression slipped a bit, replaced by an uncertainty he saw there now and then. "James wouldn't like it," she said quietly.

"I won't tell him. You won't either, will you, Ma?"

"Tell him what?" she asked innocently.

Ryan motioned toward his little three-year-old niece. "Nessa isn't paying us the least heed. She won't say anything."

"He doesn't like when you pay for things." Ennis wasn't saying anything they didn't already know.

"He also doesn't like when I *eat* things, so I'm in the muck no matter what." He smiled at his sister-in-law, hoping to take any edge out of his words. "I'll fetch you some sugar, and none of us'll say a word to James about where it came from." He bent and pressed a kiss to his ma's cheek. "I'll be home in time to help you prepare for bed," he assured her.

"A bit earlier than that wouldn't be unwelcome, lad."

He, too, wished they had more time together. But his fields required a great deal of work, and they weren't exactly conveniently located. "I'll do m'best."

In that moment, James stepped inside. "Are you off to the Claire place again?" He tromped across the room, sparing Ryan only a brief glance.

"I am." Soon enough the Claire place would be Ryan Callaghan's place. That was the plan, at least.

"I'm telling you, if you'd put that time and effort in *here*, we'd be able to grow more crops and expand some fields. We'd have enough yield to be living easier." James always grew noticeably annoyed when Ryan spoke of his plans.

"And I'm telling you that your growing family needs a house of your own, and I'd like my own corner of this world to claim."

How the man couldn't understand a longing for one's own land, Ryan couldn't say. They'd come West together, along with Ma, chasing that very dream. They'd eagerly claimed this humble farm, built this small but sturdy home together. Then James had found a wife and started a family, and Ryan and Ma had been reduced to interlopers in the house they'd once had claim on as well as on the land they'd all intended to put their mark on.

"This year's crop will be enough for me to finally begin buying the

16

land." Ryan held up one hand and marked his list one finger at a time. "Make my arrangements with Gallen. Buy the extra seed. Plant m' crop. Tend and harvest. Sell it." He moved to the other hand. "Negotiate terms for buying the farm on time. Move into the house. Start m' own life."

"You always have a plan," James muttered.

Of course he had a plan. How could he expect to claim a future for himself if he hadn't any direction? James always acted as if there were something horribly wrong with that. He, of course, had managed to secure the life he wanted almost by accident

Ryan stepped past his niece. He bent and kissed the top of her head. "See you tonight, sweetie."

"See you too, Uncle Ryan." She was a gem.

Ma loved the little one deeply. 'Twas a bright spot in their current arrangement. The new little baby would be as well.

Oh, saints. Don't let the premonition be anything bad regarding the baby. Or Ennis.

He stepped out into the morning sun and the unending Wyoming wind. Shutting the door behind him always brought a sense of relief, which in turn brought a heavy dose of guilt. For the hours he spent away from the house, he felt free. Ma had no such escape.

Ryan stuffed his hands in his jacket pockets and walked down the dusty road, whistling and taking in the scenery. No matter that he'd been surrounded by the beauty of the Hope Springs valley for five years now; he was still awed by it. He'd grown up in the city of Cork, then lived a number of years in Boston. Until coming to Wyoming Territory, he'd never known such open spaces and distant horizons. He'd even learned to love the muted greenery here. And he'd soon have his own land to lay claim to.

My own place, he told himself, though his mind didn't fully believe it. *My own land. Freedom.*

The day after James's wedding, Ryan struck the arrangement that allowed him to work the land that had then belonged to ol' Mrs. Claire. She'd been too aged and frail to look after it herself. He'd taken a portion of the profits he'd made selling his crop at market and paid Mrs. Claire for the use of her land. She was gone now. Her grandson had inherited the farm, but had no use for it. Ryan hoped to buy it from him, putting up what he had now and paying the rest over time.

He and Ma would have a home, away from the tension they lived in now. She would be near enough to James and her little grandbabies to watch them grow up. With a bit of distance between her and Ennis, they'd likely get along better. And Ryan would have his own corner of this valley. He'd belong to it in a real and permanent way.

His daily walk to the home that had once belonged to Mrs. Claire took him past what he'd come to silently call "O'Connor Row." House after house belonged to members of that large and growing family. The senior Mr. and Mrs. O'Connor were among the original founders in Hope Springs. Each of their children, excepting the very youngest, had established homes of their own, all in a line, one after the other. They were connected to on another without being suffocated. He knew all too well the difference.

Thomas Dempsey, one of the O'Connors' sons-in-law waved to Ryan as he passed. Ryan offered a good morning, receiving one in response. The Dempseys' oldest was undertaking chores and called out a, "Good morning to you, Mr. Callaghan."

"A good morning to you as well. How is everything at the Dempsey house?" he asked the lad.

"Busy."

Ryan smiled. "'Tis the way of farming, isn't it? Always being busy."

The young man nodded. "Ma's been crying, so I'm trying to be real helpful."

That sounded worrisome. "Has something happened?"

Thomas joined them at the fence. "It's her brother Patrick's birthday. He's one of the two who died in the war."

Ah. "Special days can be mournful when we've lost someone we love." His da's birthday was always a touch sad.

"She misses him," Thomas said. "I do too. He was a good lad, Patrick."

"And Colum, here, is a good lad to be looking out for his ma," Ryan said.

Thomas gave his son's shoulders a squeeze.

"If you need anything," Ryan said, "even someone to see to your evening chores so you can give Mary your time and love, you need only tell me."

Thomas gave a quick nod. "I will." Though the answer was one of acceptance, his tone spoke more of memorization, as if he'd offered the response after one-too-many insincere offers of help.

"I'm in earnest, Thomas Dempsey. Anything you need. Anything."

The tension in his shoulders eased noticeably "I will." There was the bit of relief Ryan had hoped to hear in Thomas's voice. "And I thank you."

Upon passing Mr. and Mrs. O'Connors' home, he received another friendly greeting. No one stood outside the next O'Connor home, but he'd had waves and greetings from that branch of the family before. Tavish and his wife, Cecily, lived in the next house.

Cecily stood inside the chicken coop, tossing feed to the eager flock. The gate sat a mere inch from closed, just enough of a gap that, once the chickens noticed, it'd be chaos. He moved quickly off the road and up the short distance to the coop. Cecily turned her head a bit in his direction, though she didn't turn fully.

"Just Ryan Callaghan," he told her. "The gate was open." He pulled it closed. "I didn't think you wanted your hens running all over Hope Springs."

"Thank you, Ryan," she said.

He paused a moment. "I'm told it's a difficult day for the O'Connors. How are the lot of you holding up here?"

"Hearts are heavy, but we are passing through well enough."

"I'm nearby if you need anything." He hoped she could hear that he meant it.

"Thank you, again."

"Any time, Cecily." He walked back toward the road.

Cecily was the most recent addition to the O'Connor family. Though it was likely a little childish of him, Ryan sometimes imagined what it'd be like to be one of them, to belong to that family.

Tavish and Cecily lived almost directly across the street from the land he worked and the house he hoped would be his one day. He needed to take only a few steps, and his corner of the world would spill out in front of him, warming his heart as it always did. He'd poured himself into the keeping of these fields. He'd worried and toiled over them. He'd studied the land and tracked its production. Using his records, he'd made changes, choosing different placements for crops and different rotations than had been used before. He knew this land so well that it was part of him now.

He turned up the short walk that led to the front of the house. He never went inside—the house was not included in his current arrangement—but walked alongside it on his way to the barn, where he kept a few tools, and where he always began his day.

Once he owned the place, house and all, he meant to make some improvements. He'd widen the house on the west side with tall windows, giving the parlor a view of the mountains rather than merely the road. He'd build a barn large enough for more than a cow and a single horse. He'd add a pig sty and build the chicken coop. And he'd make whatever changes were needed to allow Ma to get about the house easily and safely no matter how her condition worsened.

They'd both have their freedom, something they needed badly.

He took a moment to look out over the bare fields spreading out before him. His profit had been a tidy one thus far, but not enough to make the needed changes to the house. His plan simply had to work. He'd no other idea how to claim the future he dreamed of.

On the edges of the valley were a number of ranches. All of those people's land and efforts were dedicated to running their cattle. They grew nothing. Every crop they needed had to be purchased at market.

Ryan's experiments had significantly increased his yield of hay, something the ranches bought in tremendous quantity to stock for the winter. If he arranged to sell directly to them, he would save himself a trip to the depot. They, in turn, would not need to make that same trip and pay the higher prices the traders there charged. No one in the valley depended on the sale of hay for their own living. He'd not be hurting anyone else's profits, but he'd be improving his own.

That afternoon, he was meeting with Mr. Gallen, the owner of the largest of the ranches, to make his proposal. If the man agreed to put up a bit of money upfront, Ryan would purchase extra seed and plant vast amounts of his preferred mixture of grasses. He'd not be putting in the usual cash crops. 'Twas a risk, he knew it was. But he'd studied the matter. He'd looked at it every which way. The investment would pay off quickly. He'd have enough by the end of this season to buy the house and land.

Make arrangements with Gallen Ranch. Then plant his crop. Tend and harvest it. Sell it to the ranch, knowing others would follow in the years to come. He need only do those things.

He'd have land. Ma would have a home.

They'd at last have a future. If only he could be certain that that morning's bolt of premonition wouldn't prove to be an omen of utter disaster.

Chapter Three

Maura could hardly catch her breath as she dragged herself through the door of her tenement after cleaning two houses in one day. She never knew when the next job would come, so she worked every chance she got. Sometimes that meant asking more of her body than it could give.

She hadn't yet closed the door when Eliza came down the narrow stairs in the corridor. "Maura!"

With a smile of welcome ready despite her exhaustion, Maura turned and greeted her friend. Though she'd be willing to watch Lydia if need be, she hoped that was not what Eliza had come down to ask. Maura was tired and worn and ready to drop.

"You'd best come up." Worry tugged at Eliza's words. "Aidan returned while you were gone. He's in a bad way."

Maura pulled her door closed once more and moved as swiftly as her pained feet and struggling lungs would allow. The single flight of stairs nearly did her in. Each breath clawed at her from inside. One cough after another only added to the misery.

"Stop to catch your breath," Eliza insisted.

Maura shook her head. Something was the matter with Aidan; she would not be delayed from seeing him.

Eliza's room was smaller even than Maura's, a heartbreaking feat.

The size made Aidan all too easy to spot on a spindle-back chair, a damp rag held against his mouth.

She knelt on the floor in front him. He was scuffed and dirty, and his shirt was torn. A new hole marred the knee of his trousers. "What's happened, lad?"

He said something, but the cloth muffled his words. She pulled his hand, and the cloth it held, away from his face.

"Oh, mercy," she whispered through her wheezing struggle for air.

His upper lip was split. Only the few inches around the cut were clean, the rest of his face was filthy. Eliza had likely washed away blood. Some continued to trickle down his chin.

"What happened?" Maura repeated.

"I tried a new corner," he said.

"And corners aren't shared." Maura remembered him saying as much a few days earlier when discussing his time spent shining shoes for what pennies he could earn. She'd not expected him to be beaten for such an infraction, though. "Have you any other injuries?"

He held up his other hand, the one not holding the rag. Two of his fingers were tied together with strips of cloth. They were bruised and swollen and, she'd wager, broken.

She took a breath, deep as she could manage without her lungs seizing. A few blinks. A pushing away of anything but the most necessary course of action. She'd see them through this crisis. "Anything else?"

"They took my shoe shining kit."

"*They*?" Good heavens. He'd been set upon by more than one attacker?

He nodded. "Three lads. Big ones. They said they'd be looking for me now. I won't have a corner anywhere. Wouldn't matter, though. I don't have anything to shine with."

He'd worry about their finances. Though she'd tried to keep the desperation of their situation hidden, he was clever and observant. He knew they were a breath from destitute.

"We'll think of something," she promised. "We always do."

His eyes, light blue like his da's, but heavy and worried like hers every time she caught a glimpse of herself, watched her closely. "Not the factory, though?" he pressed. "I don't want to go to the factory."

She glanced at Eliza, who pressed a hand to her heart, her brow pulled in concern for the lad. Everyone loved Aidan. How could they not? He was dear and kind and tender.

And he was miserable.

"Not the factory," she vowed. "We'll find something else."

"There's always something else," he mumbled. 'Twas far from an expression of hopefulness.

She stood and motioned for him to do the same. He obeyed, but without enthusiasm.

"Have you said hello to Lydia yet?" she asked.

He shook his head.

"You should," Maura told him. "The sweet baby loves you, and that smile of hers would do you a world of good."

He held the cloth against his lip once more and moved to the blanket the baby was lying on. He sat down beside her and tickled her chin. Though the weight hadn't left his posture and the cheer in his expression looked a bit forced, some happiness appeared in his eyes again. How long would it last? She saw less and less of it every day.

Eliza joined Maura near the chair Aidan had vacated.

"Thank you for tending to him," Maura said quietly. "Does me good to know he wasn't alone."

"You've tended to all of us here," Eliza said.

Maura watched her lad playing with the baby. His moments of happiness were growing farther apart. She very rarely saw the lighthearted boy he'd once been.

"I still can't believe anyone would hurt Aidan," Eliza said. "He's such a dear boy, so sweet and kind to everyone."

Maura coughed, but managed to get her lungs under control again swiftly. "Perhaps 'sweet and kind' don't belong in the slums of New York. Perhaps he was always meant for somewhere else."

"The city has a way of stealing futures, doesn't it?" Eliza's loss was still so fresh; her husband had been gone less than a year.

"If you could leave the city, would you?" Maura asked.

"Without another thought." She offered a quick, sad smile. "But where would I go? And how could I possibly afford to get there?"

"Poverty has a way of stealing futures too," Maura said.

"And what would I do without you if I left?" Eliza added. "I've not another friend in all this world."

Maura squeezed her hand reassuringly. "With your sweet heart and kind nature, you'd make friends anywhere. But I would miss you something fierce."

"Maybe we could go somewhere together," Eliza suggested with a light laugh. "We could tell everyone we're sisters."

Maura could smile at that. "I suspect our differing accents would give away the ruse."

"Where would you go if you could?" Eliza asked.

Where would I go? She'd need to choose a place where Aidan had someone to look after him when her health inevitably fell to bits. If she could find a place with a doctor, so much the better. And her boy wanted open spaces, and peace and quiet. He'd likely be pleased as could be to claim a bit of land as his own; his father had longed to return to working the land as he'd done in Ireland.

"Hope Springs," she answered.

"Where's that?"

"Wyoming Territory," Maura said. "It's where my husband's family settled. Out there, Aidan would have people to look after him. He'd have land and peace and a future."

"Have you no other family nearer here?" Eliza asked.

"I've a brother-in-law in Canada, though he moves about too much for us to settle with him. My parents and sister have been dead for years. Aidan has only me and relatives he doesn't remember in the West."

And if she didn't find a way to pay for a doctor and medicine, he'd not have even her much longer.

She watched her sweet son playing with little Lydia. *I hate it here.* His whispered confession haunted her. She saw the truth of his words in his face every day. Heaviness. Misery. Growing desperation.

"This city is killing him, Eliza, and I don't know how to save him from it."

With an expression that spoke of barely held-back tears, Eliza pulled her to the table and bade her sit. "We'll think of something. I'm certain we can."

But Maura shook her head. "I've been trying for weeks to think of an answer but keep hitting the same uncrossable ravine. I can't afford to replace a small shoe-shining kit. How could I possibly afford to move us away?"

Eliza's brow tugged low, her lips pressing together as she thought. "What if we took up a collection?"

"No one in the Tower has so much as a penny to spare." Maura knew that better than anyone.

"What if you sold your furniture?" Eliza suggested. "You wouldn't be taking it with you anyway."

Maura had occasionally thought of that. "It wouldn't fetch nearly enough."

"Do you have anything else of value?"

She did her best to ignore the twinge she felt at that. The last few days, she had pushed Grady's ring from her mind as much as possible. She'd accepted that it would have to be sold; there was no avoiding that. When the time came that she could no longer survive without a doctor's care, then, and only then, would she sell the ring. The delay was the only thing that made the decision endurable.

"You've thought of something," Eliza said, watching her closely.

"Not the miracle you're thinking. I know a way to pay for my medical care when the time comes." As if to punctuate her words, a heavy cough rose, followed in quick succession by several more. With what little breath she could manage, she pressed forward. "There would be barely enough for that, perhaps not even enough, and certainly no extra for moving across the country."

An empathetic sadness filled Eliza's face. "It's one or the other, then?"

Heaven help her, it was. "Without medicine for me, Aidan will be an

26

orphan. But leaving him here will tear him to bits. And, no matter, how hard I try, I cannot save him from both."

"Oh, Maura," Eliza sighed. "I am so sorry. What a choice to face."

If they stayed, she could have a doctor's care, she'd have a chance to live, but Aidan's soul would wither. If they went West, she wouldn't live long, but Aidan would at least have a chance of being happy. Her life or Aidan's well-being. How could anyone possibly make such a decision? Her gaze returned once more to her son. He was lying on his back beside little Lydia. His eyes were on the ceiling, and his hand yet held the cloth to his poor, battered face. A single tear slipped from the corner of his eye, trickling downward into his hair. How long before the beatings and cruelty of this place no longer pulled this grieving sadness from him? How long before he simply hit back, surviving the misery by giving it to someone else? She had seen that transformation before.

And I do have the means of saving him from it. If she sold Grady's ring, if she did it now rather than waiting...

There would be nothing left for doctors and medicine. Hope Springs might not even have a doctor. The O'Connors might not welcome them. Choosing this path would be a tremendous risk.

She rubbed her temples, overwhelmed by the weight of their predicament. "I cannot keep him here. I cannot watch him fade away."

"Of course you can't," Eliza said.

Taking Aidan far from the city, giving him a chance to start new, was the only real option, the only right thing. She'd have to sell Grady's treasured offering, the link he'd forged between them through sacrifice and love. But she would do it to save their son. She was risking her very life to save Aidan's. Grady would have understood. He had risked his life, after all, fighting alongside his brother to try to save a nation, so she and Aidan would have a future. He'd given everything for them; he would forgive her for having to do the same.

"Will you write to me?" Eliza asked. "I'll be far less lonely if you do."

Maura squeezed her hand and nodded. "And you'll write to me?"

"As any pretend sister would."

27

Maura was grateful for a reason to smile after everything had crumbled around her in the past moments.

"Once I'm settled, if my health holds, and if I can save a bit of money," Maura said, "would you consider coming West, joining us there?"

"That's a lot of ifs." She spoke with hesitant hopefulness.

"I'm afraid I can't change that."

Eliza squared her shoulders. "You work on those ifs. I'll work on setting a bit aside to help. If I can get Lydia out of this city, I'll do it."

Maura hugged her friend fiercely. "It'll all be grand in the end. You'll see."

She hoped Eliza believed it. She hoped, in time, she would as well.

Chapter Four

MAY

Maura was even more nervous than she'd been the day Grady first introduced her to his parents fifteen years earlier. On this day, like that one, she desperately hoped the O'Connors would open their hearts to her and make room for her. She'd doubted they would then because they'd been strangers. She doubted they would now because ten years of deafening silence stretched between her and them.

"What if I can't remember all their names?" Aidan had been peppering her with questions all the way from New York. Now, as they walked along a dirt road, following the directions they'd been given when dismounting the cramped stagecoach, she had no more answers for him than she'd had the day they walked away from the only home he remembered.

"They'll not begrudge you," she said.

"You're certain?"

"Full certain." She'd told her son a few lies of late, all to save him worry. She only hoped the heavens would forgive her for them.

"What if there aren't any jobs for us?"

"We'll find something." She hoped that didn't prove another lie.

On they walked. The town of Hope Springs, the stage driver had told her, was just over the hill they were climbing.

"What if no one has a place for us?"

If Maura hadn't been struggling to breathe, she'd likely have begged the lad to stop with his questions. His doubts fueled her own, and she could ill afford to lose her nerve now, when she'd sacrificed so much and come so far to offer him this new beginning.

Her letter asking if the O'Connors could make room for her and her son had been answered quickly but briefly.

Received your letter. We've ample room. Come as soon as you're able.

The rest had been devoted to explaining how to get to Hope Springs, with a blessed amount of detail that had helped her tremendously. But she hadn't the first idea how she and Aidan would be received, or what "ample room" truly meant.

If the heavens chose to be kind—and she prayed that proved the case—the family would be happy to see Aidan, at least, and they'd be willing to help her sort out a more permanent arrangement than being a guest in one of their homes. 'Twould all work out in the end, and it'd all be grand, just as she continually promised her boy; it simply had to be. They'd nowhere else to go and no one else to turn to, and she'd nothing to her name beyond the contents of their carpet bags and the tiniest bit of money for living until she found work.

"Stop a moment, lad." She set a hand on his arm. "I need to catch m' breath."

His worried gaze darted to her. "The stage driver should've dropped us closer to town."

"I'd've appreciated that."

This stage route, they'd been informed, was a new one, and there wasn't an official stop established at Hope Springs. They'd switched trains a dozen times. And those trains had taken them only as close as a two-day stage journey away from a town that apparently few ever visited and, it seemed, few ever left.

"I know you're nervous, Aidan. Starting over worries a soul." She paused for air. "Do you remember when we first moved to the Widows' Tower?"

He shook his head no. She wasn't overly surprised; he had been very young.

"I was a ball of nerves, I'll tell you. What if we weren't wanted? What if we never made any friends? What if the whole thing was a disaster?"

He scuffed the toe of his shoes against the dirt and nodded.

"Do you know what I did?"

He shook his head once more, eyes on his boots.

"I decided to make a place there for myself, to help where I could, to do good for the people around me. Then it would feel like home because there was love there."

He eyed her. "Did it work?"

The answer was clear if he'd give it but a moment's thought. "Was it home to us?" she asked, hoping to help him reach his own conclusion.

He smiled, a little nostalgic, a little sad. "It was."

She took a wheezing breath, wishing her lungs weren't so heavy. Her breathing had not improved since they'd left New York. Did that mean her lungs were more damaged than even Dr. Dahl suspected? Or had she simply not been away long enough for a noticeable difference?

Before they left New York, she'd seen the doctor one last time. She'd regretted the expense, but she'd needed to be certain she was strong enough to make the journey. Had her condition been rendered critical by the strain of travel, and, heaven forbid, she'd succumbed to her illness, Aidan's situation would have been beyond dire. She'd needed to know it was safe to go, even though the expense would make things harder for them now when they needed every penny to live on.

Dr. Dahl had reiterated his warning that she might not ever improve at all. She might simply discover that she'd waited too long. She'd not allow herself to think on that possibility.

"Should I run ahead?" Aidan asked. "I could find someone to come back with a wagon or a buggy or something like that."

She shook her head, then set down the carpet bag she carried. Aidan laid his two larger bags beside hers. Hands on her hips, posture a little slumped, she attempted to settle her lungs into an easier, less painful, rhythm.

"Ma?"

She waved off the worried, unspoken question. "I only need a moment, love."

He nodded and watched, face still creased with worry.

Perhaps she could distract him from the question of her health. They would have to face it soon enough. Distractions proved a bit hard to come by. Looking about, she saw little beyond a vast emptiness. "'Tis an odd thing, not seeing any buildings."

He looked out over the horizon. "Or any people."

"You'll not be lonely, will you?"

He shook his head. "It'll be nice. I won't have to fight for a corner."

How she hoped that proved true. The world had far too many "corners."

Another round of coughs halted their conversation for a drawn-out moment. She tried to smile through the onslaught so he wouldn't worry. "Are you excited to see your grandparents?" she asked once she had air enough.

He kicked a pebble. "They're strangers."

Unfamiliar people always made him nervous. She could help with that, at least.

"Let me tell you what I remember of them while we walk on. Then they'll be better known to you." She squeezed his fingers. "Though we'd best move slowly. I don't know that I've air enough to walk very fast and talk at the same time."

"We can wait some more if you need."

She shook her head and took up her bag once more. He grabbed both of his as well. One painstaking step at a time, they moved closer to their destination.

"The O'Connors love to laugh."

"So did Papa." Aidan had no actual memories of his father. Everything he knew of Grady had come from Maura's stories and recollections.

"Your Papa was the oldest of seven children. Five of them live here now."

Aidan nodded. He knew all of this, yet hearing it again, she hoped, would offer a bit of the comfort that came of familiarity.

"They like to sing and dance. They tell wonderfully funny stories." The time she'd spent with them had been amongst the happiest of her life. How she hoped that part of the family's interactions hadn't changed. "The youngest brother, Finbarr, is only five years older than you are."

"He lives here?"

"He does." At least, she hadn't heard otherwise. "They all do."

"Will they—?" Aidan pressed his lips closed, apparently not wanting to ask whatever hung on his mind.

She took a wheezing breath. "You'd best ask whatever is on your mind, lad. Unanswered questions are a heavy thing to bear."

"Will they be glad to see us?" he asked, almost a whisper.

She had decided they would be. She depended on it. "They were always happy when we would drop in for a visit. Your grandmother, in particular, was very fond of you."

"Was she fond of *you?*" He'd picked up on what she'd not said. He always had been a bit too insightful.

"She was." 'Twas an honest answer. What she didn't know was if her mother-in-law was *still* fond of her. So much time had passed. So much lay between them: Grady staying behind for Maura's sake, dying in a war he might otherwise have avoided. Maura laid a great deal of the blame for Grady's death at her own feet. Mrs. O'Connor might very well feel the same. The whole family likely did.

Make a place for the two of us. Help where I can. Do good for the people around me. She repeated her own words of advice. She knew how to make the best of a less-than-ideal situation. And the Tower had, in time, become home. This new place could as well.

She and Aidan slowly crested the hill. Her heart pounded from exertion, nervousness, and the continued struggle in her lungs. She hoped the O'Connors didn't live too much farther. She hadn't the endurance to continue on much longer.

At the top of the hill, she paused, looking out over the valley in front of them. Vast lengths of fields spread in all directions, with homes dotting the expanse. A river wound its way toward the edges. The distant mountains added a majesty to the scene.

"It is beautiful here," she said.

"And quiet." That seemed particularly pleasing to him.

Maura's gaze slid to the only collection of buildings in any proximity to one another, what must have been the town of Hope Springs itself. Except it seemed to consist of only three buildings. *Three.* She had never seen a town so small. Even her childhood village in Tipperary was larger than this.

"Is that all of it?" Aidan looked as confused as he sounded.

"Eliza would never believe such a tiny place even existed, would she?" She smiled at the idea of their friend's reaction. "She'd think we were telling her a tale."

"Do you know what this town needs?" Aidan said.

She eyed him, curious.

"A factory," he said, not quite hiding his grin. Aidan had his father's odd but delightful sense of humor.

"Perhaps we could suggest one."

Aidan's smile lasted only a moment. Bless him, he was so nervous.

The road took them down the hill and over a wide, wooden bridge spanning a river, which appeared to wind back again on the other side of the shockingly small town, crossed by yet another bridge. The short walk left her struggling for air once more.

"That *is* all of the town." Aidan looked behind them, as if half expecting to realize he'd somehow overlooked rows and rows of houses.

The first building they came upon appeared to be a shop of some kind. Dry goods were visible through the windows. Up ahead was a smithy's. Farther yet was a building she couldn't identify. A small house. A church, perhaps. The shop seemed her best option for getting directions.

"We'll ask here," she said. "I'm sure someone will help us."

"You always think so." Aidan shook his head in amusement.

"And, generally, someone does." She ruffled his hair. "You have to believe there's good in the world, lad. And you have to be willing to add good to it."

"I know, Ma. You say that all the time."

She kept Aidan at her side as a small group of people just stepping out of the shop passed by. They eyed her with confusion, but their focus quickly settled on Aidan. They stared, making no effort to hide their curiosity. Whispers were exchanged. Gazes returned again and again, even after the strangers had passed. Maura put a protective arm around her boy, though he was every bit as tall as she. In time, her sweet little Aidan would tower over her.

"Why are they all looking at me?" he whispered.

"I've no idea," she admitted. She'd hoped he hadn't noticed. He could be quite bashful, unsure of new places and people. This level of scrutiny would unnerve even the most unshakable of people. Aidan moved closer to her. His shoulders grew so tense they practically touched his ears.

A woman hovered nearby, a wee one on her hip. Her gaze, like everyone else's, continually returned to Aidan.

Maura faced her straight on. "Begging your pardon, ma'am."

The woman met her eye. "Forgive me. I'd not meant to stare, I swear to you." She was Irish. That was a promising thing. "'Tis only that your lad . . ." Her dark brow pulled low. "He looks very like . . . a man who lives here."

A painful squeezing seized Maura's heart. "A man named O'Connor, by chance?"

The still unnamed woman grew wide-eyed. "Tavish O'Connor, in fact."

Tavish. One of Grady's younger brothers. Dear, kind Tavish. She'd missed him fiercely. Would every family name she heard pierce her with the pang of loneliness? "Would you point us in the direction we'd find him, or any of the other O'Connors. We've come here looking for them."

Realization lit the woman's eyes. "You're their kin who've come from New York, aren't you?"

The O'Connors had mentioned their anticipated arrival to others in town. That, she hoped, was a good sign. At least, nothing in the woman's expression indicated the O'Connors had grumbled about the burden of providing for distant family.

The milling crowd had begun to disperse. That would set her poor boy more at ease.

"I'm Maura O'Connor, and this is Aidan."

The woman offered a dip of her head. "I'm Katie Archer. This wee'un is Sean."

"A pleasure to meet a fellow Irishwoman," Maura said.

Katie smiled broadly. "You'll meet a great many around here."

'Twould be wonderful having a bit of home to comfort her in her difficulties. Some of Maura's unease melted away.

"The O'Connor women are having their quilting day today," Katie said. "They'll all be at Ciara's."

Little Ciara was old enough to have a home of her own? That change was difficult to imagine. When the family left New York, Ciara had been Aidan's age. She would likely be nearly unrecognizable now.

"Would you point us in the right direction?" she asked.

"I'll take you up there my own self," Katie said. "Won't they be surprised? Last I heard, you weren't expected for another week or more."

"I made my best guess about how long the journey'd take. Having never attempted to cross this vast country, I didn't do a very good job of estimating." This was not the sure footing on which she'd have preferred to undertake the coming reunion.

Katie stepped away from the shop and back onto the dirt road. Maura followed, motioning for Aidan to do the same.

"When I first came to Hope Springs," Katie said, "I estimated wrong as well, though I was wrong in the other direction. There was no stage line this way back then. I simply had to wait at the depot for someone, *anyone* who was coming this way."

"Oh, dear."

Katie smiled as they walked on. "I'd come to take a job. You can imagine the impression I made arriving late as beggar desperate for a wagon to ride in. Heavens, but things were difficult in the beginning. It turned out well in the end, though."

Maura looked to Aidan. "You see there, lad? It turned out well."

"Hope Springs has a way of managing that," Katie said. "We have our share of troubles, but somehow, it all ends grand."

Aidan adjusted his hold on both bags. His eyes darted about, studying the wide expanse of land. She couldn't be certain he was even listening. He'd dreamed of open spaces and life away from the chaotic bustle of the city. This tiny place fit the bill. Perhaps having this bit of his dream fulfilled would make up for her uncertainty.

"Such a tiny town, Hope Springs" she said quietly.

"Especially when one has lived in the cities back East," Katie agreed. "Takes some getting used to."

"You lived in America's East?" Maura asked. How easy she found conversation with this chance-met stranger. Even if her late husband's family wasn't particularly keen to see her again, she might at least have a friend here in Hope Springs.

"In Baltimore for a few years," Katie said. "It's not as large a city as New York, but vast just the same."

Katie shifted little Sean to her other hip. Doing so freed her left hand, giving Maura a glimpse of it for the first time. She hadn't a single finger on that hand, only the palm and her thumb. Maura had seen similar horrific injuries on the hands of former factory workers. Had Katie worked in one?

"School is held there in the church during the week." Katie motioned with her fingerless hand behind them at the building they'd just passed. "Aidan, you'll be right welcome there, I'm sure of it. We've a number of children your age in town. My oldest is but a couple of years younger than you are. Ian and Biddy's oldest is as well."

"They have children?" Maura felt an utter fool after the question slid from her lips. Ian and Biddy were her family: Grady's brother and sister-in-law. She had once been very close with them, yet she hadn't even heard about the birth of any of their children.

Katie didn't press, though she did appear a little surprised at her ignorance. "They've three who are living and one they lost a few years ago to a fever."

"Oh, I am sorry to hear that."

A sadness touched Katie's eyes as they walked on. "This town has lost a great many."

A town that had known tragedy, the O'Connors included. Maura was bringing them more of it, though they didn't realize as much. In her letters, she hadn't said a word about the troubles marring her future or that the O'Connors would likely be the ones seeing Aidan through the grief of losing his only remaining parent. Dr. Dahl hadn't left her entirely hopeless, but she'd seen enough people succumb to brown lung. She knew what awaited her.

The dirt path led them farther from the three buildings of town. Maura could spy houses spread out in either direction, separated by sprawling fields. A tidy farm house sat just ahead at a fork in the dirt road.

"This is my home," Katie said, "if you're ever in need of anything."

"Thank you." 'Twas an unlooked-for but much-needed bit of kindness.

"The O'Connors all live down the road to the right." Katie made her way that direction. "Across the bridge."

"Though I hate to ask, I'm needing to." Maura set a hand against her rasping chest. "Could we walk a pace slower? I've something in m' lungs, and I keep finding myself out of breath."

Aidan's eyes were full on her again. Would the lad live in a fret for the rest of Maura's life? 'Twasn't how she wanted him to pass his childhood.

"Of course." Katie didn't sound the least put out by the request. "Travel takes such a toll on a body, doesn't it?"

If only her weariness were merely a matter of travel.

True to her word, Katie continued on at a much slower pace, which eased some of the burden on Maura's weary lungs.

"Ciara's is the first house after the bridge," Katie said. "From there, you can knock on one door after another and find an O'Connor behind it."

Aidan would be surrounded by family. He would never be alone. He would be cared about and cared for. He might have a happy future yet. The first flickers of hope warmed her heart. Aidan could be happy here.

They crossed the wooden bridge, the river running swiftly beneath their feet. Trees grew in clumps along its banks. A valley spread out in all directions, farmland reaching the river's edge as it flowed away from the tiny town. In the distance were tall, snowcapped mountains. Snow. In May. Spring, it seemed, came late to Hope Springs' mountains.

Below, the river splashed against rocks and the posts of the bridge. She'd not have been able to hear the rush of water in the midst of the ceaseless rumble of New York. It was peaceful. Calming. The air smelled of earth and the approach of rain. It tasted of nothing at all; not soot, not chemical-laden steam from the mills, not the press of too many people in too small a space. The air was clean.

She looked to Aidan. His face was filled with wonder. Though questions still hung in his eyes, they held excitement, too. Enthusiasm. Seeing that change in him already, after mere minutes, put to rest many of her doubts. Moving to Hope Springs would be good for him. This would bring Aidan back to life. It would be worth the sacrifice.

In little more than a moment, they reached the first house past the bridge. Aidan stopped beside Maura. The house wasn't made of wood or bricks or anything else Maura could easily identify, neither was it built in the style of the cottages seen all over Ireland. Flowers didn't grow along the front path. No moss-covered stone walls covered in moss dotted the land nearby. The version of Hope Springs that she'd created in her mind's eye looked nothing like this.

Katie stepped up near the door. Her little one began to fuss. "Hush now, Sean. You've been an angel 'til now."

Little Sean looked over his mother's shoulder, facing him. Aidan pulled a silly face. Sean stopped his fussing, clearly intrigued. Aidan scrunched his features in a different humorous expression. A baby giggle answered the effort.

An unexpected surge of comfort filled Maura's heart. Aidan was nervous, even a little afraid, yet he'd already warmed to a tiny someone in this place. Her flicker of hope was growing.

Katie gave a quick rap on the door. Maura took a breath, triggering yet another cough. She held it back with every bit of strength she had until the seizing stopped. Aidan eyed her, no longer distracted by his new little friend.

"You don't need to be afraid," Maura whispered.

"What if they stare at me?" The curious looks in town must have unnerved him even more than she'd thought.

The door opened. Aidan tucked himself a little behind her.

"Katie," the woman in the doorway said. An Irish voice. "Are you joining us today?"

"I'd not planned to, but I've come with such news that I couldn't help m'self. I simply have to watch this play out."

Maura leaned the tiniest bit to the side to see better. She knew the woman in the doorway as soon as she was afforded a good look: Mary, the O'Connors' eldest daughter and the sibling nearest in age to Grady. In the months before the O'Connors left New York, Maura had come to think of Mary as her own elder sister, a mentor, a friend.

"You've tickled my curiosity," Mary said.

Katie stepped to the side, revealing Maura and Aidan and motioning to them. "I found these two in town, asking if there were any O'Connors about."

Mary's eyes all-but popped out of her head. "Maura! As I live and breathe." Her gaze moved almost immediately to Aidan. "Oh, mercy," she whispered.

Poor Aidan, stared at again.

Mary spun about, calling into the house. "Ma! Only look who it is!" She turned back again. "Come inside, both of you."

Maura had to give Aidan a nudge before he'd move. He dragged himself forward, but stopped only a step inside the door. That would have to be good enough. For her part, Maura faced the room with all the courage she could muster.

Mrs. O'Connor was impossible to mistake. Hers were the same happy eyes and warm expression Maura remembered so clearly. Time had aged her, as Maura was certain it had her, as well. The curiosity in Mrs. O'Connor's face slid away as her eyes settled on Aidan.

"Saints above," she whispered.

"He looks like Tavish," Mary said, still standing in the doorway, with them.

"No," Mrs. O'Connor said, emotion crackling in her voice as she shook her head. "He looks like Grady."

Maura had seen the resemblance in Aidan to her late husband, but she'd not seen Tavish in ages. Had he grown to look so much like his eldest brother?

"My dear boy!" Mrs. O'Connor crossed to Aidan and put her arms around him.

He stood frozen, still holding a large traveling bag in each hand, eyes pulled wide in shock. He looked to Maura, silently pleading with her.

They are strangers.

"This is your grandmother," Maura said quietly, gently.

Mrs. O'Connor pulled back, though she didn't look away from Aidan. "I ought to have introduced myself first. Of course, you'd not remember me. You were but a wee thing last we saw each other."

Maura waited, watching for some indication of her own reception. An embrace. A smile. A kind word. Mrs. O'Connor, however, seemed unable to look away from her grandson.

"Saints be praised." Mrs. O'Connor set her hands on either side of Aidan's face. "Only look at you. I can hardly believe this is our little Aidan, grown and tall as you are."

He didn't move, didn't speak.

His grandmother was undeterred, unhurt by the cold reception. She took his hands in hers. "You're the very image of your father. The very image. And, oh, so grown. I can hardly countenance it. Mary, is he not so very much older than he was?"

Mary laughed. "You'd not expect him to arrive still a baby, would you?"

Mrs. O'Connor swatted at her playfully. "Stop, now. I'm allowed a moment of shock at how grown he is." She turned her attention back to Aidan. "Are you hungry, lad?" Mrs. O'Connor shook her head in amusement. "You're a growing boy. Of course you're hungry. Your aunts Ciara and Biddy have gone up the road to fetch a bit more thread, but

41

they'll be back in a shake. We'll feed you while we wait for them, then chat a piece when they return."

Maura likely should have agreed. She could have offered some help either with quilting or preparing the food. And Aidan would have been able to spend time with his grandmother and aunts, getting to know them better. But she was exhausted. Her lungs ached even more than usual. She absolutely had to lie down and rest before she simply collapsed.

"We've walked a far stretch today," she said. "I'd be grateful if we'd a chance to lay our heads somewhere and rest first."

Mrs. O'Connor turned and faced her fully for the first time. "Maura." The kindness, the fondness with which she filled Maura's name eased some of the weight on her heart and mind. "It's good to see you again."

"And you as well." No matter her nervousness in this uncertain situation, she truly was grateful to see her mother-in-law. Maura had always been shown kindness in her home.

Mrs. O'Connor took her in a gentle, quick embrace. "You're most welcome, you know. Most welcome."

Maura closed her eyes and allowed some of her ever-present anxiety to lessen. How she needed those words. This was not the overwhelming expression of pleasure Aidan had received, nor a return to the full comfort she'd once known amongst her husband's family, but she and her son were welcome; they were wanted.

"I thank you for making room for us. I hope we've not put anyone to too much trouble."

"Not at all." Mrs. O'Connor motioned to the two bags Aidan carried and the smaller one in Maura's hand. "Is this all you have?"

She nodded.

"We've a house for you to use for a spell," Mrs. O'Connor said. "I'll show you to it."

"A house?" She must've heard wrong. "All to ourselves?"

She fully expected laughter at the absurdity of her misunderstanding. But Mrs. O'Connor just smiled and nodded.

"All to yourselves," she said, "while you settle in."

A house they'd not need to share. A place of their own, however temporary.

A regular miracle.

Chapter Five

The countryside was dark as Ryan walked along the road toward the home he meant to make his own later that day. Word had spread of his arrangement with the Gallen ranch and, in the end, he'd forged an agreement with a second of the nearby ranches to provide their winter hay as well. Come autumn, he'd harvest and sell it. He'd have more money to his name than he'd ever known.

But today, he would be asking Tavish and Cecily O'Connor to sell him the land and home he'd thought of as his own the past four years. He couldn't imagine they'd say no. Once the property agreement was settled, he'd return to James's house, pack his and Ma's belongings, and claim this place for their own.

He'd left for his fields earlier than usual. A great deal of work awaited him, work he did on his own. The cow at the Claire place needed milking, and he needed to be done sooner than usual, so he'd have time enough to go make his proposal to Tavish and Cecily.

No one was outside as he passed their homes, though lantern light peeked out from the barn at the senior O'Connors' place. Morning chores were a necessity at any farm. They'd all be seeing to them in the quiet of morning. Once Ryan lived on the land where he worked, he'd not begin his day already behind schedule, owing to the long walk he had to make before beginning.

And Ma would be able to sleep later, save her strength. Ryan would likely even have time enough to take her to neighbors' houses for regular visits. He might, in time, have enough money to purchase a wagon and team of his own instead of relying on James's.

Everything would be better after he and Ma were in their new home. Everything would be calm. They would have pleasure instead of merely surviving.

Not enough light illuminated the landscape for his fields to be truly visible, but he knew them well enough to be perfectly certain at what point his land stretched out beside him. He could sense it—that undeniable feeling of coming home. A few moments later, the outline of the house broke the dimness of dawn.

Ma will be happy here. So many years of struggle will be behind her at last. They will be behind both *of us.*

He stepped into the tiny barn. The lantern waited for him on the peg where he always hung it. The metal box of matches sat on the stool beneath. He pulled the match. The snap of the flame lighting echoed in the space around him. He lit the wick, turned it up, and looked over this corner of his domain.

The cow gave him the same look she did every day, one of annoyance at the interruption but relief at knowing she'd be milked soon.

"I'm not late," he told the beast, "so don't give me that disapproving look."

He hung the glowing lantern on the stall wall and pulled down the milking pail and stool. Whistling a very jaunty version of "Sly Patrick," he set to his work. How long had it been since that particular tune had been played at the weekly *ceílís*? He'd have to suggest it. 'Twas a difficult tune to keep up with on his pastoral pipes if the other musicians chose too fast a tempo, though he enjoyed the challenge of it.

Thomas Dempsey was possibly the most talented tin-whistle player Ryan had ever encountered. The two of them enjoyed doing their utmost to out-play each other, whether it be in terms of the complication of a tune or the speed of it. They'd not yet competed over "Sly Patrick."

At the thought of proposing a new tune to try their hands at, a grin pulled Ryan's mouth, making continuing to whistle it rather impossible. He'd come to love the *ceilís* over the past years. Ma loved them even more. 'Twas her opportunity to be surrounded by people, to join in laughter and gladness. He couldn't imagine living anywhere else, not when so much about this place brought both him and Ma such joy.

With the milk in the pail, he patted the cow on her flank, thanking her as he always did for her generosity. "How'd you like a bit of hay, ol' girl?"

Again, a look of annoyance. The cow had a mind of her own; there was no denying that.

He set the pail on a small table he'd placed in the barn for things: the food he brought each day sat there as well, easy to find and grab. He took up his thick slice of bread and allowed himself a few generous bites before turning to fetch the cow her breakfast.

When he was only a step shy of the hay pile, the dim lantern light glinted off something metal high off the ground, not at all where he expected one to be. He looked up to find the dual tines of the pitchfork. Pointed at him.

"What are you doing in here?" a woman's voice demanded. Irish. And angry.

He held his hands up in a show of innocence. "I'd ask the same of you, but I've a good idea what it is you're doing."

The fork inched closer. "And what would that be?"

"Taking a prisoner."

"Mighty brash for one facing the sharp end of a pitchfork." The woman didn't lack for grit, he'd give her that.

"And you're mighty forceful for one standing unannounced in another person's barn."

"I'd say that boot's on the other foot, stranger."

This back-and-forth was getting them nowhere. "I don't know where it is you think you are, miss—"

"Ma'am," she corrected, sounding just a touch out of breath.

"*Ma'am*," he acknowledged. "But this is my barn, sure enough. And you're keeping me from doing my chores."

She stood too much in the shadows. The pitchfork remained all he could see clearly of the madwoman holding him captive. "Aidan," she said.

Just as Ryan opened his mouth to tell her that she had his name wrong, he heard rustling a bit to the side, over by the door. How many people had snuck in without him noticing? He pivoted a bit in that direction. The lantern light vaguely illuminated a figure: a lad not quite grown but no longer a child.

"You remember where Tavish's house is, don't you?" the woman asked Aidan.

"I remember." His voice was not Irish like hers.

"Run over there and ask him to come here straight off."

"I won't leave you here with—"

"She has the upper hand, lad," Ryan said. "A pitchfork can make quick work of a fellow. You'd best fetch Tavish. He'll straighten this all out."

The lad's footsteps moved quickly and not at all silent this time.

"You know Tavish?" the woman pressed.

"I do. Quite well, in fact." Most everyone knew Tavish. He was a friendly sort, personable. And Ryan's position on Mrs. Claire's land meant he'd had ample opportunity to interact with Tavish over the past years. He considered them friends. Indeed, Ryan considered himself on friendly terms with most everyone in Hope Springs. "Do *you* know him?"

"I did." An odd way of phrasing things.

"Do you mean to tell me your name, at least? I think most captors do as much."

"I don't mean to do anything but wait." She took a few steps to the side, the pitchfork never wavering. The movement placed her directly between him and the door. There'd be no escaping until Tavish arrived and explained things.

Ryan didn't truly feel threatened; he simply had no desire to make their situations more difficult than necessary. He suspected that underneath her bravado the woman was a little scared. He couldn't begin to guess at the cause of their current misunderstanding, but he'd grant her

47

the security of not pressing her for answers to his growing list of questions.

"Mind if I sit?"

"Please do; you'll make an easier target."

He couldn't help himself; he laughed. "I'll take the risk."

He slid a bit to the side and took a seat on a low stool. She adjusted her position as well, keeping him within easy range of her chosen bit of weaponry. A shaft of morning light illuminated her, letting him see her for the first time. Though he made vague note that she was pretty and somewhere near his age, any details beyond that were lost. The same feeling of anticipation, the premonition he'd not managed to sort out weeks earlier, crashed over him once more. The force of it temporarily pushed all other thoughts from his mind.

Who was she?

He could see her well enough now to be certain that he didn't know her. Her mouth pulled in a tight line, her gaze didn't waver, her pitchfork remained utterly still. Eyes gave people away; hers showed determination, but also unmistakable worry. He didn't know what she had to do with his most recent bolt of frustratingly unspecific insight, but he felt absolutely certain she wasn't a threat.

He leaned back against the wall of the barn, tucked his arms behind his head and closed his eyes. He would far rather be seeing to his chores, but he'd not let a rare chance to rest pass him by.

"You mustn't be overly concerned that I mean to murder you." A hint of amusement touched her words.

"I only figure, if I'm going to die an inglorious death in this barn, I'd do well to be comfortable while I wait for the end to come."

He opened one eye a tiny sliver, allowing him a glimpse of her without giving him away. She'd lowered her pitchfork a bit, though not entirely. Her posture had slipped. The fearsome warrior of a moment earlier looked deeply tired.

She was a mystery and no denying it. His premonitions had never proven empty. When he felt the winds of change begin to blow, the storm *always* arrived. And the moment he'd truly seen her, those winds had become a gale.

"Are you certain you won't tell me your name?" he asked.

The pitchfork resumed its previous position, though, with him now tucked more in a shadow, the woman could not have known he was watching.

He sighed rather dramatically. "Tell me when brave Sir Tavish arrives to rescue me."

He closed his eyes fully once more and settled in as comfortably as he could. The moments stretched out in silence between them. He'd spent long, exhausting days in his fields the past few weeks. Every day he awoke more tired than he'd been the day before. Sitting still and quiet, he could feel himself beginning to drift off, as much as one could while waiting to be impaled.

His captor coughed. Not the light cough of one with a bit of dust in her throat or from feeling a bit under the weather. Her chest rattled, emitting a sound that made his own lungs hurt with sympathy.

He opened his eyes. "Are you needing to sit down?"

"I'll survive."

He looked at her a touch more closely, as much as the dim barn light would allow. A fragileness in her belied the fearsome picture painted by their current arrangement. The puzzle she presented grew more complicated.

Footsteps echoed in from just outside. A moment later, Tavish stepped through the doorway. He crossed the small barn, with a young man of likely thirteen or fourteen at his side—Aidan, no doubt. As they approached, Ryan couldn't help staring. The lad could've been Tavish's own son, they looked so much alike.

"I'm told we've a situation." Tavish sounded on the verge of laughter, a not unusual thing for him.

The woman lowered the pitchfork, even set it against the wall, and turned to face the new arrival. She froze, then she whispered, "Oh, my heavens."

"Maura." Tavish rushed to her and wrapped his arms around her. "Welcome to Hope Springs, darling."

Darling? Something odd was going on here. Tavish was married, and not to this "Maura." Furthermore, Tavish was quite happy in that marriage. She must be connected to him some other way. A sister, perhaps? Ryan hadn't heard of any O'Connor sisters not already in Hope Springs. The only siblings who hadn't come West were two brothers, both killed in battle.

Maura—it was nice to have a name to put with his assailant—leaned a bit into Tavish's embrace. "'Tis a fine thing to see you again."

Tavish squeezed her tighter for a bit, before loosening his embrace and giving her a look-over.

She spoke again before he could. "You've grown up, lad."

Lad? Tavish is older than I am. How old was Maura? She hardly looked ancient.

"This boy here, is the one who's grown." Tavish motioned to Aidan. "Mercy, he looks like his da."

Maura sighed. "So do you, Tavish. So very much."

Tavish grinned. "Grady always was handsome."

That brought an answering smile to Maura's face. Ryan watched them both, fascinated. He didn't know the exact connection between them, but it was clearly a close and affectionate one. Somewhere in the back of Ryan's mind, he knew that name—Grady—but couldn't be certain where exactly he fit in the O'Connor family.

"I'd wanted to come by and greet you last evening," Tavish said. "But Ma told us not to bother you, as you needed to rest from your journey."

"I'd meant to rest a bit longer, but I caught this interloper in the barn." She motioned with her head to Ryan. "He says the place is his."

Tavish adjusted his hat, returning his attention to Ryan. "In a manner of speaking, it is."

That revelation did not appear to meet with Maura's approval.

"The land and house belonged to my granny," Tavish said.

Maura's mouth twisted in disbelief. "I happen to know that none of your grandparents left Ireland."

"A long story, Maura. I'll explain it in full later."

Maura pointed at Ryan. "As that story likely explains him, you'd best tell me the details now."

50

"And," Ryan jumped in, "as her hearing the details will mean I can get back to work, I support the telling as well."

Maura glared him near to his grave for that bit of cheek.

"This house and land belonged to a dear old woman who meant all the world to me," Tavish said. "She was too old and frail to work the land herself, so it was arranged with Ryan, here— Ryan Callaghan," Tavish abruptly added. "Ryan, this is Maura O'Connor."

O'Connor. She is *family.*

"We've an arrangement with Ryan," Tavish continued. "He works the land, growing crops and making what profit he can. A bit of that is paid back for upkeep on the house and barn and such, and was used by Granny while she was still alive. The land was left to my wife and me."

Maura's fierce expression gave way to a bright smile. "You're married?"

He beamed. "Eight months now."

"Oh, Tavish." She hugged him again. Prickly, pitchfork-wielding Maura O'Connor hugged Tavish with all the tenderness of a doting sister. "It's right happy I am for you. Right happy."

"Once you're settled and rested, you can come have supper with us. I'll introduce you to my Cecily. I'll warn you though, she's fearsome."

"Fearsome enough to hold a pitchfork to a man's throat?" The moment the remark slid free, Ryan pressed his lips closed. At Maura's hard glare, he held his hands up in a show of surrender, and leaned back against the wall once more.

The boy, Aidan, stepped up beside Maura, keeping close to her side. She put an arm around him in a gesture too maternal for him to be anything but her son. To have a lad of likely thirteen or fourteen, she must've been older than he'd first guessed.

"Finish your story, then," Maura said. "Ryan Callaghan works the land. Will he be in the barn every morning?"

"I'd imagine so," Tavish said. He turned to face Ryan. "The family's given Maura and her lad use of the house now that they've come to town, while they're sorting out just what they mean to do in the long term. We've every intention of keeping our agreement with you about working the fields and such."

Their agreement never had included the house. Ryan had meant to change that. What was he to do now?

Ryan stood. "I'd hoped to talk with you about that, actually."

"Walk back with me," Tavish suggested.

Ryan nodded. He turned to Maura. "The cow's been seen to. You're welcome to the milk, if you're needing it, though I'd ask you to save me a glass. Payment for my efforts, if you will."

She eyed him with suspicion. They'd not begun on a good footing, and she didn't appear ready to change that.

Another chest-rattling cough, stopping Tavish in his tracks.

"That doesn't sound good, Maura."

She waved him off. "It'll pass. Have your chat."

Tavish hesitated a moment, but resumed their walk. Ryan strode alongside Tavish out of the barn into the light of morning. He had so many questions that he didn't know where to begin.

Ryan glanced back one more time, though he could no longer make her out in the dim interior of the barn. Her arrival was the change he'd been anticipating for weeks. He felt it in his very bones. Everything had just changed.

"That made for an interesting morning," he said. "Strangers with pitchforks are not a common occurrence."

"I'm guessing my ma didn't warn her that you'd be around," Tavish said.

"To be fair, you didn't warn me that she'd be around, either. Nearly gave me a heart attack, she did."

Tavish tucked his hands into the pockets of his jacket. "Seems we made a mull of the entire thing."

"I'll accept an explanation now," Ryan said. "Better late than never."

"She's family and fallen on a bit of tough luck. They were needing to leave New York and wanted to be around family. We couldn't countenance making them live in the corners of someone's home when there was an empty house amongst us."

He could appreciate that. "Living in someone else's house would be a burden, for sure."

52

"I don't know what she'll do in the end, but for now, they've a roof over their heads."

"*This* roof?"

Tavish nodded. "It's put everyone's mind at ease."

'Twasn't putting Ryan's mind at ease. "You said you mean to keep our arrangement even with Mrs. O'Connor and her boy living in the house."

"You'd best call her Maura," Tavish said. "There're a few too many Mrs. O'Connors around for anything else."

Which brought up another question. "How's she connected to you? Her boy is your spittin' image. It's a little eerie, truth be told."

"Seeing him walk into my barn nearly knocked me over, I'll tell you that." Tavish shook his head in obvious shock. "Aidan is my brother Grady's son. Maura is his widow."

"Grady's one of the two who died." Of course.

"Both killed at Gettysburg." A deep sadness filled his eyes. "Grady, Patrick, and I looked a fair bit alike. Seeing Aidan is like seeing a ghost . . . two of them."

Far too close a connection for Ryan to believe the O'Connors would ever toss Maura and her boy out of the Claire place if she had even the slightest desire to stay. That didn't bode well for him.

"Any inkling what Maura's plans might be?" he asked.

Tavish shrugged. "We're simply going to give her time and see what she decides."

This was uncertainty Ryan hadn't anticipated. *Make plans, then adjust* had been his philosophy for as long as he could remember. But he wasn't at all certain how to adjust for this.

If Maura O'Connor was eventually granted a permanent claim to the house, the land would no doubt be given to her as well. All he'd worked for and dreamed of would be snatched away. He'd lose everything.

Again.

His blurry second-sight had proven painfully correct once more. Maura had blown in, not as a wind of change, but as a tornado of destruction.

Chapter Six

Maura's first morning in Hope Springs was proving more than a bit tumultuous. Holding a stranger off by pitchfork was not something she'd ever imagined herself doing. If only someone had thought to mention that a man would be wandering the place at all hours of the morning.

She didn't like the arrangement one bit. Yet, she had no room to complain. Her trek across the country had been made on the promise of a room. That she'd been granted an entire house for her and Aidan had been an unforeseen blessing from heaven itself. To argue that Mr. Callaghan's presence in the barn and out in the fields was a great invasion of her privacy felt rather petty.

Should he insist upon full access to the house, however, she would make her objections widely known. 'Twasn't merely a matter of privacy, but safety. She was a woman living alone, with a child to look after. Though she preferred to think the best of people, the decade since Grady's death had taught her to be cautious.

"Time to be going," she called to the loft overhead.

Though the home had two bedrooms, Aidan had taken an immediate liking to the open loft. If he felt at home there, she would let him make it his own.

"Do I have to go to school?" He climbed down the ladder.

"You must. At school, you'll learn useful things. You'll be a better reader and writer. You'll learn to do more complicated ciphering."

Aidan dragged his feet as they moved toward the door. "I don't need to know any of that."

"You might. Most people living out here farm. You'd need ciphering to know if you'd money enough for living on. You'd use your reading and writing to order seed and equipment." They stepped outside. "Or you might find yourself pursuing a different line of work that needs those things even more. 'Tis best we prepare for whatever lies ahead."

"*You* never needed all that much schooling," Aidan said as they made their way up the dirt path leading to the road. "You didn't learn to read until you were grown, and you've never done any fancy ciphering."

"Which is why I know how important it is." She linked her arm through his, knowing his objections rose far more from nerves than actual disapproval. "If I'd had any learning, maybe I'd not have needed to work in the factory. Maybe you'd not have needed to shine shoes for pennies."

"I don't mind working, Ma."

She patted his arm. "I know it. And I love that about you. I simply mean to see to it you're prepared for the twists and turns of life."

He needed to be ready to support himself, to survive more or less on his own. He would have the O'Connors around him—she was determined to build a relationship between him and his father's family—but once she was gone, he would be an orphan. Without immediate family. She would not leave him helpless. He had an opportunity to return to the schooling he'd had to give up when hardship forced him to go to work. She would not throw away that chance.

They'd left with ample time to reach the schoolhouse before class began, so she didn't walk quickly. As the days grew shorter, this walk would be made in the dark and cold. Aidan would need to be convinced enough of the importance of school to be willing to undertake the trip without her there to nudge him along.

A number of children, more than Maura had expected based on the size of the town, were gathered around the building.

"Look about you, Aidan. You'll make a great many friends today,

I'm certain of it. Some of these children are your cousins," Maura reminded him. "You'll get to know them better. And I see a couple of boys who look to be your age."

He nodded silently.

They walked to the schoolhouse steps, where a woman, the only adult in the gathering, stood, looking over the children. Maura climbed the steps, but Aidan hung back.

Though a touch out of breath, she greeted the woman she suspected was the teacher. "Good morning. My boy, Aidan, has come to be part of the school." Heavens, but those few words were difficult to get out. Her lungs meant to fight her.

"Has Aidan had schooling before?" A thoroughly American accent, the first Maura had heard since arriving in Hope Springs.

"A bit," Maura said. "He's been away, working, these past few years, though. I don't know how much he remembers from before."

The woman smiled kindly. "He'll catch up quickly, I'm certain. Young ones rally more quickly than adults."

"They've resiliency, there's no denying that." She was counting on Aidan being quick to adapt.

"I am Mrs. Hall," the woman said. "My husband recently took the position of preacher here in town, and I am the new teacher."

"Maura O'Connor."

Mrs. Hall's features lit. "We have a number of O'Connors in our school."

"Aidan's cousins," Maura explained.

"He should feel right at home, then."

She certainly hoped so.

"Will he be leaving early to help work fields?" Mrs. Hall went on. "Many of our older students do this time of year, when so much is being planted."

"That is not currently our plan." She would need to think on it, though. If he were to make a life for himself here, he would need to know how to work and maintain fields. Maura couldn't teach him that. Perhaps Tavish would be willing, though it would be a burden for him to spend his time and effort on someone with so little experience. Aidan would be more of a hindrance than a help.

"Should your plans change," Mrs. Hall said, "you need only tell me. Many of our students also do not attend during harvest, there being too much work to be done. Let me know if Aidan will be gone then. I'll see to it he doesn't fall too far behind."

Maura nodded. She had far more to sort out than she'd realized.

"Mrs. Hall, will you help?" a child's voice called from nearby.

The teacher offered Maura a quick dip of her head before slipping away to answer the child's pleading.

Maura turned her own focus on Aidan. He stood at the base of the stairs still, eying the other students with uncertainty. The children were playing in the schoolyard, a bit apart from where Aidan stood. Even from that distance, he was receiving ample attention.

A boy, likely quite near him in age, looked at him repeatedly, but made no effort to introduce himself. Another small group of boys, younger, but not by too much, eyed him while whispering among themselves. The older girls noted him and watched him with unabashed curiosity—and an obvious reluctance to bridge the gap. Mrs. Hall was occupied with fixing one of the student's long braids.

Please, someone speak to him.

A little girl, likely half Aidan's age, skipped over to him, her braids bouncing against her back. "You look like Mr. Tavish." Another American voice. Perhaps Hope Springs wasn't entirely Irish.

Aidan nodded silently. He'd heard the declaration often enough the day before to not be the least confused or surprised. Seeing him standing beside Tavish in the barn that very morning had driven home to Maura how very true it was. Tavish looked so much like Grady had, though he was older now than his brother had lived to be. 'Twas an odd thing seeing a version of her Grady that would never exist.

"Mr. Tavish gives me butterscotch," the little girl told Aidan.

"I don't have any." Aidan sounded disappointed not to have something to offer her. He'd always had a soft spot in his heart for young ones. Though he hadn't siblings of his own, he'd been an older brother to many children over the years.

The darling little girl offered him a gap-toothed smile. "Mr. Tavish will give you one. He always does."

That sounded like the Tavish that Maura had known: thoughtful and tenderhearted.

"Do you like peppermints?" the girl asked.

"Never had one." Aidan spoke to with less misgiving now. Bless the dear little child's heart, she was easing the way for him.

"Finbarr always has peppermints," the girl said. "He'll give you a peppermint. He gives them to us, but Emma won't take them. Emma's my sister. She's quiet too. She likes peppermint, but she doesn't like Finbarr so much anymore. He got angry at her, and she's still sad at him."

Most of that made no sense to Maura, but the name "Finbarr" held her attention. No doubt the name belonged to Finbarr O'Connor, the youngest of the family. He'd been only six years old when last she'd seen him, about the same age as this little girl. He would be grown now. Eighteen or nineteen years old.

"I'm Ivy. You can be my friend."

Aidan shot Maura a look of amused helplessness. She did her best to return the expression with one of empathy. Being forced into a friendship with a child so much younger than he was could not be how he'd hoped to begin his time at this school, yet the offer gave Maura such a feeling of relief. In time, he would find his footing. And for now, this dear little Ivy would help him at least feel wanted.

"I'll see you after school," Maura said.

"See you then," he answered.

"Be safe."

"I will."

Ivy took Aidan's hand and pulled him toward the youngest group of students. Maura slipped away, heading toward the mercantile. They were in need of food and supplies, and she meant to have the house set to rights, with a warm meal ready when Aidan returned that afternoon. She would make a home for him.

The shop was not as busy as it had been the day before. In their corner of New York, the shops had predictable times of busyness and quiet. Maura would eventually learn the pattern of this one. Once she did, she could come when it wasn't busy. A quick trip would be less exhausting than one during which she had to wait in long lines.

A man stood behind the counter. "Good morning, ma'am. Welcome."

She couldn't place his manner of speaking. He was absolutely not from Ireland, but neither did he sound like anyone she'd encountered in New York. His words were slow without dragging, slipping smoothly one into another.

"You must be the newly arrived Mrs. O'Connor."

She nodded. "I am."

"A pleasure to meet you. I'm Jeremiah Johnson, proprietor here. What can I do for you?"

"I'm needing a few things." She made a quick accounting. Her list was longer than she'd have liked, but she and Aidan had not been able to bring much with them, and the house was empty of even the most basic of necessities.

One by one, Mr. Johnson set her requests on the counter, or, in the case of the barrel of flour, nearby on the floor. Bacon and beans would make a perfect supper that night; they were one of Aidan's favorite meals.

After a bit of quick adding, Mr. Johnson said, "That'll be twelve dollars and three bits."

Her heart sunk. *Twelve.* She couldn't spend so much on her first day, not when she didn't have an income yet. "I cannot spend more than seven dollars." Embarrassment burned hot in her cheeks.

Mr. Johnson simply smiled with an expression of familiarity and empathy. She, apparently, was not the first customer unable to pay for everything she needed. "Is there anything you want to remove entirely? The rest we'll just cut back on."

She thought it over as she eyed her much-needed items. "I can manage without the coffee." She'd miss it, but she could get by without coffee far easier than flour or soap. "And perhaps we might reduce the bacon by half."

He nodded and made adjustments to the receipt. In like manner, she evaluated and adjusted each item. She would have to work hard to make these supplies last as long as possible; she could not allow herself to spend her money too quickly, or she would run out before she had income to replace it.

"That brings you to seven dollars, ninety cents."

Still too much. She shook her head. She'd sold the most important item in the world to her, and she wouldn't waste a single penny she'd received for it. "How much if we take out the bacon entirely?"

Aidan would be disappointed not to have their beans cooked with bacon. But what could she do?

"Still over seven dollars, Mrs. O'Connor."

She rubbed her temples, trying to ease a breath through her tense and uncooperative lungs. Food and goods were surprisingly expensive out West.

They made more adjustments, more cuts.

Mr. Johnson added it up again. With a pleased smile, he said, "Six dollars and fifteen cents."

She might have felt relieved, but the remaining collection of foodstuffs and supplies looked so small. How long would it last? She'd thought her money would see them through a few months, if they were careful. At this rate, she'd be penniless in a matter of weeks. Yet, she couldn't scrimp any further.

"Could I increase the bacon to bring the total to seven dollars?" Aidan was a growing boy. He needed something more substantial to eat.

While Mr. Johnson set a crate on the counter and began arranging her things inside it, Maura counted out her precious coins. Not far distant, she spied a grouping of jars with sweets inside. She recognized anise candy and what she felt certain was butterscotch. The small white ones were likely peppermints. In the schoolyard, Aidan had admitted to never having one.

"Are the white candies peppermints?" she asked.

He nodded. "Four for a penny."

Four for a penny. Aidan would love the candy, but she couldn't justify it. Not out of Grady's money. Once she had a job, perhaps she could save enough to get him a peppermint for Christmas. That was more than half a year away. Surely she'd have a job and an income by then.

The crate was full to bursting. The sack of flour was too large to fit.

Mr. Johnson eyed it. "You cannot possibly carry this all the way back the Claire place," he said.

He was right, of course. How was it, even living with this disease day after day, she still sometimes needed to remind herself of the limits it placed on her? "Could I leave the items here and find someone with a wagon to return and fetch them?"

"Of course."

"I thank you, Mr. Johnson."

"Any time."

She set her stack of coins carefully beside the crate. Mr. Johnson counted them into his own hand as she put her remaining money back in her drawstring bag. It grew lighter all the time. She began her slow walk back toward her new home. Children were no longer outside the schoolhouse. How she prayed that Aidan was happy inside. New York had been destroying him, but would Hope Springs give him the new start at life that he so needed?

The day's excursion was taking its toll on her, and it was still early. She held out hope that the longer she lived away from the city, and the longer she spent not breathing heavy factory air, the more she would improve.

How long she'd debated during her final visit with Dr. Dahl whether she ought to spend even more of their funds on a bit of medicine he said might help her when the disease progressed nearer its final stages. In the end, she'd opted not to. Nothing would prevent the brown lung from reaching its inevitable conclusion. She couldn't justify spending money they desperately need to simply prolong what could not be avoided. Once in Hope Springs, she'd reminded herself, Aidan would have family. Her time could be cut short, yet he would not be alone.

She'd not think on her difficult future now. She had a house to set in order, a supper to cook. A boy to raise and to prepare for whatever lay ahead of him. She had an income to secure. Meager supplies to stretch as long and as far as possible.

And a town she hoped would eventually feel like home.

Chapter Seven

After his discouraging conversation with Tavish outside the barn, Ryan found no joy in working his fields. 'Twas an odd experience for him, who'd loved most every moment he'd spent on his land— rather, the *Claire* land.

He'd been so sure of his future right up until Tavish unknowingly snatched it away. How confidently Ryan had told Ma again and again that he'd have a home for them both soon enough. He'd made plans, and now, as always, he was adjusting those plans to account for obstacles he'd not seen coming. And adjusting meant he and Ma would have to undertake an uncomfortable conversation that evening.

"Forgive me, Ma," he'd have to say. "A woman with a pitchfork stole our house."

Four years he'd worked this land. Four. And on the very day he'd intended to truly claim it, the land was snatched out of reach once more.

Early in working the Claire land, Ryan discovered a large, flat rock along the riverbank. He'd made a habit of taking his midday meal there, listening to water flow past, watching the occasional townsperson cross the bridge, feeling the breeze rush over him on its way to rustle branches of the sparsely clumped trees, and, as it turned out, insufficiently grateful for the years he'd passed without having had any of his blasted premonitions.

He sat there now, unenthusiastically eating his thick-cut sandwich. If a man had to have "insights" they ought to at least come with enough detail to avoid disaster.

All he'd done to change out his fields and his crop, his arrangements with two of the ranches with the hope of eventually convincing more— his original plan depended on all of it, and now he faced losing the land and the house and his entire plan, curse it all. Now what was he to do?

Across the river and up a piece, schoolchildren were outside, running and chasing one another and eating their lunches. He'd often sat in this spot and imagined having little ones of his own at the school. He pictured himself coming to this spot each day at the very time they were outside, enjoying a bit of play. They would look out across the river and wave, and he'd wave back. It'd be their own little moment of connection. He could see it so clearly in his mind.

His father died when Ryan was only five years old. He'd spent the twenty-two years since imagining his da being part of the important moments of his life. If Da had lived, the family might not have left Ireland. And if they had left, they might've found more success in Boston with Da working too. And, in the end, if they had still come to Hope Springs, the house Ryan and James had built together would have belonged to the entire family. Ma wouldn't've been reduced to the role of interloper. Ryan wouldn't be racing a clock so he could continue to pursue his own dreams and Ma's well-being and happiness.

He wanted his one-day children to have a da. He wanted them to have the things he never did: stability, certainty for the future, their father nearby to hold them when they were afraid, to share their happiness, to love them.

You can't sit here all day moping. You've work to do. He sat only a minute longer before shaking off his heavy mood. The best way to face any trouble was directly and with a strategy. He needed to think of a new one.

He walked along the edge of his fields, reassessing the situation. Tavish said that their arrangement with him, as far as the land was concerned, would continue. So Ryan would move forward as planned for this year, excepting the bit about moving into the house. By harvesttime, Maura ought to know what she meant to do. He simply needed an expanded approach to prepare for two possibilities: Maura staying, and Maura going.

He reached the front of the house just as Maura herself approached. "Good afternoon to you, Maura O'Connor."

She didn't immediately reply, but stood silently on the path leading to the house, just breathing. She wasn't flushed like she would be if she'd been running. Why, then, was she so out of breath? He recalled her bad cough that morning.

"Are you unwell?" he asked.

She shook her head but still didn't speak. Frustration pulled at her features. She coughed like before. The sound of it would worry any person who heard it. 'Twasn't a simple tickle in the throat or a need for water. Again she insisted she wasn't ill, but he doubted that.

"Truly, lass. Let me fetch you a bit of water."

She summoned her voice at last. "I need chickens."

He'd've laughed if he weren't so confused. "I can't say I've ever heard that particular cure for a cough."

"My mind is running so many directions at once." A quick cough. An even quicker few breaths. "I find myself forgetting to explain where a thought's come from."

He leaned against the post of the front porch. "I'm full dying to hear where chickens originated."

"Chickens come from eggs. Hadn't you heard?" She spoke with enough cheek to pull a partly-formed smile from him. She coughed again, then pressed onward. "I think I'd do well to have chickens. I'd rather not spend money buying eggs if I don't need to." She paused for air. "But I haven't the first idea where to obtain chickens, how to keep them, what to feed them."

No matter that she stood between him and everything he'd worked for, the woman had a dilemma to solve. He'd not refuse to help. "If you've neighbors with a rooster and hens, you could get yourself some chicks to raise. If you're wanting eggs sooner, though, you'd need to buy mature laying hens."

She nodded. "Where would I keep them?"

"In a coop."

Her eyes darted to the barn. "There isn't one."

"No." 'Twas on his list of improvements he meant to make around the place—for himself. "One would have to be built."

A breath wheezed from her. The sound was worrisome, yet she'd made quite clear she didn't mean to discuss it. "What else do I need?"

"A henhouse for them to lay in and stay warm. And feed."

She rubbed at her pressed lips. "That is a great deal of work for eggs."

"It's an investment," Ryan said. "'Twould be worth the cost in the long run."

"But one must have the money in the short run."

And the first idea how to raise chickens. "Have you never lived on a farm before?"

"Not since I was a tiny child in Ireland."

She might, then, not be interested in claiming this farm for her own. A little bubble of hope expanded in his chest. He kept his expression and tone calm, though. "Is it your dream, then, to live on a farm again?"

She watched him for an unexpectedly long moment. The woman was clearly trying to sort out something about him. Her brow pulled steeply, and she let her gaze wander away out to the distant horizon. "It's been a long while since I let myself dream."

He'd not expected that response at all, nor her tone of weariness. This was a woman carrying a burden, and one, he'd wager, she carried alone.

He found himself wanting to pull her into a reassuring embrace. 'Twasn't a romantic inclination in the least, but a strictly human one. She was hurting, and in that moment, she looked rather desolate.

"You've come to the right town, then, Miss Maura. Hope Springs is a place for dreamers."

She met his eye again. "Is it?"

He nodded. "The dreams don't come easy, and they aren't promised, but they're possible here."

She smiled briefly—minutely, but sincerely. "At the moment, my dreams are centered on chickens."

"Those chickens are known to break a person's heart, though. Always strutting around, promising a person eggs then changing their wee little minds. The worst of all the birds, they are."

"I'll take my chances." She coughed again. After a wheezing breath, she returned to her more earnest tone. "I'm sorry about the pitchfork this morning. If I'd been warned that you would be in the barn, I wouldn't have—"

"I wasn't offended, Miss Maura. In fact, I'm tempted to have you teach my ma your pitchfork technique. Seems an efficient way of defending oneself."

Again, she smiled. The expression suited her far better than the pensive one he'd seen most during their two brief interactions. "I do need a job. Perhaps I should offer to teach all the women in town to use pitchforks as weapons."

"That would be a new one in Hope Springs," he said with a laugh.

She stepped up onto the porch. "I really am sorry about the pitchfork."

"And I'm really sorry my being in the barn gave you such a fright."

With a nod, she disappeared inside the house.

Though there was work enough to be done, Ryan couldn't force himself out to the fields again. Rather, he stood there, thinking. Maura seemed a decent person. She also seemed more than a bit desperate. He rubbed at the back of his neck.

A two-pronged plan was decidedly best, he decided: the first assumed her desperation meant she'd need to claim the house for the longer term, and the other assumed that he was somehow granted a miracle and she wouldn't need the place after all.

He made his way back to James's to sit and think.

When Ryan returned Ma was lying in bed. Retiring early wasn't unheard of for her, but it was unusual. He offered only the briefest of greetings to his brother and sister-in-law then made directly for Ma's small corner.

He pulled back the hanging quilt, determined to make a quick assessment of the situation. Her features weren't pulled in the intense pain she sometimes experienced, but she did look very uncomfortable.

He sat on the edge of her bed. "What's laid you low?"

She was paler than he'd like, but didn't appear truly ill. "Merely tired, is all. We ought not to have laid this house out so long and narrow. I feel as though I've walked miles and miles by day's end."

They'd not yet reached nightfall. This house, and, truth be told, its occupants, were taking a toll on her. Heaven help him, he no longer knew how to save her from it.

"The Claire place is very nearly square," she said, the smallest hint of hope in her voice. "No part of the house is terribly far from any other. Sweet Mrs. Claire often praised her husband for that bit of foresight. It'll be a good change on that score. A bit less walking." She sighed, clearly anticipating the joy of living there.

His stomach couldn't have sunk faster if he'd swallowed a cannon ball. "I don't know that we'll be making that move when we'd hoped."

She didn't seem overly worried. "Mary— O'Connor, mind you, not Dempsey; the mother, not the daughter—"

He nodded, indicating that he understood. The O'Connors, like most Irish families, shared names amongst themselves, which made confusion easy and frequent.

"Mary would empathize with my plight, I'm sure of it. If I explained, she'd talk to Tavish and Cecily. And they would listen; I know they would."

No avoiding telling the truth of the matter. "There's been a complication, Ma. The house is being used now."

She held perfectly still. She didn't appear to breathe. "They've given it to someone else?"

"Not exactly. They've allowed someone else the use of it for the time being, a daughter-in-law newly arrived from New York. I don't know how long she means to remain or if she has plans elsewhere."

"They're taking your land away?" Panic punctuated her words, and with it, her volume grew.

He didn't care to make James and Ennis privy to his current setbacks. With nothing but a hanging quilt separating him and Ma from their would-be audience, he needed to keep this conversation quiet. "No, Ma," he said. "I'm to continue working the land. For now, at least. I don't know what will be decided in the end."

She lowered her voice to a desperate whisper, no doubt remembering they weren't alone in this house. "I cannot live like this much longer, Ryan. I simply cannot."

He gently squeezed her fingers. "I know it. I'll not be giving up on your wellbeing and happiness. I'm adjusting my plans."

"Something you've had to do far too many times, lad." She spoke with equal parts worry and frustration.

He did his best to smile. "'Tis the reason I'm so exceptionally good at it." He patted her hand gently, on account of her rheumatism. "Try not to fret, Ma. I'll prepare us for whatever we face in the end. We'll be ready for it. And it'll all be grand in the end."

She nodded, but didn't look fully convinced.

"When've I ever let you down, Ma?"

Her gaze softened, and she relaxed a bit. "Not ever."

"And I don't mean to start now." He pressed a gentle kiss to her cheek. "Rest up, then."

He tucked her quilt more securely around her, then stood, leaving her to sleep if she could. She weighed on his heart.

He returned to the other side of the hanging quilt. His niece sat on the floor, playing with a carved dog. Ryan dropped onto the floor beside her.

"How are you, sweet thing?" he asked.

"This is my puppy." She ran the figurine up his arm.

"A fine-looking dog," he said. "I missed you today, Nessa."

"I missed you too, Uncle Ryan."

She gave him a kiss on the cheek, something she did almost every day. Nessa was his favorite part of this house and the young family who'd laid claim to it.

"Did you watch the children at school today?" she asked.

He'd once told her that he enjoyed watching the children's games while he ate his lunch, and she often asked him about it. "I did. And they were very happy today."

"Did they have a puppy?" She held her figurine up once more.

"I did not see one. When you're older and going to school, you can take yours and show them."

"And I can show you," she said. "You'll be watching from over the river."

He nodded. "I'll watch for you in particular, lass."

Ness looked over at her ma. "Uncle Ryan likes my puppy."

"Of course he does," Ennis said. She turned her attention more fully to Ryan. "You're back early. Nothing's amiss, I hope."

"I've a few things to sort out, is all. A few adjustments to make in m' plan."

She glanced at the door. "Don't let James hear you talking about your 'plan.' You know it aggravates him."

"You'd think he'd be grateful I'm working so hard to get out of the house and stop being a bother to him—and to you."

She tapped her spoon against the side of the pot. "You've not ever given me a moment's difficulty. 'Tis simply an uncomfortable arrangement."

"And that, my dear sister-in-law, is why I have a plan." He leaned one elbow on his crossed legs. Sitting on the floor wasn't particularly comfortable, but keeping Nessa busy helped Ennis. "Soon enough, you and James will have a home all to yourselves to raise your wee family in. Ma and I will have one as well."

"That'd be grand." Ennis actually sighed. He hated that she was so miserable in all this too. Everyone was. "We'll be a bigger family soon enough. I can only imagine it'll be more difficult even than it is now."

"We'll sort it," Ryan promised her. "I'm adjusting my plan. I'll think of something."

Nessa climbed onto Ryan's lap. She ran her wooden dog up his arm again then over his shoulder. She smiled at him, and he smiled back. Someday he'd have children of his own, his own little family. A wife who got on well with Ma and wouldn't get upset having her around.

Maura's dreams might have been centered around chickens, but his dreams were far bigger. He had to find a way to not let them slip out of his grasp.

Chapter Eight

Maura hadn't found a wheelbarrow or pull cart or anything she might use to fetch her purchases from the mercantile. She wasn't certain she'd have had the breath or the energy to pull it anyway. Nothing for it but to go begging a favor of someone. How she disliked asking for help when she had so little to offer in return.

Tavish was nearby and had been welcoming, but he'd proven difficult to be around. He looked so very much like Grady. The sharpness of her grief had ebbed in the decade since Grady's death, but seeing his face again, hearing a voice so like his, had pricked painfully at her heart. It would again and again until she grew more immune to the shock of the experience.

But she needed the supplies she'd purchased, and she couldn't get them home on her own. If life had taught her anything over the last ten years 'twas that survival trumped convenience. She would, once again, do what needed doing.

No other two houses sat so near each other on this long road as the one she'd been granted use of and the one Tavish called home. She had a near neighbor; that was reassuring.

She crossed the road and walked apace, arriving at her brother-in-law's door without feeling any less unsure of her errand. To begin her time here as a burden wouldn't set her on a very sure footing. Yet, what else was to be done?

'Twasn't Tavish who answered her knock, but a woman Maura didn't know. His wife, perhaps? Her shape had the tell-tale roundness of one anticipating a child. She was beautiful, her posture sure and confident. On her dainty nose sat a pair of green-tinted spectacles.

Green spectacles. Maura'd never seen such a thing.

"I've come looking for Tavish," Maura said.

The woman stood quietly, not responding. Her head tipped to one side, even as her mouth pressed tight and her golden brow scrunched behind her glasses. "Forgive me," she said after a moment, "but I cannot place you by voice alone. You'll have to tell me who you are."

An Englishwoman in Tavish's home. Maura'd not been expecting that. She'd no objection to English people being around—Eliza was English, after all—she'd simply been caught unaware.

"I'm Maura O'Connor."

Understanding lit the woman's face. "Ah, yes. Tavish told me you had arrived. Please, come inside." She stepped back, motioning for Maura to enter.

"I'm not wanting to intrude," she said, keeping to her spot outside. "I'd hoped to ask him a favor. He said I could if I needed anything."

"Of course. Of course."

Again Maura was motioned inside. This time, she accepted the invitation.

The woman closed the door and turned to face her. "I am Cecily," she said. "Tavish's wife."

"I thought you might've been." Though she'd guessed at the connection, she still needed a moment—the length of a heartbeat—to settle the truth of it in her mind. Tavish's wife, an Englishwoman. But also a welcoming neighbor. A stunningly beautiful woman even with the odd spectacles. "A pleasure to meet you, Cecily."

"And I, you. Tavish has spoken often of Grady. His watch once belonged to your late husband, I believe."

Maura hadn't thought of that watch in nearly thirteen years. Before leaving Ireland, Grady had been given it by his grandfather. Tavish had always loved it. When the family went West and Grady remained behind, he'd given it to his younger brother, a token of his affection and a means of connecting them across a continent.

"He still has it?" she asked.

Cecily nodded. "He treasures it."

That was both comforting and heartrending. An item of value Grady had entrusted him with, and Tavish had kept the watch all these years, guarding it, while she'd sold the ring, which he'd saved and scrimped for and so had proudly and tenderly given her.

"Tavish is larking about somewhere, likely up to the barn." Cecily spoke the Irish turn of phrase in her English accent, which somehow chipped away at some of Maura's nervousness. "I can call for him, if you'd like."

There ended up being no need. In that very moment, Tavish stepped inside. Maura's heart lurched, as it likely always would when seeing him. She summoned a smile. His gaze, however, was entirely on his wife. The look of deep, abiding love on his face would have warmed even the most cynical of hearts.

Cecily had turned in his direction, but didn't look exactly at him. "I wasn't expecting you yet. Has the weather turned bad?"

He crossed to her and slid his arms about her rounded middle. "I've come back for my kerchief. The wind's picked up something fierce."

"Making up sweet to me isn't going to get you your kerchief any faster."

He kissed her forehead. "The kerchief's an excuse, love."

"We have a visitor, Tavish. Behave yourself."

Tavish turned his head enough to look at Maura. "You'll not begrudge me a wee cuddle with m'wife, will you, Maura?"

She shook her head.

"Maura says I can go right on sparkin' with you," Tavish said to Cecily.

"Why should I believe you?"

"She'll vouch for me."

"Out loud?" Cecily pressed.

Tavish chuckled. "What's a man to do when his wife won't trust his translation?"

This was a decidedly odd conversation.

"I think we've confused our guest," Tavish said. "You have a tendency to do that, Cecee." He tucked his wife up against his side, his arm draped lovingly around her. Then he turned and faced Maura once more. "Cecily's blind."

He might have said any number of things that would have surprised Maura less than that blunt declaration. Cecily moved about freely, had looked at Maura while they were speaking—at least, she'd appeared to look at her beneath her glasses, had known that Tavish was the one who'd entered the house without being told and before he'd spoken.

"That leaves to me the task of telling her if someone's shaking her head or nodding," Tavish further explained to Maura. "She, however, has a horrible tendency to not believe me. Unfair, it is. Fully unfair."

"Behave," Cecily said. "Maura's come needing a favor."

Tavish actually looked hopeful, as if he was excited to have a woman he'd not seen in more than a decade come asking him to do something for her. "What are you needing?"

"I bought a few things at the mercantile, but haven't a means of bringing them back to the house."

"Say no more, Maura." He pressed a kiss to Cecily's cheek, then pulled away. "I'll hitch my wagon and fetch your things."

"On one condition," Cecily quickly added. Amusement pulled at her features. "That Maura and her boy have supper with us tonight."

"You will, won't you?" Tavish watched Maura closely. "It'd be grand."

She bit back the refusal that rose to her lips. Though she'd intended to prepare a meal special for herself and Aidan, making certain her son knew his family—knew them well enough to lean on them—was far too crucial. She couldn't toss away an offered hand of welcome. There'd be many nights when she could have a meal alone with her lad. Connecting him to his family needed to begin now.

"We'd be most appreciative," she said. "And I thank you."

"School'll be out in a bit," Tavish said. "Do you think Aidan'd be willing to ride up with me? He could help load the wagon and unload at your place."

"There isn't a great deal to unload," she warned him, "simply more than I could carry."

"No matter. It'll do the lad good to work at setting his new home to rights; makes a fellow feel connected to a place."

How very much Tavish reminded her of Grady in that moment, so giving and caring and insightful.

And Aidan will have him nearby when I am gone. There was tremendous comfort in that.

"May I help prepare supper, then?" she asked. "It seems only fair."

Her offer was readily accepted, much to Maura's relief. Being useful was important to her. No place would ever feel like home if she didn't have a purpose.

Tavish kissed his wife and offered a whispered, "I love you, darling."

She brushed her fingertips along his jaw. "I love you too, dearest."

The tender display upended Maura more than she would have expected. She'd not been held that way nor spoken to with that tenderness in so long. She didn't often allow herself to long for it, but the need, the wish, the loneliness was always there, hovering unacknowledged beneath the surface.

She'd been so consumed with grief in those first years that her heart hadn't had the capacity for even the thought of loving again. By the time the acute ache had dulled a bit, she'd been focused on her and Aidan's survival. True healing had come as she'd helped the women of the Tower. Their needs had often been greater than hers, a humbling and motivating reminder. Someone had needed her, and that had given her strength to keep going. She hoped there'd be opportunities for helping here, too, and she prayed her health would last long enough for her to seize them.

Tavish left, the same spring in his step she remembered seeing on him in New York.

"He's happy." She didn't realize she'd spoken aloud until Cecily responded.

"He was utterly broken when I first met him, to the point I worried he would never be whole again. For a long time, it seemed likely he wouldn't— that he *couldn't* heal, but he did. And my heart is grateful every day that he is happy."

Something enormous— something *horrific*, by the sound of it— had happened to Tavish in the years since they'd seen one another, and she hadn't the first idea what. Katie had told her that Biddy and Ian, who'd been infinitely dear to Maura in New York, had lost a child, and she didn't have the first idea when that had happened.

What of the other O'Connor siblings? What did their families look like? How far away did they live? Ciara had a home of her own, but was she married? Where was Finbarr in all of this? What was his situation?

She wanted to be part of this family again, but she wasn't sure how to bridge the chasm that time and life had created between them.

"If Tavish is as much like my Grady as I suspect he is," Maura said, "he will be a wonderfully loving father."

Cecily's hand dropped to her rounded belly, and a soft smile touched her features. "He is both excited and a little bit terrified. He has lost so many people he loved. I suspect he is quietly preparing himself for something catastrophic."

Bless his heart. "I have worked as a midwife. I've delivered more than two dozen babies, and several of those deliveries were very complicated. Tavish's mind might be set at ease to know that I am able and willing to help if I'm needed or wanted."

"Truth be told, that sets *my* mind at ease," Cecily said. "Though I have no intention of admitting as much to Tavish, I am a little nervous myself."

"Every woman is," Maura said. "And, I stand by my offer. I know we are not well acquainted, but—"

"But that can be rectified." Cecily smiled broadly. "I suspect you and I are going to get on famously."

While they prepared supper, they spoke easily on a number of topics:

where in New York Maura had lived, where in Ireland, questions about Aidan's likes and dislikes. Cecily shared much of her own history, and the extensive traveling she'd done.

Maura found she liked her new sister-in-law, a realization that brought as much relief as it did joy. She'd lost her husband, then her father, followed by her mother, and lastly, her sister, all within three years. Sometimes she felt as though grief had filled every available space in her heart, leaving no room for friendships. Eliza had been the only real exception over the years. Even the other women at the Tower had been neighbors and associates, not true friends.

She and Cecily had nearly finished preparing supper when the door opened again. Maura was bent over a bowl, stirring, and didn't look up immediately.

"If you'll wash up, you can help us finish," Cecily said. Then she added, "We're to have guests."

Was it not Tavish, then? He, after all, knew she and Aidan were staying for supper. Maura turned her gaze to the doorway. The man who'd walked in was certainly not Tavish. Whereas Tavish's hair was black as night, just like Aidan's, just like Grady's, this new arrival sported wisps of ginger poking out from beneath his broad-brimmed hat.

Ian, perhaps?

"I need a moment first, Cecily. I'll help, I just need a moment." A nearly American accent. Ian would not have lost the Irish in his voice, not as deeply rooted as it was. His voice hadn't the timbre of a fully-grown man, but the mere beginnings of it. Could this be little Finbarr? Tiny, darling Finbarr.

Tears sprang unbidden to her eyes, and a deep pulsing grief. The little boy she'd adored was grown. She had missed his entire life.

Cecily had abandoned the kitchen area of the room and crossed to him. "What's happened?"

He shook his head. "Nothing to do with my vision."

"I'll ask a hug if you're willing to give one," Cecily said.

Finbarr set his hat on a hook. "You're beginning to say things like an Irishwoman."

"I'm not sure that could have been avoided, living where I do."

He turned back from the hook to face Cecily, meaning he faced Maura as well. Finbarr's face was horribly scarred, his skin twisted in misshapen ridges on the right side of his face. A thick scar ran from his forehead, over the bridge of his nose, and beneath his left eye, ending at a patch of discolored, scarred skin along his left jaw. Her heart dropped to her toes.

Saints of mercy, what could have caused such injuries?

She did her utmost not to study overly long the change in him. She'd no desire to embarrass him. He, however, hadn't taken note of her at all.

As requested, he gave Cecily a hug, one that spoke far more of affection than obligation.

"I'm sorry you've had a difficult day," she said. "Take the time you need. I can always put you to work after the meal."

"Oh, I have full confidence in your ability to 'put me to work.'" The merest whisper of teasing hung in those words, so small it was almost unnoticeable. He stepped away from her, moving toward the fireplace.

Practicing in her mind a few different ways of greeting this nearly grown version of the little boy she'd loved so dearly, Maura waited for him to notice her. But he walked to the ladder and simply climbed it to the loft above.

Cecily's mouth pulled downward in a tight line as she walked back toward the stove. "I wonder what went wrong today." She clearly spoke to herself.

Maura was wondering about things far bigger than the events of *today*. What had happened to Finbarr's face? Did Cecily know he was scarred?

Another question jumped to mind, one she felt more comfortable asking. "Does Finbarr live here, then?"

Cecily nodded. "Since before I came to Hope Springs."

"And he lives here still? Even now that you and Tavish are married?"

Cecily set the pot of stew on the table. She moved with perfect confidence. "He's not yet ready to live on his own."

"He must be eighteen or nineteen now." She kept her voice low, as did Cecily.

"It's not his age he struggles against," Cecily said. "Life in the dark, especially when thrust upon someone unexpectedly, requires a great deal of adjustment."

Life in the dark, Maura repeated in her mind. He *had* been in a heavy state of mind. Perhaps that was a perpetual state for him. She hoped not; he'd been a joyous child.

Cecily pulled bowls from a shelf, then spoons from a drawer. 'Twas so easy to forget she couldn't see. Maura doubted she'd be half so capable were she in the same situation.

Again, the door pulled open. This was a busy house, considering only three people lived here. With Finbarr and Tavish, Cecily had known who'd arrived without a word being spoken. Could she manage the thing again?

Tavish stepped inside, with Aidan trudging in behind him. He held out his arm to stop the lad from moving any further, and pressed a finger to his own lips, indicating they should keep quiet.

Cecily tipped her head in contemplation. "Must be Tavish. Only he would try to trick me by keeping so quiet."

Still, no one spoke or moved. The amusement in Tavish's eyes nearly pulled a laugh from Maura.

"There were two sets of footsteps, though," Cecily continued. "I'd wager you managed to convince your nephew to come along after all."

He sighed quite dramatically. A twinkle evident in his eyes, he shook his head. "One of these days, *mo mhuirnín*, I'll manage to fool you."

Cecily tipped her chin up, her lips pursed in arrogance. "I wouldn't place any wagers on that, if I were you."

Tavish resumed his entrance. Though he crossed directly to his wife, he spoke to Maura. "We've delivered your goods to the house. This lad, here, is a hard and willing worker."

"He always has been," she said.

Deep splotches of red touched Aidan's cheeks. He always had been put easily to the blush. Would he outgrow that tendency? She wasn't sure if she hoped he would.

Her brother-in-law set his hands atop Cecily's, still holding the bowls. "I'll set these out."

She nodded and let him take them. She kept near his side as he crossed to the table. "Finbarr's home," she said quietly, "and he's in one of his moods."

"Combative or despondent?" Tavish asked.

Both descriptors were difficult for Maura to reconcile with the boy Finbarr she'd known.

"Despondent," Cecily answered. "And frustrated, I'd say."

Tavish glanced up at the loft, though Finbarr was not visible, having made his way into the shadows. "He intended to try his hand in the fields today. I'd wager it didn't go well."

Worry tugged at Cecily's mouth. "I am at such a loss as to how we might help, having never faced that particular challenge. No one I've written to for help has any insights to offer either. Short of tying himself to a fence post, I'm not sure how he'd navigate fields he cannot see."

Mercy. Of course. So much suddenly made sense. Cecily's comment about living in the dark, Finbarr not yet being on his own... How had she not pieced together the truth of the situation sooner? He, like his sister-in-law, was blind. Maura would wager that his lost sight was related somehow to the horrific injuries he'd sustained to his face. Heavens. The idyllic life she'd imagined the O'Connors living in this corner of the world had apparently been anything but.

What does that mean for the kind of life will Aidan have here? What if it proved no better than his fate would have been in New York?

Finbarr didn't join them when the time came to take their meal, which did not seem to surprise either Cecily or Tavish. Aidan didn't talk, which was normal for him. They all kept to very neutral topics: crops, neighbors, the coming harvest. Perhaps it was just as well. She'd missed so much of the O'Connors' lives that trying to explain it all to her was likely beyond the scope of a single meal.

Though Maura would have preferred not asking even more of her brother- and sister-in-law, she required more of their help. Pride and comfort would have to be set aside. "I'm needing a job," she said. "But I haven't the first idea where to begin looking. Are either of you aware of anyone that might be hiring."

They both sat quiet a moment, thinking.

"Jeremiah Johnson is sometimes looking for some extra help," Tavish said after a moment. "But I haven't heard he's looking just now."

"The ranches on the outskirts hire help now and then," Cecily said.

"Only ranch hands and cowboys," Tavish countered.

Aidan looked from one of them to the other. His food, a larger meal than either of them had seen in years, sat all-but forgotten as he watched, anxiousness pulling at the corners of his mouth. He was too aware of the state of their finances to have the least doubt she needed a job quickly.

"If you hear of anything," Maura said, "please let me know. I've experience cleaning houses, delivering babies—"

"Delivering babies?" Tavish interrupted.

Cecily reached for his hand, needing two tries to find it. "She and I spoke of it already. It is a fine thing having a midwife so nearby."

"It is indeed."

Perhaps they weren't the only people who would feel that way. "I've also worked in textile factories and taken in sewing and laundry. I'll not balk at any honest work available to me, no matter how menial. Truly, anything you hear of."

"We'll keep our ears open," Cecily said. "And we'll have the rest of the family do the same. Everyone will do whatever they can to help, I am certain of it."

"That was always the O'Connor way," Maura acknowledged.

"Still is," Tavish said. "It still is."

Chapter Nine

Friday afternoon, Ryan sat in Joseph Archer's dining parlor, papers spread out on the table before them. Joseph was a man of business, Ryan was an uneducated and inexperienced farmer, and he'd come to rely on the expertise of his neighbor. Joseph had helped with the details of Ryan's plan to sell hay to local ranches. He only hoped the man could help him now, when so much of his planning needed to be redone.

"Do the numbers still work if I'm not here in Hope Springs?" Ryan asked.

"You mean if someone else works your land while you're away?"

Ryan shook his head. "I mean if the land where I'm growing my crops is somewhere other than Hope Springs."

"Are you leaving?"

"I've no idea." He pushed out a tense breath. "The O'Connors have a daughter-in-law living in the Claire house now. They may very well give her the land."

Joseph made a sound of pondering, even as he leaned back in his chair, eyes a bit unfocused. "That does toss a great deal of uncertainty into your situation."

"There is still land not yet being farmed in the Hope Springs valley." Pointing that out was probably not necessary. After all, Joseph owned nearly every bit of this valley. If Ryan meant to attempt to purchase a piece of it, Joseph would be the one he'd be buying it from.

"The land here, so near an established town and community, combined with the recent addition of a stage line running nearby and the rare and valuable presence of a river, make that land very valuable," Joseph said. "And I paid a pretty penny for it. I can't sell it to you cheap."

Ryan understood Joseph's situation well enough, though that didn't help his dilemma. "I used up a fair bit of my savings purchasing the sickle-bar mower so I could harvest my hay faster. I've so much of it now; it's too big a task by hand. If I lose the land I've been working all these years, I don't have enough money for buying land at a premium." He tried not to be angry at the possibility—at again losing something he'd worked hard for—but it was difficult.

"Perhaps I might be able to find something less expensive elsewhere," he thought aloud.

"More isolated land would be cheaper," Joseph acknowledged.

At last, a bit of good news.

"But your business arrangement wouldn't work if you don't live here."

The sentence landed like a brick. "It wouldn't?"

"Your profits rely on the cost of delivery. Hay that ranches buy at market is usually grown very near to where it's sold, saving the growers the cost of delivery. By growing the hay near ranchers, you're saving them the cost of hauling it back. If you aren't near them, you'll have to factor that extra cost back in."

A number of very colorful exclamations ran through Ryan's mind. "And that cost…"

"Would essentially eliminate your profit," Joseph said.

Ryan rubbed his eyes with his palms. 'Twasn't the direction he'd wanted this conversation to take. "So, if I lose the land I've worked these past years, I'm sunk."

"You might very well be," Joseph said.

"Well, that's a right kick in the bread basket, isn't it?"

The door to the kitchen behind them swung open, and Joseph's little

84

girl Ivy bounced into the room. "Pompah! Guess what I did at school today."

Joseph scooped her onto his lap. "You wrote your name on your slate."

"I do that every day." Ivy sounded just a touch indignant.

"Then I haven't the first idea."

Proud as could be, Ivy declared, "I ate my lunch with a boy."

Joseph clearly didn't know whether he ought to make a show of being impressed or being shocked. "Did you?"

She nodded. "And he said he would be my friend even though he's very old."

"As old as I am?" Joseph asked.

Her nose crinkled up, lips twisting tightly. "No one at school is as old as that."

Joseph's older daughter, Emma, had stepped into the room. She was as quiet as her sister was excitable. "She will not leave him alone."

"This boy she ate lunch with?" Joseph asked.

"Aidan O'Connor," Emma said. "It's embarrassing."

The little one was uncowed. "He's *my* friend. Not Emma's. He said, 'good day' to her today, and then she turned red and ran away. Everyone laughed."

Emma's face crumbled, and, as her sister had so eloquently described, she ran away. Joseph set Ivy on her feet and followed the path his older girl had taken.

Ivy, undeterred, turned her attention to Ryan. "Good afternoon, Mr. Callaghan."

"Good afternoon, Ivy," he said. "It seems you had a fine day."

She nodded. "You look sad."

Was he so transparent? "I'm trying to sort some business matters."

She climbed onto her father's vacated chair and looked over the papers spread across the table. Her brow pulled into a look of pondering very like the expression her father wore when discussing finances and evaluating risks. No matter that his mind was heavy, Ryan found himself smiling at the sight.

"Are you going to be a businessman?" she asked, still bent over the papers, studying them.

"I am hoping to be a farmer."

She nodded solemnly. "Finbarr wants to be a farmer, but he gets lost in the fields because he can't see them."

"That does make things more difficult." All the town wondered what would become of Finbarr O'Connor. The lad, no doubt, wondered that himself.

"I asked Aidan if he's a farmer," Ivy said.

Ryan attempted to answer in a casual tone. "What did he say?" He could plan much better if he knew the answer to that.

"He said he's not a farmer. And when I asked what he was, he said he wasn't anything. He said it with his shoulders down like this." She slumped forward, sporting a frown.

How easily he could hear those words. *I'm not anything.* 'Twasn't Aidan's voice he heard, but his own. He'd felt that sense of not belonging, that struggle to know who he was and what he was meant to be. He'd felt it in Ireland after his da died. He'd felt it when they first came to America, and again when they arrived in Hope Springs. Truth of it was, he felt a touch of that ol' struggle even now.

But feeling a kinship with Aidan O'Connor would not help Ryan's situation in the least. His only fully developed plans depended on Aidan and his mother finding a different place to live.

Again, the kitchen door swung. Katie, Joseph's wife and the girls' stepmother, came in, a wee baby fussing in her arms. "Ivy, where's your father?" she asked, a frantic edge to her words.

"He went after Emma. Her face was red."

The little one let out a screech like a banshee. Frustration and exhaustion touched Katie's already harried expression. She stood in indecision. Having seen this play out in James's house a few times, Ryan had little trouble sorting it: Katie had something that needed doing, but the baby wasn't allowing her the freedom to see to it.

"Allow me to look after your little handful," he offered.

"I'd not put you out, Ryan."

"Nonsense." He held his arms out for the child. "I love little ones, and I haven't any of my own. It'd be a treat."

Still, she hesitated. "He's in a difficult mood."

"It's no matter." Ryan stood and accepted little Sean, who objected quite vocally. "Now," he said to Katie, "you don't worry the least if you hear him in here fussing. Just see to whatever it is you're needing to see to; I'll not be felled by his complaining."

She smiled a little, the strain in her face easing for the first time since she'd stepped into the room. "You mean to have a battle of wills with him, do you?"

"I do." He eyed little Sean with an overblown look of challenge. "And I mean to be victorious."

Katie set a hand on his arm. "Thank you."

He nodded, and she slipped back into the kitchen. Sean's cries of outrage turned to whimpers of dismay. The drool this child was producing would put a Saint Bernard to shame. He popped his little hand in his mouth, gumming it even as he continued mewling.

"He's my brother," Ivy said, pride evident in every syllable.

"I know.- And a fine brother you have, even if he thinks his hand is tasty."

Ivy giggled. "Pompah says Sean is getting his teeth. That's why he's such a miserable tyrant." The unexpected turn of phrase pulled his gaze to the little girl, who grinned unrepentantly. "Mama calls Sean that, and it makes Pompah laugh."

The tyrant was, at that moment, leaning his head against Ryan's chest, crying in the most despondent way. Ryan gently patted his back, walking slowly about the room. Ivy watched his every move from her spot in her father's chair.

"Mama says we'll have to do without clean clothes and meals if Sean doesn't stop being fussy. I think she's saying it bigger than it is. She's examertating."

She was likely searching for the word *exaggerating*. Ryan didn't correct her; doing so hardly seemed necessary.

"Mrs. Smith left, you know," Ivy continued. "Her sister wanted her to live with her, and she thought it was a good idea."

Mrs. Smith had been their housekeeper. Joseph had come West from Baltimore, where he still owned a very profitable shipping firm. The Archers were the only family in the valley who could afford a housekeeper. Ryan, as it was turning out, couldn't even afford a house.

Sean was settling a bit. Ryan began humming "Nil Na La," hoping a touch of music would soothe him further.

Ivy rested her head on her hands, which lay on the table. A little smile touched her lips. "I know that one," she said. "Katie plays it sometimes."

"Do you now the words?" he asked.

"No."

He began to sing, keeping his voice soft and the tune nice and slow. *"Níl 'na lá, tá 'na lá. Níl 'na lá, tá ar maidin."*

His was not a voice that'd earn him any accolades, but neither was it unpleasant. Sean hiccupped between his increasingly quieter whimpers, which Ryan chose to take as approval of his efforts. Even Ivy had stopped talking, which was something of a miracle. He had vague memories of her being far quieter in the years before Katie had come into their lives. Joseph had kept his distance from the rest of the town then, so it might simply have been Ryan's inexperience with her rather than the true way of things. He did, however, firmly believe the fierce and strong Irishwoman had done a world of good in this family.

What would that be like? He thought often of how much he'd appreciate having a goodhearted, fearsome woman at his side, building a life and a home and a family with him. The two of them walking the floor with their babies. Those imagined waves across the river when the little ones were old enough to be at school.

'Twasn't the sort of thing most men admitted to longing for. Why not? Why was wishing for love and family and home so often considered a strictly feminine desire? It ought not be. Men wanted those things as well. They were simply seldom permitted to express as much.

Joseph returned to the room, holding Emma's hand. Her eyes were puffy and edged in pink. The tell-tale tracks of dried tears showed faintly on her cheeks. Still, she seemed comforted. Both their eyes settled first on Ivy, who had, without Ryan's realizing it, fallen asleep.

Joseph's attention next turned to the little one in Ryan's arms. "How did this arrangement come to be?"

"Katie came in looking for you. Seems this unhappy fellow was making trouble for his ma."

"He does that," Joseph said. He looked from his son to his youngest daughter a couple of times before settling on a course of action. "Emma, will you take Sean? I'll carry Ivy to the sofa."

Emma nodded and moved slowly toward Ryan. She was quiet and cautious, always had been. Hers was also a widely acknowledged tender and caring heart. Joseph picked up his sleeping daughter and carried her from the room.

Ryan offered Emma an empathetic look. "I'm sorry your sister was teasing you, lass. 'Twasn't kind of her."

"Papa says she doesn't realize that she embarrasses me. She isn't easily embarrassed, so she doesn't understand."

"Knowing that doesn't make it hurt any less, though, does it?"

She shook her head. "But it helps me not be mad at her, and that's good."

"That is very good."

Her smile was quick and subtle, but genuine. She reached out for little Sean. The transfer was made with little incident, though Sean did toss Ryan a look of utter betrayal.

"I believe your brother is put out with me."

Emma held the little one firmly in her arms. "Katie says he has a mind of his own, which is how we know he's Irish, even though he won't likely sound that way."

"What does your da think of that?"

"He likes everything Katie says. He just smiles and hugs her. Sometimes he kisses her, which makes Ivy squirm." Emma adjusted her hold on her brother, who was beginning to fuss again.

"You'd likely best take him to your da. He'll be screaming the roof down on top of us in a minute."

Emma sighed. "He screams a lot lately."

She walked from the dining room in the direction of the kitchen. Ryan was alone again. He gathered his papers, careful not to miss any. He'd labored over the ciphers for days.

He meant to leave by way of the kitchen, having come in that way and, admittedly, he felt less out of place there than if he'd walked through the formal sitting room. Katie stood over the stove, stirring sharply at something. The poor woman did look done in.

She looked up as he passed. The smile she offered was edged in exhaustion, though she clearly meant to make an effort to be personable. "Are you leaving, Ryan? You are welcome to stay for supper if you'd like."

Though he'd have appreciated a warm meal and company, he could see the strain in her eyes. "I thank you, but I've work yet to do on the land today. I'd best get to it while the sun's still shining."

She nodded. "Did you know Cecily hadn't the first idea you worked that land in all the months she lived with Granny? Even when I lived there, you did have a tendency to slip about unnoticed."

"The newest occupant certainly noticed," he said, with a laugh. "Held me at pitchfork-point until I could prove I belonged there."

Katie laughed, the traitor. "Maura O'Connor does strike me as a woman ready and willing to go to battle if need be."

That was precisely what he was afraid of. Fighting with a widow over land they both needed was hardly an experience he wanted to have.

"A good evening to you, Katie," he said with a dip of his head.

"And to you, Ryan."

He tucked his papers inside his jacket as he stepped outside, knowing the wind would be blowing, as it always did in Wyoming.

If I lose the land, I'm sunk. Those words, in all their horror, repeated in his mind over and over. Were he on his own, were it only *his* future that depended on the outcome, he might have accepted the loss. But Ma needed a home. She needed the support of this community. She needed to live near both her sons and her grandchildren. She needed what joy she could claim, having suffered as much and for as long as she had. He had to fight for her.

As had become his motto over the years, he'd make plans and he'd adjust. But this time, what if all the adjusting in the world wasn't enough?

Chapter Ten

Maura could hear what must have been dozens and dozens of voices not far up the road. She and Aidan were walking to her mother- and father-in-law's home late on Saturday evening. Tavish had told her the town held a weekly party, a *ceílí*, like they'd once known in Ireland. Everyone came, he'd insisted, and she and Aidan would be missed if they didn't attend. The idea of a *ceílí* had appealed to her from the moment Tavish mentioned it. 'Twould be such a good opportunity for Aidan. He would come to know his family better, as well as his neighbors far and near. And there was nothing so joyous as a *ceílí*. She ought to be eager and excited.

Why, then, was she so nervous?

"Michael told me yesterday that he would be at the *ceílí*," Aidan said as they slowly approached the edges of what appeared to be a very large group of people. This was the party, then.

"Who is Michael?"

"One of the lads at school."

Hope bubbled inside Maura. This was the first time Aidan had spoken of any of the school children other than Ivy, the little girl who had insisted on being his friend that first day and, according to the mumbled reports he'd made each evening over their admittedly meager meals, had continued her efforts in the days since.

"Is he your age?" she asked.

"A little younger. They're all a little younger. I'm the oldest."

She'd worried over that possibility. The children of this town had been blessed with the chance for schooling their whole lives. Aidan had been required to give up school years ago to supplement their income. She insisted he take it up once more in the hope that he could finish and learn all he'd been prevented from learning in New York. That meant, however, being grouped with children younger than he was, sometimes considerably younger.

"Is Michael a nice lad?"

Aidan nodded. "He said we're cousins."

"Truly?" She watched him closely, trying to gauge his feelings on the matter. "Did he say who his parents are?"

"He said Da was his da's brother."

Ian and Biddy's son, then. They hadn't had any children in New York. Biddy must have been expecting when they'd left, though she'd not said as much. "You've a cousin near to your age. That's a fine thing."

"Two, actually," he said. "Colum's my cousin too, but he and Michael aren't brothers. And his name's not O'Connor."

"He must be your aunt Mary's boy." Two nephews Maura hadn't even met. Thirteen years of separation had left quite a gap.

Aidan watched the nearby townspeople with both interest and uncertainty. There'd been an eagerness in him, a hope that been growing ever since they left New York. In that moment, the conflicting responses filled his expression.

"Let's scout out the food, shall we?" she suggested conspiratorially.

"I'll agree to that." His voice hardly rose above a mutter. He was as nervous as she.

He was likely also hungry. Knowing there'd be food, she'd opted to skip making supper to stretch their supplies further. They already needed more of several things. Her remaining money would not last long, and she hadn't the first idea what she would do for work when it was gone.

They wove through the gathering. So many people took note of Aidan, no doubt taken aback by the resemblance to Tavish. What would they all have thought of Grady? Would the similarity between uncle and nephew be less noteworthy if the town had been accustomed to the resemblance between the brothers? And if Patrick had also been here over the years, no one would likely have given a second thought to Aidan's appearance. The three brothers had looked as alike as triplets.

She and Aidan had not gone very far when a tall, lanky lad, brown-haired and tender-eyed, stopped them.

"You're here," he said to Aidan. More of Ireland lay in his voice than in Aidan's, yet there was still so much of America.

Aidan shrugged. "I heard there'd be food." His humor had always been dry and subtle. She recognized the jest for what it was. Did this new arrival?

"I can show you where it is," the boy offered.

Aidan looked to Maura, hopeful. "May I, Ma? May I go with him?"

"If you tell me who he is."

Aidan's brow pulled a bit. "I thought you'd know him."

Ah. "This must be either Michael or Colum."

Both Aidan and his friend—his *cousin*—nodded. Now that she knew the lad belonged to the O'Connors, she could see bits of Ian and Biddy in him.

"Michael, I believe."

Aidan made a sound of confirmation.

"'Tis a pleasure to meet you, Michael."

He dipped his head. "And you, ma'am."

Why *ma'am* and not *Aunt Maura*? He must have known their connection. He, after all, had been the one to tell Aidan they were related. Perhaps, given time, she'd feel more like family to him and the others. Time, however, was not something she had in abundance.

"Run along then, you two," she said with a smile. "Fill your bellies."

Her heart warmed to see Aidan rush off so willingly. He'd made a friend, and he'd made it amongst his family. She attempted a deep breath, but it ended in a cough. The walk here had proven quite a trek. She was worn and weary, and the night had not even begun.

If her condition grew worse—she refused to think of it in terms other

94

than *if*—she'd need to ask Tavish's or Ian's families to make certain Aidan still participated in these gatherings. It wouldn't do for the lad to be cooped up at home because *she* wasn't there.

Not far distant was a grouping of chairs, many of which sat empty. Maura made directly for them. She swore she could hear her lungs thanking her as she lowered herself into a vacant seat. She was away from the city now, but felt only marginally better. If only Dr. Dahl had given her a more definitive idea of how long she'd need to be away from the city for her lungs to calm as much as they were able.

People milled about on the far end of the chairs, all holding various instruments. Tavish had said the *ceílís* featured music. She'd enjoy that bit, having always been fond of music, especially that from home. Aidan had not grown up hearing as much of it as she would have liked.

That first day, Katie Archer had indicated that the town claimed a great many Irish families. 'Twas another reason to be grateful Aidan would be settled here. He would come to know the culture of his parents and grandparents in a way he hadn't in New York. Many of the tenements there had been filled with Irish, but the Tower had been a mixture of people from many different places. The experience had been a good one—Aidan had learned to be accepting and open, had learned to love the differences in people rather than fear them—but he didn't feel a particularly strong connection to the land of his ancestors. She regretted that.

Someone approached her from the side. She didn't wish to be obtrusive, so she kept her gaze a bit lowered. The person spoke anyway. "Begging your pardon, Miss Maura."

She thought she knew the voice, but looked up to be certain. As she'd suspected: Ryan Callaghan. She offered a single nod.

"Would you mind if my ma sits beside you?" He indicated the woman leaning heavily on both his arm and her cane.

"I'd not mind in the least," she said.

A painstaking rearranging took place, with Ryan holding fast to his ma as she carefully lowered herself into the chair beside Maura's. The woman wore a look of unmistakable pain.

"Are you comfortable?" Ryan asked his mother.

"I'll do."

He watched her a breath longer, as if unconvinced. After a moment, he seemed to accept her answer. "I'd best join the musicians, or Seamus'll have my neck. If I see Mrs. O'Connor—the *senior* Mrs. O'Connor—I'll send her your way. I'm sure she'd love to gab."

"I'd be obliged to you, lad."

"Seeing as you gave me life, I'll consider us even."

Mrs. Callaghan laughed and shooed him away. "Go join the others. I've a yearning for some music, and they'll not start without you."

"I *am* very important." With a laugh of his own, he sauntered away, greeting people as he passed. He was personable and obviously well-liked.

She wasn't surprised. Though she and he had not begun their acquaintance on a positive footing, he'd not ever been unkind. He'd even come surprisingly close to making her laugh, something she'd not done often enough the past years.

"Mary O'Connor's been eager for your arrival," Mrs. Callaghan said. "She's spoken of it again and again for weeks."

Her mother-in-law had been anxious to see her? Maura wanted it to be true, but no one in the O'Connor family outside of Tavish and his wife had come by. And none had written to her in the years since Grady's death.

"She couldn't quite bring her mind to picture your boy as anything but a baby, though she knew he'd be grown."

"He's not *quite* grown," Maura said, with a small smile. "*My* mind's not ready to picture him that old yet."

Mrs. Callaghan looked over at her son, standing amongst the musicians. "It happens faster than you think."

"Is he your oldest?"

She shook her head. "Youngest. I've three others. The first is in Ireland yet. The second remained in Boston after we left. The son just older is here in town. Ryan and I live with him and his wife and their little one."

Exactly the situation Maura had expected to find herself in. "That has the makings of either a cozy arrangement or a" —she allowed her tone to reflect the discomfort possible in sharing a house with another family— "*cozy* arrangement."

Mrs. Callaghan nodded. "It is decidedly cozy." Though her tone was neutral, Maura suspected 'twas the uncomfortable kind of cozy she meant.

The musicians were beginning to tune up. Ryan had opened the large drawstring bag he'd carried over his shoulder. What instrument could be inside? The bag couldn't've held a fiddle. 'Twas too large for a pennywhistle. He reached into the bag. Maura recognized the instrument he pulled out.

"He plays the pastoral pipes." Maura made the observation aloud, though she'd not intended to.

"He does, and he plays them well." Mrs. Callaghan's pride in her son was touching.

Maura's mother used to speak of her that way. She missed that feeling, the knowledge that someone in this often-cruel world thought highly of her. She missed having a parent to simply love her the way her parents had. She'd lost her sister so soon after her parents' deaths and all of that on the heels of Grady's death. Life had asked so very much of her. Too much, at times.

"Do you play an instrument?" Mrs. Callaghan asked.

"Yes, actually." She couldn't help a grin, what earned her a look of curiosity from her companion. "I happen to play the pipes as well."

Mrs. Callaghan's eyes pulled wide. "Do you, now?"

"I've not had the opportunity in nearly twenty years. We didn't bring them with us from Ireland." She mourned that loss, but they'd been able to bring only what they could easily carry. Clothing and food had been more important than her precious pipes. "Can't say I've heard pastoral pipes more than a couple of times since leaving Ireland, and not at all in the last ten years."

"You are in for a treat tonight," Mrs. Callaghan said. "My Ryan plays like a dream."

"And the others?"

Mrs. Callaghan shrugged a little. "They do their best to keep up."

Was this the pride of a mother speaking, or an accurate description of his talent?

Ryan strapped the bellows to his right arm with the ease and familiarity of one who'd been doing so a long time. Maura hadn't played in so long, she'd likely have needed a moment to remember where all the bits went. Ryan talked with Thomas Dempsey, the O'Connors' son-in-law. Though she couldn't overhear their words, the conversation appeared to be a jovial one.

Every instrument that she associated with the Emerald Isle appeared to be accounted for. She also spotted a banjo and guitar, which she'd first seen in this country, as well as a small metal instrument close in size to a pennywhistle, but rectangular and flat. She wasn't at all certain what it was.

A man Maura hadn't met yet, which was an accurate description of most everyone there, stood in the midst of the open area between the musicians and the chairs. He called out but wasn't heeded. His pulled his lips in tight and let forth a shrill whistle. That went unnoticed as well.

Into the din of voices, the sudden loud drone of pipes called everyone to attention. Pipes were good at that.

The man who'd attempted to catch everyone's notice turned back to the musicians. "My thanks to our piper."

Ryan pressed the remaining air out of the pipe bladder, emitting a sound closer to that of a dying bird than any kind of music.

The man turned to the crowd once more. "We've new arrivals amongst us this week, and we all know what that means, don't we?"

The crowd enthusiastically agreed. Trepidation tip-toed over Maura. As one of the new arrivals, was something expected of her?

The man, whose name she still did not know, but who was clearly something of a leader amongst the people of Hope Springs, looked directly at her. "Where's your lad, then?"

She managed a shrug and a slight shake of her head. She'd not seen Aidan since he'd run off with his cousin.

"He's over here, Seamus!"

Everyone turned toward the voice, including Maura. Her boy stood beside a man she knew on the instant: Ian, the O'Connor brother nearest in age to her Grady. He still had his ginger hair, though it now contained a few strands of white. And he was smiling the same quiet, understated smile he'd so often worn in New York, though strain lay beneath it, and an unmistakable dose of weariness.

Beside him, Aidan stood with his hands stuffed into his trouser pockets, his shoulders hunched forward. She knew that posture well: he was not happy at being the focus of so many eyes. Her lad wasn't unfriendly, but he *was* bashful and far preferred quiet anonymity, something he'd not often been granted since their arrival in Hope Springs.

"Ah, yes. There's 'Tavish Jr.'" Seamus, as Ian had called him, likely didn't realize how unappreciated that nickname would be. He looked back to the musicians. "What do you say, lads and lasses? Shall we favor our newest arrivals with 'The Gallant Tipperary Boys'?"

Odd that he'd choose that one in particular. She hailed from Tipperary, but this stranger didn't know that. Perhaps he'd asked her in-laws. She liked the thought of the town putting in effort to welcome her and Aidan. And, as any self-respecting Tipperary lass, she quite liked the tune they'd chosen.

A moment later, Ian stood in front of her, Aidan at his side.

His gaze was kind but uncertain. "Did Tavish warn you about the traditional 'Welcome to Hope Springs' ritual?"

She shook her head. "He did not." This had been expected by the others, but she'd not been told about it. She'd also not been told about Ryan, either. How many other things had they neglected to tell her?

"Then you're likely unaware that the song isn't the entirety of it," Ian said.

Begor. "There's more?"

"You're meant to lead the dancing." Ian, bless him, appeared apologetic. He always had been one of the most considerate people she'd known.

"Do I have to?"

99

"No one will force you, but it is tradition. That part has been intentionally skipped but once, and then only because that welcome wasn't truly a welcome."

Her heart froze for just a moment. "Is *this* one a welcome?"

Though he and Grady hadn't looked a great deal alike, when Ian smiled, as he was doing now, the resemblance was there. "This is absolutely a welcome, Maura. From the town, and from us."

She needed a welcome from this family she'd once felt such a part of. This past week had held too much silence and distance. As had the past decade.

"Am I permitted to dance with Aidan?"

Ian shook his head no. "Aidan has to lead out the dancing as well, but separately."

That brought wide-eyed panic to her poor lad's face. "I have to dance?"

Ian nodded. "Best pick a partner quickly."

Aidan turned to his mother, pleading in his expression. She knew perfectly well how difficult this was for him. His was a quiet nature. This degree of attention would send his tender heart into a panic.

"If you can't think of anyone you could endure asking, I'll insist you be excused."

He thought a minute. The musicians struck the opening notes of "The Gallant Tipperary Boys." Something passed over Aidan's features, a mingling of hope and relief. He looked over the crowd and, after the tiniest of moments, crossed to one side of it.

Before him little Ivy Archer, the wee girl who'd insisted he be her friend. How Maura hoped he meant to ask the sweet child to be his partner for this welcome dance. She was too young for any embarrassing whispered speculation involving a romantic interest, which would save Aidan some potential distress. And Ivy would be endlessly entertaining, keeping what could've been a difficult moment lighthearted instead.

"What of you, Maura?" Ian asked. "Are you needing me to scout you a partner?"

Whom could she ask? This might be a nice opportunity to spend time with one of the family members she'd not seen in ages. Would any of them welcome an invitation? Would offering one simply be awkward?

Of all the brothers, one in particular had always been very fond of dancing. She took a risk on that still being true.

"Is Finbarr near about?" Only after she asked did she remember that he could no longer see. She hadn't the first idea if he was able to dance.

Sadness touched Ian's face. "He'd begun attending again at the end of last summer, but he's stopped again. No one's certain why. Life's laid a heavy burden on him."

The song was in full swing now, but no one was dancing. Aidan stood watching Maura, Ivy bouncing with excitement at his side. She could not leave him to undertake this welcome entirely alone, no matter that she wanted to ask Ian question after question.

"Would Biddy begrudge me asking you?" She hoped not.

Ian dipped his head. "Not in the least." He motioned to the open area.

She stepped out, and Ian kept at her side. She met Aidan's eye and, to her relief, saw less fear there than she would have expected.

The evening hadn't gone as she'd planned, but neither was it proving a misery. She'd seen a few more of her extended family members. Aidan seemed surprisingly pleased to be there. They were being welcomed to the town.

For the first time since arriving in Hope Springs, she felt truly hopeful.

"I don't know how we're meant to dance to this," Aidan admitted.

"I do." Ivy's eyes were lit with anticipation. "We hold hands and spin in a circle."

Maura looked to Ian.

He shrugged. "Everyone in Hope Springs knows better than to argue with Miss Ivy."

"I feel I should warn you," she told Ian, "I've a bit of something in my lungs just now." The *just now* was a lie, but she wasn't ready to tell anyone what lay in her future. Time enough for that once there was no hiding it.

"We'll move as slow and easy as our instructor will allow," Ian assured her. Ivy assumed control of the situation quickly. They linked hands as she told them to and moved in a wide, fast circle. Quick as a flash of lightning, the townspeople flooded the dancing area, taking up the lines and intricate weavings one generally saw in group dances. Ivy pulled Aidan over to a gathering of dancers, tugging him through the motions.

Ian, bless him, didn't insist Maura do the same. She'd begun wheezing, something he couldn't have helped but notice, but didn't mention. He simply walked back with her to the chair she'd abandoned.

"'Tis good to have you among us again, Maura," he said. "Too many years have passed."

And too few remain. For now, though, she'd think only on the welcome they'd received and the near miracle of Aidan making two friends so quickly. This would be a good place for him, she was certain of it. And that certainty eased a bit of the too-heavy burden pressing on her too-oft broken heart.

Chapter Eleven

"The roof ought to be right as rain, now." Thomas Dempsey looked up at his barn. "If the wind in these parts would stop acting as though it has something to prove, I'd not need to mend things so often."

The wind was little more than a breeze at the moment. Ryan set his hat on his head. "Mother Nature certainly keeps us on our toes, doesn't she?"

"I believe that's the job of any woman." Thomas grinned. "Don't go telling my wife I said that."

"I'm not one for landing a man in the stew."

They walked together toward the road. Ryan had been on his way to his land when he'd spied Thomas climbing onto his barn roof. A couple of questions had revealed the man's predicament: a roof in need of repairs that he had to make on his own. Ryan understood all too well the struggle to maintain a farm alone. He'd happily insisted on helping. But now, half the day was gone; he needed to get to his own work.

"How's Maura faring?" Thomas asked.

Ryan shrugged. "I don't see much of her."

Thomas rubbed at his stubbled chin. "Word around the family is she's needing a job, but none of us knows of any. Without an income, she'll be in a tough situation right quick."

Most people hereabout subsisted off the land, but the land Maura lived on was worked by Ryan, and he claimed the profits. If Maura grew desperate enough, the O'Connors might find themselves in the difficult situation of deciding between keeping him on and supporting their kin. Maura might soon be granted ownership of the land. Ryan had no desire to be relegated to the role of worker, assuming she even wanted to keep him on at all; he'd not have money enough for a place of his own.

"Thank you for your help, Ryan." Thomas shook his hand.

"Any time."

He walked on, down the road, toward his fields. He hadn't yet pieced together a plan that accounted for the possibility of the O'Connors giving Maura the land as well as the house. Without the land, Ryan had no real future here. But leaving Hope Springs would mean losing everything he'd worked for. Ma would have to choose between going with him, which would also mean leaving behind the remainder of her family, or continuing to live in an often-miserable arrangement. And, to add urgency to the situation, Ma hadn't been doing well. Her health was uncertain on the best of days, but she'd had fewer good days lately.

How am I to adjust this time? What solution could possibly exist if Maura's chosen over me?

He'd not yet reached the turnoff that lead to the house and barn when he spotted young Aidan moving with a swift, panicked step onto the road.

"Lad!" he called, drawing the boy's attention.

Aidan crossed directly to him. One look at his face told Ryan that whatever had happened was no small thing. "I don't know what to do," Aidan said.

"Tell me what's happened. I'll help you sort it."

Aidan took a quick, deep breath. "School let out early because the teacher wasn't feeling well. I came home, and Ma was out by the barn, crying. She doesn't cry. Something awful must've happened."

"Did you ask her what?"

"I—" Another deep breath did not calm him any more than the first. "Ma doesn't cry. I can't remember the last time. She just doesn't."

Ryan thought he knew what Aidan said between the words. He'd seen his mother's apparently rare tears and had panicked, running for help rather than talking to her. Ryan scratched at the stubble just beginning to form on his jaw. He likely ought to send the lad to his uncle or grandparents. Yet, he, himself, was headed to the barn and would be there in only a moment. He couldn't simply walk past someone in distress.

"I think our first task should be discovering why your ma's crying," he said.

"How do we do that?"

Heavens, had the child never attempted to soothe his mother? Surely he'd seen her sad or upset before.

"Well." Ryan pointed the lad toward the house once more. He set his arm around Aidan's shoulders and walked with him. "I thought we'd begin by sneaking about and trying to catch her talking to herself about all that's ailing her. If that doesn't work, I'd sort of figured on just asking."

Aidan smiled a little. "If she tears anyone to strips, I mean to make certain it's you."

He and Aidan turned the corner and walked up the narrow footpath toward the house and the barn just to the side of it. Sure enough, there stood Maura, eying a collection of posts and a bent, half-unspooled roll of wire netting. Ryan wasn't near enough to see if she was, indeed, crying, but her posture spoke loudly of frustration.

"She'll give you a mighty tongue-lashing," Aidan warned in a whisper.

"I'll take m' chances." Ryan sauntered over to her, assuming a greater confidence than he felt. He didn't particularly care to press himself into Maura's private concerns, but Aidan seemed to need an ally in that moment. "Good afternoon to you, Miss Maura."

Her eyes shifted to Aidan then to Ryan. Though she was not crying now, he could see enough red edging the rims of her eyelids to know that she had recently.

"What's this project, then?" Ryan motioned toward the wire.

She squared her shoulders. "A chicken coop. At least, it will be once I've sorted what's wrong with it." Her voice held more than frustration.

He heard the tension of pain. Was this from the lingering cough he'd heard time and again, or had she injured herself somehow?

"You've managed to set two posts." He eyed the planks of wood leaning heavily to the side. "In a manner of speaking."

"I couldn't sort out how to dig deeper without also digging wider."

He looked around the area, at the hammer and nails, the wire and posts laid out there. "Where's your post-hole digger?"

"I *am* the post-hole digger." The woman spoke with such firmness. She was no shrinking violet, that was for certain. But she was also lacking some vital information.

"'Tisn't a person I'm referring to. I mean a tool designed specifically for digging post holes."

Her mouth turned down sharply. "That can go deeper *without* going wider?"

He nodded.

She closed her eyes in a show of exhausted frustration. "Next you will tell me there is a tool for straightening wire netting so it can be stretched between posts."

"That requires brute strength," he answered.

She looked at him once more, an eyebrow raised. "I've been trying that, but it hasn't worked."

He smiled back at her. "You might be the Goliath of our day, and you'd still struggle with it. Stretching wire netting between posts is done by at least two people working together. You're attempting the impossible."

She took a breath, though it turned to a cough. As always.

"Ma, why are your hands bleeding?" Aidan's question pulled Ryan's gaze to Maura's hands. Blood had seeped between her fingers.

"What've you done?" Ryan asked, closing the distance again.

"The wire was uncooperative," was all the explanation she gave.

He took her hand in his, carefully, and turned it palm up. Scratches and cuts crisscrossed her palms and fingers. None appeared to be terribly deep nor dangerously long, but she'd certainly done damage.

"Merciful heavens, woman." He met her eyes once more. Beneath her determination, he now clearly saw the pain and misery. "Why'd you not wear gloves?"

"I don't own any," she said.

"I do," he said. "And I'd not begrudge you them. Better yet, I'd've helped you with the posts and netting. Rather, I'd've explained to you how people in this town get coops made and fences laid and barns raised. Neighbors gather and work together and manage the thing in no time."

"I've only newly arrived. I can't ask them to do that."

The stubborn colleen was, though she likely didn't know it, tugging at his heart something fierce. He'd felt just as alone when he'd first come to Hope Springs. He and James and Ma were the new arrivals, hardly acquainted with anyone. He and his brother had labored for so long building the home James now claimed for his own. They, like so many other new arrivals, had made do in a drafty, dirty, tiny sod house while they slowly pieced together something more lasting. He'd watched others with family and friends in town get the help they needed quickly and escape much of the suffering he'd endured. To hear she felt the same, despite having more family here than nearly anyone, made his conscience niggle ever more uncomfortably. He couldn't wage battle with a fellow sufferer.

"You'd best bandage these," he told her.

She shook her head. "I've too much work to do."

Stubborn, stubborn. "If you don't take care of the wounds, they'll turn putrid. Then what good would your hands be to you?"

With that, she broke. She didn't cry, didn't rage. Her shoulders drooped, and she sighed, a sound of soul-deep exhaustion. "I have to finish this. We need the chickens. I can't keep buying eggs. And keeping a large flock would mean having meat now and then. Aidan's a growing boy. He needs meat. He needs eggs."

He turned to look at the lad. "Are you goin' hungry?"

The same stoic determination Ryan had come to know well in the lad's mother pulled at those young boy's shoulders. "We're making do."

Which likely meant they weren't making do at all. He was hanging his hat on the hope of uprooting not merely a widow, but a *starving* widow and her child. *I've been made a regular villain.*

"You tend to your hands, Maura," he said. "I'll see if I can't root out someone with a post-hole digger. You'll have your chicken coop, but it might not happen for another few days. Perhaps not until next week or the week after."

"But I need the eggs sooner than that."

"This is a very busy time in the fields," he said. "You'll get the help you need—I promise you will—but you'll have to be patient."

"I told you I didn't intend to burden anyone with this." She looked ready to fight him, bloodied hands and all. If she'd had a pitchfork handy, he'd have been pinned to the wall like a flesh-and-blood *Wanted* poster. "If I can have the borrowing of the post-hole digger, I'll manage it alone."

"With these hands?" He lifted the one he still held to emphasize the state of things. "If you're going to survive in a place like this, Maura O'Connor, you'll have to learn to ask for help *and* accept it. No one survives here alone. No one. 'Tisn't a matter of being weak or lazy or any such thing. The land here asks too much of people for anyone to last without help. You learn to depend on your neighbors, or you fail. Sometimes that failure means leaving. Sometimes it means dying."

Here he was offering advice to a person in a position to see to it that he failed in a very significant way. Yet he didn't want her to suffer or even to have to leave Hope Springs entirely. No matter where she eventually settled in the valley, she needed to understand the interconnectedness of the people who lived here.

Her gaze was on her son, unwavering, worried, heartbreaking. In a tone far less defiant, but no less determined, she asked, "Will you teach Aidan how to dig the posts and stretch the wiring and all that?"

"He likely ought to learn it," Ryan answered. Though he was more than willing to help build the coop, he knew with utter certainty that when he asked the O'Connors if any of them had a post-hole digger—and he had no doubt one of them did, and it was regularly lent out between them all—they'd want to know why it was needed. The moment they knew Maura needed a coop built, they'd organize in force and see the job done.

If the O'Connors didn't think to include Aidan in the effort on their own, Ryan would suggest it, though he doubted that would prove necessary. "This'd be a good opportunity for him."

"Thank you," Maura said.

She pulled her hand from his, then turned and walked almost regally to the house. Her strength would do her a world of good here. Her stubbornness, however, might prove her undoing.

Chapter Twelve

Maura wasn't at all certain what she was going to do. She was out of food and nearly out of money. She'd gone to the mercantile, hoping Mr. Johnson might be willing to accept a trade. She'd do some work for him, whatever he was in need of that her still-healing hands would permit her to do, in exchange for the barest of necessities to see her and Aidan through the next little while. He'd been kind and apologetic, but unable to make such an agreement.

"During the winter I can barter," he'd explained. "But this time of year, I need cash on hand. I stock my shelves during the summer months, buying things from the merchants at the depot. They require cash."

"I understand," she'd assured him. "'Twas worth the asking."

And so she sat on the banks of the Hope Springs river, catching her breath and fretting. A cough rattled her chest. That'd happened less often of late, or perhaps she'd simply grown so used to it that she didn't always notice. She pulled in a breath and found she could do so the tiniest bit more deeply than before.

Hope began to surge, but she quickly pushed it back. She knew better. She'd indulged in the hope that her mother would live despite the obvious deterioration she'd seen day after day. She'd clung to the hope that her sister would survive childbirth, even as the delivery grew more and more dangerous. And she'd hoped—heaven help her, she'd hoped against all logic against all reason—that Grady would simply knock at the door one day and tell her there'd been a miscommunication on the battlefield and he'd not been killed after all. She knew it could happen. She knew of soldiers who had returned after being declared dead. It was possible. But she had received confirmation that Grady had, indeed, been killed, confirmed by a soldier who'd seen him die.

Hope was an all-too fragile thing, and she couldn't afford to be breakable.

"Maura," a woman's voice said, sounding both surprised and pleased.

She looked up. "Good afternoon to you, Katie. As you see, I've trespassed a bit on your land here. I needed to rest a spell."

"You're welcome to do so. Though on a hot day like today, you might prefer sitting among the trees a bit farther down the river."

She shook her head. "I've no intention of trespassing as far as that."

Katie sat down, adjusting so little Sean could sit on her lap. "I'll be very clear, then. You're welcome to sit under the trees any time you'd like. 'Tis a bit of a magical place. I practice m' fiddle there. I'm nearly convinced it's a fairy circle like those we had in Ireland."

"You play the fiddle?"

Sadness touched her eyes. "I did." She held up her left hand, the one missing every finger but the thumb. "Lost them all in an accident. I've been trying to learn to play with m' other hand, but it's frustrating."

She could appreciate that, though not fully understand it. "I once played the pipes. We had to leave them in Ireland, though. I've not touched a set of pipes in twenty years. If I tried my hand at them now, I'd likely make a noise that'd send the neighbors running, thinking the cow was dying of dysentery or some such thing."

Katie nodded knowingly. "My first few efforts after this"—she raised her fingerless hand again—"bore a horrible resemblance to an alley cat losing a fight."

"Perhaps you and I could play at the next *ceílí*." The idea made her laugh in spite of her heavy mind. "Though we'd best wait until the very end when the O'Connors wish for everyone to leave."

"They'd run for their homes." Katie bounced little Sean on her legs. "Though an early night wouldn't be such a bad thing. I could use the sleep."

Katie did look tired. Exhausted, even.

"Are you unwell, Katie?"

She shook her head. "I confess, though, I'm swimming against a tide. I know that women the world over manage to keep home and look after their children, even with working long hours in factories or as maids, some juggling their demands all on their own. I've none of those extra burdens, but I'm having a terrible time keeping up with the house and the little ones. I thought, perhaps I was simply struggling to relearn how to do things one-and-a-half handed. But it's been over two years since I lost my fingers. I can't still be struggling because of my lost fingers. Not after so long."

Maura knew well the burden she heard in Katie's voice. "My Grady had been fighting in the war for years when word came that he'd not survived Gettysburg. Though I'd cared for Aidan and the home and earned the money we needed while he was away, something about knowing he'd not be coming back changed everything. What I'd managed to do before, I suddenly couldn't. Every task was harder. Every setback loomed larger."

Katie, to Maura's surprise, wiped away a tear.

"Your life has changed," Maura said. "After I lost my husband, my mother told me that change, especially *tragic* change, leaves a person different from before. A different person can't approach life the same way. Until you sort out who you are after that loss, you can't begin again."

"So much has changed in the last two years," Katie said. "Not all of it has been bad, though."

Maura shrugged. "Even good change is change. The fact that any of it was bad would make all of it harder."

Katie took a shaky breath, gently running her hand over Sean's hair. "Joseph says we should hire another housekeeper. We had one before, but she left to live with her sister."

"Why don't you?"

"My mother never had a housekeeper. No one I've ever known has. We've many of us *worked* as housekeepers, but . . ." Misery tugged at her brow. "I ought to be able to do this on my own."

The famous Irish stubbornness. "Would hiring a housekeeper put your family in the poor house?"

"It wouldn't." Katie actually smiled again. "That alone is a struggle to accustom myself to. I've lived a breath away from disaster all my life."

How well Maura understood that. "And would having a housekeeper help you pull your head above water again?"

"'Twould be a breath of air to one who's drowning," she said. "Yet, saying I'm needing the help feels like admitting defeat."

Again, Maura understood all too well. "What is it you'd say to one who was drowning but fully refused the air that would save her?"

Katie pulled Sean into her arms once more. "You are telling me to stop being so stubborn and accept the help I'm being offered?"

"I suppose I am. Though if you tell Ryan Callaghan that I've talked at such length on the very topic he lectured me on only a few days ago, I'll deny the whole thing, swearing on the saints if I have to."

Katie laughed. Maura kept herself to a smile, afraid her unusually cooperative lungs would fall to bits if she tried to laugh.

"What is it you need help with?" Katie asked. "Ryan's not one to lecture for the sake of lecturing."

Though Maura was one who normally kept her concerns to herself, she found Katie to be an easy person to talk with. "I was trying to repair something around the house, something that would help save us money as time went on. Money's in short supply, and I was a little desperate. Managed to tear my hands up."

"I'd wondered about the bandaging," Katie admitted.

"I had opportunities enough for employment in New York, even if none of them were truly enjoyable. I'd not anticipated Hope Springs being devoid of options." Maura coughed quickly. Then once more. After a moment, she had breath enough to continue. "We don't know how to farm, so we can't earn a living from the land. There're no factories; that's not a bad thing, really, but it is one less option."

"Did you work in a factory?" Katie's tone turned deeply empathetic.

She nodded. "I'd been working as a maid, but getting from the neighborhood where we lived to the home where I worked took too much time. The factories were drudgery and dangerous, but they were close and the work was reliable. 'Twas what I needed."

Katie's head turned sharply to look at Maura. "You worked as a maid?"

"I did. I returned to that work the last few months we were in New York."

"Have you ever considered being a housekeeper?"

Understanding hit her in a flash. "Oh, Katie. You're needing a housekeeper."

"I am."

"And I'm needing a job."

"That you are," Katie said. "Now, mind you, once I manage to get myself sorted, I'll not need a housekeeper. This wouldn't be a permanent arrangement."

Maura turned enough to be facing her instead of the river. "It needn't be permanent. I'd have money to live on while I looked for something else, while I found my footing." And who was to say how long she'd be able to do the work? If her health began to fail, she'd have to quit anyway.

"I think I could bear the thought of having a housekeeper if I knew that the housekeeper understood why I struggle with the idea."

Maura nodded. "And I'd be grateful having a job, especially one so near both my house and the school."

"When could you begin?" Katie asked. "I know your hands are hurt, and that would make things difficult for a time."

She'd not thought of that difficulty, but it was a real one. "Beginning of next week?" She didn't know what she and Aidan would do until then in terms of food, but they'd make do.

"You can come up to the house and talk with Joseph about what you'd be paid. He's in the fields, but I could find him."

Maura shook her head. "We'll sort out the details later. I'm simply relieved to know I'll have something to live on. That worry has been suffocating me."

"It seems to me, Maura O'Connor, we're both about to get the air we've so desperately needed."

Chapter Thirteen

Maura walked home after her gab with Katie. Her heart felt lighter than it had in months. Heaven help her, she was letting herself hope again.

She'd not yet reached the house when a sudden burst of distant laughter reached her. She might have only vaguely wondered about it, but she was nearly certain the voices had come from the very destination she herself was aiming for. Were people at the house? That seemed unlikely. Other than Tavish on that first morning, and Ryan Callaghan, who kept mostly to the fields, no one had ever come by.

The voices grew louder as she approached. Too many sounded at once to be discernible, but the tone could not be mistaken. Whatever the gathering she would momentarily be interrupting, it was a jovial one.

She stepped up the path and saw the O'Connors at the side of the barn. Tavish and Cecily. Ian and Biddy. Mary and Thomas Dempsey. Ciara and the man Maura felt certain was Ciara's husband though she'd not yet met him. Mr. O'Connor was there, calling out instructions.

"Pack the soil in tight, or that post'll never stand," he called to Thomas and to, presumably, Ciara's husband. "Don't allow too much slack in the meshing," he warned Tavish and Ian. To the women, who stood in the middle of what would soon be a chicken coop, building some kind of small lean-to against the side of the barn, he said, "We can fetch you more nails if you need."

"I think we've enough, Da," Mary answered.

Maura watched the scene in shock. They were building her chicken coop. They'd made such progress in the two hours she'd been gone.

Neighbors gather and work together and manage the thing in no time, Ryan had said. He'd been entirely correct on that score.

"Maura, there you are." Mr. O'Connor waved her over.

"I can hardly believe this," she said, looking over the family's accomplishments.

"We weren't certain when you'd be back, but we wanted to get started straight off."

"But you all must have work to do on your own land." She knew they did.

Mr. O'Connor gave her a sweet smile, a sight she remembered so very well from their years in New York. He was, quite possibly, the kindest man she'd ever known. "Don't you fret over that. The lads feel they ought to be done with the fencing in another hour. The women'll be well on their way with the henhouse by then. We mean to stop for lunch. Ryan Callaghan says he can see to finishing whatever's left to be done on the henhouse in the next few days."

In silent shock, Maura turned once more to watch the family accomplish what she could never have done alone. "How did you know?"

"Ryan told us."

Embarrassment filled her. "He wasn't meant to spill that in your ear."

"He wasn't gossiping," Mr. O'Connor said. "Not truly. He came asking if any of us had a post-hole digger. Being insufferable busybodies, we harangued him until he told us why he needed one. After that, there was nothing for it but to gather everyone together and come see to the coop. Of course, upon realizing you didn't have a proper henhouse, either, we added that to the list."

"The last thing I want is to be a burden to you." Life would make a burden of her soon enough.

Just as Maura's own father used to do, he set his arm around her shoulders. "Don't you ever feel you can't come ask for anything you're needing, even if it's nothing more than someone to talk to."

"I won't be much help to them today," Maura said. "My hands didn't fare well when I tried managing this on my own."

"Ryan might've mentioned that as well." Mr. O'Connor turned her toward the house with gentle pressure on her arm. "And that you're needing to obtain laying hens and a rooster. Between all of us, we can piece together a small flock for you to begin with."

What an unexpected blessing that was. She wouldn't have to go searching for chickens. She didn't know if Mr. Johnson sold animals and hadn't had the first idea where else to look. "If you'll tell me what it is I owe you—"

"None of that." Mr. O'Connor motioned her inside. "We know you're still trying to get settled. Beginning again in a new place is not without expense."

"Did Ryan also tell you I'm short on money?"

Mr. O'Connor smiled gently. "He didn't have to, dear."

All the town had likely noticed how famished she and Aidan had been at the *ceílí*. The other students couldn't have helped but notice Aidan's sparse lunches. She hadn't yet obtained lye, so their clothes were in need of washing.

"Go inside, lass. Your mother-in-law's there seeing to lunch for the lot of us, and I'd guess she'll want to help you tend to your hands."

She turned back to face him again. "Thank you for this."

"Our pleasure, Maura. We've missed having you among us."

He nudged her on, and she climbed the steps to the house, entering to the aroma of a very traditional potato stew. Mrs. O'Connor stood at the cast-iron stove, checking a pot simmering there.

"There you are, Maura," she said. "We thought you'd be by in a spell."

"I would've been back sooner, but I stopped for a gab with Katie Archer." Besides, she hadn't known anyone was at the house.

"How is our dear Katie?"

"She and I may have worked out a job for me."

Mrs. O'Connor shot her a look of excitement. "Truly?"

Maura nodded. "I've been worrying over that. 'Tis a relief to have such a promising possibility."

Mrs. O'Connor stirred the pot on the stove again. Maura had only ever cooked over a fire. She hadn't the first idea how to use a stove. A difficulty suddenly entered her thoughts, weighing heavily on her mind.

"Do you know if the Archers have a stove like this one?"

"Aye." Mrs. O'Connor set her spoon aside. "Theirs is larger and newer, though. Joseph is quite successful, you know, and wealthy as can be. He owns nearly all this valley, excepting *this* house and land, mine and Thomas's" —the senior O'Connors shared both their Christian names with the eldest of their daughters and her husband, a fact that had provided any number of entertaining moments during their time in New York— "and the mercantile and church house. He even owns the land the ranchers use."

'Twas little wonder, then, that Katie had been confident of her family's ability to pay a housekeeper.

"What sort of man is Mr. Archer?" Maura asked.

Mrs. O'Connor moved to the wash basin and began cleaning knives, the cutting board, and spoons. "Joseph's very like our Ian, though a bit less jovial. He's quiet, thoughtful. As loyal a friend as you'll ever meet. And he's fair."

That sounded promising indeed. "Katie strikes me as much the same."

"Peas in a pod, those two, though we'd once thought she'd make a good match for Tavish."

Maura very nearly laughed to hear that. "Tavish, with someone you describe as quiet? I can't imagine it."

A quick smile did little to hide the pain in Mrs. O'Connor's eyes. "He's changed in the years since you knew him, Maura. Not in the most fundamental ways—he's still the first to rush to the rescue or to lift a person's sagging spirits, and he's still good to his very core—but life has taken a toll on the lad. It has on all of us, truth be told."

"I've—seen Finbarr." Maura made the statement hesitantly, carefully.

Mrs. O'Connor grew very still, washrag hovering over a dirty spoon. "Did he speak to you?"

"No. He climbed into the loft at Tavish and Cecily's house and didn't come back down."

"He was nearly killed just over a year ago," Mrs. O'Connor said quietly, resuming her washing. "In some ways he's doing far better now than he did during those first terrible months afterward. But he struggles mightily. Cecily says it's to be expected. That he'll have times when he pulls away and times when he draws near. But seeing him suffer so mightily breaks my heart. Sometimes I worry that we'll still lose him in the end. Not to his injuries, but to his sorrows. I'm not certain he can bear much more. I'm not sure any of us can."

Then Maura would not tell them of her diagnosis, not yet, of her own uncertain future. They would know soon enough. This family, with their big, loving, vulnerable hearts did not deserve more worries, not when they were being so kind to her and her son. She would tell them later. For the moment, she would simply treasure their loving kindness.

"I'm ever so grateful to Tavish and Cecily for giving Aidan and me the use of this house. We'd've been in dire straits otherwise."

"You could have stayed with us, if you'd needed," Mrs. O'Connor assured her as she dried the dishes. "Though you'd've been far less comfortable, of course." She laid down her kitchen towel, then crossed to the table, motioning for Maura to sit with her. "Having Ryan seeing to the land makes it far easier for you to adjust to life out here. It's so very different from New York. This way, you need not take on the burden of crops and such when you're so newly arrived."

She had to admit that, no matter how uncomfortable she'd been at having a man hanging about all the time, Ryan's role had proven a helpful one. Yes, it meant she couldn't make a living off the land, but that wouldn't have been immediately possible anyway. She hadn't the first idea how to go about farming, nor the ability to work the land on her own. Aidan knew even less than she did.

"Do many families in the valley hire out the working of their land?" She didn't know if the arrangement Tavish had with Ryan was a common one.

"None. Ryan began working the land when old Granny Claire lived here, after the last of her family died. She couldn't manage the crops herself, and he needed the money. After she died and left the land to Cecily, he continued on, seeing as Tavish had his own land and income there. It saved Tavish the burden of working two farms, which he couldn't've done anyway. And it's afforded him and Cecily a bit of extra income. Ryan's been a godsend."

"You make him sound like a saint."

Mrs. O'Connor laughed. "Wouldn't he be amused to hear that? Ryan's a good man, mind you, but none of us is a saint. Besides, he's not working the land out of the goodness of his heart. If I'm not mistaken, he's always intended to save enough to buy it for himself."

That was news to Maura. "Truly? The land and barn, too?"

"And the house, I'd imagine. The old soddie would hardly make a comfortable home."

She wasn't certain what a *soddie* was, but that was hardly the most pressing thing Mrs. O'Connor had revealed. "He wants to buy this place?"

Mrs. O'Connor nodded, her expression too light for the difficulty she'd revealed to have truly wriggled its way into her mind. "As far as I know, they've not spoken of it specifically, though Tavish thought Ryan was going to make an offer last year. He suspects Ryan might not've saved quite enough money to put toward the purchase."

"I hadn't heard that," Maura said quietly.

Mrs. O'Connor hopped up and crossed to the hearth. She pulled back a tea-towel set over two loaves of dough rising in the warmth of the nearly extinguished fire.

Maura sat frozen in her chair. Shocked. Ryan Callaghan meant to buy this house. From the sound of things, his offer would likely be accepted. What, then, would happen to her and Aidan? Mrs. O'Connor had said they'd've made room for her and her boy if this house hadn't been available. They'd likely do so again. But how long could such an arrangement be endured? When Aidan was grown enough, he'd likely have to leave and look elsewhere for work. Her dreams of giving him a life among his family would all come to naught. They needed the stability of a home of their own, here, near his aunts and uncles, cousins and grandparents. She'd let herself begin to believe it was possible. She'd let herself hope.

Questions and doubts began multiplying. What she'd seen as a kindness—Ryan rallying her extended family to help her build the coop—no longer felt so generous. He'd made certain Tavish knew that she was out of her element and had managed to get a much-needed improvement done on land he hoped to call his own. The point of her poverty had likely not helped her cause either, and his pointing out her struggle to get the chickens she needed would have only reinforced that. He would easily be seen as the better choice to assume full possession of this farm.

She'd been going head-to-head with someone in a position to take everything from her. She hadn't known it.

But *he* had.

Chapter Fourteen

"Would you be terribly put out if my ma came and sat very quietly in the house during the day?" Ryan shook his head, sighing in frustration at the admittedly weak version of the question he intended to pose to Maura.

Despite practicing this speech for nearly a quarter hour out in the fields, pretending Maura was standing in front of him rather than his crop, he'd not yet hit upon the best approach.

Perhaps if I tried a less pleading approach. He set his shoulders and, in firm tones, told a particularly tall stalk of grass, "Ma's in need of being closer to me, as her health is not reliable. I need her here during the day, in the house, where I can check on her."

That was less a question and more a demand. He knew enough of Irish women, and Maura O'Connor, in particular, to know that such an approach would likely go about as well as a mouse herding cats.

He addressed the absent lady once more. "Miss Maura, I've come begging a favor on behalf of my mother. She's ill and a bit frail and needs me nearby to look in on her during the day. Would you be willing to let her stay in the house when I'm here working the fields? She'll be no trouble, I promise you."

'Twas neither demanding nor groveling. The underlying difficulty was posed without pity or polish. He was no scholar, but that seemed to him a wise approach.

She'd not turn Ma away after hearing that plea. He hoped.

One thing he was certain of: the hay was coming in beautifully. He'd have some crop loss—that couldn't be avoided—but the fields were producing well. He'd have plenty enough to fill the ranches' orders. He'd easily make back the money he'd invested. And heaven knew his sickle-bar mower would cover more acres this summer in far less time than he'd manage by hand.

It truly was a brilliant plan, as Joseph had said. But losing the land would mean his efforts would all be for naught.

He walked the length of the row, checking for signs of distress or trouble, but found none. A very good sign.

Emerging from one of his fields, he came face-to-face with the very person he needed to talk with. "Maura. What brings you 'round here?"

A jumble of emotions filled her expression, frustration and disappointment being chief among them. And the look was aimed at him.

"What've I done now?"

"Why'd you not tell me you're looking to buy this land?" Of all the answers she might have given, he'd not expected that one.

"For one thing, I assumed your family told you," he said. "For another, I like to keep my own peace, not go spilling my troubles to all the world."

"But you've a taste for telling all the world *my* troubles, don't you?" That question held more than a hint of accusation. "It seems all of the O'Connor family knows I've little money and no idea how to do any of the things necessary to run this land."

"I needed a post-hole digger *and* hands to help build the coop. You couldn't manage it alone, no, but neither could I. 'Twasn't a job for one person. Asking for help when help is needed is the way things are done in this valley. Needs don't stay secret for long."

"Yet convincing Tavish and Cecily that I'm ill-suited to this place would help your cause tremendously," she said. "You can't deny that."

"I've not done anything to undermine your cause," he said. "I'm not that kind of person."

Some of her frustration softened, but that only made the worry in her expression more obvious. "I need this house."

"And *I* need both this land and the house that sits on it," he said. "I've worked for it, for it *specifically* for five years. Five years."

"And I've a son who needs stability and a roof over his head, one that won't simply be snatched away." Though she wasn't precisely pleading with him, a hint of it lay in her words. "This house puts my son near family, puts *us* near family. We need that as well, and I don't know that we can find it anywhere else."

He nodded calmly. "You're reading me my own story, lass. This land puts my ma and me near *our* family. It will give her back some independence and hope she's sorely lacking. This land is my only source of income. We need this land and house too."

She pushed out a short, deep breath. "What do we do, then?"

He shrugged a shoulder and stepped past her. "I don't know."

She walked at his side with a silent but swift step. Her breathing still sounded awful. Whatever bit of lung inflammation she'd arrived with hadn't abated. And she looked every bit as tired as she had then. That exhaustion, and the age of her son, had convinced him she was significantly older than he was. Realizing what he'd been seeing was the weight of worry not the actual passage of years, he now believed her to be likely no more than five years his senior. Not much older, at all. She was simply so burdened and seemed so very alone.

He reminded himself that worrying about her would do him no good; he had plenty enough to be worrying about as it was. Which only served to remind him that he had something to ask her.

"I realize the timing of the request I'm about to make is unfortunate," he said, not bothering to begin less abruptly, "but I'm in need of a favor."

"You're bold, I'll grant you that."

"I'd not bother, but it's for m' ma. I'd endure nearly anything for her." He shot Maura a quick look. Certain that she was listening, he pressed on. "She's not well. It's nothing catching. Her joints are rheumatic and have been for years. It's growing worse, though. She needs me to check on her during the day and to help her with things, see to it she's not suffering overly much."

"She told me the two of you live with your older brother," Maura said. "Cannot he look after her?"

"He and his wife have all they can manage looking after their own place and growing brood. Though they do not do so on purpose, they . . . neglect her a bit." He felt terribly disloyal speaking ill of his brother, but Maura needed to be convinced to accept an inconvenience, and the truth seemed the best way to manage it. "She's made to feel a burden, which only makes it all worse. I need her close by during the day. So I'm asking if you'd allow her to stay in the house while I'm in the fields. She'll not give you trouble, and I'll come inside regularly to see to whatever she needs."

He looked to Maura again. Her brow was drawn, and her face twisted in thought. She at least appeared to be considering his request. Ryan held his breath as they walked onward.

"My mother-in-law said something about there being a soddie?"

Ryan bristled on the instant. "I'll not consign her to stay in that. It's dark and poky, hot in the summer and bitterly cold in the winter. Even the soddie that once sat on our family's land when we first settled in Hope Springs wasn't as shabby as the one here."

Embarrassed color heated Maura's face. "I was going to ask what a soddie is, as I'm not entirely sure. I hadn't meant to imply that your mother should be made to pass her days anywhere so miserable."

He took a calming breath. He believed her explanation, but the thought of his ma confined to those cramped quarters pricked sharply at him. "A soddie is a building made of sod, of dirt. Most of the families here about began in them, living half underground while they built proper homes. Some simply built nicer, bigger soddies. But the one on this land—" How could he adequately describe it? "This one's currently being used as a vegetable cellar, and it's better suited to that purpose than for living in."

She shook her head. "That'd not do for your mother."

126

Her assessment showed her to be a thoughtful person and increased the chances of the arrangement he was proposing not being a complete disaster.

"She's more than welcome in the house. In fact, I've a job, beginning Monday, so I'll be gone during the day as it is."

"You have?" He didn't know whether to think of that as a positive development. "What is it you'll be doing?"

"Grave robbery." She made the pronouncement so solemnly he almost believed her. But a moment later, he spied devilry in her eyes.

He knew how to play along. "An old profession, that, though not a terribly honorable one."

"Hadn't you heard, Ryan Callaghan? The Irish are not honorable people. Violent and ignorant and lacking in any morals, every last one of us."

"You know, I *have* heard that. Nearly every American I encountered when I first arrived in this country told me as much. 'Twas eye-opening to realize I, who'd spent my life surrounded by Irish, had been so mistaken in their character." He picked a blade of feed grass in passing, examining it as they walked on.

"'Tis a fine thing the Americans are willing to explain about us to ourselves," Maura said. "Why, without them, we might've started thinking we were people."

Ryan ran his fingers over the grass. The blade had the right thickness and texture—pliable without being wilted. "Looks like a good crop this year."

"I'm glad to hear it." She sounded sincere.

"I really do love this land, Maura. I can't just give it up."

"I know. But neither can I. A life here, with his family nearby, and a future free of factories and crippling poverty—that's all I have to offer my son."

He stopped at the path leading to the next field. "We're at an impasse, then? Both of us are fighting for what only one of us can have in the end?"

Sadness pulled at her brow. "Unfortunately, it seems life means to make enemies of us."

"I'd've far better liked being your friend, Maura," he said. "I wish fate had dealt us a different hand."

She nodded. "So do I."

He motioned with his head toward his field. "I need to check more of the crop."

"I'll not keep you." She walked away, head a little lowered, not in defeat but in thought. Life was uncertain at the moment for both of them, and Ryan hadn't the first idea who would emerge victorious in the end.

Chapter Fifteen

Maura swept the floor for the second time in a single morning. Mrs. Callaghan was coming that day and would have a full view of how Maura ran her house, of how suited, ill- or otherwise, she was to the life she was trying to build, a life the same woman's son stood in a position to snatch away. Maura would make certain even the most critical eye could find nothing in her housekeeping to disapprove of.

Aidan's spoon scraped his bowl over and over again as he dug for every last bit of porridge. With food in too short supply, her boy was always hungry, even after finishing a meal. That would change on Monday, or at least, as soon as she received her first pay. She and Aidan would have what they needed at last. For a time, at least.

"I could stay home today, Ma," Aidan said. "Then you wouldn't have to be here alone with her."

She'd told Aidan about the arrangement with Ryan, not wishing the boy to be caught unaware. As anticipated, he'd been uneasy, questioning. He'd come short of outright objecting, but she could see he was as nervous as she.

"I'll not be felled by a granny," she told him.

He smiled at that. The expression both warmed and pricked her heart. Grady had been gone for a decade, and he'd been away fighting for two years before that. She'd not seen his face in ever so long. But when Aidan smiled, Grady's face grew sharp and precise in her memory once more. They'd spent only three years together before he'd left for war, and only two of those as a married couple. Two years out of her thirty-three.

Aidan's smile faltered. "You look done-in."

She pulled out a lighter expression once more, crossing back to the table to ruffle his hair and give him a one-armed hug. "My mind was simply wandering, is all."

"I can stay home," he repeated.

She snatched up his bowl and spoon. "Nonsense."

"But I want to help."

She set his dishes near the pot she'd clean before the morning was out. "I've something you can do for me. You've made the trek to school for more than a week now. I think you're well able to manage it on your own without me going with you."

He laughed. Not loudly or boisterously, but with simple, quiet amusement. "I walked the streets of New York City alone, Ma. That was far more difficult to manage than a stroll down one dirt road leading directly to school."

She offered him an apologetic look. "I forget sometimes how far grown you are."

"I'm taller than you now." He rose as if to prove it. The lad was of a height with her. That would change quickly. He'd grow and grow.

"Are you willing, then? To walk to school and back?" That would make her schedule a bit easier when she began her new job. She'd need a bit of time after he left for school to see to chores at home before rushing out the door.

"I can do it." His dark brow angled a bit, and his mouth turned down at one corner the way it did whenever he pondered something. "I think I know the time Michael and his sister would be passing by. I could walk with them."

How perfect that would be. Aidan's daily treks would bring him closer to his cousins. They would forge a friendship and connections.

She wrapped up a thick-cut slice of brown bread in a tea towel. A quick knot held it all together, and then she handed him his lunch. Though he clearly tried to hide his disappointment in such a meager offering, she saw it clear as anything in his eyes.

"I'll have a job come Monday," she reminded him. "We'll soon have money enough. You'll have a proper lunch each day."

"I could find work too, Ma."

They'd had this discussion before. She didn't know if he took the stance so often because he disliked school or because he worried. She wished she knew the answer. How could she ease his mind if she didn't know what was weighing on it?

"I know you're willing to work and help, and I vow to tell you if that becomes necessary," she said. "Until that happens, you're to put that mind of yours to the task of learning. You are doing exactly what I wish most for you to do."

He nodded but, she suspected, didn't truly mean to leave the topic alone. She'd likely be fighting him on the matter until the day he finished the last of his studies. Her Aidan was quiet and gentle and tenderhearted, but, blessed fields, the lad was stubborn.

The sound of wheels and hooves pulled both their attention to the window. A wagon had come to a stop just beside the barn, very near the newly finished chicken coop and henhouse. Maura didn't recognize the driver, but she knew the woman beside him as well as the man riding in the back. Ryan and his mother had arrived.

"Mr. Callaghan is later than usual," Aidan whispered, shrinking back from the window.

Maura stiffened her spine and raised her chin. "We'll keep to our schedule and leave him to keep his." She didn't like that they had been placed in the role of rivals and enemies. Ryan seemed a kind and good man, but she would hold her ground regardless. Too much depended upon her being successful in this new life she'd chosen for Aidan.

Outside, Ryan had climbed down and moved to the wagon's front bench. He carefully helped his mother down, much the way he'd assisted her at the *ceílí* the week before. He'd said her joints were rheumatic. The condition, it seemed, was advanced enough to cause her difficulty.

Maura opened the door and assumed a welcoming expression. Aidan kept to the corner, watching through the window while making himself as unobtrusive as possible.

Ryan and his mother made the painstaking walk to the house. Each of the three steps to the porch required effort and planning. Ryan held fast to Mrs. Callaghan, his features pulled and strained, not with effort but anxiety. He was careful with her, worried for her. Maura had heard it said that one could tell a great deal about a man by watching how he treated his mother.

Maura looked away. She simply could not allow herself to feel anything for Ryan Callaghan other than a determination to best him in their unasked-for competition.

He means to take this home from us. He means to take away Aidan's future.

The reminder had its intended effect: she held firm. He could show kindness to every ailing person in all of Wyoming Territory, but that wouldn't change the fact that he would ruin their lives if she allowed him to.

Behind Ryan and Mrs. Callaghan, the driver of wagon they'd come in set it in motion once more, pulling away from the house.

"I thought the rocking chair might be the best option, Mrs. Callaghan," Maura said as they stepped inside, "but I did not know where you might prefer it to be placed. I'll happily move it wherever you'd like it."

Mrs. Callaghan looked over the space for a brief moment. "By the window, I think."

Maura nodded and moved the rocker from the fireplace to the window.

"Maybe turned a bit toward the room," Mrs. Callaghan said. "I'll feel I've been banished to a corner otherwise."

Maura turned the chair enough to offer a view of both the room and the window at once. She stepped back and allowed Ryan to see his mother settled. Mrs. Callaghan's hand bumped the chair, sending it rocking. Afraid it might shift and topple Mrs. Callaghan, Maura took hold of the back and held it still.

132

Once situated, the older woman actually sighed, a sound of sheer relief. The effort of getting from the wagon into the house had, it seemed, been even more painful and exhausting than it had appeared. The neglect Ryan had hinted at must have been significant for this much effort to be warranted when she would have been far less pained if she'd stayed home.

He remained a bit bent, keeping himself at eye level with his seated mother. "Are you in need of anything? I'll come back a few times to look in on you, but let me know if you're wanting anything just now."

She shook her head. "I'll do."

He stood upright, and his gaze moved slowly to Maura. "I'm for the fields."

"The cow will be disappointed." Truth be told, the cow would be pained and miserable.

He winced a bit. "Nearly forgot about the cow. I'm usually moving out to the fields about now. I'll stop at the barn first."

"James ought to have just let you take the wagon," Mrs. Callaghan said. "He doesn't use it during the day. He has no need of it. Requiring you to wait for him to be ready to bring us—"

"We're here now," Ryan said. "I'll hitch everything my own self tomorrow while James sees to his chores. If he's as hard-nosed and unreasonable tomorrow, at least we'll be able to leave a little sooner."

"Where'd I go wrong with that one, Ryan?" Mrs. Callaghan sighed.

This was a very personal conversation. Maura slipped a bit away, giving them as much space as possible in a house consisting almost entirely of one large room.

"You didn't go wrong at all, Ma. And he's not a bad sort. It's a difficult arrangement we're in, is all."

"He's not making it any easier," Mrs. Callaghan said.

"Time away will do all of us good." Ryan moved to the door but didn't step out yet. He turned to Maura. "I'll be back by near lunchtime, but Ma and I've brought our own food, so you needn't be worried about that."

"I wasn't," Maura said. She had been, though. The matter of food hadn't been discussed, and she'd wondered if she would be expected to feed her guest.

Aidan emerged from the spare bedroom. When had he stepped away? He crossed to Mrs. Callaghan, a blanket under his arm and deep color touching his cheeks.

He set the blanket on the floor beside the woman. "The window can be drafty." He kept his eyes lowered. The edges of his ears turned a deep shade of red.

"Thank you, lad," the woman said, as surprised as Maura felt.

Aidan nodded quickly and without another word moved to the door. He snatched up his slate and tea-towel-wrapped slice of bread and ran from the house. Maura spared the other two only the briefest of glances before hurrying after him.

"Aidan O'Connor, you come back here and give your ma a proper farewell." He'd left without even the tiniest of goodbyes.

He stopped but didn't turn back. "Ma." The moan was as much one of embarrassment as it was complaint.

She held firm. "Do as I've asked, lad, or I swear to you, I'll set a curse on your head so mighty you'll think the banshee—"

"—is real?" He finished her sentence with a bit of cheek.

"*Buachaill*," she said firmly, motioning him back. A cough racked her body, as always. Rushing about made it worse.

He dragged himself back to where she was. Under his expression of annoyance was enough apology to soften her own frustration with him.

She set her hands on his arms. "You're not ever to leave without saying farewell, lad. Not ever. You know that."

"Nothing would've happened," he said.

"That's America talking," she countered. "Here, they don't believe in anything. I know what I know, and I'll not take such a risk."

His forehead scrunched up even as he looked more closely at her. "It wasn't not saying farewell that kept Da from coming back to us. He'd have died anyway."

"Hush." She pulled Aidan into a fierce embrace. "Always say goodbye when you leave. Indulge me in this, no matter how foolish you find it."

"I will."

"Come home safe to me," she said.

"I will."

She squeezed him tighter for good measure before letting him go. He stepped back. His eyes darted to look at something behind her. Blushing once more, he said, "Goodbye, Ma. I'll see you after school," and hurried off.

She knew what she'd see when she turned around, yet she did it anyway. Sure enough, Ryan stood too nearby to have missed a single word.

Maura set her hands on her hips. "Has America stripped you of the old ways as well? Do you now find a woman foolish for not wishing to cross fate?" He shook his head. "I can't say I believe entirely in all the stories we were told as children—changelings, banshees, wee folk—but I've a healthy respect for the possibility of 'em."

She maintained her defiant stance. "Requiring the lad to bid me farewell is not such an outrageous thing to ask of him."

"Not at all." Ryan tipped his head to her and began walking toward the barn. "I'll see you about lunchtime, Miss Maura. And I won't bid you farewell, as that'd leave you less time to celebrate my departure."

"Something I fully intend to do," she said.

He laughed. Loudly. Maura had to fight back a smile. Feeling an affinity for the man twice in one morning would never do.

When she stepped inside, Mrs. Callaghan sat in the rocker, watching her arrival. Maura gave a quick nod of acknowledgment and crossed directly to the dishes waiting for her across the room.

"'Twas kind of your son to bring me a blanket," Mrs. Callaghan said.

"He's a good lad, though I say it myself." She gathered up the dirty dishes and moved to the large pot hanging over the fire. She'd left enough water behind for washing the dishes. "He's also a quiet lad. He grows anxious around people he doesn't know well."

"M' oldest is the same," Mrs. Callaghan said. "There're some very fine people in this world who're the quiet and keep-to-themselves sort."

If the Callaghans continued to refuse to show themselves to be terrible people, this was going to be more difficult than she wanted it to be. She needed this house. But leaving good-hearted people without the home they'd counted on would never sit easily on her mind or heart.

Chapter Sixteen

"I've milk for you," Ryan said to Maura the next afternoon. Heavens, he was worn to the bone. "Tell me where you'd like it."

"I'll see to the milk," she said. "Your mother likely would appreciate her lunch."

The last two days, he'd arrived late, owing to the need to wait on James. Even having the team hitched and ready hadn't convinced his brother to leave any earlier. So Ryan didn't get the milking done until long after the cow had grown uncomfortable and a great deal of precious daylight had been lost. 'Twas lunchtime already, and he'd not even been to the fields yet.

"It'd be a helpful thing, Miss Maura, if you or your lad could see to the milking in the mornings. I can't say if I'll ever get m' brother to move faster or allow me the use of the wagon, so I'm bound to be arriving late from now on."

She took up the pail, not looking at him. "If I can find someone to show either of us how to milk the cow, I'd be happy to see to that bit of work."

"You—you don't know how to milk a cow?" How did she plan to survive on a farm when she didn't know how to do one of the most common of tasks?

"'Twasn't one of my chores on our bit of land in Ireland when I was very small, so I didn't learn." She turned to face him, with that oh-so-familiar combination of pride and uncertainty in her eyes. "After that, I lived in a city, where we bought our milk, like everyone else in the tenements."

"Farming in arid land leaves little room for error," he told her. "If you don't know what it is you're doing, you'll lose everything."

"I've buried every member of my family, including my husband, and left New York, our home of over a decade with only what we could carry and with no certainty for the future. I assure you, Ryan Callaghan, I've already 'lost everything.'"

Mercy. With such a history, she carried a great weight on her heart. "What about your son?"

"I will make certain he has something to cling to," she said. "Coming here has always been about *his* future. And if you know anything about Irish mothers, that ought to give you a great deal of pause."

It did, indeed.

A knock at the door saved him from needing to respond. He looked back at Ma, who sat near enough the front window for a full view of the porch.

"'Tis Tavish," she told him.

"Wave him inside," Ryan said.

"This isn't your home," Maura said. "It's not for you to decide who enters or when."

But Ma had already motioned the new arrival inside. Ryan knew perfectly well that Maura had no objection to her brother-in-law coming inside. 'Twas Ryan's welcome of him that upset her. Yet if he didn't act as though he had a claim equal to hers on the place, he'd soon enough have no claim whatsoever. An impossible situation, no matter how he looked at it.

"Mrs. Callaghan." Tavish greeted her with a smile. "Do you know, my Granny used to sit in this chair just where you are now and wave me inside the same way you've done."

She reached out and took his hand. "I hope I've not caused you pain by dredging up those memories."

"Not the least pain. And I'm pleased to see you here. This house and this chair have been empty too long."

Ryan crossed to him. They shook hands as they always did. "How are you, Tavish?"

"Grand. How are your crops coming in?"

"Faster than I can keep up with them," he said, "though I'll manage well enough."

Tavish nodded. "Better that than crops dying in the fields." His gaze moved to Maura. "I've something for you, *deirfiúr*."

Deirfiúr. Sister. Family was of great importance to the O'Connors, which was not good news for Ryan.

"What is it?" Maura asked while pouring milk from the pail into her milk jug.

"A flock." Tavish spoke, as was customary for him, with a laugh beneath his words.

She eyed him with confusion for a moment before her mouth dropped open in understanding. "Chickens."

"Aye." Tavish poked his thumb toward the door. "Shall we go put them in their coop?"

"We'd best not put them in the house," she countered, a smile touching the cheeky remark.

"Come on, then." Tavish returned to the door and pulled it open. "Let's give the birds a bit of freedom."

She swept past Ryan and Tavish, leading the way out to the porch.

"You'd best go as well," Ma whispered when only she and Ryan remained. "Tavish needs to remember that you've also a claim to this land."

Wise counsel. He stepped out, following the others' path. The wind blew something fierce. He eyed the horizon and billowing clouds. The valley was in for a storm, it seemed.

Tavish pulled something from the back of his cart—the loudest crate Ryan had ever encountered. It must've held a half-dozen hens, none of which sounded the least pleased about their current arrangement.

"The rooster's in his own box," Tavish told his sister-in-law.

"I didn't know these were coming today," she said. "I haven't any feed."

Tavish lugged the large crate to the coop. "Cecee scolded the lot of us for not warning you. Insisted we each send feed enough for one of the chickens for the next week so you'd not have to worry over it."

"She did?" Maura's amazement was as evident as her relief.

Tavish grinned broadly. "My wife sounds enough like Queen Victoria that we all obey out of habit."

Maura laughed, something Ryan had never heard. There was a musical quality to her laughter, one that settled on his very heart like a warm, comforting blanket.

Pull yourself together, man. This is the enemy.

He grabbed the crated rooster from the cart and carried it to the coop, where Tavish and Maura already were. Once inside, he pulled the gate closed behind him.

Tavish pried open the top of his crate. Chaos immediately erupted in the box. Maura took a large step backward, eying the birds with misgiving. Did she also not know how to look after chickens? How could a woman so ill-prepared to look after this land be the one in a position to snatch it away? Surely fate didn't hate him so entirely.

As Ryan released the rooster to join the others, he attempted to hold back his annoyance. Once free, the rooster pecked aggressively at his feet. He nudged it away with his boot and a mild Irish curse.

Maura continued watching the new arrivals with unmistakable distrust. When the rooster moved her direction, she slipped swiftly to the other side of the gate, closing it with a snap.

Tavish joined Ryan in the midst of the frantic flock. "I don't imagine she has much experience with chickens, living in New York for so long," Tavish said.

'Twas the perfect opportunity to stress how ill-suited she was to this life, how much wiser Tavish'd be to let Ryan have full claim to the land. He wouldn't even be planting the doubt; the doubt was already there, clear as day.

Yet he heard himself saying, "We were all new to this at one point, yourself included. 'Twould be unfair not to give her a chance to learn."

Tavish slapped a hand on his back. "True enough." Smiling and content, he crossed to his sister-in-law.

What is the matter with you, Ryan Callaghan? You'll not secure your future or Ma's by being soft-hearted.

Chapter Seventeen

As Saturday evening arrived, Maura prepared herself for a fight with Aidan. 'Twas time for the weekly *ceílí*, Aidan's opportunity to build friendships and spend time with his extended family. She, however, felt too ill to attend. Her cough was worse, and she simply had to rest. She also desperately wished to avoid the inevitable questions that would come if the entire town listened to her hacking for hours on end.

Aidan needed to be welcomed and part of this community *before* they knew how soon he was likely to become a burden to them. If he could be loved and wanted for who he was and for any joy he brought to their lives, he could be more than the orphan left on their doorstep.

He needed to attend the *ceílí*, even if he had to do so alone. She stood at the front door, squared her shoulders, and called out to him.

"Come on down here, lad."

He was up in the loft. He had truly come to love the space, with so much room all to himself. He'd only ever known cramped quarters in their one room at the Tower. 'Twas a luxury having the whole loft to his own self. Maura was so very happy for him.

"We're for Tavish's house," she said. "I'm meaning to ask him and your aunt Cecily to take you to the *ceílí*." Before he could ask questions or make any objection, she pressed on. "M' cough's been fierce today, and I'm needing to rest. Going to the party would be a fine thing for you, Aidan. Michael and Colum will want you to come. Your grandmother and grandfather will as well."

He shrugged a little. "I know how to get to Grandmother's house. I could walk there alone."

He didn't mean to object? "I've full confidence in your ability to walk down the road a few miles," she said, "but I'd like you to go with your aunt and uncle."

"We'd better ask them first." He rolled his eyes as he reached past her and opened the door.

"You're not going to argue with me?" She'd fully expected him to do exactly that.

"I liked the *ceílí*," he said. "And Ivy said her mother's bringing tarts. I've never had one, but she said they're the best thing I'll ever eat in all my life. Emma says her sister's exaggerating only a little."

Maura ought to have known that food would be the key to getting Aidan's cooperation, especially as there hadn't been any eggs that morning, and the cupboards were basically bare. They were both hungry.

"Let's go see if Tavish and Cecily have left yet," Aidan said, already to the edge of the porch.

She pulled the door closed behind her and walked at his side. "You and Ivy Archer seem to be good friends."

"That's what she tells me." He flashed a smile, one heavy with embarrassment. "Michael has a little sister. She pesters him same as Ivy pesters me."

Ah. He spoke so seriously that she didn't dare laugh, though she felt sorely tempted to. "So Ivy's rather like a little sister to you."

"I suppose." Far from bothering him, he seemed pleased.

"I'll be working at the Archer house starting Monday," she said.

"Did you know Uncle Finbarr works there?"

Now that he said it, she thought she remembered hearing something like that. Perhaps Finbarr would tell her a bit about the Archer family, about what working for them was like, how she'd best prove a helpful but unobtrusive addition to their household.

Before even reaching the road, Maura began coughing again. That day her lungs had felt more like they had in New York. Heavy. Tight. Painful. She'd been doing better, yet had watched for this to happen. Dr. Dahl had warned her not to be fooled by periods of improvement.

"Too many workers see a little improvement after leaving the factory and think they're healed enough to go back," he'd said. "They do not last long."

She stood at the edge of the road, coughing and wheezing, trying to take small enough breaths to get the air she needed without further irritating her lungs. Her shoulders heaved with the effort. Sometimes these bouts lasted for so long that every muscle in her upper body hurt and ached for days afterward.

Aidan set his hand on her back. When she'd first been afflicted with these body-shaking coughs, he'd thumped her back, wanting to help. The effort didn't improve her breathing and only added to her misery. She'd finally convinced him to try a different approach.

"I can walk the rest of the way alone," he said. "I can see Tavish's house there. I'll not get lost."

His turns of phrase grew more Irish whenever he tried to comfort her. Did he know he did that? Did he realize how much that tiny connection to her homeland touched her?

"I only need a moment." She managed all five words without stopping to gasp for air. "I want to offer them a good evening. And thank them for taking you. And—" 'Twas too many words, too much air. She breathed slow and shallow through the tightness and pain. A bit of calm came to her lungs. "And I'd like to speak with Finbarr."

"But if you should be resting—"

"I'll not stay long." The last emerged easier and more whole. And, thank the heavens, she'd not coughed up any blood. Everyone knew what it meant. The other women at the factory had called that "the red mark of death."

She'd regained enough control to resume their journey. Neither of them spoke. She knew Aidan worried, but she didn't know what to do about it. He knew of her illness, but he didn't know how potentially dire the situation truly was. She would not allow him to carry that burden. But how could she set his mind at ease without lying to him?

They reached Tavish's door and knocked. Very little time passed before it opened.

Cecily was beautiful. That truth always surprised Maura, though she couldn't say why. Perhaps because she was *strikingly* beautiful, not merely pleasant-looking. Perhaps because Tavish was also rather shockingly handsome, and two such fine-looking people finding each other in such a tiny place seemed too unlikely to be real.

Perhaps because Cecily's green spectacles would, on anyone else, have been the aspect of her appearance that most pulled one's notice, but on her they weren't.

Perhaps because when she spoke, it was an almost aristocratic English voice that emerged and, being Irish, Maura had been brought up to associate the well-to-do in England with all that was ugly and horrid in the world. She'd unlearned those lessons to a large extent, living as she had amongst so many different people from different places in their rundown tenement. But underneath all the learning and unlearning, a person still struggled with the way she'd been first taught to respond to certain voices, certain languages, certain appearances.

"I will need you to tell me who you are." Cecily spoke both firmly and gently. She clearly was not ashamed of her blindness, but she also acknowledged that people were unaccustomed to the accommodation and often needed reminding.

"'Tis Maura and Aidan," she said.

Cecily's mouth tugged down at the corners. "Are you unwell, Maura?"

How could she possibly tell that? "A little." She didn't care to share the extent of it; she didn't dare. "That's why we've come by."

"Please, come inside." Cecily motioned them in.

They slipped past her. All of the easy confidence Aidan had exuded upon leaving their house had disappeared. That often happened. When only the two of them were together, he was sure of himself, talkative. He grew far more uncertain with other people.

"I'm hoping you and Tavish would be willing to take Aidan with you to the *ceili*," Maura said. "I'm not feeling equal to it this evening."

"You sound as though you have a little bit of a tickle in your lungs or throat," Cecily said.

"Yes." That was as detailed an explanation as she would offer. "Would you mind terribly if he went with you?"

"Not at all." Cecily smiled at Aidan. How did she know where he was? He'd not spoken. "Tavish should be done hitching the cart in a moment."

Knowing Aidan had a means of arriving at the party, as well as someone to look after him, Maura's worries eased. For the first time, she truly looked around the room. There, facing the empty fireplace, sat Finbarr. He'd not said a word in greeting, nor turned toward them. Cecily was blind as well, yet she faced them as they spoke. Why didn't he?

"Good evening, Finbarr," Maura said.

His head moved the smallest bit. "Good evening, Maura."

'Twas still so odd to hear such a deep voice coming from the lad she'd known at a time when his words had emerged in the high-pitched tone of a six-year-old. That he was broad-shouldered, tall, and a touch lanky, like Ian, was equally jarring.

She moved to an empty chair adjacent to his. "Are you meaning to go to the party tonight?"

He shook his head in mute denial.

"Would you mind, then, if I sat here a spell? I'm in need of a rest, but I'd also appreciate some advice."

That clearly surprised him. He turned fully toward her for the first time. Saints, the scars on his face. She would likely grow accustomed to them in time, but they were extensive and thick and dark. Something truly terrible must have happened to him.

"I'm to begin working for the Archers on Monday." A cough—one blessedly small—prevented her from continuing.

"Joseph said you were." Finbarr spoke into the silence that followed her cough. "He's grateful to you. Katie's been struggling. He worries a lot about her."

Maura didn't yet know Joseph Archer, but from all she'd heard of him, she liked him already.

"I know you work for them," Maura pressed forward. "What can you tell me of the family? What is most likely to gain their approval? What ought I do to make certain they'll be pleased to have me there?"

He rubbed at the back of his neck, making a sound of pondering. "Don't be late," he said. "They'll not scold you or even begrudge you, but Joseph's always pleased when I arrive on time or a bit early."

Arrive on time. That would not be difficult. Working in the factory taught one the importance of being punctual.

Tavish stepped inside. The man was forever smiling. Grady had been the same way.

"We're to take Aidan with us tonight," Cecily said without needing to be told who'd arrived.

"Are you not coming, Maura?" Tavish asked.

"I'm feeling a bit poor this evening." She made certain to show none of her actual concern. "And I'm of a mind to ply Finbarr for information about my new employers."

"He's the one to ask," Tavish said. "Though anyone in town will tell you the Archers are fine, good people."

Cecily held her hand out to her husband. He took it without hesitation.

"We would do well to be on our way," she said. "Your parents will be quite upset with us if we are late bringing their grandson."

Tavish kept her hand in his as he moved back to the door. He pulled a cane off a hook and set it in her hand.

"Come along, Aidan," he called over. "Your aunt's right; your grandparents'll have our necks if we're late. They like you better than they like either of us."

Aidan flushed a deep red, but he also laughed. He and Maura had always been happy together, but he didn't laugh often. *She* didn't laugh often. How might he have been different if he'd had his father around, or at least the O'Connor family? They'd'd've made him laugh, would've brought a smile to his face. He'd only had her, and instead of laughing, he was often withdrawn and uncertain. Had she done that to him? She didn't consider timidity a failure in a person by any means. But his quietness was often more than simple bashfulness. 'Twas doubt: in himself, in the world around him, in the future.

He'll have the O'Connors now, though. He'll have them after I'm gone.

The door was closed, and they were gone. Finbarr sighed, deeply. If she was not mistaken, his was a sigh of disappointment.

"Is something the matter, lad?" she asked.

He started the tiniest, minutest bit. Apparently, he'd forgotten she was there.

"I'm just glad they're gone," Finbarr said. "Tavish never stops talking. It's peaceful only when he leaves." He was not the least convincing.

"I enjoyed the *ceílí* last week," Maura said, keeping her tone neutral. "'Twas a bit chaotic, though."

"They usually are."

She heard no longing in his voice. Perhaps the disappointment from before had not been about missing the party.

"Ivy Archer told Aidan that her mother would be bringing tarts, and that those tarts were the most delicious food in all the world. Makes me wish I felt well enough to be there, to find out for myself."

"Katie had a business for a time baking breads and tarts and things like that. She really is very good. But Ivy is also a born storyteller. Everything is theatrical with her." Finbarr smiled, though it was brief and marred by his scars.

"I look forward to knowing her better."

His brow pulled in thought once more. "That's another thing that'll help with your new position. Katie loves those girls. Treat them kindly, and she'll praise you to the heavens."

"And Joseph? Does he love them as well?"

"Of course he does." Finbarr spoke as if that ought to have been obvious, despite his having only specifically mentioned Katie. "They're *his* daughters."

148

His words didn't make sense.

"And hers," she added.

Finbarr shook his head. "They're not, though she thinks of them that way."

Joseph is the girls' father, but Katie is not their mother. More than the mystery of it, Maura clung to the promise. Here was someone in this town lovingly raising another woman's children.

There was hope that someone would do the same for Aidan.

Chapter Eighteen

Agreeing to teach Aidan O'Connor how to milk a cow most certainly made Ryan's list of ill-advised decisions. The lad and his mother stood between Ryan and his future, between Ryan and his ability to look after his ma. More than that, though, teaching these things to a lad 'twas the work of a father, not that of a neighbor.

He knew nothing about being a father. He indulged in dreams of one day having his own children and the moments he'd share with them. But in his heart of hearts, he knew he'd fumble his way through fatherhood, trying to pull from fuzzy memories of a man he'd never really known.

Aidan was in the barn when Ryan arrived Sunday morning as they'd arranged at the *ceílí* the night before. The boy stood only a few steps inside, holding himself stiff and uncertain.

How well Ryan remembered the first time he'd milked a cow. Before Hope Springs, he'd lived in large cities all his life, buying milk, just as Maura had in New York.

Only five years ago Ryan had dropped himself onto a milking stool for the first time, when they'd moved here at the urging of Seamus Kelly, a friend to the Callaghan brother just older than James. Seamus had come to this tiny Irish oasis and started a blacksmith shop. Once the family arrived, their neighbors, anxious to add another Irish family to the precarious balance in the then-feuding town, had undertaken the Callaghan brothers' farming education with a fury.

That first time, Ryan had confidently approached the cow he'd been charged with milking—and had been promptly kicked for his efforts. Only by a miracle had the kick gone wide, grazing him rather than truly injuring him. That taught him to treat the animals with a healthy degree of respect. Now, the least he could do was teach Aidan how to avoid getting himself knocked around by an angry cow.

"Have you greeted the cow yet?" he asked Aidan.

The lad's brows shot up. "Greet the—" His mouth dropped open. He turned wide eyes to the cow before looking at Ryan once more.

Ryan must've had a bit of the devil in him that morning; he couldn't resist teasing the boy a bit more. He nodded solemnly. "The cow, lad. She's a cow."

A tiny smile made a fleeting appearance on Aidan's face. "Is she?"

"She is, and a fine animal." Ryan spoke more seriously again. "Taking a moment for a kind word shows her you acknowledge that she's a living creature with concerns, and that you're grateful she's providing your family with something you need."

Aidan eyed him a bit sidelong. "Cows don't understand words."

"You certain of that?"

"Yes . . ." But Aidan's statement tipped up at the end in a hint of a question.

Ryan waved him toward the animal. Aidan followed but at a slower pace. He eyed the animal through narrowed eyes, his mouth pulled in a tense line of uncertainty.

"Cows are simple beasts," Ryan acknowledged, "but they've hearts and minds like people do. They know when they're being mistreated. They can feel worried, unsafe. Speak soft and kind to her, and approach with words so she knows you're coming, and offer a gentle pat on her side. That tells her she's nothing to fear from you."

Aidan nodded, but looked ever warier. He kept his distance from the cow, just as his ma did from the chickens in the yard. Heavens, but they were ill-suited to life on a farm.

Ryan approached the cow to demonstrate. "A fine good morning, love. Have I kept you waiting too long, then?"

The cow turned her head enough to give him the look of annoyed impatience she always did. He patted her flank, then, keeping his hand on her so she'd know where he was and not be scared, he passed to the side of her stall, snatching the milk pail off its nail and the stool from the corner.

He looked over at Aidan. "Come wish the girl a bit of a good morning, Aidan."

"I'd rather not." 'Twasn't stubbornness punctuating the words. The bit of a wobble in his voice, and the careful distance he kept from the cow, spoke far more of nervousness.

Da had laughed whenever Ryan was afraid. Not to mock his fear, but to cheer and reassure him. That laugh was one of his most clear memories of the man who'd died so long ago. "You either need to greet the cow, or undertake a druid sacrifice. Those are your only options."

Aidan's shock quickly gave way to a small twinkle in his eyes and a shake of his head. His posture relaxed a bit "Cows don't understand words, but they respond to pagan rituals?"

"Odd creatures, I'll admit."

Though the lad still looked wary, he approached, with his hand out in front of him, clearly hoping to give the obligatory pat without getting too close. He gave the cow the briefest tap Ryan had ever seen. The cow couldn't possibly have felt the touch.

Aidan would warm up in time.

Ryan set the milking stool in position. "You need to sit near enough to reach the teats," he said, "but not so close that you're under the cow. That'd be a misery for both of you."

"I imagine." To Aidan's credit, he remained in the stall.

"The bucket goes directly beneath the udder." Ryan placed it there. "There's a bit of a trick to milking. Give us a watch." He leaned back so his hand and the udder were fully visible. More slowly than he usually milked, he grasped, pulled, and squeezed the teat by rolling his fingers from top to bottom, sending a spray of milk into the bucket. "You'll not want to pull hard or sudden. She'll not like that, and you'll not get much milk from her. But you do need a firm squeeze."

He repeated the motions a few times, pointing out some of the small little tricks he'd learned the hard way over the past years. Aidan watched, leaning a bit away. His features turned into a nervous grimace. Hoping to give the lad at least a sense of how milking should look and sound when done properly, he picked up his pace. *Thwank. Thwank. Thwank.*

Aidan's mouth pulled tight. "Couldn't I just make the pagan sacrifice?"

Ryan laughed. Aidan's was a subtle sense of humor, one a person might miss if he weren't paying close attention. One Ryan liked. 'Twas like a quiet gift, but those wanting to enjoy it had to work for it.

"I'll not make you milk today," Ryan said. "But tomorrow morning, I expect you out here before school. I'll make certain I'm here early enough, and I'll have you try your hand."

Aidan shook his head and backed up. "I'm not ready to try. I'll just watch for a few more days."

Ryan had been where Aidan now stood: fatherless and facing uncertainty. Others had been firm with him, insisting he learn what he needed to survive. Ryan could do the same for Aidan. He could offer that to the boy, one fatherless child to another. So he held firm.

"It's not a skill you learn from watching," Ryan said. "You'll master it only if you do it."

Aidan released a tense breath. "Ma's always saying I have to learn things, and I won't learn if I don't do them."

"She has the right of it. Life, especially life on an arid farm, asks a lot of us. We have to work hard."

"I *do* work hard." He watched Ryan's movements closely. Studying. "I shined shoes on the streets in New York for years. If you don't work hard there, you don't make any money. I always made money." Aidan reached out and gently patted the cow. A show of bravery and determination. "I won't be good at milking for a time."

"I know," Ryan said. "But, given some work and practice, you'll be able to do *this*." He tilted a teat and shot a stream of milk at Aidan's shoes.

He jumped backward. His wide, shocked eyes stared at the wet tip of his boot before returning to Ryan's face.

"Learn to do that," Ryan said, "and I'll consider you as having put in the work you need to have learned."

Aidan appeared intrigued. "And if I do, then I won't have to milk anymore?"

He couldn't make that agreement with the lad. Milking was one chore that never went away. Aidan lived on a farm, so he'd have to get used to that. "Squirt my boots, and I'll trade you milking a few days a week. You'll get to sleep late now and then."

The boy smiled at him, a look of comforted reassurance. "Do you know how to bake bread?" Aidan posed the question hopefully and hesitantly.

Ryan took up the milking again. "I can make a soda bread, and what our American neighbors call johnnycake."

"Cake?" He whispered the word, almost like a prayer. What fourteen-year-old lad could resist the idea of cake?

"'Tisn't truly cake, but cornbread."

"We need bread for the week," Aidan said, "but Ma's too ill to make it."

The last of the milk splashed into the pail.

"I thought I'd try making some bread, but I don't know how." Aidan had never spoken to him so much. "Ma will try to get it made, but she'll wear herself thin and be even more ill than she is now."

Ryan stood, taking up the pail. He made the mistake of looking into the boy's tired, worried face. He knew that expression. He'd worn it for twenty-two years himself, ever since his father died and left the whole family without the tiniest bit of stability.

"Your ma didn't come to the *ceílí* last night." Though he'd not admit it, even to himself, Ryan had looked for her.

"She starts her job tomorrow. She's worried she won't be well enough."

Ryan's ma had often been in similar straits. Her health had never been good, even before Da died. She'd lost a few positions because of days missed to illness. Ryan knew all too well the weight sitting on Aidan's mind. He'd borne it too.

"Let's go check on her," he suggested. "We'll make certain there's nothing she needs."

He gave the cow his usual pat and word of gratitude. Aidan stepped from the stall first. Ryan followed and closed the door behind them.

In silence, they walked to the house and through the front door. They were greeted by a chest-rattling cough. That didn't sound good at all.

Ryan set the heavy milk pail on the table and crossed to the open doorway of an adjacent room. Sunlight spilled in from a small window, illuminating Maura, curled in a ball on the bed, a quilt tucked firmly around her.

She looked up when he entered. "Oh, saints have mercy," she muttered.

"Your coughing disturbed the cow," he said. "You'd best keep it down, unless you're wanting sour milk."

"And you had best make your way to church, Ryan Callaghan." She took in a wheezing breath. "Those lies are falling too easily from your lips."

She closed her eyes once more and pulled the quilt more tightly around her shoulders. She coughed. Ryan's chest hurt simply listening to it.

Aidan stood outside the room, just to the side of the doorway. Ryan looked at him. The boy shrugged, but not with dismissal. He didn't know what to do.

I really should leave and go to church, he told himself. Yet looking at Aidan, a young lad helplessly worrying over his mother, Ryan saw himself at that age, younger even. Though he wished he could say otherwise, he saw himself *now*.

"Let's make your ma a bit of broth," he said. "And we'll make a soda bread you can eat for a few days."

Aidan exhaled. "Thank you." He spoke almost silently.

Ryan didn't leave for church like anyone with any degree of self-preservation. Rather, he stayed and helped Aidan make food from the painfully meager supplies on hand.

Through it all, Maura's coughs filled the house. How long would she be ill? Did Aidan have what he needed to feed himself, and to look after her? What if Maura couldn't start her job in the morning? Where would she and Aidan go if they hadn't any money? This home was theirs to use through their family's generosity. Going anywhere else would require a significant income. How could they fill their almost-bare cupboards if Maura didn't have employment?

And how, he silently demanded of himself, was he to keep focused on his plans for his own future now that he'd let himself come to care about this widow's son?

Chapter Nineteen

Maura felt ghastly. She'd coughed too much and too long the past two days to rest at all. Her throat and lungs were raw. Every time a new tickle began, her heart seized, terrified that this would be the cough that brought up blood. In the end, the past days had proven exhausting and frustrating, but nothing worse than that.

Except for Ryan Callaghan.

The day before, he'd spent hours at the house. Several times she'd attempted to get out of bed to go see what he was doing, but she'd been too weak. Her son had been left to shoulder the burden of the household, and she'd been so frail. Yet the man meaning to steal her home had been the one Aidan had received support from.

The past ten years, she'd stood tall as her world crumbled again and again. After surviving what would have felled someone less determined, her body was betraying her. And she could not let anyone see it. Mrs. O'Connor had come by after church to look in on them, allowing Ryan to return to his brother's home. Maura had done her utmost to convince her mother-in-law that she needn't be overly concerned, an impression she hoped to convey everywhere she went. She needed everyone to believe she was equal to the life she'd come to claim.

Aidan had been out at the barn early that morning, where Ryan was teaching him to milk. 'Twas difficult to be fully angry with the man when he was helping with something desperately needed. She, however, intended to find someone to help her sort out how to care for the chickens. None had produced any eggs, and she hadn't the first idea why.

Maura pushed all these heavy thoughts from her mind as she approached the Archer home. Making a show of being equal to whatever task she was assigned would go a long way on this first day. In her, they would see competence. They would see ability. She would keep her lingering feebleness hidden as much as she possibly could.

She went directly to the back door, through which she'd always entered the fine houses she'd cleaned in New York. Her knock was not quickly answered, so she tried again. She felt certain she heard little Sean crying inside. Perhaps Katie couldn't hear her knock.

Ought she to simply go inside? In time, expectations would be established between them all. But for today, she was at a loss as to what to do. She stood on the back porch, thinking. The sound of her own wheezing filled the air around her. There'd be no hiding the fact that she was ill, but she'd do her utmost to make it seem a small thing, the lingering effects of a common bit of a cold.

And if that doesn't work, what am I to do?

She spied Finbarr stepping from the barn. He held a cane in his hand, but didn't use it in the typical manner. The tip rested at an angle, sweeping the ground in front of him. She'd seen Cecily do the same with her cane. Surely some kind of aid for those with limited vision.

"Finbarr." She called, grateful she had the air to do so.

He paused. His head tipped to one side. Too much of his face was hidden beneath the wide brim of his hat for his expression to be readable. "I'm not sure who you are."

He did not yet recognize her voice. That realization ached her heart. He had once known her so well. Did he remember that in the weeks before the family left New York, she and he had developed between themselves a secret knock? Back then, he knew when she had arrived before the door was even opened.

Perhaps, working here for the same family, they could reclaim some of that connection.

"It's Maura," she said. "I'm here for my first day of work, but no one's answered my knock."

Finbarr didn't hesitate to motion her over. "Joseph's in the barn. We can ask him if he knows where Katie might be."

Mr. Archer. Though Maura knew she'd be working for Katie more than for Katie's husband, the prospect of meeting Joseph made her nervous. Approaching the barn, she felt as though she were about to find herself on trial. He, after all, would be the one setting her salary. He would also have a say in whether she continued her employment; she knew he would.

She smoothed the front of her dress, attempting to neaten herself a bit as they stepped inside. The dim barn was very large inside, far larger than hers. Did she need a bigger one? Was that an expense she ought to anticipate? How was it possible that Hope Springs could prove to be more expensive than New York City?

"Maura's here," Finbarr called from behind her.

A man stepped to the edge of the hay loft above, looking down at them. "Good morning, Mrs. O'Connor."

"Maura will do, sir," she said.

He climbed down with the swiftness of familiarity, then turned to face her. He held out a hand for her to shake. She accepted it, keeping her grip firm enough to convey that she had the strength to do the work asked of her, and hiding the fact that her hands had not fully healed from her difficulty with the wire mesh the week before.

"A pleasure to meet you, Maura," he said. "I despaired of ever convincing Katie to hire on a housekeeper again."

"And I despaired of finding a job in this town," Maura said.

Joseph nodded. "Katie had the same difficulty when she first arrived. Farming or ranching are nearly the only sources of income here."

"Other than being the Archers' housekeeper, that is," Finbarr quipped from the doorway. 'Twas the first lighthearted comment Maura had heard from the lad since her arrival in town and far more like the young Finbarr she remembered.

"We are doing our part for the good of the community." Joseph's was a dry response, but a humorous one.

159

"I'll fetch the tools you were wanting," Finbarr told Joseph.

"When you grab the plainer from the lean-to, search around for the bag of nails. It wasn't where it ought to be."

"I'll try," Finbarr muttered. Quick as that, the lighthearted version was gone.

Joseph watched Finbarr step out of the barn. His lips set in a grim line, and his brow wrinkled.

Maura looked back to the empty barn door, feeling a bit worried herself. "Did something happen today? You look suddenly more concerned for him."

Joseph nodded slowly. "Cecily has helped him a great deal. He is functioning now, which was not the case for a long time. But he's not happy. He has moments of lightness, moments of hope, but overall . . ." Sadness filled his voice as it trailed off.

Finbarr had been the happiest child she'd ever known. She best remembered his cheerfulness more than anything else. Hearing of his struggles broke her heart.

"I'm not certain what Katie will want you to do today," Joseph said, changing the subject. "In my experience, it's usually best just to ask her what she wants, as she always has very firm ideas on that score."

Maura smiled at the picture he painted. "You have yourself a very Irish wife, then."

"That I do."

They walked into the bright sunlight of the outdoors.

"I knocked at the back door when I first arrived," Maura said, "but no one answered. I could hear your youngest fussing inside, so Katie likely couldn't hear me."

"Likely not," Joseph said. "That child is louder than Ryan Callaghan on his pipes."

"That is mighty loud."

Joseph nodded solemnly. "And now you know why Katie is so near her wits' end." He pushed open the back door and motioned her inside ahead of him. His were the fine manners of one born to a degree of comfort above anything Maura had known.

160

The door led directly into a kitchen, one finer and larger than any she'd worked in before, though smaller than the one that had graced the large house in which she'd been an upstairs maid. She could accomplish a great deal of work in a room so large. But this kitchen had a cast-iron stove, not a fireplace. The home most certainly had a fireplace somewhere, but not in the kitchen. Maura didn't know how to cook on anything but a fire.

Joseph held another door, one on a swing hinge. She passed through into a dining room. She'd never seen a separate dining room in any house but those belonging to the very wealthy and influential. To see one so far west and inside a comparatively humble home was wholly unexpected.

Beyond the dining room was a sitting room, with tall windows—and a large, stone-surrounded fireplace her eyes lingered on. 'Twasn't in the most convenient location for cooking, but she could manage it if that was one of her jobs. The house boasted many rooms: a large kitchen, a formal dining room, and an expansive sitting room. Bedchambers were abovestairs, no doubt.

'Twas a lot of space to tidy and clean. If Katie's littlest was as difficult as she and Joseph made him seem, it was little wonder Katie felt overwhelmed. Add to that the amount of laundry little ones produced and the mountain of food they required, and it was a miracle Katie didn't spend her days constantly in tears.

Joseph had stepped to the foot of a narrow staircase at the far end of the room. Looking up, he called, "Katie?"

Quick footsteps followed. "By the saints, Joseph. Keep your voice down. If you wake Sean, I swear to you—" She hurried down the stairs, a little frantic, a little flustered.

"Maura's here," Joseph said.

Katie looked to her and sighed, not entirely in relief. "We've had quite a morning, Maura. I meant to have everything prepared to make this first day a smooth one."

Joseph watched his wife with concern, much as he had Finbarr. This was a man who cared deeply for the people around him, who wished to relieve suffering where he could. Maura could help with that.

"You leave it to me, Katie," she said. "I'll see to whatever work you wish me to do. You need only tell me what it is you want done first."

Here was a surer footing. Housework was familiar.

"All the floors need sweeping." Katie spoke hesitantly.

Maura nodded. "And what else? That will not even fill the morning."

"The kitchen shelves and cupboards are a mess," she said.

"What of lunch?" Maura pressed. "I can easily prepare a meal in the midst of all those tasks, and then you needn't worry about that."

"I don't wish to ask too much." Clearly she was still uncomfortable with the idea of handing over the duties she, herself, had been attempting to juggle.

"I am not here as an act of charity, Katie Archer. I mean to work. Joseph." She met his eye. "When you return to the house for your lunch, we can discuss pay."

"An excellent plan," he said.

She turned to Katie once more. "I fully expect you to give your morning over to the task of taking a nap. I remember all too well how rare and precious sleep was when my Aidan was your Sean's age."

Actual tears formed in Katie's eyes. "I am so tired."

Maura smiled gently. "Rest. I'll see to the house."

Joseph mouthed a thank you, then, with an arm at Katie' shoulders, guided her back upstairs, no doubt to make certain she lay down and rested. Maura missed that—missed having someone who treated her tenderly, who looked after her when she forgot to look after herself.

I'm what I have now, and what Aidan has. I'll be enough.

A cough arose. Why was it every time she attempted to reassure herself, her lungs put the lie to it?

She allowed but a moment for catching her breath, then set herself to her work.

Katie's cupboards were hardly the disaster she'd hinted they were. A bit disorganized, certainly, but nothing so horrible as warranted the embarrassment Maura had seen in her eyes. Bringing in a housekeeper, no matter that she'd had one before, was clearly a blow to the woman's pride.

Maura could tiptoe around that. She knew what it was to be deeply humbled by life. Everything she'd received since arriving in Hope Springs was given out of charity, in large part because she'd begged for it. She'd make certain Katie knew that she was grateful for the work, that it was a blessing to have a job and the ability to provide for herself and Aidan.

Her not-yet-healed hands made her work slower than she'd have preferred, yet she took extra care, knowing if she pulled the wounds open, they'd have to begin healing all over again. As she straightened cupboards and shelves, she made an accounting of the food, planning an easy meal she could cook on the fire without the family suspecting that she didn't know how to use the stove.

By lunchtime, she had decided to make a soup to serve with what remained of a loaf of soda bread she found in a covered basket.

Maura was stirring the pot hanging over the low-burning fire in the sitting room when Katie came downstairs, Sean on her hip, his dark brown hair sticking up every which way. He looked over the room with wide, eager eyes. This was a child, Maura would wager, who never missed a detail, large or small.

"Did you rest, Katie?" Maura asked.

"I did, and I cannot tell you how desperately I needed it."

"I remember the exhaustion of having a little one," Maura assured her. "And I had only the one, not three as you have. My Aidan was no older than wee Sean, here, when m' husband left to join the fighting. 'Twas only the two of us after that, which comes with its own set of difficulties."

"I can imagine." Katie watched Maura a moment. "I've not cooked over a fire in ages."

Would Katie ask why she'd not used the stove? If Maura had to admit she didn't know how, she might be deemed ill-suited to this job she so desperately needed.

"I should again," Katie said. "Nothing tastes quite as much like home as a fire-cooked meal. My ma only ever cooked that way."

"Mine as well." Maura left it at that. Katie's nostalgia for fire cooking was a stroke of unforeseen luck.

The remainder of the day was long and quiet, though Maura had no complaints. She'd steeled herself against hearing a worryingly low offer of pay from Joseph, only to be shocked by the generosity of his proposal. She and Aidan wouldn't live in high cream by any means, but they'd no longer be hungry, and she'd likely even have enough to buy them coats for the coming winter. In time, she might save enough to expand the barn if that, indeed, proved necessary.

She'd not heard anyone mention a doctor in Hope Springs, which was just as well. The money from Grady's ring was gone. And while her income was more generous than she had anticipated, it wouldn't stretch beyond the necessities of home to doctoring and medicines. She'd known when making the decision to come west, that she was giving up her hope for medical treatment in order to save Aidan from a future of misery. Yet facing again the truth of it dealt her a blow. She'd watched friends die of brown lung, and, if she were fully honest, she was a little afraid of the fate. 'Twas a terrible way to die.

She finished the work assigned her for the day just as the Archers' daughters arrived home from school, meaning Aidan was likely on his way down the road as well. She took off the work apron she'd borrowed from Katie, not having brought one from New York, then stepped into the sitting room and waited for a break in Katie's conversation with her girls.

"If you've no objections," Maura said, "I'll be returning home now. If you're needing longer workdays in the future, I'll have Aidan come here after school while I work. He'll keep out of the way."

"Thank you, Maura," Katie said, a genuine smile on her still-weary face.

Maura offered a nod.

Ivy hopped off the sofa and rushed to her, throwing her arms around Maura's waist in an enthusiastic hug.

"What's this for?" Maura was both pleased and utterly confused.

"For Aidan," the little girl said, hopping back to her spot beside Katie. "Tell him it's from me. Then he'll shake his head and twist his eyes about like this" —she demonstrated— "but then he'll smile a little."

How easily Maura could picture Aidan doing precisely that. "He does this often, does he?"

Ivy nodded. "Emma tells me not to torture him, but she's just embarrassed because he is 'very handsome' and that makes her flustered."

Emma muttered her sister's name through clenched teeth. 'Twas likely for the best that the discussion not be drawn out any longer.

"I will offer Aidan your greetings, Ivy," Maura said. "And I will see you tomorrow, Katie."

She stepped back through the dining room and the kitchen and out onto the back porch. Her first day at this new job had gone well. She'd maneuvered her way through the challenge of cooking for the family. She felt she'd done an admirable job of not pricking Katie's pride. She'd worked exceptionally hard at holding back every cough and hiding every hint of illness.

And she was exhausted.

Chapter Twenty

Maura's first week working for the Archers had gone well. She'd managed her tasks without too many coughing fits. and Katie seemed pleased with the work being done. On Friday, Maura was sent to the mercantile on Katie's behalf. The list of needed items was blessedly short; carrying too many things back from town would have been difficult to manage.

Mrs. Johnson set a cake of lye soap in Maura's basket beside the bag of nails, small stack of parchment, inkwell, and bottle of liniment she'd placed inside already. The proprietress checked the list once more, then stepped to the jars of sweets. She placed a few peppermints and butterscotches on a small bit of paper, which she folded and tucked into a little packet. She set that in the basket as well.

"That's the entire list," Mrs. Johnson said. "Unless you're wanting something for yourself."

Maura wanted a great many things, but she couldn't afford any of them. She wouldn't be paid until the end of the day and refused to buy on credit. "I'll be by tomorrow with a list of my own. And I'll bring m' Aidan so he can carry the heavier items."

Mrs. Johnson thought a moment. "If you'd like, you can tell me what it is you intend to buy tomorrow. We can have your purchase crated and ready for you. Then you need only send your son to make the purchase."

Her first inclination was to refuse. She wanted so much for Aidan to have the childhood he'd been denied. To be carefree. To spend his days in play and laughing with his friends. But life had not afforded them that luxury. Even here, away from the weight of the city, he was having to grow up quickly. He had a sickly mother, though he didn't realize how sick yet. She had to admit to herself, and she had to accept, that she had limits, and that those limits would only grow.

"I will send him in the morning." How she wished that weren't necessary.

Mrs. Johnson pulled a small pad of paper from her apron pocket, along with a stub of pencil. "Tell me what all you need."

Maura knew her list by heart, having reworked it time and again in the past few days, searching for the best way to balance their needs and wants against the price of goods and the size of her income. She wanted the money she made to last. She would save everything possible so Aidan would have a bit set by to live on. Should her lungs fail quickly, while he was still in school, he'd not have to abandon his education. She wanted schooling for him. Grady would have wanted that for him.

She meticulously listed each item and their amounts she'd previously determined. Mrs. Johnson took a moment to calculate the total, then told her what each selection would cost. The total came to exactly what Maura had anticipated. That, at least, had gone according to plan; so little had lately.

"I am hoping soon to send a letter or a telegram back to New York," she said. "But I'm not certain how to do that."

Mrs. Johnson nodded. "Any letters or telegram messages you'd like sent you can leave here. Once a week our oldest makes a trip to Bartonville, a few hours from here. They have a telegraph line now and a stage stop where mail is collected."

Maura had sent letters across that same distance and knew what price to expect to post them. But she had no experience with telegrams. "Is a telegram terribly expensive?"

"One to New York would be quite expensive," Mrs. Johnson said.

Maura nodded. "When does your son leave with the letters?"

"On Tuesdays."

She would have a letter ready for Eliza by then. Though the pennies required could be put to use elsewhere, she needed that connection with her "sister." She missed her and worried about her. She wanted Eliza to know she wasn't forgotten, that someone, however far away, yet cared about her. And if there was any way for Eliza to join her here, she wanted her to.

She had another bit of business as well. "Do you sell coats, by chance? My boy outgrew his at the end of last winter."

Mrs. Johnson shook her head. "We seldom have ready-made clothing. I have wool, though. Two different bolts, both thick enough for a fine coat."

Maura had made most of their clothes until recent years, when there'd simply not been enough time in the day. Factory hours were long, and her health had been even poorer in New York. But she could make him a new coat now. If she sized it a little large, it'd last more than one winter.

Next winter, he would have it and would think of her when he wore it. 'Twould be a little piece of her, a reminder that she'd loved him.

"I'd like to see the wool, if you'd not mind."

Mrs. Johnson stepped around the counter and walked with Maura to a nearby table, one laden with bolts of fabric and a large basket of sewing notions. She indicated the two bottom-most bolts, one gray and one green. "These are both well-suited to a coat for our winter weather."

Maura knew on the instant which one she'd pick. The green. She ran a finger along the folded length of the fabric. "It's quite soft."

Mrs. Johnson nodded. "And not so itchy as wool often is."

"It likely still needs to be lined." That would add to the expense.

"And not only for comfort," Mrs. Johnson said. "We've found that coats are blessedly warmer when lined in thin flannel. Winters are shockingly brutal here. Lining is a necessity."

"Have you any?"

Mrs. Johnson pulled another bolt of gray fabric from the pile. "This is our most popular choice for coat linings. Soft, again, but not overly expensive."

Maura knew all too well that "expensive" was a relative term.

The door chimed, meaning another customer had entered. Mrs. Johnson would need to help the new customer but Maura needed a bit more information first.

"How much is the green wool?"

She checked a list on the table. "Two bits a yard."

Maura swallowed hard. 'Twas far more costly than in New York. "And the flannel?"

"Fifteen cents to the yard." Mrs. Johnson anticipated her next question. "Buttons are two cents apiece. A spool of thread is ten cents."

"Thank you."

Mrs. Johnson slipped away. Maura did some calculating in her head. She'd need nearly five dollars to make Aidan a coat. It wasn't enough to put them in the poor house, but she'd labored over the numbers. They would have mere pennies left over after buying food, feed for the chickens, supplies for the house. They couldn't do without those things, but neither could Aidan go without a coat. He needed one desperately. Hers still fit—one of the benefits of being fully grown—but it was thin in the elbows and worn to threads at the cuffs and collar. His need was more pressing by far.

"What can I do for you, Ryan?" Mrs. Johnson asked.

Maura didn't know how many Ryans lived in Hope Springs, but had her suspicions she knew which one of them this was. She looked out of the corner of her eye. Sure enough, Ryan Callaghan stood at the counter.

"I'm needing some Dover powders," he said. "For my ma. Her joints are aching something fierce. I think I'd best find something stronger than the teas she's been using."

Maura hadn't been home during the day the last week and therefore had seen very little of Mrs. Callaghan. When Maura returned home with Aidan each day, the woman had generally been napping. The day before, Maura came home to find that Ryan had already taken his mother back to her other son's house.

"I haven't any Dover powders," Mrs. Johnson said. "Jeremiah will be bringing some back with him, but he won't return for at least another week."

Ryan shook his head. His posture spoke of worry and frustration. "You haven't anything?"

"Only more of the tincture she's been using."

Ryan rubbed his mouth and chin. "I hate the idea of her hurting so much for another week. Sometimes the pain subsides, eases a bit, but you can't know when that'll be. Right now, she can't even sleep. A good night's rest always helps."

"I'm sorry," Mrs. Johnson said. "Is there anything else you need while you're here?"

"Likely. Give me a moment. M' mind's spinning a bit too fast for clear thinking."

Mrs. Johnson returned to Maura. "Would you like the wool and flannel?"

Of course she would like it, but she had to be careful. "Just the wool today," she said. "I can start on the coat, and eventually have enough to make the lining."

"Any thread?" Mrs. Johnson pressed.

She did need thread. Fortunately, she had needles and a good pair of scissors.

Mrs. Johnson pulled her notepad out once more. She talked through the items on Maura's list. By reducing the bacon and molasses, as well as slightly reducing the flour and sugar, Maura brought the total down to a number that made adding in the purchase of wool and thread possible.

"I'll send Aidan for everything in the morning."

Mrs. Johnson nodded. Once more, she returned to Ryan, not too far distant. Though the mercantile was not a large space, running the business on her own certainly kept the woman on her feet. "Have you decided on anything else you need?"

"There likely is something," he said, "but, lands o' mercy, I can't think straight. I'm wanting to get back and check on my ma."

"I'm so sorry I don't have any powders," Mrs. Johnson said.

"We'll manage something." Ryan looked to Maura. "Are you heading to the Archer place?"

He'd not bothered with any kind of greeting, and he didn't usually forget the niceties. The man might've been her rival for the house, but she couldn't deny that he was usually personable. This level of distraction made Maura wonder if his mother was suffering even more than he'd hinted at.

"I'm walking back there now," she said.

He gave a single, firm nod of his head. "Would you be put out if I walked with you? I'm needing to talk to Joseph."

"You'd be no bother." Though she didn't know why his need for a conversation with her employer required him to walk with her.

She took up the basket of Katie's purchases, thanked Mrs. Johnson, and repeated her promise to send Aidan for her own supplies in the morning. Ryan held the door as she slipped outside. He followed close on her heels.

"I'm sorry to hear that your mother's feeling poorly," she said, once he walked at her side. "My mother's health was very fragile the last couple years of her life."

Ryan paled a little, and she realized what she'd inadvertently implied.

"I've not any suspicion that your ma's in so delicate a state as that," she quickly insisted. "I only meant to say that I know the worry of seeing one's parent ailing, and it's an experience I'd rather no one have to endure."

"Including me?" he asked a bit dryly.

"Well . . ." She pretended to mull over the possibility of excluding him from her declaration.

He laughed a little. "You've a subtle sense of humor, Maura O'Connor," he said. "I like it."

"And you've shown my boy kindness," she said. "I like that."

He nodded solemnly. "A saint, that's what I am."

'Twas a wonderful thing, feeling herself smile so easily. She'd done precious little of that the past years.

"And to further prove how upstanding I am, I'll even offer to carry your basket for you. It looks a bit heavy."

It was at that. "Thank you," she said, and allowed him to take it.

They walked on at a blessedly slow pace. Her lungs would not have been equal to much else.

"I don't know what to do for Ma," he said. "The daily journey to the house is taking a toll, but I can't leave her with Ennis—that's my sister-in-law," he explained. "She's a good person; she truly is. But we've a difficult arrangement. The house was once ours—my ma's, my brother's, and mine—and Ma was once mistress of it. Now it, in essence, belongs to my brother, and his wife has assumed the role that once belonged to Ma."

Maura understood that experience well enough. "I lived with my ma for a time. The sharing of a home is a difficult balance to manage."

"Harder when it's a mother- and daughter-*in-law*. And in so small a house, there's no way to carve out a bit of space for them both. I'm afraid they've come to resent each other a bit."

That was, indeed, unfortunate.

"I'd imagine your ma thinks herself a burden, too. Being poor in health makes a person feel that way. When you've less to contribute than you'd wish, 'tis far too easy to feel you're not contributing at all." She'd meant the observation to help Ryan understand the hidden struggles his ma was likely enduring beneath the difficulties he could see. Her explanation of the connection between health woes and feeling a burden came too close to a confession, however. A new topic was absolutely necessary, so she said, "How's Aidan coming along with the milking?"

"He's not so nervous around the cow as he was, though I can tell she still puts a bit o' the ol' fear in him."

"Will he need gloves for the job when the winter comes?" The possibility hadn't occurred to her until that exact moment. Heavens, she'd never get ahead of expenses.

"He'll need a good pair for simply going about outside, whether to school or church or simply wandering about town. He'll pull 'em off to milk though. Being tucked up against that beast is blessedly warm."

A small group of people had gathered outside the blacksmith shop. School would end soon, and parents with very young ones gathered to fetch them at the end of the school day.

"Would you mind terribly if we waited for the children to come out?" Maura asked. "It'll be but a moment."

"Not at all," he said. "That Ivy Archer is such a mischievous little sprite; I'd not pass up an opportunity to walk with her apace. She'd lighten even the heaviest heart.'"

"She's been a dear to my Aidan," Maura said. "I can't put in words how grateful I am to her for her determination to be his friend."

An odd, secretive sort of smile touched Ryan's face.

"What is that look for?" she pressed. They'd stopped very near the group of waiting parents.

"I was only thinking that *she* is not the Archer sister whom your lad's mentioned most. Leastways, not to me."

This was news. "He's spoken to you of Emma?"

"Only a mention here and there, but enough that I've wondered." He smiled fondly and with a bit of amusement. "He's a good lad, more talkative than I expected him to be."

So Aidan was speaking with Ryan, and enough to be described as "talkative." This conversation continued to grow more and more surprising.

"What did he have to say about Emma?" Maura pressed. She was full dying of curiosity, not only about the possible state of her son's affections, but also about the oddity of his being so social with a near-stranger.

"He's mentioned that she's very clever and knows the answers at school. I think he likes that about her." Ryan's brow pulled in thought. "He told me she's patient with the younger children, but is a bit shy with those her own age. I imagine he relates to that."

Maura knew for a fact he did.

"And . . ." Ryan lowered his voice. "He even said once that he thought she was pretty."

"Truly?" Something about knowing that her lad felt a pull to the sweet girl brought a bubble of excitement to her heart. "Both of them are of so quiet a nature. I can hardly imagine them having a conversation."

Ryan's smile hadn't slipped. "I remember the first time my heart was pricked by a lass. I was about Aidan's age. Talking to her was entirely out of the question, as my tongue simply tied itself in knots any time I so much as thought about her."

"You, at a loss for words? I don't believe it."

He eyed her sidelong, but with a twinkle of devilment in his eyes. "Are you sayin' I talk too much?"

"Might be," she said with a one-shouldered shrug.

He went right on grinning. They'd not always had jovial interactions, but she was discovering Ryan Callaghan to be a lighthearted person. He laughed and smiled a great deal. He buoyed her spirits.

He was also the obstacle standing between her and the future she meant to give her son. She needed to remember that.

The door of the schoolhouse, which doubled as the church on Sundays, flew open, and a stream of loud, excited children rushed out. Parents gathered theirs up. The older children stood about a bit longer, chatting.

Ivy spotted Maura and Ryan and ran over to them. "Are you walking home with us?"

"We are, *ceann beag*," Ryan said.

"Mama calls me that sometimes too," Ivy said. "But I don't know what it means. Does it mean 'mischievous?' That's what Pompah calls me."

Ryan laughed. "It means *little one*."

Ivy's shoulders popped backward in a posture of offense. "I'm not little anymore. I'm in school now."

Ryan hunched down, placing himself more on her level. "I only mean that you're littler than I am."

She reached out and patted the top of his head, which was in reach now. "You're *older* than me too."

He laughed. Maura did as well; she couldn't help herself. Ivy was a delight.

Ryan looked up at her from his still-bent position. "You've a nice laugh, Maura O'Connor."

Heat touched her cheeks. "I don't know that anyone's ever said that to me before."

"Likely because few people get to hear it."

There was too much truth in that for her to entirely dismiss the observation. "I've not had a great many reasons to laugh of late."

He stood once more, facing her, watching her with curiosity. "Have you missed it?"

"Laughing?"

He nodded.

Had she missed laughing? Without warning, a tear sprang to her eye. She turned her face away, not wanting him to see the emotion she couldn't quite hide.

"Oh, Maura." He set his hand gently on her arm. "I'd not meant to make you cry."

"I *have* missed it," she whispered. "I've been crushed by too many things for too many years."

He took her hand. To her own surprise, she clung to it.

"I'm sorry," he said. "Life is seldom easy, is it?"

She took such comfort in the words of understanding and the friendly support of his touch. Loneliness took more of a toll on her than she would generally admit.

Beside them, Ivy spun about in a circle, arms outstretched. She didn't take any notice of them, having lost herself in a moment of simple, childish play. Emma wandered over, far less sure of herself than her sister. Still, she offered a wee smile. Maura offered one of her own to Ryan, then slipped her hand free.

"I've not seen Aidan yet," Maura said to Emma. "Do you know what's keeping him?"

"He's helping Mrs. Hall. He shouldn't be much longer."

Aidan's heart had ever been one eager to serve, a trait he'd inherited from his father.

"Why don't you come visit us?" Ivy asked Ryan, taking her hand in his. "You did before, when it was winter."

"When it was winter, I didn't need to be out in the fields, working. And I was planning my crop then. I needed your father's opinion on just what that crop ought to be, and how large, and what to do with it."

Ivy didn't seem fully satisfied with that answer. Her sister, however, was the one who spoke next.

"Papa says you have a mind for business, that you know when a risk is a risk and when it's an opportunity." Emma was clearly speaking the words nearly verbatim. "He talks about Mr. Tavish that way, but you two are the only ones."

"'Tis a fine compliment coming from your da." A mixture of pride and embarrassment filled Ryan's eyes. Was there anything about him that wasn't a contradiction?

Aidan emerged from the schoolhouse in that moment. His eyes darted about, likely searching for Ivy and Emma, since they walked to the Archers' house together each day. He spied Maura, and, to her heart's utter delight, he smiled broadly. He hurried across the small distance to where she stood.

"Ma, why are you here?"

She motioned to the basket Ryan held. "I was doing some shopping for the Archers."

Emma watched Aidan, a smile in her eyes. Perhaps his tenderness toward his sweet classmate was not entirely one-sided.

Ryan met Maura's gaze. He motioned subtly with his head toward Emma and allowed a knowing smile. He'd noticed as well.

Aidan, however, seemed oblivious. "Lead the way, Ivy," he instructed, grinning at his tiny friend.

She did not need to be told twice. She marched ahead, snatching Ryan's hand and fairly dragging him along with her. Aidan walked at Maura's side, Emma silently on the other.

In the midst of it all, Maura felt a deep sense of contentment. She wasn't sure exactly what the future held, but her Aidan was finding his place in this town. He was happier than she remembered him being in some time. Life in the city had taken a greater toll on him than she'd been willing to admit.

He was free of that now. So was she—a comfort and a reassurance. Even if time proved that they'd waited too long, and that losing access to medical care shortened what time she did have, at the very least, for this moment in this place, she and her son were free.

Chapter Twenty-one

It'd been a decidedly awful day. Ma was in pain. Ryan was behind in every chore he had. The mercantile still hadn't had any powders. And Joseph had thought it too great a risk to invest in building any additional hay sheds while Ryan's claim on the land remained uncertain. Joseph was right in that, should Ryan lose his claim to the farm, he'd need what few pennies he had left to begin again somewhere else, if that was even possible. But not having storage sheds meant that if the weather turned while his hay was drying, he might lose too much of it to meet the ranches' orders. He'd be ruined, bankrupted.

An awful, disappointing day.

He had to admit, though, that the time he'd spent walking home from school with Maura and the children had been an unexpected highlight. She'd been empathetic when he'd told her of Ma's plight. She'd laughed with him. She'd confided a few of her struggles and difficulties. He had friends in Hope Springs; he was part of so many lives. Yet he often felt like an outsider among them, not having his own little family or land to truly claim as his own. He appreciated the tentative connection she'd forged with him more than she likely knew.

Upon reaching the barn, he hung his tools up and set his gloves in their usual spot. He made certain the milking stool and pail were where he'd need them in the morning. Now that he was bringing Ma with him, he started late every day, and usually ended early to fetch the wagon to take her back to James's. He was far behind schedule today, though. He had too much to do, and he'd lost so much time.

Ryan quickly returned to the house, needing to let Ma know he'd only then be leaving to get the wagon. She was likely near to starving. He was more than a bit hungry himself.

When he went inside, she was not, however, in her usual rocker. Aidan sat on the floor near the fireplace, eating from a bowl he held carefully in front of him.

Maura looked up as Ryan closed the door. "Your ma's not feeling well," she said. "It took a bit of doing, but I convinced her to lie down."

Ought he to look in on her, or let her rest? He wasn't at all certain. How often he'd wished Hope Springs had a doctor. "I can rush to James's and return within an hour with the wagon. She'll be horribly hungry by then, though."

Maura smiled a little. "I fed her already. She's warm and comfortable. I'd wager she's asleep by now."

Ma'd not been sleeping well at all of late. He hated the thought of waking her, but if she'd finally lapsed into much-needed sleep, what choice did he have?

Maura crossed to him. She eyed Aidan for only a moment then lowered her voice. "She didn't look well, Ryan. I think you'd do best to leave her sleeping rather than make her endure the rickety drive and an early morning return."

"You're offering to let her stay?" He was almost too shocked to ask the question.

"I know what it is to be ill," she said. "I'd not toss her out while she's ailing."

'Twas a kindness, but she could not know what she was taking on. "Ma sometimes passes difficult nights," he said. "I'll not ask you to give up your own sleep. You're still fighting a cough."

"You know, for two people trying to steal each other's land, we're being surprisingly considerate." She smiled a little then motioned him toward the fireplace. "Have a bowl of soup," she said. "It's nothing fine, but it'll take the edge off your hunger."

He knew perfectly well she was struggling for money. Though she would have been paid that day by Joseph, Aidan wouldn't fetch their supplies from the mercantile until morning, and those supplies were clearly slimmer than she'd hoped. He'd overheard her giving up some foodstuffs to purchase wool for a coat. Still, he *was* quite hungry and didn't particularly want to fight with her over a single meal. He could simply return the favor at some point to make things even between them.

He dished a bit of soup into a bowl. "I thank you for this. I'm not ever back to my brother's house in time for a hot meal. They've always already eaten when I get there, and I'm too hungry to spend time heating anything back up."

"Your ma says she's not had a hot supper at all this week." Maura glanced in the direction of one of the doors, no doubt the one behind which Ma was resting. "She also says she hasn't been sleeping much."

"And you managed to address both today." Though his conscience pricked at him, he needed to ask another favor of her. "Would you be willing—and, mind you, I'll understand if the answer is no—to allow me to sleep on the floor in the room Ma's using? I'd not need anything but a blanket. It'd let me be nearby tonight in case she needs something."

She gave his request a long moment's thought. He could very nearly hear the debate raging in her mind, and he understood it. They were rivals, after all, vying for the same bit of the world. They'd not truly gotten along the past two weeks. Having him in the house might be too uncomfortable. But his worries for Ma were too great to not at least ask.

"I suppose it wouldn't hurt for the one night," she finally said.

His tension eased in a swift wave from the top of his head to the soles of his feet. Ma wouldn't suffer unduly that evening, leaving one less worry on his mind. "I'll get started on chores early so we needn't be here any longer than necessary."

"Do what you need to do," she said. "We've a load of chores to see to ourselves on my day off tomorrow."

They'd be back to tiptoeing around each other come the next day.

'Twould be more familiar footing, yet he found himself disappointed. More than once that day, they'd been on friendly terms.

As the night grew late, little more was said between them. Aidan wasn't talkative. Had Ivy exhausted his supply of words, or was he simply not as comfortable with Ryan as he'd thought? Again, he felt a twinge of disappointment. He liked the lad and had enjoyed their early morning talks over the milking. He felt like something of a mentor to the boy.

What a gawm I am, fooling myself. Showing a lad how to milk didn't make a man important his life. Ryan needed to pull his head out of the clouds and ground himself again. He was a little lonely, and he longed for the day he'd have a family of his own, but letting his imagination run amuck wouldn't help anyone.

A bit of sleep would do him good. He excused himself, then slipped inside the room where Ma slept, careful not to wake the exhausted woman. She slept deeply, thank the heavens. By the time they reached home other nights, she was rattled and pained and suffering, making sleep difficult to claim.

I cannot keep forcing that journey on her. But what choice did he have? He lay on the floor, staring at the dark ceiling. What could he do? Leaving Ma at James's every day wouldn't do at all. Making the twice-daily journey had proved a source of suffering for her and a drain on his time.

He wove his fingers together, then set his hands on his forehead, his elbows jutting out in both directions. Heaven help him, he needed this house. Did Maura have the first idea how badly he needed it? Did Tavish and Cecily? 'Twasn't merely the livelihood offered him by the land, but the nearness of this house *in particular* to the very fields he'd made successful. It was a roof over Ma's head. It was her long-term health and happiness. And, owing to the income he'd have and the stability that income would provide, this house was likely his best chance to someday have the family he dreamed of.

Ryan hadn't, in all the years he'd worked the Claire place, been able to begin his day at the early hour other farmers usually did. Arriving from James's house always set him behind the usual schedule, and even more so of late. The morning after he'd been permitted to sleep in Ma's bedroom, however, he was not only awake long before the sun, but he was also already at work.

He'd just finished forking hay off the loft for the cow when he heard footsteps. He'd not milked, wanting to give Aidan the chance to continue improving his skills there. But he didn't think the lad would be up this early.

Ryan leaned his pitchfork against the barn wall and crossed to the door. Instead of seeing Aidan, he found Maura. She'd stepped into the chicken coop, heading for the henhouse. She'd wrapped herself in a blanket. Did she not have a coat? He'd heard her negotiating for the material to make a coat, but thought the coat was meant for Aidan. She clearly needed one as well. Wyoming winters could be punishing. Lands, if she hadn't a proper coat, she could freeze to death.

He crossed to the coop, then leaned forward against one of the posts. "I can fetch the eggs for you in the mornings, Maura, especially as the weather turns colder."

She stepped gingerly over one hen, then another. "I don't mind," she said. "In fact, I like feeling as though I'm beginning to understand at least this part of living on a farm. We haven't had any eggs yet. Finbarr tells me it can take a little while."

"He's right about that."

"I come out each morning, choosing to be hopeful."

He adjusted the collar of his coat, hoping to keep out a little of the cold morning air. "That's a mighty optimistic viewpoint for a woman who insisted only yesterday that she's beaten down by her struggles."

She smiled at him. Saints, that smile of hers did odd things to his heart. "Perhaps I'm growing senile in my old age."

"You're that ancient, are you?"

"Some days, I feel old as the mountains themselves." She pulled open the hatch of the henhouse and peeked inside. He heard her take a sharp breath. "There's an egg." She couldn't have sounded more excited if she'd discovered a gold nugget.

"That's a fine bit of luck, isn't it?" Sometimes a new brood of hens took ages to start laying. He slipped inside the chicken coop and made his way to where she stood.

She reached in and pulled out the egg, only to exclaim, "Another one. And another." She pulled out several, setting them in her upturned apron. "Seven." She turned and faced him, carefully holding eggs in her hands. "Oh, Ryan. We have *seven* eggs."

"Were you optimistic enough to bring a basket?"

She nodded and motioned toward her feet. Sure enough, a basket sat there waiting. He reached down and picked it up, holding it out while she set her precious discoveries inside.

"We have eggs," she repeated in an excited whisper. "I've been so worried I'd bungle the chickens; they're the only thing I am solely overseeing, and I just knew I'd do something terribly wrong."

Guilt clutched at him over how he'd pointed out her inadequacies, reiterated how ill-suited she was to run a farm. He'd been frustrated by her sudden arrival and how it had upended his carefully laid plans. He'd been unfair. "I haven't exactly been encouraging, have I?"

"No one is required to encourage a thorn in their side." She set her hand on the basket, clearly intending to take it back.

He set his hand over hers. "You haven't been a thorn, Maura. Ours is a difficult arrangement, is all."

A degree of empathy he hadn't been expecting entered her expression. "Like your living arrangement with your brother?"

"I seem to collect difficult arrangements."

She smiled a little. "Do you like eggs? We could have eggs for breakfast. It'd make *our* arrangement a little less uncomfortable for a morning."

"I won't take your eggs, Maura." He knew all too well how much she struggled with food.

"You're not *taking*. I'm *offering*. Besides, you are the reason I have a coop and a henhouse and eggs. I think it fitting you should enjoy the first fruits of that undertaking."

She was giving him too much credit. "The O'Connors did nearly all the work."

"After you told them I needed the help," she countered. "I'll accept no arguments."

He could see by the set of her shoulders that she really wouldn't bend on this. "You let my ma and me stay. You fed her and me last night. You're making it mighty difficult to remember that we're at war over this place."

"I know the cost of war." Her expression had turned more somber. "I'm not willing to fight."

"I'm sorry, Maura. I ought to have chosen my words with more care." He knew she'd lost her husband to war. Like a fool, he'd tossed that word out so casually. "I didn't mean to cause you pain."

She hooked her arm through the handle of her basket, and, to his surprise, took one of his hands between both of hers. "You didn't cause me pain. I meant what I said. We're both hoping to claim what only one of us can have in the end. That makes us rivals. We can't avoid that. But I don't want to be enemies. I don't want to fight."

"Neither do I." He held fast to her hand. "What do we do, then?"

She smiled a little. "We have breakfast." She slipped her hand free. "And we do our best not to hate each other." She stepped toward the gate.

"Is that how you feel about me?" His heart dropped to his feet. "You *hate* me?"

She looked over her shoulder at him. "No. But our situation can only end well for *one* of us. In the end, someone is going to lose."

He rubbed the back of his neck. "Sometimes I wonder if anything in life is ever going to 'end well.'"

He crossed to the gate, and they stepped out of the coop.

She watched him with drawn brow. "Has something happened, Ryan?"

He wasn't particularly keen on baring his soul, but speaking his worries out loud made them easier to sort through. "I don't know what to do about Ma. She's too worn to make the journey here and back every day, but she's also in need of having me nearby, so she can't remain at

James's during the day. And the time I spend fetching the wagon and taking her back and forth means I'm running short on time to do m' chores, and, if I can't make up the work, I'll start losing crops. I've tried to formulate a solution, but I haven't the first idea what could be done."

"I've been thinking about that, actually." She tugged the blanket more firmly around her shoulders. 'Twasn't an overly cold morning, but neither was it warm.

"Let's go back inside," he suggested.

She didn't argue. "We agree that your ma needs to not have to move about so much," she said as they took the first of the porch steps. "My Aidan needs to learn more about working on a farm. Both would be accomplished if you and your ma lived here."

That was true, but what was she suggesting? He didn't dare hazard a guess.

"But Aidan and I would need to live here as well." She stepped inside. He followed close behind as she went on. "I've not been able to think of a way for us to share this house that wouldn't be both horribly uncomfortable and more than a touch scandalous." Shrugging, she set the basket of eggs on the table.

If Ryan stayed in the house day to day, that would strengthen his claim on it. Perhaps she hadn't thought of that. She'd not have suggested it if she had. Living here would also save him time and Ma significant suffering. But Maura was right: an unmarried man and a young widow could not share a home without raising eyebrows. Neither of them wanted that.

"I could sleep in the barn until the weather turns too cold for comfort," he offered.

She eyed him doubtfully as she pulled a mixing bowl off a shelf. "How long before the nights are uncomfortably chilly?"

"They are a little already," he admitted.

"That won't do, then," she said. "Besides, your ma would never agree to an arrangement where you slept with the animals. She speaks fondly enough of you for me to know that for certain."

Ryan's head was beginning to ache. "I won't stay at James's while Ma stays here. That wouldn't be fair to you or to her."

"Or to *you*," Maura added. "You'd still have the difficulty of losing time in traveling back and forth."

That was as true as the day was long. Heavens, this whole thing seemed so impossible.

"There doesn't happen to be a secret house tucked away somewhere among the fields, does there?" she asked.

He smiled at the jest. "Only the soddie."

In a flash, his own words settled on his mind. *The soddie.* Though 'twas used as a shed now, it had once been a house.

His mind spun, attempting to fill in the bits of the fast-forming idea. "My ma wouldn't do well in the soddie, but I could make it do for me. I'd be nearby. Were something to happen to Ma in the nighttime, you could send Aidan for me."

She eyed him closely. "And you'd not be living in the house, which should meet with the approval of even the preacher."

Begor, this might work. "We could at least try," he said.

"You're willing to continue helping Aidan?" she pressed.

"If you're willing to help Ma."

"Agreed." She held out her hand.

Uncertain, but with a growing measure of hope, he shook the hand she offered. "Agreed."

"See how much better this is, not being entirely at odds with each other?" she said.

"Much better." He kept hold of her hand, finding comfort in it—and a surprising amount of pleasure.

"And we get to be neighbors instead of enemies," Maura said. That smile of hers sent his heart flipping.

An awareness of her grew, expanding in his chest. His pulse thrummed in his neck, heat stealing up with it. Maura was compassionate and beautiful, clever and kind, fierce and determined.

And he . . . was quickly finding himself on unfamiliar footing.

He stepped back and offered a quick nod before moving to the door. Making his claim on this land was part of the plan. Moving Ma into this house was part of the plan.

Growing tenderly attached to Maura O'Connor was not.

Chapter Twenty-two

The O'Connor family held weekly family suppers on Sundays, rotating from one house to the next. Today was Maura's turn to be hostess. She fully suspected 'twas not actually her turn in the rotation, but rather a ploy to get her and Aidan to attend an O'Connor supper at all.

They'd been invited before, but she'd not felt ready herself yet. She was finding her footing, accustoming herself to being with Grady's family again, of hearing voices so like his, smiles matching the one she'd loved so well. She might have demurred again when Mrs. O'Connor gently informed Maura that her turn had come 'round. But looking at Aidan's hopeful face when his grandmother spoke of the family being together, Maura knew she couldn't refuse. He was ready to truly join his father's family; she would not deny him that.

They would arrive any moment. She'd prepared all she could, but was still nervous. Suppose there wasn't room enough, or she'd forgotten something significant? She wanted the evening to be a success.

Her gaze fell on Mrs. Callaghan. "Are you certain you'll not suffer for enduring company?" Maura must've asked her that same question four dozen times over the past week.

Mrs. Callaghan had insisted again and again that she wasn't worried about overtaxing herself or having her peace disturbed. "I enjoy the O'Connors. It'll be lovely to have them here."

"Why is it you've not asked me how *I* feel about being overrun with O'Connors?" Ryan sat near the fireplace, eying Maura with mingled amusement and, if she wasn't mistaken, a bit of playfulness.

"In that case, do tell, Ryan." She sat on a chair facing his and gave him her most overdone look of eager curiosity. "How do you feel about having this house filled to the rafters with O'Connors? Have you had trouble sleeping with so exciting a prospect before you?"

He leaned back in his seat, crossing his boots at the ankles. "You, Maura O'Connor, are funnier than you first let on."

"Ma's always been funny," Aidan said. "Lydia giggled and giggled whenever she looked after her."

"Who is Lydia?" Mrs. Callaghan asked.

"The wee daughter of a dear friend of mine back in New York," Maura said. "Eliza—that's the lass's mother—is like a sister to me."

"You must miss her," Mrs. Callaghan said. "I've a sister in Cork, and I miss her fiercely."

"I'm hoping, if I can save a bit of money, that I can send for her. She would love Hope Springs, and this town would love her, I'm certain of it."

"And Ivy would insist that Lydia be her friend," Aidan tossed in.

Ryan gave Aidan a commiserating look, one that barely concealed his mirth. "Ivy is a force of nature."

Aidan smiled, something he did more often and far more easily than he used to. "I think she drives her sister a little mad."

She detected the hint of tenderness that Ryan had mentioned hearing in Aidan's voice when he spoke of Emma. Ryan hadn't imagined it. She met his gaze with wide-eyed amazement. He silently nodded in acknowledgment, a half-hidden smile on his lips.

"You know, Aidan," Ryan said, "when your family's here, you could give them a milking demonstration. I'd wager you'd receive a rousing round of applause."

"And you could give 'em a tour of your soddie," Aidan tossed back. "You'd be the envy of the entire town."

"We'd have to manage such a tour with only a couple of amazed visitors at a time," Ryan said. "Three, if the third was of the narrow variety."

More than once, he'd mentioned the soddie was small. He'd also commented on it being cold at night. Neither observation, however, had been made in a tone of complaining. Indeed, Maura wondered if he even realized how often he spoke about the size and temperature of the mud-built house he currently called home.

She felt bad about the discomfort he was enduring. Truly, she did. Yet she couldn't yield. She had so little to leave Aidan as it was. At the very least, he needed a place to live, land he could one day live on, and a ma who wasn't whispered about for having a man she wasn't related to living in her house.

"I'd be willing to forego the luxury of my very fine soddie to join the gathering, if that's permitted." Ryan posed the idea with just enough hopeful uncertainty to tell her that he wanted to be included but hesitated to set his heart on the idea at all. 'Twas a bit of vulnerability she understood all too well. She wasn't certain what her own welcome would be that day. The O'Connors had been friendly to her whenever she crossed paths with them, but she didn't see them often.

"Everyone is welcome at my supper table," she said, "provided they know the secret code."

Ryan fought back a smile. "I'll do my very best ferreting."

He had such a knack for lightening her spirits with a simple glance or a quick-witted comment. Her heart had begun flipping about every time he tucked away one of his smiles. Something about the way he hid them gave the expression added charm.

Maura turned away and set herself to the unnecessary task of checking the colcannon hanging over the low-burning fire. Though the supper was to be held at her home, she hadn't been tasked with providing the entire meal. Not even *most* of it.

"A pot of colcannon will do perfectly," Mrs. O'Connor had said. "Everyone will bring bits and pieces. We'll have a fine meal among us all."

Maura didn't know if that was the family's usual way of things on

Sundays, or if they simply realized how very short of funds she was. Feeding their large brood—twenty counting herself and Aidan—was beyond her ability.

Her next breath came in oddly, thick and dry. Coughing seized her immediately, so strong, so violent, she doubled over with it.

"Ma?" Aidan's worried voice penetrated the sound of her struggle for air.

'Twas Ryan, though, who reached her first. "Sweet heavens, Maura. Are you choking on something?"

She managed to shake her head even as she kept fighting her lungs. "What do you need?"

She rasped out, "Water," though she didn't know if it would help.

"Aidan, lad. Fetch your ma a glass of water, quick-like."

Ryan set his hand on her back and rubbed it gently. Somehow, he knew—or guessed—that thumping wouldn't help. It would only leave her more sore and miserable.

"Your cough never seems to get better," he said quietly.

One breath came a bit easier. Then another. Though she hadn't stopped coughing, she managed to stand straight again. Ryan kept his arm around her, keeping close to her side.

A moment later, Aidan was there, holding out a glass of water to her. She took it and sipped slowly between coughs, praying her lungs would calm and that the water would settle the tickle in her throat. She hated seeing Aidan worrying about her.

"She'll fare fine in a moment," Ryan told Aidan in a calm and reassuring voice. "The ceaseless Wyoming winds put a great deal of dust in the air. Sets a body coughing something fierce."

'Twasn't at all the reason for her struggles, but it was an explanation Aidan wouldn't have to fret over. Thank the heavens Ryan had thought to offer the boy that much.

"You've quite a group heading up the walk just now," Mrs. Callaghan said.

An instant later, Maura heard their voices. She looked to Ryan. Though she was no longer entirely at the mercy of her latest lung-seizing, she was in no condition to greet her in-laws.

He tucked her tenderly against him. "Don't you worry yourself over this," he said softly, walking her in the direction of her bedroom. He called back over his shoulder. "Aidan, see to it your grandparents, aunts and uncles, and the whole lot are let inside and made to feel at home. Your ma's needing to catch her breath."

Quick as that, he led her to the quiet solitude of the bedroom. The coughs hadn't entirely subsided, but they were far fewer and less frequent. She kept sipping at the water.

"Can I do anything else for you, Maura?" Ryan kept near her side, watching her, not with pity, but with unmistakable compassion and concern.

"I hate being weak," she said.

"Weak?" His expression turned scolding. "Not a word that can honestly describe the Maura O'Connor I know."

"You don't know me that well."

He leaned his back against the closed door. "Then what do I know of you?" The question was asked too theatrically for him to sincerely want an answer. "I know you raised a fine lad on your own. You crossed the country. Held a man at pitchfork point."

"He deserved it," she said with a smile.

He grinned back. "You've also found a job and negotiated a living arrangement that keeps a roof over the heads of two families while we wait for our claims to be decided upon. Those are not the accomplishments of a weakling."

Her lungs hurt, but they were calmer. She set the glass on the bureau and let herself breathe a moment.

From the other side of the door, she could hear the O'Connors' voices. They were a boisterous clan, no denying that. They would enjoy themselves; they always did. But heavens, she was nervous. She could feel Ryan's gaze on her face. She glanced at him before looking away again.

"Is it pathetic that I want so desperately for them to like me?"

"They love you, Maura." He joined her at the bureau. "I've seen it in their faces, heard it in their words, again and again. They love you, just as they should."

She met his eye. "'Tis a very good thing you're not abandoning us for the grandeur of the soddie for supper. I may need you to remind me of all that a few times."

"I've had your colcannon, Maura," he said. "Simply ply them with that, and they'll be singing your praises all evening."

"If nothing else, their mouths will be too full to wage any complaints," she answered dryly.

He nodded toward the door. "Face 'em down. You've bearded fiercer lions."

"Fiercer than you know," she whispered.

"I've no doubt."

Maura took a few shallow breaths, allowing her lungs to regain their normal rhythm. She led the way from the room.

The O'Connors had, indeed, arrived, a large, milling crowd of them. Maura moved, not toward them, but to the side of the room near the stove and away from the highest concentration of family members. Her courage, it seemed, was deserting her a bit. Ryan moved about the group.

Thomas Dempsey shook his hand heartily. "Pleasure to see you, Ryan."

"And you."

Ian thumped him on the back and offered a greeting of his own. Mrs. O'Connor gave him a very motherly hug. Mr. O'Connor shook his hand as well. They all liked Ryan; she'd known as much from the beginning. As she'd come to know him better, she understood why. Ryan was a good man. A deeply good man.

"Tavish." No mistaking the English voice that called his name from somewhere in the house. Would it ever stop being strange to hear so refined an accent amongst so many Irish voices?

He stood and turned to face the gathering. "Where are you, love?"

"You're asking *me*?" Cecily laughed. "I can't sort my way through so many people."

Tavish wove through them, finally pulling his wife free of the hoard and over where Maura stood. More O'Connors continued pouring in through the door.

"We'll be tight as fleas on a hound in here." Maura spoke to herself but, apparently, Cecily overheard.

"We always are, but happy fleas, which helps." She looked directly at Maura.. "Thank you for hosting us."

"Yes, thank you," Tavish said, standing at Cecily's side. "We do appreciate it."

"I don't know that I had a choice."

Cecily laughed quietly. "Our mother-in-law is rather tenacious, isn't she?"

"Says a woman who's rather tenacious herself," Tavish tossed in with a grin.

Sometimes having him nearby was unnerving, as his resemblance to Grady swirled up a few too many memories. That evening, however, his presence was comforting. He was kind and friendly, always eager to lift the burdens around him, and did so expertly.

Though, somehow, not Finbarr's burdens. Maura had seen for herself the heaviness in the young man's expression.

"How are arrangements here?" Cecily asked. "We hadn't intended to place you in so difficult a situation. Ryan and his mother didn't let on that they were having so miserable a time in his brother's home."

Maura waved off Cecily's obvious concern over her and Ryan's situation as if it mattered not at all. Tavish and Cecily would, in the end, decide who kept this house and the land it was on. She wanted them to know that she deeply appreciated their generosity in letting her use it and of her intention to be generous to others in return. "Mrs. Callaghan is very kind and sweet. 'Tis a pleasure having her with us. And Ryan lives out at the soddie, so we've no awkwardness on that score. Plus, he's able to begin his work earlier in the day, which I understand is important for a farmer."

"When one lives off the land, one does what the lands demands." Something heavy lay in Tavish's tone.

"Has something happened?" Maura asked.

"Nothing too unusual."

More concerned than reassured by Tavish's dismissive answer, Maura turned to her sister-in-law. "What's he not saying, Cecily?"

"There was a bit of a cold snap a couple of weeks ago."

Maura nodded. "I remember."

"We lost a good bit of our crop to it."

A knot formed in Maura's stomach. Everyone in this valley depended on the yearly crop. "Ryan didn't mention any loss."

"He grows hay," Tavish said. "We grow berries. His crop is likely fine."

"And yours isn't?" Maura pressed.

"We'll have a tight year, Cecily and I, but we'll not starve," he said. "We'll likely not even truly suffer. I'm simply too much of a farmer now not to worry over these things."

"Even with a wee one on the way?" Maura asked. "That must put a burden on the mind."

Cecily's hand dropped to her ever-expanding belly. "We have family enough to look after us if things grow truly terrible. I have every confidence in the O'Connors' compassion."

"I'm an experienced midwife," she reminded them. "Please let me help when the time comes. And Aidan has a tender spot for babies. He'll gladly help you look after your new arrival. We've little to offer beyond that, but what we have, we'll happily give."

Tavish put an arm around her shoulders and gave a very brotherly squeeze. "You've a kind heart, Maura. You always did."

She leaned a bit into his hug. She hadn't realized until he offered it how much she'd needed a bit of familial affection. "During those dark walks back from the factory in New York, did you ever think that you'd one day have a farmer's heart?"

"I knew I'd never have a factory worker's heart." He slipped his arm away. "I'd best go help Ma set out all the food, or she'll begin lodging generally directed complaints meant to guilt us all into action." He pressed a kiss to his wife's cheek, then crossed to his mother.

"That is a good man, there." Maura said as he retreated.

"The very best," Cecily said.

"Are you wanting to sit?" Maura asked. "Or are you also likely to fall under our mother-in-law's guilt umbrella?"

Cecily smiled. She did that a lot, something that made her utterly perfect for the lighthearted and jovial Tavish. "I struggle to navigate through such a tightly crowded space, a fact that has freed me of a great many obligations at these gatherings. Makes me think I ought to have gone blind decades ago."

"Have you not always been?" The moment Maura asked the question, she realized how prying it was. "Forgive me, I—"

"Talking about my sight doesn't upset me," she said. "I lost it slowly, over many years. I've been fully blind for only about a year now."

"And Finbarr? How long has it been for him?" Maura watched Finbarr tucked into a corner away from everyone else. Was he keeping a distance because he couldn't navigate the crowd either, or was he clinging to isolation as she'd seen him do before?

"It's been two-and-a-half years for him. He was doing well, but something changed at the beginning of the summer. We're not at all sure what."

"My Grady could be that way sometimes," Maura said. "Not self-isolating, necessarily, but reluctant to open up when troubles weighed on him. He kept so much tucked inside."

Cecily had turned to face her. Maura had to continually remind herself that Cecily couldn't actually see; she was so adept at appearing as if she did. "Did you ever discover how to get through to him when he closed himself off like that? If so, perhaps Finbarr could be reached the same way."

Maura swallowed down a lump of emotion. "We were married only two years when he left to fight in the war. I would have learned so much more about him, had there been time."

"I am sorry," she said. "Losing someone we love never truly grows easy, does it? Time dulls the ache a little, but doesn't wash it away."

"No, it doesn't." She didn't know who Cecily had lost, but could sense the depth of her empathy. "I'm glad Aidan will now get to know his family. He'll come to know his father better that way."

"He didn't know his father?"

They were delving further into this topic than Maura generally allowed. Somehow speaking of Grady felt easier with Cecily. Perhaps because she, too, had known sorrow. Perhaps because she was not connected to Grady the way the rest of the O'Connors were. Maura felt guilty speaking to his parents and siblings about him. They were his family and had been long before Maura met him, long after she'd convinced him to remain behind when they'd left. They were so achingly close to the grief of his loss. With Cecily, she felt freer.

"Aidan was so little when Grady left that he doesn't remember him at all. He has only the memories I've shared with him." Memories that felt horrifically inadequate. "I've told him how much Tavish looks like his da, and now sometimes I catch Aidan staring at him, and I know it's because he's trying to make a memory of his father, using Tavish as a surrogate. Shatters my heart every time."

"If ever your Aidan wants to come visit, even if only to stare"— Cecily smiled, adding a layer of humor to the situation—"send him over. Better yet, you come too. I would love to know you better, and I know that to the O'Connors, you and Aidan being here means having a bit of themselves back that they thought they'd lost forever."

"A bit of Grady?" she guessed aloud.

"Yes, but the two of you, as well."

She understood the pull the family felt to Aidan. He was blood to them. Knowing they wanted her here as well did her heart good.

Chapter Twenty-three

Maura took a spot in the corner beneath the front window opposite the one where Mrs. Callaghan sat in her rocker. She ate and watched her husband's family interact. Love permeated every look, every word, every laugh. Aidan sat with the cousins his age: Ian's oldest, Michael, and Mary's oldest, Colum. Maura couldn't overhear every comment but had no difficulty interpreting their smiles and laughter. Her boy was happy, and he was home.

Somehow a place was found for everyone despite the insufficient number of chairs and the small table. The O'Connors were adept at making do. Ryan and Mrs. Callaghan were included in the group without any hesitation—a testament to the family's kindness but also a source of worry for Maura. They cared about the other two people who shared this land and house. That affection would complicate the decision of whom to grant it to permanently.

"A fine colcannon, Maura," Ciara said. "I don't know what you do differently than I do, but it's heavenly."

"I add a pinch of mace," Maura said. "Grady preferred it that way."

Hearing his father's name pulled Aidan's attention to her immediately. "He did?"

Oh, how it pained her that he knew so little of his da.

"And he couldn't get enough shortbread," Mrs. O'Connor jumped in. "I had to hide it any time I made it, or he'd finish the whole tray before anyone else had a chance for a single piece."

"I like shortbread too," Aidan said. "Did he like it a certain way?"

"With cardamom." Mrs. O'Connor, Mary, and Ian all answered in near unison. The whole family burst out laughing.

"'Twasn't cheap making it that way," Mrs. O'Connor said through the laughter. "I made it plain most of the time, adding in the cardamom only on very special occasions. He'd eat it, all the while making the most ridiculous noises of enjoyment, telling me I was an angel and hugging me over and over. That man enjoyed his food, I'll tell you that much."

"And he could eat more coddle than all of us combined," Tavish said. "Though, blessedly, he liked the potatoes best and left plenty enough sausage and bacon for everyone else."

Maura dropped her gaze to her plate, trying to breathe through the burning behind her eyes and in her throat. Remembering him didn't usually hurt, but now and then, reminders of Grady pierced her.

"What else do all of you remember?" Aidan asked. Something like desperation filled his voice.

"He was a hard worker." Mr. O'Connor spoke with palpable pride. "He took joy in working, in accomplishing things. The harder the task, the harder he worked."

Aidan listened with rapt attention. "What kind of work did he like best?"

"He worked the land when we lived in Ireland," Mr. O'Connor said. "Up before the sun, out long after it went down. He loved the land. Loved working the soil and harvesting what he'd planted."

Guilt joined the grief Maura struggled with. Grady *had* loved working the land. He'd spoken of it often. He could have had that satisfaction again here if only she hadn't held him back, insisting they remain in New York.

"And in New York," Mrs. O'Connor jumped in, "he drove a delivery wagon. He enjoyed that. He saw so many parts of the city and came to know so many people. He loved meeting new people."

"Sounds like Tavish," Cecily said. "I think that is his favorite part of his berry business: traveling the territory and meeting people."

While they were all sharing more memories of their oldest son and brother, Maura slipped quietly and, she hoped, unheeded out the door and onto the porch. She sat on the swing and wrapped her arms around her middle.

Grady would have been in heaven had he been here these past years. Aidan would have had a family and a father. She was the reason her son had to beg for the tiniest details of Grady. She was the reason he so often looked lost and lonely.

Tears flowed unchecked. She'd wondered over the past decade if staying in New York had been a mistake. Now she knew it had been a catastrophic one. She'd stolen both Grady's future and Aidan's past, and nothing she did could ever give them back.

The door opened. She braced herself. Somehow, she would have to explain her hasty exit and raw emotions. Doing so would require opening old wounds she'd rather leave untouched.

The swing shifted as someone sat beside her. She glanced over. Ryan, of all people, had joined her. What could she possibly say to him? Why had he come outside?

"How long has it been?" he asked after a long moment.

She didn't need to ask what he referred to. "Ten years."

"Do you talk of him often?"

"No." She wiped away another ear. Heavens, this should not be this painful.

"My ma doesn't talk about my da often either. But my brothers did, and it helped." He leaned forward, his elbows on his legs. His feet planted on the porch kept the swing still. "Having the O'Connors tell Aidan about his father will ease some of the boy's pain, but it's adding to yours, and I'm sorry for that."

Maura dropped her gaze to her clasped hands. "I have tried to help him know his father," she said quietly. "But I didn't realize until watching him in there just now how poorly I managed the task."

"You likely did better than you think."

198

She tucked her legs up beside her on the swing. Doing so pushed her a bit closer to him. The proximity brought her a measure of comfort. "He never asked me as many questions as he's asking them. I couldn't have— I couldn't have answered all of them anyway. I didn't know that Grady's favorite part of coddle was the potatoes. I knew he liked working the land, but I didn't know just how much until today. I can't even—I didn't—"

Ryan slipped his hand around hers. "They knew him as a child and a very young man. You knew him as Aidan's father. You can give your lad that."

She bent her fingers more tightly around his, needing the reassurance of his firm, steady clasp. "It's difficult to talk about."

"Yes, but I also know you are not one to shrink from something simply because it's not easy. You'll find a way."

She shook her head. He didn't understand the complications—that it was her fault Grady was gone. Entirely her fault.

He set his other hand atop the one he held. "Let the O'Connors fill in some empty bits while you catch your breath. Aidan will eagerly take whatever you can offer, and I promise you he'll never stop wanting to hear about his da. Not ever. Whenever you're ready to tell him more, he'll listen with every ounce of his heart."

If she'd had all the time in the world, she might have taken greater comfort in Ryan's words. But the violence of that day's coughing fit made her evermore unsure of her own future. Brown lung, once it took full hold of a person, was unforgiving and brutal. She might be gone long before she was ready to break her heart by opening it up on this topic with her son.

"I need to find my courage," she admitted to herself.

He leaned a bit closer to her. In a tone of warmth and encouragement, he said, "You've courage enough, I've no doubt. What you need to find is your voice."

She laid her head on his shoulder. "Where does one find a voice in the midst of such heartache?"

"We all find ours in our own ways and on our own paths. Each of us simply has to be willing to walk it."

She closed her eyes, attempting to capture the peace that came from the simple blessing of not being alone with her sorrows. "There's nothing simple about walking that path, Ryan Callaghan."

"No, there isn't."

Chapter Twenty-four

Maura had settled into her role as housekeeper at the Archers'. She still cooked the meals over the fire, and she didn't know how much longer she could do so without raising suspicion or plain wearing herself out. Moving from the kitchen to the sitting room and back as often as she had to when seeing to both meals and kitchen chores was burdensome and time-consuming. She'd need to swallow her pride eventually and ask someone to show her how to use the stove.

Furthermore, she struggled with the laundry, a physically demanding task, and one she never managed without returning home drained and coughing and worrying anew about her health.

Outside of the times when she'd pushed herself too hard, she felt stronger. Her cough came less frequently, though it didn't calm any quicker than before. She wanted to believe she was improving, but laundry day in particular called that belief into question.

On a bright Friday morning, more than six weeks after coming to Hope Springs, she sat in the Archers' kitchen, Aidan's yet-unfinished coat on her lap. She'd finally saved enough to purchase fabric for the lining and was beginning to piece it together. Little Sean Archer was sleeping in the housekeeper's room, a furnished but unoccupied bedchamber directly off the kitchen. The Archer girls sat at the kitchen work table, bent over their slates, working on a bit of schoolwork. Katie had taken her fiddle out to the copse of trees where she practiced nearly every day.

Earlier that week, Joseph had pulled Maura aside, emotion thick in his voice, to thank her for giving Katie the freedom to practice again.

"She used to play the fiddle exceptionally well, shockingly well, in fact," he'd explained. "But when she lost her fingers in the same fire that cost Finbarr his vision, she lost her music." His voice had broken on those last four words. "She's attempting to teach herself to play with her other hand. I've wanted so badly for her to have the music back, but there hasn't been time for her to practice. She'd all but given up, until now. You've given that back to her, Maura. Thank you."

Listening to Katie now did Maura's heart good. Working for the Archers was making a difference in a real and personal way, and that mattered to her.

Emma paused in her schoolwork, her head turned a little toward the open back door. She wasn't watching anything; she was listening.

"Katie's music has improved this week," Maura said.

"She is getting better," Emma acknowledged. "I've missed hearing her play. She used to play a lot before—" She didn't finish. Her gaze dropped to her slate, though she didn't take up her chalk. "She's different since then. Everyone is."

"But Pompah is happier," Ivy chimed in, "because Katie is here. He was sad when she wasn't here with us. And Finbarr is here again. After the fire, he went away for a long time."

Finbarr had been gone? "Where did he go?" Maura asked, pausing in her stitches.

"He just didn't come visit," Emma explained. "He didn't know how to work anymore because his eyes didn't see very well. And he was sad." Emma's brow scrunched in thought. "Not just sad, though, he was . . . angry. He still is, sometimes."

Maura wouldn't have used those words, but then, she hadn't been here long nor seen enough for her assessment to be perfect. "To me, he seems lost more than anything."

Emma bent over her slate once more. She didn't seem to be writing anything, though.

Ivy took up the conversation her sister had abandoned. "He said angry things to Emma, so she won't be his friend anymore."

"Ivy, stop."

Ignoring her sister, Ivy went on. "Sometimes they talk again like they used to, but then they always go back to being quiet around each other." Ivy climbed off her chair, abandoning her slate altogether. "And he went to the *ceílís*, but then someone said something—I don't know who it was—and it made him grumpy again. Then Emma tried to talk to him—"

"Ivy." Again, Emma's protest made no difference.

"—and he was just grumbly, and then she was sad again, and he was sad again, and now he doesn't go to the *ceílís* anymore. He doesn't come to the house, either, unless we're at school."

In some way, Emma was connected to Finbarr's distance from everyone; Maura was sure of it. Did the O'Connors realize as much? She might be able to help them reach out to him. Then again, Ivy spoke of Emma and Finbarr's difficulties as longstanding and repeating. Perhaps pulling Emma back into Finbarr's struggles would only make things more painful for both young people.

The possibilities spun about in Maura's mind as she continued sewing. Ivy pulled a chair up beside her, content to talk without any replies.

"The Scotts have a new puppy," she said. "Seamus Kelly's dog had a litter, but only two puppies lived. Mr. Scott got one of them. The other one is at Mr. Gallen's ranch. Mr. Callaghan was there when the puppy came. He told me the puppy was happy, and that made me glad. Mr. Callaghan said he was glad I was glad."

"Mr. Callaghan is very kind." The night of the O'Connor gathering, Maura had sat with her hand in his and her head on his shoulder for long moments. He'd shown her kindness and tenderness again and again. "He is helping Aidan repair a bit of the henhouse, since I don't know how."

"Was it damaged by the wind this week?" Emma, apparently, found this topic far safer than discussions of Finbarr.

Maura nodded. "'Twasn't enough to damage the house or barn or, he says, the crop, but it pulled up a bit of the henhouse roof."

Ivy patted her hand, as if consoling her. "Mr. Callaghan will fix it."

"I have every confidence in him," Maura said.

The kitchen door opened, and Joseph stepped inside. His girls both jumped up and rushed over, throwing their arms around him.

He kept them in his arms as he addressed Maura. "I've been instructed to tell you that you needn't remain, as it's past your usual time to return home. Katie is finishing up and will be back shortly, and I will be here until she returns."

Maura didn't intend to argue. She needed to get home to prepare a meal for herself and Aidan. And she hoped to make more progress on his coat while light still spilled inside their small house. Keeping lanterns lit cost too much to justify the oil while days were still long.

"Sean is sleeping in the housekeeper's room," she said. "He was worn out, poor lad."

"Thank you, Maura."

She nodded. With her basket over her arm, Aidan's unfinished coat tucked inside, she slipped out the back door and moved quickly along the side of the house and to the road. Quite to her surprise, she came upon Finbarr. That he made his way back to Tavish's house each day on his own ought to have occurred to her sooner, yet she'd never seen him make the journey and was, somehow, caught off-guard by the sight.

He walked with his cane stretched out ahead of him, searching the ground.

"Finbarr," she called out to him, moving quickly to catch up.

He stopped and waited. That, she hoped, was a good sign.

"May I walk with you?" she asked.

He nodded, not seeming put out by the request.

"Those Archer girls are dears," she said as they moved toward the bridge.

"They are," he said. "They've been like little sisters to me for years." Loneliness filled the quiet declaration. He spoke of them as family yet was separated from them. Not unlike he was with his own family.

"Aidan has said the same about Ivy," Maura said.

Finbarr continued his forward trek but turned his head a little toward her. "Not about Emma?"

"He's fond of Emma," Maura acknowledged, "though I think it is a different sort of fondness than with Ivy."

"He sees Emma as a friend, then?" The answer seemed to matter to Finbarr.

"Most certainly a friend. They get along quite well, which I think is good for both of them. Aidan is trying to find his footing in this town, and Emma strikes me as a little lonely."

Finbarr's scarred countenance pulled in worry. "She's always been very quiet, worryingly so at times. I hope Aidan treats her with kindness."

Very interesting. Ivy indicated that harsh words had pulled Finbarr and Emma apart, yet he spoke in such fierce defense of her. Theirs was clearly a complicated relationship.

"I'm likely overstepping myself," Maura said, "but I'll tell you something I think you ought to know. Emma's heart is heavy regarding you, Finbarr O'Connor. I don't know the exact nature of that ache, but it's powerful heavy. I believe a kind word from you would do her a world of good."

"I don't think she wants any words from me, kind or otherwise."

For reasons she could not entirely explain, his muttered bit of self-pity set Maura's back up. "She's not the only one who could use a bit more of your time and effort. All of your family misses you. They miss you, lad, even though you're among them. Give them a bit of yourself. It'd lift burdens I don't think you're even aware of."

"Well, then, let me do a bit of overstepping and tell you something I think you ought to know," he tossed back. "The entire family wonders why it is you dislike being among them so much. They debate at length whether to press themselves into your life. They love you and miss you and hope that you actually want them in your life, but they're not entirely certain you'd rather the whole lot of them go to Hades."

"I've never wished any of them to Hades." She was shocked at the very suggestion. "I'm a little uncomfortable, I'll admit, after being apart so long, and I worry about being a burden on the family, but never have I ever wanted anything but the best for all of you."

"Then it seems we're both giving impressions we don't intend to." He had a point she couldn't refute.

"Then you aren't purposely avoiding them?" she pressed.

"Are you?" The lad was a stubborn one.

She could be quite determined herself, especially when doing so would help someone. And Finbarr, whether he acknowledged it or not, needed help.

"I'll do better if you try to as well." Opening herself up was a risk, but she'd make the effort if it meant bringing a measure of happiness back to this young man, who had once been such a sweet and cheerful child.

"I'll try." His was a half-hearted agreement, but it was an agreement nevertheless.

Eventually they reached the point where she'd turn off the road in one direction, and he in the other. He dipped his head and bid her a good evening, then made his way up the walk, his cane guiding his way.

When she walked past the chicken coop, Aidan and Ryan were inside it. Both looked up at her. No matter that she'd rather go straight to the house and begin her work, she'd taken to heart Ryan's gentle prodding, and was doing what she could to be more open around her son.

"How is the repair coming along, Aidan?" she asked, making certain her pride in him showed in her tone and expression.

"We're done," Aidan said, crossing to where she stood and speaking to her across the mesh wiring. "But Ryan has a bone to pick with you."

He did, did he? She quirked an eyebrow as she turned to look at him. "What complaint have you to lodge today, Mr. Callaghan?"

He shot Aidan a look. "You've landed me in hot water now, lad."

"You're the one who said you meant to give her quite a talking."

Maura folded her arms across her chest, her basket hooked over her elbow. "Did you?"

"My soul, you two. You'll dig me a pit so deep I'll never escape." He mimicked Maura's stance. "The lad, here, told me you play the pipes, a bit of knowledge you never mentioned despite knowing I played. I was

206

shocked enough that you'd leave that out that I told him I meant to find out why. He's the one who twisted it all about."

Then Aidan did something he seldom did: he laughed. He genuinely, fully, deeply laughed. All Maura's bluster died at the sound of it.

Her boy shoved Ryan, who jokingly shoved back. They were jostling and teasing. They'd developed a friendly interaction. She'd wanted her son to find his place amongst his family. He was exceeding that hope by finding friendship amongst the Archers, the other schoolchildren, and now with this man who continually surprised and upended her.

She ought to have been overjoyed, yet her heart dropped.

Maura spun about and moved toward the house. How Ryan caught her before she stepped onto the porch, she didn't know. He must have run, perhaps even hopped over the coop fence.

"I wasn't actually upset," he said. "Truly."

"I know. I realized after a time that Aidan was only baiting you."

"And I did want to talk to you about the pipes," he said, "but not to scold you. I've been the only piper in this town in all the years I've lived here. To know another . . . that's a fine thing."

He'd be sorely disappointed.

"I've not played the pipes in twenty years, Ryan," she warned him. "I'm not the musician you are."

"It's no matter, Maura. The pipes get in your blood. They make you love them, and that love doesn't die off simply because years have passed."

She did miss the pipes. She'd often longed to try them again. But fate had not been kind on that score. Fate hadn't been kind on many scores.

"I also meant to talk to you about it because"—he glanced at the coop and lowered his voice—"Aidan said he might want to learn. I didn't know what you'd think of that. If you'd object."

For a moment she couldn't find her voice. "He's never expressed an interest in pipes before."

"He has now." Ryan watched her closely. "I'd be happy to teach him, but I thought maybe you'd prefer to do it yourself. Or maybe you'd rather he not at all. I'm not looking to make trouble."

Her first inclination was to insist that any teaching be done by her. She was so accustomed to keeping her lad close, struggling to be everything he needed. She hadn't yet fully adjusted to the reality that he had many people looking out for him now.

She swallowed her pride. "If he'd like to learn, and if you're willing to teach him, I'd be obliged to you. I've no money to pay you, but I could arrange some kind of trade."

He was already shaking his head. "Aidan is the one wanting to learn. Let him and me work out between us a trade of some kind. There are chores enough to be done."

"Chores you'll have to teach him to do," she pointed out. She didn't care to be beholden to anyone, nor a burden.

"I'll not let a thirteen-year-old swindle me." His smile worked its usual magic, turning her worries and prickles into calm warmth.

"I'm not certain Aidan would have the first idea how to swindle anyone." How she loved her sweet-natured boy. Life had not always been kind to him. "His tender heart made him such a target for the harder and harsher boys who worked the street corners. They made his life such a misery."

Her gaze fell on Aidan, standing at the edge of the chicken coop, watching her with anxious eyes. Learning to play the pipes would bring him a bit of much needed joy. And for him to learn more about running a farm would be an answer to prayer.

"I'd be grateful to you," Maura said. "And though I know perfectly well you'll be stubborn about it, I'll find a way of evening things up with you over this."

He raised an eyebrow. "Is that a threat?"

"A promise."

A corner of his mouth twitched upward. "I've been warned."

"You don't look worried."

"Far from it." He turned to walk back toward the chicken coop. "I'm looking forward to it."

Chapter Twenty-five

Ryan pulled on a thicker pair of stockings. 'Twas July, yet the night was a cold one. The weather had been unpredictable this season. He wasn't overly concerned about his fields. Not yet, at least. But he knew others, who had more sensitive crops, were beginning to get nervous. Tavish, who harvested the first of his fields long before anyone else, had already suffered some losses.

A cold draft sliced through the air. Ryan had found most of the cracks and holes in the soddie's walls, but clearly not all of them. Some, like the edges of the greased-paper windows, couldn't be fully sealed. It was going to be a long night.

And a quiet one.

He felt rather like a hermit, tucked up in the fields as he was. No matter that James's house was overly crowded, he found living in this soddie took things too far in the other direction. He was, in a word, lonely.

Someone knocked at the door. The sound was so unexpected that at first, he couldn't convince his brain that his ears weren't playing tricks on him. No one ever visited here. Not ever.

"Ryan?" As surprising as the knock had been, Maura's voice proved even more so.

She wouldn't have come so far for no reason. Something must've happened. Had Ma grown ill or terribly pained?

He pulled the door open, his heart pounding an anxious rhythm.

She stood there, uncertainty in her expression. Her hair hung down in waves, something he'd not seen before, and a sure sign that this was not truly a planned visit. She held a pile of what looked like two folded quilts.

"What's the matter?"

She shook her head. "Nothing. I've brought you blankets." The wind kicked up, a mighty gust nearly blowing her off balance.

"You came all this way to deliver blankets?"

She shrugged as if her efforts didn't matter, but she was shivering enough to tell him with certainty 'twas a sacrifice to bring the quilts out to him. "You've mentioned that the air gets quite cold in here. We're a bit cold up at the house, so I assumed you'd be miserable."

"It is a chilly night," he acknowledged. "You'd be cozier if you weren't out in it."

"That, I would be," she said, "so let me come in and set these down rather than leaving me out here in the wind."

He motioned her inside. Another gust pushed its way in with her, setting both their teeth to chattering. He popped the door shut. "Thaw out a moment before braving that again," he insisted. "It's not toasty in here, but it's better than being out in Mother Nature's embrace."

She set her armful of blankets on the bed in the corner.

Her presence upended him more than he'd've expected. She looked softer with her golden-brown hair hanging loose, and the sight tugged at him.

"Is Ma keeping warm enough?" he asked. "She aches terribly when it gets cold. Can't hardly move for the pain and stiffness."

Maura nodded. "Aidan and I searched out every blanket we could find in the house. Your mother has several. Aidan has an extra—he insists the loft is fairly warm—and I've an extra two in my room. You were the only one without."

He motioned to the stack. "I have plenty now."

She looked around the humble, nearly empty sod home. "You don't have a fireplace."

210

No, he didn't. "The Claires used the cast-iron stove when they lived in here. But then it was moved to the house."

Her deep brown eyes turned to him, real concern in their depths. "You can't live in a place without heat. When winter comes, you'll freeze to death, quite literally."

Did she not realize? They'd been getting along so well of late. He hated to bring up the topic most likely to push them apart again. Yet, she needed to understand. "This'll not be our situation that long. A decision will have to be made before winter sets in."

"Oh." Her countenance fell a little. "For a moment, I'd forgotten about that." Apparently, she wasn't entirely certain of the outcome of that decision. He wasn't either. "How soon do you think Tavish and Cecily will make their choice?"

He shrugged. "Likely not until after harvest."

She nodded a bit absentmindedly. Her gaze remained unfocused as she turned and sat on the edge of the bed. The only other bit of furniture in the soddie was a single spindle-backed chair.

"I understand why you need this land, Ryan, and the house for your ma. I truly do. But"—she turned pleading eyes on him—"we need it too. Aidan and I have nowhere else. I can't afford to buy us a home. I can't afford to purchase land for him to one day make his own. And I simply cannot live on the charity of my relations. You, of all people, must know the misery of living in someone else's house."

"You mean because Ma and I have been living in James's house?"

She nodded.

How little she understood the situation. He sat in the chair, turning it to face her. "The house isn't his. Not really. Ma and I and James all put every penny we had into buying the land and the materials for the house. I spent as much time as he did building it. I put in as much effort. The house was *all of ours*. It should be still."

She watched him with growing confusion.

"Then James married and started a family, and, somehow, it all slowly became his. I'm not sure he even remembers that it wasn't always."

"The cruelty of fate has forced you from the home you always meant to be your own?" Maura asked.

That hit closer to the truth of the matter.

"I always meant to stay in New York," she said. "The tenement we lived in was poky and a bit rundown, but I never imagined living anywhere else. Fate forced us away as well."

He didn't know what, precisely, had made her decide to come to Hope Springs. "What was it fate tossed at you?"

"Aidan was slipping away." Her gaze dropped to her fingers, fidgeting with the ties on the quilt beside her. "He was so very unhappy. I could tell that the life we were living—one of poverty and hopelessness—was changing him. He felt broken by it already, and he was so young. I had to get him out of that place. I had to give him something to believe in and a place to belong."

"A lot of people in Hope Springs, the Irish especially, came here looking for a future they could believe in." That same optimism had brought Ryan and his family west. "Aidan does seem very happy here."

A tiny, fleeting smile lightened her heavy expression. "Just as I hoped he'd be. He has family here, and he is making friends. And, thank the heavens, he'll not ever have to work in a factory like I did."

Ryan had heard terrible things about the mills and the toll they took on people. Maura said that only *she* had worked there, but she'd indicated 'twas Aidan's future that had weighed on her mind. Had she not wished to escape their circumstances as well?

She coughed, that same deep, rattling one he'd heard from her so often. As always, the attack seemed to drain strength from her, as if the simple act was exhausting. Her shoulders drooped and her posture grew heavy.

"You've been here weeks and weeks, Maura, and that cough's not gone away yet."

"I've a bit of something in my lungs, is all."

He watched her taking one shallow breath after another, her open palm pressed to her chest. "You'd be on the mend if it were so simple a thing."

She rose abruptly. "I'd best begin walking b—" The sentence ended in the middle of a word as another coughing fit seized her. She tried to take a deep breath, but that only made things worse.

He moved to her, rubbing her back as he'd done a few times lately. He didn't know if it helped, but hoped the gesture at least brought her some comfort. Ma had often said that being ill made her feel alone.

Maura's breathing settled a little, though not entirely. He continued to rub her back, standing beside her, unsure of what else he might do. "If you wanted to stay a bit longer in the soddie, love, I'd've let you. You needn't attempt coughing up your very lungs to avoid going out in the cold and wind."

His teasing quip did not have the effect he'd hoped. She looked up at him, and, to his horror, a tear fell from her eye, another threatening in the other.

"Merciful heavens, Maura. What's this?"

For the first time since he'd met her, she looked truly defeated. In all their sparring, in all the moments of struggle he'd seen her pass through, she'd never looked anything but determined. Even when she'd teared up during the O'Connors' visit, she'd not looked this broken.

She stepped closer to him. He set an arm gingerly about her, ready to withdraw it if she objected. Maura leaned into him, so he pulled her into a true embrace. Her breathing still hadn't fully settled.

"This isn't a cold," she said quietly.

His heart clenched, concern creeping in faster by the moment. "What is it, then?"

"The doctor called it brown lung."

Ryan didn't at all like the sound of that.

"People get it from working in the textile factories," she said between lingering coughs. "Bits of cotton get stuck in the lungs and eat away at them. I had to leave. *We* had to leave." A wheezing breath followed. "Staying would have made it all worse."

"But you'll get better now? Now that you're away from the factory?"

She held very still in his arms, her head tucked enough to hide her face. Wind whistled through the cracks in the walls, mingling with her labored breaths to fill the silence that stretched out between them. A long moment passed. He waited for an answer, one he grew increasingly nervous to hear.

"Brown lung doesn't get better," she whispered.

His mind refused to make sense of her words. They jumbled about, crashing against his heart with unexpected force. *She isn't going to get better.*

"Will you—will it grow worse?"

"There's some hope that I've not left too late."

"Too late?"

"Brown lung kills." She spoke from within his embrace. "I've seen it my own self. There's no way to know for sure if a person's time will be short except to wait and watch for the signs."

He couldn't tell if his head was spinning or simply empty. No solid thoughts formed.

She took a surer breath than she had in a few minutes' time. "The coughing will grow worse. Breathing becomes permanently belabored. Blood comes up with the coughing. When that happens, there's no stopping it. There's no outrunning it, no matter how far from the factories a person's gone."

His heart thudded a fear-filled rhythm against his ribs. "Have you been coughin' blood?"

She shook her head against him. "Not yet."

Not yet. Those weren't words of encouragement.

"I've seen this before," she said quietly. "I can't ignore the symptoms I already have."

He was reeling. Maura was dying. *Dying.* "Aidan's never mentioned it."

He felt her tense in his arms. "He doesn't know."

"Maura—"

She stood fully straight, pulling back to look him in the eye. "Don't you dare tell him, Ryan Callaghan. It'll be clear enough to him in time. Worry eating at him beforehand will do him no good; it certainly won't heal me. Let him have his childhood while he still can."

"He needs to know."

She stepped back, forcing his arms to drop away. "He's seen it, too, Ryan. He likely has his suspicions. But so long as I'm not in a panic, he won't be. Once my lungs take that turn—that final turn—he'll know well enough what it is."

Good heavens. She was looking death in the face. He could hardly comprehend it. "Do the O'Connors know?"

Again she shook her head. "Once it's certain and coming fast, I'll talk to them. Aidan will need them then."

"Until then?"

"I'll not be a burden, and I'll not be defined by this illness. I've strength enough to hold out a bit yet, and I'll make this journey on my terms." She moved to the door. "Let me know if the blankets are enough tonight. If not, we'll try to scout out more for tomorrow."

"Maura, wait. You can't simply tell a person you're dying then walk out the door as if nothing has changed."

She held his gaze firmly, unapologetically. "Nothing *has* changed. I'm no sicker now than I was before you found out; I'll be no less sick now that you know."

"Maura." He reached out and gently touched her face, unsure if she'd pull away or let him hold her again. Not knowing which he'd prefer.

She closed her eyes, both pleasure and pain in her expression. The burdens she carried too often went unseen and unacknowledged. 'Twas little wonder she looked so crushed by them in that moment.

He closed the gap between them. "I'm sorry, Maura. I'm sorry the factory took such a toll. I'm sorry your Aidan was so unhappy. I'm sorry the future isn't as bright as you deserve it to be."

"And I'm sorry our arrival ruined so many of your plans for the future." She spoke without opening her eyes or pulling away.

His griping and grumbling had all but guaranteed she would blame herself for that. It wasn't fair of him. "That's the way of life: we make plans, and then we adjust."

She set a hand softly on his chest, looking up at him at last. "Have you done a lot of adjusting, then?"

"Heavens, yes." He set his hand atop hers. "When I was a lad, I'd planned to live out my days in Ireland, but that changed. In Boston, I worked as an assistant gardener in a fine house and had plans to one day be head gardener."

"What changed?" Her thumb rubbed absentmindedly along the edge of his button. "Coming here?"

"No. The butler caught me sleeping in the servants' stairwell when I was supposed to be working."

She smiled. "How old were you?"

He made a show of pondering. "Twenty-four. Twenty-five."

She raised an eyebrow, clearly not believing him.

He set his arms around her, entwining his hands behind her back. "I was eleven."

Empathy and amusement filled her gaze. "I'd wager you never napped in a servants' stairwell again."

"You'd make money on that bet, Maura."

"Does it bother you?" she asked. "All the plans you've had to change?"

"I'm feeling pretty content with things at the moment," he said.

The smallest hint of a blush stole over her cheeks. "I'm not entirely discontented myself."

How excruciatingly tempting it was to kiss her. She was in his arms, smiling, sharing with him her hopes, her worries . . . herself. This was everything he'd dreamed of for so long. A strong, dependable, loving woman who pulled fiercely at his heart strings, in what was, at the moment, his home, and who had found an inarguable place in his affection. How easily he could let himself fall more deeply under this spell that was being woven between them. How very, very easily.

She said his name. Quietly. Earnestly. Hopefully.

He bent closer. His pulse pounded in his head, his heart thudding punishingly against his ribs. Her hand slid up his chest, her fingers brushing his neck. His next exhale trembled from him. He turned his head enough to feel the warmth of her breath against his lips.

"This is likely a bad idea," she whispered. "We're simply lonely."

It was just the splash of cold water he needed. "You're not wrong."

He stepped back. His arms felt immediately bereft without her. He hadn't even the briefest moment in which to bid her farewell or to express the hope that he'd see her in the morning, or to mourn the need for her to go. She was simply gone, out into the brutal wind and cold.

Ryan dropped onto his bed and pushed air from his tense lungs. "What are you doing, man?" he asked himself. "You can't go making up sweet to her like that. It'll only complicate things further."

Yet, when he closed his eyes, willing sleep to quiet his uncertainties, thoughts of her saturated his mind. The feel of her in his arms, the sound of her quiet voice saying his name. He flipped over onto his side, trying to force himself to think about his crops or his ma or any number of things. He didn't manage.

No matter that he and Maura had sworn to not be enemies, they *were* rivals. That would change only after one of them was declared the victor. Not even mutual loneliness would be enough to bridge the chasm that fast-approaching day would create between them.

Chapter Twenty-six

Ryan's thoughts were in a jumble and had been ever since Maura visited the soddie. The state of her health weighed on him, as did the state of his heart. They were rivals, but they were also friends. The first hint of something more had grown between them, but too many questions remained unanswered for either of them to move forward. A couple of weeks had passed, and still he hadn't the first idea what to do.

Aidan returned home at suppertime on a drizzly summer day, but his mother was not with him. The rain had let up enough that he hadn't been soaked on his walk. He carried a basket, one Ryan had seen Maura carry to and from the Archer home. Aidan set it on the table. He pulled out two large jars of what appeared to be soup.

"Ma says if we put a pot over the fire and pour these in, it'll warm up quickly and make a good supper." He then pulled out a cross-cut loaf of soda bread. "And we're supposed to eat this with it."

"She's not expecting to be home for supper?" Ma asked from her rocker, watching Aidan with concern.

He shook his head. "It's laundry day."

Ah. Maura did laundry at the Archers' once a week, and on those days, she always came back late. Late *and* exhausted. Ryan had tried to tell her that she didn't need to worry over fixing supper here at home, as well. She, however, had wrapped her stubbornness around herself like a battle cloak and told him she would do precisely what she felt she ought, and he'd best have nothing contrary to say about it.

Ryan would have argued with her, but, knowing what he knew of her struggles, he simply nodded. She was a woman coming to terms with a very unkindly dealt hand. Clinging to her ability to feed her son and the people with whom she shared a home was not a matter of contrariness. She was, rather, showing strength in the face of overwhelming difficulties.

He admired that. He admired it deeply.

"Do you know how to build a fire, Aidan?" he asked.

The boy nodded. "I built them in our tenement fireplace nearly every day."

Ryan slapped him on the shoulder. "Get at it."

Aidan jumped to the task.

"I'll set out bowls and spoons," Ma said, rising slowly from her chair.

"You needn't," Ryan insisted. "Aidan and I'll see to it."

"I'm having a good day. I'll help while I'm able." She leveled him a look Maura'd be hard-pressed to equal in its determination. Far be it from Ryan to stand between an Irishwoman and something she meant to do.

He, instead, carried the heavy iron pot to the fireplace, then hung it on the pot hook. He set the jars of soup on the mantel shelf, waiting for the fire to take. Aidan saw to his task quickly and easily. Here was one thing he'd not need to be taught how to do.

He spotted Ryan watching him. "Ma says I'm an expert fire maker."

"She's right about that. You've stacked the wood just as you ought, laid the right amount of kindling. Making the fires was my task from a young age. I know a fellow expert when I see one."

Aidan stood, having started the flame. They'd have a nice, low fire going in a moment more. "Did your da not see to the fires?"

"My da died when I was a young boy," Ryan said.

"So did mine." Aidan stuffed his hands in his trouser pockets. "I was a baby. My grandparents have been telling me about him, though."

"Does your ma tell you about him?"

"A little. She grows sad if she speaks of him too long." He chewed at his bottom lip. "But not sad like she's still grieving. More that she . . . I don't know how to explain it. She feels bad that he's gone. She maybe feels a little guilty."

'Twas an insightful observation for so young a lad. Ryan hadn't recognized the misplaced guilt in his own ma's mourning for a very long time.

Aidan pushed out a breath. "She doesn't let on, but I think she's a bit lonely, too."

Her words had repeated in his head again and again the past days: "We're simply lonely." She'd reached out, not because she felt the same pull he did, but because she, too, was lonely. The moment they'd shared, the kiss they'd *nearly* shared, had been about loneliness.

She'd kept her distance since. The regret she'd spoken of hadn't been avoided, but his regret wasn't quite the same as hers. She clearly wished they'd not had that tender moment together. He, on the other hand, wished he hadn't realized how much his affection for her had grown. Unrequited feelings were difficult enough in the best of circumstances. Falling even the tiniest bit in love with a woman when, in the end, one of them was going to crush the other's hopes for a future . . . that was a complication in the plan he did not know how to adjust for.

"Ma misses Eliza, her friend in the Tower."

Ryan opened the first of the jars, trying to set his mind on his task rather than his dilemma. "What's 'the Tower'?"

"The building we lived in," the lad said. "It was old and falling apart, so the rent was low. Most people wouldn't live there, except widows like Ma who were too poor to live anywhere else."

A slum. He'd seen plenty enough of those in Boston.

"I didn't earn much money shining shoes," Aidan said, "but she wouldn't let me work at the factory, even though I'd've earned a lot more that way. She was always saying I needed to be a child a little longer."

"She's bang on the mark there, lad." Ryan poured the soup in the pot. "This ol' world will force you to grow up before you know it."

Aidan leaned his back against the wall beside the fireplace. "'Any place you live should be better because you lived there.' She always says that, but I didn't make the Tower any better. I didn't help people the way she did."

He set a hand on Aidan's shoulder. "In case you don't hear it often enough, I'll tell you that your mother is powerful proud of you. That pride shows in her eyes when she watches you and when she talks about you."

"Truly?"

"Truly." He poured the second jar of soup in the pot.

"She says I look like my da," Aidan said. "I really do, at least a little."

Ryan eyed him, confused. "How is it you know what he looked like?" Aidan had lost his father far younger than Ryan lost his, and Ryan had only the vaguest idea what his father had looked like.

"Ma has a photograph."

"She does?" That was not a common thing.

Aidan nodded. "I know where she keeps it. I'll show you." Without waiting for a response, he rushed from the room and through the door to Maura's bedchamber.

Ryan stirred the soup. Heavens, but the lad was desperate for a connection to his da. What would he do if he lost his ma, as well? He'd be devastated.

Ryan's ma shuffled to where he stood and gave him an unexpected hug. "You're very good to the lad. I suspect he needs it."

"I know all too well what he's feeling."

Ma offered a sad sort of smile. "'Tis a difficult thing, losing a father."

Ryan nodded. "That it is."

Aidan returned quickly. He must have gone in after the photograph often to have found it as quickly as he did. Ryan waved him to the chairs near the fireplace. They sat, each beside the other. Aidan carefully unlatched the tiny metal hook holding the book-like leather frame closed. He slowly opened it, nervousness in his movements. Behind an engraved tin oval matte and thick glass lay the image of a man in the uniform of the Union army, his eyes looking directly at whomever opened the frame. Dark hair showed beneath his army cap. The eyes were very light, like

Aidan's. He looked shockingly like Tavish and precisely as Aidan would in another ten years or so.

"You look *very* much like him," he told the lad. "Strikingly so."

"Ma says he was very handsome."

"He was," Ryan confirmed. "And brave to have fought as he did."

Aidan carefully closed the frame again. "Ma said he fought because my uncle did. He was trying to keep his brother safe."

"He was protecting his family while serving this new country of ours. 'Tis an admirable thing."

Aidan held the frame tenderly, the way one would a treasure. "Do you think he—?" Emotion cut off the question.

An answering ache echoed in Ryan's heart. He didn't know precisely what Aidan meant to ask, but he recognized the worry underneath it. He, too, longed to connect to a father he'd never truly known. He desperately wished to understand him, to please him. So many questions pressed on Ryan's mind and heart where his da was concerned, but there would never be an opportunity to ask the man any of them. 'Twas a weight and a sadness he carried with him, one Aidan likely did as well.

Ryan gave the lad's shoulders a reassuring squeeze. "It's a fine thing having a photograph of your da."

Aidan nodded and smiled a little. "Sometimes I pull it out and just look at him."

"If I had a photograph of my da, I'd look at it every day."

He nodded, a gesture that acknowledged how deeply they both understood this particular pain.

"I should put it back. Ma doesn't mind if I look at it, but she's always tired on laundry day. She grows sad more easily when she's tired."

While Aidan returned his treasure, Ryan stirred the soup again. He met Ma's eyes and saw both sadness and pride in her eyes, precisely what he'd seen in Maura's expression time and again when she'd watched her son.

The door opened; Maura had returned. He'd seen her on previous laundry days and knew she'd be tired, as Aidan had predicted. 'Twas different this time, however. She looked utterly done in. Exhausted. She had almost no color.

"Laws, woman, are you ill?" He moved quickly toward her, but she held up her hand to halt him.

"Only tired. A moment or two and a bit to eat, and I'll be fine."

He didn't fully believe her but knew better than to say as much. "I'll fetch you a bowl of soup. You set yourself down somewhere."

Aidan stepped back out in the next moment. "Ma, you're home."

Maura didn't answer, which was odd enough to pull Ryan's attention back to her. What little color she had drained in an instant. She dropped, without a word, to the floor.

"Ma!"

Ryan was closer and reached Maura before Aidan did, though the lad ran to where she lay crumpled on the floor. Ryan knelt beside her and set a hand on her shoulder. She was breathing, that immediately settled some of his worries.

"Maura?"

A quiet, quavering voice answered. "What happened?" She was sensible enough to speak. A good sign, that.

Ryan brushed her hair away from her face, hoping to get a better look at the state of her. She was still worryingly pale. A small trickle of blood slid from beneath her hairline.

"You've hit your head, love," he said.

She attempted to reach up and touch it, but seemed to run out of strength, her hand dropping away.

Ryan met Aidan's eye. The poor lad looked nearly panicked. "She's bleeding."

"Only a bit, lad." He hooked his thumb toward the kitchen. "Fetch us a rag."

Aidan did so without hesitation. He handed the cloth over. Ryan wiped away the blood rolling down Maura's forehead, then pressed the rag to the wound. "This hasn't happened before," Aidan whispered.

Maura struggled to sit up. Ryan slipped an arm around her, offering her his support in her weakened state. Watching her struggle, Aidan didn't appear the least reassured. She was very nearly seated, still on the floor but upright. She swayed a bit. Ryan tucked her up beside him, and she leaned against him.

"What do we do?" Aidan asked.

"I'll look after your ma. You run across the road and have your uncle Tavish ride up to your granny's house and send her down here. She'll know what's best."

Aidan didn't look away from his ma, his brow pulled in lines of worry.

"Go, now," Ryan insisted. "And be quick."

At last Aidan shook off his shock and rushed for the door. He was gone in a flash.

Maura leaned more heavily against Ryan. The blood had not stopped, though it was a thin line, likely a small cut. He suspected she wasn't feeling well enough to remain sitting without his support. She certainly couldn't stand. Though she wasn't coughing, her breaths rasped. And she was overly warm. Was fever a sign of the brown lung progressing? Saints, he hoped not.

"I'd really rather you not collapse like that again, Maura," he said quietly.

"I'd rather not either," she whispered.

He kept her in his arms, trying not to think about what this deterioration might mean.

Chapter Twenty-seven

The next day, Ryan returned from the fields at lunchtime as he usually did. Today, though, he'd come not merely for food nor to look in on Ma. He was worried about Maura. She had not been left to fend for herself; Mrs. O'Connor was there looking after her. But Ryan had to see for himself whether she was improving.

"Hello there, Ryan," Mrs. O'Connor greeted when he stepped through the front door. "Come for a bite to eat?" She exchanged a look with Ma that told him she knew perfectly well that food was not his primary motivation. With mischief twinkling in her eyes, she turned back to Ryan. "A bit of brown bread, perhaps? A boiled potato? Bite of sausage? What is it you're interested in?"

"I'll assume our patient isn't too poor off," Ryan replied. "Else you'd not be spending your effort giving me grief."

Ma took pity on him. "Maura's resting. She's still fighting that cough and is weary to her very bones, but otherwise seems well."

He nodded. The cough would persist the rest of her life; she'd told him as much. "How's she been sleeping?"

"No worse than usual," Ma said. "She's coughed throughout the night ever since I began living here. That hasn't changed."

'Twas little wonder Maura was so tired all the time. Was that why she'd fainted last night? From pure exhaustion?

The door to her bedroom opened. He moved there with all the dignified haste he could manage. "Maura, why're you up? You should be resting."

"All I've done today is rest." The words were quiet and slow. Her steps were measured. Weakened.

"Are you certain you won't go lie down again?"

"I'd be more than willing to sit, if there's a chair handy."

He motioned her toward the fireplace, where an empty chair sat waiting. While she made her way there, he opened the trunk under the window and pulled out a blanket. He grabbed a chair from the kitchen table and brought it and the blanket to her. He set the chair next to hers, then spread the blanket over her lap.

"Thank you," she said.

He sat beside her, grateful to see her awake and alert. Though exhaustion still hung heavy over her, she was entirely lucid and upright.

"How're the fields treating you?" she asked. "Tavish has lost a good bit of his crop. I heard Mrs. O'Connor say this morning that they've a bit of loss in their wheat." She paused for a labored breath. "Your hay really is fine?"

Wasn't that just like Maura? Fretting for others when she had worries of her own.

"The hay is fine as feathers," he said. "Berries are very different from hay. What'll ruin Tavish's yield won't make any trouble for mine."

She coughed, but only once. "I'm glad to hear it. I know you've a lot depending on this crop."

He shrugged a bit, allowing himself a hint of a laugh. "Only my entire future."

"I know what it is to gamble your future on something risky."

His gaze unfocused as the reality of her words hit him anew. She, too, needed the house and land. If only they could continue as they were, somehow. If he thought long enough, he might find a way to heat the soddie to make it habitable in the winter. It'd be lonely and a bit uncomfortable, but he could make do, surely. For a time, at least.

His gaze focused on Maura once more. She tucked the blanket more snuggly over her shoulders, then turned her head in his direction. When she met his eye, a small, weary smile touched her face.

Aidan said she'd never been courted. How was that possible? He couldn't imagine any man *not* being drawn to her. He certainly was. Did she feel that pull between them too?

"James and Ennis are coming up the walk," Ma said, looking through the front window. "And they've brought Nessa."

James was calling? That was odd enough to make him nervous. James didn't usually bother with Ryan's company unless he had something to complain about. A difficult visitor was the last thing Maura needed while recovering.

They knocked. Through the window, Ma motioned them inside. Ennis entered first, Nessa's hand in hers. James followed close behind. The man seldom looked happy; he certainly didn't now.

Nessa pulled free and rushed to him. "Uncle Ryan." She held her arms up to him.

He plopped her on his lap. "How are you, flower?"

She didn't answer, just rested her head against him. He looked to Ennis, confused. "Is she ill?"

"She woke me up long before the usual time this morning, and she refuses to go back to sleep, no matter that she's exhausted." Ennis moved slowly, one hand pressed to her back. She'd been uncomfortable in the weeks before Nessa was born, and her time was fast approaching with this new arrival. "I brought her here in the hope that you could get her to sleep. You've managed to in the past."

James shook his head, clearly annoyed. Trying to appease him was like juggling cats: precarious, exhausting, and arguably pointless. Nothing Ryan did, whether that meant tending to his crops or spending time with Nessa, ever failed to bother James. Their interactions didn't used to be that way.

"Sit with me a spell, James," Ma said patting the chair next to hers. "I don't see you anymore."

He sat. "Things've been overwhelming the past weeks. I've so much to do around the place."

"For you and Ryan, both," she said. "Who'd have thought you'd be working *longer* hours here than we did in Boston?"

"I like this work better, though," James said. His eyes settled on his wife. "And I decidedly like the company."

That tender declaration was, quite possibly, the most tender thing Ryan had heard his brother say in years. He knew James loved Ennis. He'd never harbored the slightest doubt about that. James's was a happy little family, except when Ryan was with them. Perhaps James's resentment at having to share the house stemmed from frustration: so long as the space didn't belong wholly to him and his wife, their happiness remained out of reach.

Nessa waved at Maura, who smiled back.

"This is my friend, Maura," Ryan told his niece. "I've been trying to convince her to go back to sleep as well, but I've a feeling neither of you is going to pay me the least heed."

"Does she live here too?" Nessa tucked her legs up and curled into a ball.

"Maura lives here with her son and your granny. I live in a house nearby." Describing the soddie as a *house* was something of a stretch.

"Do you like it?" Nessa asked.

He didn't *like* the soddie. But he did like living on this land he loved. He was grateful to be near Ma in a place where she was happier. He found, more and more, he treasured being near Maura. "I mostly like it."

James watched him, a look of genuine curiosity on his face. "This arrangement's working out for you, then?"

"Well enough," he said. "I'm still sorting how to heat the soddie in the wintertime."

"Surely things will be decided before then." Ennis's brow pulled in concern. "You can't go on living in that drafty vegetable cellar. And we've only just begun feeling like a family with a house of our own."

"Ennis," James struck a warning tone.

"Of course we'll have you back if need be," Ennis said, "but—"

"Don't you fret, sister," Ryan said. "If things don't work here, I'll come up with something else."

"Another *plan*?" James clearly doubted he'd sort out anything at all. "When have those ever worked?"

"That's the way of life," Maura said. "We make plans, and then we adjust."

Quoting Ryan's own words. She'd listened to him. His own family didn't always do that.

"He'll find his way," Ma said. "I've every confidence."

Bolstered by their support, Ryan pushed onward. "I'd have greater confidence if I knew whether James meant to let me use the wagon." He watched his brother but did his best to hide the hope and worry he felt.

"I can part with it now and then," James said, "but not on a regular schedule, and I can't guarantee I'll always be able to lend it to you exactly when you need it."

Frustration stiffened Ryan's posture. "Without a wagon, I'll not be able to bring my hay in. It'd be a disaster."

"I need the wagon for my crop as well," James insisted. "And you're borrowing my horses to pull your mower as it is."

"I paid for half that team and wagon," Ryan tossed back. "Why is it I have to beg for the use of them?"

"Lads," Ma scolded.

Nessa shifted about, her movements made jerky with frustration. She let out a plaintive cry. Ryan tried adjusting his hold on her, suspecting she was too tired to be comfortable, and too uncomfortable to sleep.

"Come sit with me, sweetie," Maura urged. Nessa didn't hesitate but crawled quickly from Ryan's lap onto Maura's.

"Maura, you're not well," Ryan insisted.

"I'm well enough to hold a child on my lap."

Ryan hadn't the energy for two arguments at once. He took a calming breath and addressed his brother once more. "Could I not have the use of the wagon only one afternoon a week for the time being?" Ryan pressed. "Only one, and I'd not have it for long. When harvest comes, we can sort out something more."

"I must be able to look after my fields," James said. "Everything depends on the harvest." As if that weren't just as true for Ryan.

"Believe me, I understand that. But your harvest covers weeks and weeks as different crops come ready. I've one crop, and every bit of it will have to come in at the same time." Ryan tried to speak calmly, not wishing to upset Nessa or Ma. "Without a wagon, I'll lose everything."

James paced a bit away. "We'll have another mouth to feed soon enough. I'm having to be very cautious."

Ryan took a slow breath in through his nose, trying to stay calm enough to not tear a strip from his brother. James never saw anyone's struggles but his own, never allowed Ryan even a moment of consideration.

"How are you faring, Ennis?" Ma asked.

"Well enough."

The focus of the conversation shifted immediately to James and Ennis and their coming arrival. The question of Ryan's crop, along with the team and wagon he'd helped pay for, was to be ignored, it seemed.

Ryan leaned forward, his elbows on his legs. He rubbed at his throbbing temples.

"Seems it's time to adjust your plans again," Maura said quietly.

"That's the exhausting part," he said. "It's *always* time to adjust."

Chapter Twenty-eight

Maura considered avoiding the *ceilí* at the end of the week, knowing she'd be answering one question after another about her health, and not wishing to lie over and over again. But in the end, she knew her absence would only fuel speculation. People would begin thinking too closely on her health since her arrival, and they'd begin being more aware of it moving forward. Attending the party and showing herself capable of participating was her best course of action.

She put extra effort into tidying her appearance and even prepared a plate of scones to add to the table of victuals. The undertaking required her to stop to rest a few times, something that frustrated her to no end. She'd raised a son on her own, worked long hours at a factory, and seen to the needs of dozens of families in the Tower, all without slowing a single step. Now, she couldn't make a simple plate of scones without being felled by fatigue.

Upon reaching the gathering and watching Aidan dash off to be with his cousins, she found a chair near the dancing. *A lighthearted expression,* she reminded herself. *Upright posture. Chat amicably.* If she appeared healthy, hardy, and enthusiastic, then the people around her wouldn't realize she wanted nothing more than to go back home and sleep for days on end.

Within moments, Katie and Joseph sat beside her.

"I'm so glad to see you here and looking so well," Katie said. "I've been worried over you these past few days."

Maura had known she would be. "I can't say what the culprit was on Tuesday. I've felt better each day since then, though the trouble is lingering a bit."

"Ryan is convinced that laundry day is what's doing you in," Katie said. "Bless his soul, he tried to convince that brother of his to allow him use of the wagon to drive you home on Tuesdays. Seems he couldn't talk James into it."

"Is that why he wanted the wagon?" Maura hadn't had any idea that was his reason. He'd argued for the use of it once harvest arrived. Was this truly why he wanted it now?

"Ryan Callaghan is a good man," Joseph said. "Life hasn't been kind to him, though things have been looking up lately."

Maura didn't need an explanation for that observation. Ryan had negotiated a fine arrangement with the ranches, one that would see him and his ma living in comfort with land and a home of his own at last. She, however, stood in the way.

"Finbarr spoke to Tavish," Katie said, "He'll happily come by on laundry day to take both you and Finbarr back in his cart."

Maura shook her head. "Tavish is having difficulty with his crop. He needs to spend his time tending to *it*, not to *me*."

Katie shrugged. "He did offer to send Cecily in his place, but in the end, it seemed a bit misguided setting her and Finbarr to the task of driving a horse and cart."

"'Twas kind of Finbarr to try to help me," Maura said. "I've wondered these past weeks if he notices much to do with the family, and I'm barely part of it."

"He notices." Joseph spoke with quiet firmness. "He simply doesn't know how to be part of that family any longer. He doubts his value. Something happened earlier this summer—he hasn't told me what—that strengthened those doubts."

"He's afraid of becoming the family's object of charity." She needn't phrase the thought as a question; she knew what Finbarr was feeling. She felt it herself.

Joseph's mouth turned downward. He rubbed a hand over his chin and jaw. "Tavish is more likely to be the next one in need of their support."

She turned to look at him. "Is his situation so dire as that?"

"He's lost almost half his crop. He lost nearly all of it the season before last and hasn't yet recovered from the blow. He's already told me he won't be able to make his land payment until after Ryan sells his hay and makes his payment to Tavish and Cecily. Which means he's now worried not only over his crop, but also over the hay across the road, all the while knowing that he'll have a little one to care for and feed and clothe before long. That's quite a burden to bear."

"Poor Tavish," Katie said quietly. "And Cecily's likely beside herself as well. The land can be a cruel mistress."

"Tavish is buying his land from you?" Maura was struggling to sort out the tangled web. "And Ryan is 'renting' the land he works from Tavish and Cecily?"

Joseph nodded. "When Mrs. Claire lost all her family to the fever a few years ago, I paid off her note on the land, wanting to remove that burden from her. I generally can't do that; I'd lose my shirt. But I could in this one instance. When she passed on, she owned the land free and clear and was able to do with it whatever she chose. She left it to Cecily."

"And the income from leasing that land to Ryan helps Tavish and Cecily meet their own needs?"

"It helps them look after Finbarr too," Katie said. "An extra mouth, one belonging to a nineteen-year-old lad who's growing and works up quite an appetite each day, is no small thing."

Maura hadn't the ability to pay Tavish and Cecily for the land and house. Choosing to let her have the place would mean losing money they desperately needed. The plans Ryan was so busy adjusting because of her impacted more than *his* life. Ryan was the key to many futures. His and his ma's. Tavish and Cecily's. Finbarr's.

"Miss Maura." She startled to hear Ryan's voice. He stood in front of her, grinning the mischievous grin he sometimes wore. "The musicians are striking up a tune they don't care to have a pipe for, and Ma says she won't dance with me. You'll take pity on me, won't you?"

Taken word for word, it wasn't the most gallantly spoken request, yet the twinkle in his eyes told her he was teasing. "You don't truly want to dance with me, so stop your mocking."

To her surprise, he actually looked hurt. "You think I would play such a dastardly trick?"

A surge of heat stole over her. "I'm no dancer. Haven't been for years."

He eyed her with confusion. "Did you never dance in New York City?"

She could feel Katie and Joseph's gaze on her. Confessing to her loneliness had not been on her list of things she meant to do at the *ceílí*. She'd already told Ryan, and she'd regretted it since. "I was a widow who wasn't getting younger, raising a child on my own. I had little opportunity for dancing and such things."

"That child is currently perfectly happy amongst the lads and lasses his age," Ryan said. "And I'm fond of aged women."

She ought to have been offended, but there was too much laughter in his voice for that. "How old are you?"

"Twenty-seven," he said.

"Don't ask her how old *she* is," Joseph warned. "That won't end well."

Ryan grinned broadly at her. "I wouldn't dare."

Twenty-seven. He was six years younger than she was. Six.

He held out a hand to her. "Will you dance with me? I really would like you to."

"I suppose it wouldn't do to shun the younger generation."

He helped her to her feet. "'The younger generation?' You're not so old as all that, Maura."

She walked with him out amongst the dancers. "I'm thirty-three."

He gasped. "Thirty-three. Faith and truth and saints above! I never heard a number so high in all my days." His expression turned gentler, more heartfelt. "I've two brothers older than that, you know, and I don't consider them ancient."

The musician struck up the opening strains of "Irish Lamentation."

"This is a waltz?" She hoped she was remembering correctly. Waltzes were less taxing.

Ryan nodded. "I didn't know that you were feeling well enough for a jig or a reel."

"Likely not."

He slipped an arm around her middle, keeping her right hand in his left. As the music began, he pulled her a touch closer.

"I'd not wanted to say anything when I'd be overheard, knowing you mean this to stay a secret, but how are you feeling, Maura? Truly?"

"I still have my cough, and I wheeze a bit when I breathe, and, blessed fields, I'm tired, but I'm not feeling any worse than I did before that fainting spell." Having someone she trusted enough to talk with about her struggles was a blessing. She'd felt so alone before meeting him. "I think I need only to give m'self more time to see to the laundry so it'll not be as taxing, maybe split the chore in half and do it over two days."

"I hope that helps, Maura." He kept perfect time to the music as they took a turn about the dance area. "I wish I could do more to ease your burdens."

She smiled up at him. "You were very sweet to try. I'd've welcomed a wagon ride rather than that long walk."

His eyes narrowed a bit. "How'd you know I was looking to borrow the wagon for that in particular?"

She shook her head. "I'll not reveal my sources. 'Twas a fine idea you had, though."

"Well, we young folks are very thoughtful."

She laughed a bit. She'd done that a lot since coming to Hope Springs, mostly in his company. She appreciated that likely more than he knew.

"Don't ruffle up at me, lass, but I do think you ought to tell the O'Connors what it is you're facing." He held her a bit closer. Her heart simultaneously jumped and melted. "I've seen them rally in support of those they care about. They're a force, that family."

235

"The one they need to bolster is Finbarr. He needs their love and strength more than I do. He deserves it more."

He didn't argue, didn't try to convince her to change course. He simply continued with their dance. The movements were slow, which her struggling body needed. Her legs were growing a touch wobbly, but she didn't want the dance to end.

She found such comfort in being held again, even as part of a dance. She'd not felt truly safe with anyone the past ten years. With Ryan, she did. With Ryan, who was likely to be granted the final claim to the home she needed. Ryan, who sometimes frustrated her like no one else, and more often comforted her to an even greater degree. Ryan, who was . . . twenty-seven.

"Are you truly only twenty-seven?"

He laughed, a deep, rumbling laugh. "Rather shocked by that, aren't you?"

"That would mean when Aidan was born, you were only fourteen." Good heavens. "And Aidan is nearly fourteen now."

Ryan touched his cheek to hers, whispering in her ear. "Leave the cyphering for another time, love, and just relax and enjoy the dancing."

"I've all but forgotten how to relax."

"Close your eyes," he gently instructed, "and trust me not to let anything happen to you for the next minute or so."

"Depend on you, you mean?" She shook her head. "I'm even less adept at *that*."

He assumed a more proper dancing position. "I'm not surprised. Old people do get a little set in their ways."

With a wink, he continued leading her through the dance, but he didn't say much else. Had he taken offense? Or had his making sweet to her only been teasing? How close she'd come in the soddie to indulging in the urge to kiss him. She'd been lonely, and sharing her worries had forged a link between them.

She'd been right to end things quickly. He had a way of chipping away at her walls. Behind those protective barriers lay nothing but pain and heartache. All the regrets she carried, all the plans he'd had to change, the dreams he pursued, and all the dreams she'd likely not live long enough to realize. Allowing this tug she felt toward him to go any farther than that would only lead to sorrow. She wouldn't subject either of them to that.

Chapter Twenty-nine

The next Saturday morning, Maura put Aidan's still-unfinished coat in her basket, as well as her sewing supplies, and set herself in the direction of Tavish and Cecily's house. The O'Connor women were holding their weekly sewing circle, something they usually did on Wednesdays. 'Twas a rare opportunity for Maura to join them.

Though her first inclination was to keep a distance and remain at home where all was quiet and she needn't worry about her cough and wheezing drawing attention, she'd come to a conclusion. She could either spend what time remained to her in hiding, or she could seek out bits of happiness and opportunities to do some good in the world around her. Today that meant taking the time to enjoy a morning spent with her O'Connor relatives. She could work to build a relationship of trust between them all, so that, someday, when she needed to depend on them, she could do so with less guilt and as less of a burden.

She knew that going to the gathering was the right course of action, yet she was nervous.

Before she'd taken a single step, Aidan joined her on the porch. "May I come? Finbarr said Cecily made biscuits."

"I don't know that she meant any of those biscuits for you," Maura warned.

Aidan grinned. "Finbarr says she's soft-hearted when it comes to 'growing boys' wanting a biscuit."

When he was being mischievous like this, he looked and sounded so much like Grady. She saw the resemblance more often lately. He was happier and lighter than he'd ever been. Hope Springs had managed to work some kind of magic.

Maura motioned him to walk with her. He did so with a bounce in his step.

"When did you and Finbarr talk about Cecily?"

"Yesterday," he said. "He was outside when I passed by after school."

"Do you talk to him often?" As far as she knew, Finbarr didn't generally talk to anyone.

Aidan shrugged. "Sure."

This was a development. "What do you talk about?"

"Lots of things. How I'm getting on with the kids at school. What I'm learning. How you're feeling."

Worry clutched at her. "You discuss my health?"

"He knows you've had a cough—he hears it when you're at the Archers'—and everyone knows you were sick last week. He asked about that."

Joseph had said that Finbarr paid attention to the family, even if he didn't interact with them very often. That observation, as it turned out, was quite true.

They had crossed the dirt road and were quickly approaching their destination.

"What else do you and Finbarr talk about?"

"He asks about Emma and Ivy, which is odd, because he sees them as often as I do."

"Do you ever ask him questions?" Thus far, the conversations sounded rather one-sided.

"Sometimes." Aidan stuffed his hands in his pockets, a posture he often struck when feeling uncomfortable. "The questions I have are all . . . He knows about farming and living here and all of that. Those are the questions always floating around in my mind. But I don't want him to think I'm stupid."

"I will let you in on a secret, Aidan," Maura said as they made their way up the path to Tavish and Cecily's door. "Finbarr wouldn't be annoyed or unimpressed by questions about farming or living in Hope Springs or any of the many things he's learned over the years. Not at all. I happen to know he'd be eager to share those things with you."

Aidan eyed her with a mixture of doubt and hope. "How do you know that?"

Because she knew what it was to feel useless and broken. She knew the pain and loneliness of wondering if she had anything at all to contribute to the world. She'd felt that pain deeply in the time between her sister's death and their move to the Tower. Finding a way to serve, and finding someone who needed her, had made all the difference. She suspected Finbarr needed the same.

"Trust me on this one, lad. You'll both be better for it if you find the courage to ask your questions."

He nodded. "I'll try."

Maura squeezed his shoulders. "I love you, Aidan. You know that, don't you?"

"Ma." He colored a bit and pulled away. He was fast approaching that age when shows of affection from his mother wouldn't be welcomed as often and as readily as they'd once been. She dreaded the time, but also embraced it. This was part of growing up, and she was simply grateful her illness had not progressed so quickly that she would miss this part of his life.

Aidan knocked at the door. It was opened quickly. Mrs. O'Connor's eyes pulled wide and she smiled broadly.

"Come in, come in." She had a hug for both of them. "Find a seat, Maura. We're beginning a bit casually this morning. Cecily's lying down; she's having a difficult day, I'm afraid."

"Is she unwell?"

Mrs. O'Connor's gaze flicked to Aidan. "Would you mind terribly, lad, if I asked a favor of you?"

"Not at all," he insisted.

"Finbarr's out in the barn trying to get the morning chores done, since Tavish is out in his fields trying to save a bit more of his crop. Would you rush out to see if Finbarr has something you can do for him?"

"I don't know how to do very much yet," Aidan warned.

Mrs. O'Connor smiled kindly. "No matter. I have full faith he'll find something for you that you either know already or he can explain to you. It'd help your aunt and uncle quite a bit."

Aidan left quickly, though Maura saw nervousness in his expression and posture. He would have to ask a lot of questions if he meant to help at all. That would be difficult for him, but it'd be a helpful bit of practice.

Mrs. O'Connor looked to Maura again. "I know you've come hoping to do some sewing, but as I said, Cecily's feeling poorly. It's to do with the baby. She says you have experience with midwifery?"

"Quite a bit of experience."

"Would you look in on her?" Mrs. O'Connor asked. "It'd put all our minds at ease."

Maura's sisters-in-law sat in the room, watching the exchange hopefully.

"Of course," she told the room in general.

Relief touched all their faces. They clearly cared deeply for the very proper English addition to the family. As Ryan had said, the O'Connors rallied around their own.

Mrs. O'Connor led her to a room off the main one. She gave a quick knock before opening the door and stepping inside. Large picture windows filled the bedchamber with an abundance of light. The window framed a breathtaking view of the distant mountains. Cecily lay on the bed.

"Maura's come," Mrs. O'Connor said. "She means to take a look at you."

"I suspect," Cecily said, "you'll discover this was all a great deal of fuss over nothing."

Maura crossed to the bed. "The health of an expectant mother and her baby is never 'nothing.' And I told you my own self to send for me if you had even the slightest worry or concern. I meant it, you know."

241

Mrs. O'Connor mouthed "thank you" and slipped from the room, closing the door behind her.

"How far are you from your time?" Maura asked. It'd be helpful to know that before discussing anything ailing her today.

"I'd say two months or so. Not very long."

"No, but far enough that some things would be more worrisome than if you were nearer the end."

Cecily shifted up to a reclining position, pillows behind her back. She set her hand atop her rounded middle. Her eyes were closed, as they had been since Maura came inside. "I have been having pains. They're an achy and cramping kind of pain, precisely as I've so often heard delivery pains described."

False labor, perhaps? Maura had known quite a few women who experienced that in the weeks before true labor began.

"What else?"

"The baby doesn't move about as much during the pains or for a little while afterward."

"But do things return to normal after the cramping has stopped?"

Cecily nodded. "If I rest entirely: no working or even walking about."

That did not sound like false labor. "Have you had any bleeding?"

"No."

Thank the heavens. "Does anything else seem to contribute to the pains starting or stopping?"

Cecily's brow tugged low in thought. "Lifting heavy things. Riding in the cart. I had some difficulty after dancing at the *ceilí*."

That all made perfect sense. "Physical exertion sets if off, seems to me. That can happen with labor pains."

"You think this is labor?" Cecily paled further. "I'm too far from my time."

Maura understood perfectly the panic in Cecily's voice. Babies born too early seldom survived, and their mothers did not always fare better.

Maura set a comforting hand on Cecily's. "You know what brings on these bouts, and you know what calms them. That knowledge makes all the difference in the world."

Eyes still closed, Cecily took a deep breath. Her expression calmed a little. "I can stop the pains from happening again?"

"You can reduce the chance, at least." Maura turned a bit, facing Cecily more fully. "That means staying mostly off your feet—fully if you're having pains—and neglecting the work of your household until after the baby arrives."

Cecily shook her head. "Tavish has enough work with his crop without household chores and cooking placed on his shoulders as well."

"He is likely as worried about this as you are. Knowing how to help will set his mind at ease."

"He doesn't know," Cecily said. "I've just been telling him I'm tired. He likely suspects it's more than that, but . . ."

"Why haven't you told him?" From all Maura had seen of their relationship, Tavish would move mountains for Cecily's sake.

"We've lost over half our crop," she said, heaviness in her words. "The situation is growing dire. As it is, the weight he carries is already nearly crushing him."

"Is it nearly crushing you?" Maura asked.

Cecily offered no verbal response. She didn't need to. The heaviness in her expression told its own story. Stress and strain contributed to difficult pregnancies. Maura hadn't the medical training to know how or why, but she'd seen it often enough. Those at the Tower whose losses were the most raw and who struggled the most severely financially or in any other way often had more complications.

"You need to tell him," Maura said. "You can't carry this weight alone. But you've strength enough between the two of you to face this, even with your other worries."

A bit of regret touched Cecily's expression. "I likely should have told him about this sooner."

"If he's anything like my Grady—and I suspect he is—he'll not begrudge you the delay. He'll simply be relieved to know what it is you're facing and have the chance to help you feel better."

"On the subject of feeling better," Cecily said, "you haven't coughed once as we've been talking. I hope that means *your* health is improving."

Maura had been so focused on Cecily, she'd hardly noticed. She'd had a few better days mixed in with the difficult ones these past months. The brown lung wouldn't go away, but perhaps the balance of ups and downs would begin to even out a bit more. "The cough is better just now."

Cecily smiled empathetically. "I'm glad."

"So am I."

"Will you come by now and then to check on me and the baby?" Cecily asked. "I'll worry less if I'm not left to guess how our little one is faring."

"I'll come by as often as you'd like."

Cecily leaned back against the headboard. "Thank you."

"What can I do to make you more comfortable?" Maura asked. "I notice you've kept your eyes closed. I can pull the curtains if the light is causing you discomfort."

Cecily smiled a little. "The light doesn't bother me, but I suspect my eyes would bother you. I lost my sight to a disease; it disfigured them."

"Is that why you wear darkened spectacles?"

Cecily nodded. "Sometimes hiding imperfections is easier than constantly explaining them."

'Twas the reason Maura worked so hard to convince people her cough was nothing more than a lingering cold. She didn't want to be defined by the disease she grappled with. Cecily understood that as few people likely did.

As Maura came to know the people of Hope Springs, both in and out of the O'Connor family, she identified with them more and more. She hid the impact of her ill health as Cecily did. She struggled to accomplish all the things she once had, as Katie admitted to experiencing. She wondered if she had anything at all to contribute, as Finbarr so often did. Feeling a connection to them all was comforting. She felt less alone.

"I am sorry I didn't have better news for you," Maura said. "But I do think if you keep mostly off your feet, rest extra when you are struggling, and let Tavish help you carry this worry, you'll fare far better than you now fear."

"Thank you, Maura," she said.

She stood and moved to the door. "Do your best to rest. Sleep if you can. Your family will look after everything."

"It is a fine thing to have family, isn't it?"

Maura was beginning to understand just how fine a thing it truly was. They would help her—she felt certain they would—and she meant to do everything she could to help them.

Chapter Thirty

If Maura hadn't been so certain what she was about to do was the absolute right thing, she might have been more nervous. After a vast deal of pondering, she knew what needed to be done and wouldn't put it off a moment longer. She placed a plate of sweet biscuits on the kitchen table in front of the Archer girls.

"I need to talk with your father a moment," she told them. "You two look after each other, and be good."

"We're always good," Ivy insisted.

"Oh, are you, now?" Maura met Emma's gaze for the briefest of moments, long enough to exchange a bit of amusement. "My Aidan tells me you're a bit of a mischief maker, Ivy."

A gap-toothed grin blossomed across her face. "Aidan likes me."

"He likes the both of you," Maura said. "I have it from his own lips."

Emma's eager gaze captured Maura's. "Truly?"

"I swear on Ireland herself."

That brought hope to Emma's face. Aidan had said on more than one occasion that both Ivy and Emma were like little sisters to him. Maura knew with perfect clarity that Emma would not appreciate hearing that particular detail. Enough for the moment to know that she was liked and noticed. The rest would sort itself in time.

She scooped little Sean into her arms. "I'll take your brother with me," she told the girls. "Then you needn't look after him."

"He'll scream all the while you're talking to Pompah," Ivy warned.

Maura shook her head. "Sean and I have an agreement. He promises not to scream like the banshee for hours on end, and I vow to make certain there's an extra bit of colcannon for him whenever I make it."

Emma smiled a bit. "He does like colcannon."

Maura eyed her armful. "You're an Irish lad, that's for certain."

His big brown eyes twinkled back at her. Grady had always said he fully expected their children to have her brown eyes, but Aidan had his blue. Perhaps if they'd had more children, one would have had brown eyes like this wee, darling boy. So many of the things they'd planned to have in abundance—children, dreams, time—had vanished on a battlefield, gone with the smoke of cannons and the cries of war.

She held Sean a touch closer and made her way from the house. The sounds of Katie practicing her fiddle floated on the breeze. Maura's work allowed Katie time for her music. She liked knowing she was helping bring a bit of joy to Katie's life.

Aidan and Finbarr stood only a few steps inside the barn door, in a horse stall. Aidan ran a stiff brush the length of a horse's side. Finbarr followed behind with his hand, using touch to evaluate Aidan's efforts.

"Good," Finbarr said. "Be careful not to miss any spots. A clean coat is important for a horse's health."

Aidan repeated brushing, with Finbarr checking his work. Maura slipped past quietly; Sean was being very cooperative. She found the little one's da sharpening a tool at the other end of the barn.

"Maura," Joseph said, dipping his head in greeting. "Is there something I can do for you?"

"I'm needing a moment of your time," she answered.

He moved to set his tool aside.

"Please don't stop on my account," she said. "This is something I can speak on while you work."

He didn't object but returned to his efforts.

"I've been thinking on what you told me about Tavish and Cecily and their land, and I have a proposition."

He paused in his sharpening, giving her a look of deep curiosity.

"I'll preface this all by saying I haven't any experience with business or money dealings, so the whole thing might be a terrible idea."

Joseph shook his head. "I am not afraid of hearing terrible ideas."

Sean chose that moment to wriggle and quietly fuss. "Come now, little one. I'm attempting to look like a dignified business woman. You aren't helping."

Joseph chuckled. He didn't do that often, though she hadn't the least worry he was actually an unhappy person. His nature was simply quieter, like Emma's. He set down his tools and reached for Sean. Maura handed him over.

Content in his father's arms, Sean giggled and popped his fingers in his mouth. Joseph's attention was quickly back on Maura.

She firmed her courage and pressed forward. "Tavish and Cecily pay you for their land. Ryan pays them for the land he works. What he pays them helps them pay you when they have a particularly lean year."

He nodded.

"They own the land Ryan works free and clear," she said. "But they don't own the land they actually live on and live off of."

Another nod.

"What if you were to trade?" This was the part she wasn't sure was even possible. "Rather than having a note on the land they work and fully owning the land they don't, what if they were to give you the Claire land?"

His golden brow had pulled in thought. "Pay off their note with the Claire land?"

She nodded.

"That is an interesting proposition." He bounced Sean on his hip as he thought it over. "The Claire property is larger than their land. Tavish and Cecily wouldn't necessarily be getting the better end of the deal."

She'd wondered about the relative values of the properties. "But to not owe anything on their own land, to be free of the debt and weight on their minds might be worth it to them."

"Or we might be able to work something out to even the exchange,"

Joseph countered. "You do realize, though, if we trade that way, I'll have to collect rent on the Claire land—or payment against a new note if it's being purchased. I have to. I can't take a loss on that land without risking everyone else's land as well."

She'd anticipated that. "I know."

"Ryan Callaghan could make that payment," Joseph hesitantly pressed. "But I don't think you could."

She tried to appear unconcerned as her heart dropped to her toes. No matter that she'd sorted this part out in her mind; it still wrapped her heart and mind in cold tendrils of worry. "I realize I would have to give up my claim to the house and land. But Tavish and Cecily desperately need the stability. And the Claire land should be in the hands of someone who can make it profitable. Neither of those will happen if Aidan and I are granted the house and land."

"What would you do, then?" Joseph asked.

"I have an idea, but I'd need to talk to Katie first."

Joseph kissed the tip of Sean's button nose. "I'll give this lad back to you so I can finish my work here. Let me know what Katie says to your proposition. The land swap you suggest is, I'll admit, rather ingenious, but I'll not undertake it if it means you'll be tossed onto the road."

She could smile at that. "It wouldn't come to that either way. The O'Connors would take us in if need be."

Maura took Sean in her arms again. He didn't seem overly happy about the change, but didn't truly object. From behind them, she heard Aidan.

"The horse didn't like that."

"What did he do?" Finbarr asked.

"Flicked his tail at me."

"Is he still?"

"No," Aidan said. "Just the once."

"He was likely flicking at a fly, not you."

Joseph lowered his voice. "I don't know what you said to Finbarr to convince him to work with Aidan, but whatever it was, it's a godsend. He's come back to life in a way I haven't seen in months."

"He needed to know he has a purpose," Maura said. "That he can still contribute. And Aidan genuinely needs someone to help him learn these things. The two will be good for each other."

"He has always had a purpose here," Joseph insisted. "He's always been needed."

"This is different." How could Maura help him see? "When a person can't do what he has always done, when a person is facing new limitations, it is important that he feel he is able to offer something, and that what he has to offer is needed."

"He doesn't want to always be the weak link."

"Yes, but I believe it's more than that. He doesn't want to always be the one *taking*. He wants to *give* as well."

Joseph made a sound of pondering. "Anytime your Aidan wants to come learn what Finbarr can teach, he's welcome. Not only because it'll be good for Finbarr. Aidan's a hard worker and a fast learner."

"He takes after his father," she said.

"Says the woman who just made a brilliant business suggestion I hadn't thought of despite years of study and experience." He shook his head as he took up his sharpening tool once more. "Give yourself due credit, Maura O'Connor. You deserve it."

She carried Sean out of the barn once more, her heart somehow both lighter and heavier. She knew this was the right course of action, but her burden would grow as a result. She would have less to offer Aidan in the short term. If she could live long enough to see Aidan gain the farming skills he needed, he could live with his grandparents or an aunt and uncle without being a burden. That would mean a lot.

Katie's music had stopped, but had she returned to the house yet? Maura glanced in the direction of the practice copse. Katie was walking toward her, her fiddle case held securely against her. Maura waved.

"Wave to your ma, Sean," she said, demonstrating for him. After a few tries, he made a valiant effort.

Katie waved back and hurried to them. "Were you waving to your ma, dear?"

Sean reached for her.

"I'll take your fiddle," Maura offered. Holding the boy and the case would require some juggling for someone with fingers on only one of her hands.

"Thank you."

They made the swap quickly.

"May I talk with you?" Maura asked.

"Of course. Is anything the matter?"

Maura shook her head. "I'm wanting to ask if I can make a change in my arrangements here."

"Is the work proving too much? After the difficult time you had last week, I worried it might."

"No. Well . . . the change I'm thinking of would help in that regard, as I'd not be so tired from walking up and down the road day after day." She had Katie's attention. 'Twould be best to move forward. "Running a farm is far beyond mine and Aidan's abilities. This job suits my skills better. And I believe Ryan and Mrs. Callaghan will soon have ownership of the Claire land and house."

"Where will you go?" Bless Katie, she sounded genuinely concerned.

"I hoped I might lay claim to the housekeeper's room here. I'd make extra at meals for m'self and Aidan, which can be deducted from my pay, as well as the value of the laundering soap I'd use when tossing our clothes in with the rest of the family's."

Katie tipped her head in thought. "I lived in that room while working as a housekeeper here, and we took those same things into consideration. It is easier to get the work done when you're not having to walk here each morning."

Ryan had made the same observation about his land and living at his brother's house. If she lived with the Archers, she would have more time to work, but she would also have more energy, more air, more endurance.

"What about Aidan?" Katie asked. "Where would he sleep?"

That part of Maura's plan was less ideal. "He's been sleeping on the floor of the loft these past weeks, so he's not unaccustomed to a blanket on the floor."

"He'd sleep in the housekeeper's room with you?" Doubt had entered Katie's voice.

Maura couldn't afford to allow it to grow. "Not permanently, only until I sort out something better. He won't complain, and we'll not be a burden on the household. Indeed, he's been working for Joseph the past couple of days with Finbarr's help."

Katie's mouth dropped a bit open. "Finbarr's been helping him?"

Maura nodded. "'Tis a good thing for them both. I'd like to allow the connection between them to grow for a time. We can make do sharing a room; we've done it before. And we needn't rule out the possibility of finding something different if need be. But both of us staying here would help us tremendously for now."

Katie bounced Sean on her hip. "If things are too pressed sharing that room, you can always search out a more comfortable arrangement." She made the statement almost as a question.

Maura nodded. "We simply need something to bridge the gap between where we've been and where we'll eventually be."

Katie smiled and nodded. "I think we can make that work, for however long you need it."

However long *would* they need it?

That was a question she would just assume avoid answering.

Chapter Thirty-one

Ryan stepped inside the house and hung his jacket on the hook, movements fast and anxious. "I think I'll be ready to begin harvesting in the morning."

"Thank the heavens. I'd begun to wonder if the hay would ever be ready for cutting." Ma spoke from the stove, stirring something in a pan.

"It's been an odd season. The mower will be helpful. We might get everyone's hay cut, even with the crop coming in a couple of weeks later than usual." Ryan glanced around, but they were alone. Maura always cooked supper when she was home, and this wasn't a late laundry day. "Are you well enough to be up and working?"

Ma smiled at him, a look of utter satisfaction. "I've had more and more good days. The extra sleep and quiet have done wonders."

Ryan gave her a hug. "I am so pleased to hear that. I just knew if you could come here, you would feel better."

"'Twas a long time in coming, wasn't it?" She patted his cheek, then returned to her supper preparations.

Ryan slipped away toward the open door of Maura's room. He didn't know how Ma had convinced her to relinquish supper duties, but he meant to thank her for allowing it. But Maura wasn't inside. Ryan had returned from his fields later than usual; there was no reason she should still be gone. He turned to step away once more, but stopped. Something was wrong about the room.

He looked back and, in an instant, understood what had niggled at the back of his mind The room was empty. No clothes. No hairbrush. Everything was gone.

He moved to within view of the stove, though not all the way across the room again. "Why are Maura's things gone?"

Ma set her serving spoon aside. "She came by a couple of hours ago and packed everything. They've left."

"Left?" The words hardly made sense to his spinning mind. "Where'd they go? They haven't anywhere."

Ma checked a loaf of soda bread browning in the stove. "She didn't say."

"And you didn't ask?"

"I did." Ma turned to him, amusement in her expression. "But she told me I needn't worry, and should tell you that she'd found another arrangement for herself and her lad, and that they'd not be in your way any longer."

In my way? Did she think that was how he viewed them? "She said that?"

"She did." Ma shuffled from the stove to her rocker near the window. She was doing better, but she'd not be running foot races anytime soon.

"'Tell him we'll no longer be in his way,' is all she said? That's all the explanation she intends to give?"

"She's a grown woman, Ryan. She's not beholden to you."

Being beholden or not wasn't his objection. He liked that Maura was fearsome and independent. He didn't want her indebted to anyone, least of all him. "She doesn't owe me an explanation, but I'd have appreciated at least a farewell, or knowing where they went, that they are well and happy and—"

Ma watched him with an uncomfortably knowing look. "You're going to miss them."

He knew what she was hinting at, and he wasn't about to confess to anything so personal. "I'll have to start milking the cow again, is all. And your first difficult day, I'll go hungry as well."

Ma's mouth pulled in a line of disapproval. "Don't lie to your mother, Ryan Michael-Patrick Callaghan."

His shoulders drooped. No point pretending she was mistaken. "Yes, I'll miss them. But don't you start filling in gaps with anything beyond that."

"I'll let you fill those gaps in on your own." Ma began rocking.

"She truly didn't say where they were going?"

Ma shook her head.

Ryan paced, thinking aloud. "Likely to stay with one of the O'Connors." Saints, she hadn't wanted to live on the charity of her family. "Which one, though?"

"For what it's worth," Ma said, "she arrived with Katie Archer and left with her, as well. I'd wager she's there."

"At the Archers'?" It made sense from one angle, but not from any others. Maura did work for the Archer family, but they hadn't a loft for Aidan or a set of rooms for the two of them. Maybe Katie was simply driving Maura somewhere else.

Ryan snatched up his jacket.

"Don't you go chewing her up," Ma warned. "Life's been too often cruel to that woman. She's making the best of it."

"I've no intention of chewing her up. I only want to make certain she's not living in a cave or something." And he wanted to find out why she'd left without a word. How often had they shared their worries and dreams and hopes? He'd held her in his arms, danced with her tucked close to him. They'd shared something he thought was special. And she'd simply walked away.

He pulled his jacket on.

"I'll keep supper warm," Ma said.

"Thank you." He made the mistake of looking at her one more time. He didn't know if what he saw was pity or, more likely, amusement. "You're laughing at me."

"I'm curious, is all. I'm looking forward to seeing where this goes."

He wasn't about to confirm her speculation. "'Where it's going' is down to Archers', then back here for supper, then out to find someone who'll lend me a wagon over the next few days."

"Why are you needing a wagon?" she asked. "Maura's not needing to be driven back on laundry days."

She wasn't coming back even on laundry days. She wasn't coming back on any day. He didn't care for that. Not at all. He pushed the objections aside, though, and focused on the task at hand. "The wagon's for the hay, Ma. The harvest is my priority."

"Just as soon as you find and talk to Maura, you mean."

Ryan didn't take the bait. He stepped outside and set himself in the direction of Archers'.

I'll simply make certain they've a roof over their heads, that they didn't leave because they thought they had to. 'Tis simply a neighborly visit, nothing more.

But the farther he walked down the road, the more his mind spun over the situation, and the more frustrated he grew. Why would she leave without even saying goodbye? Why would she not at least tell him she was considering such a departure? She had every right to make decisions for herself and for her son, but he thought they'd formed enough of a connection for more than that.

By the time the Archer home came into view, his calm and collected intentions had shifted to frustration and, if he were being fully honest, a touch of hurt. 'Twasn't the best frame of mind to be in when he knocked at the kitchen door, but it was the truth of the situation.

Maura answered the door, and his frustration melted on the instant, replaced with a deep and unexpected surge of disappointment, not at seeing her, but in knowing how easily she'd walked away.

"Why've you left?" He could have begun the conversation more smoothly, but in the moment, his mind chose instead to hit at the heart of the matter.

"Left where?"

He let his expression turn absolutely arid. "Home, Maura. Why've you left home? You and Aidan?"

"It was not ever really home," she said. "Not ours, anyway. It was always meant to be yours; I think I always knew that. I was simply being stubborn." She stepped back into the kitchen, but left the outside door open.

He stepped inside, closing the door behind them. "You simply packed and left. Not a word of explanation or warning. You don't think I expected that of you, do you?"

"Of course not." She stood on the side of the kitchen near another door. Ryan wasn't certain what it led to. Maura went on. "But it was necessary."

"Leaving without a word was necessary?"

She looked back at him, obviously confused. "I told your mother we were moving out."

Ryan found himself at a loss to explain that speaking to *him*, in particular, had mattered so little to her, and why that oversight mattered so blasted much to him.

"Where will you stay?" He was proud of the calm logic of his response. If she was indifferent, he could be, as well.

"In here." She waved him toward whatever lay beyond the doorway.

He crossed to her and peered through the doorway into a bedchamber with only one narrow bed and hardly room enough for anything else.

"This room is for the both of you?" he asked.

"Aidan was sleeping on the floor in the loft. He'll not mind being on another floor."

She'd given up a house with privacy and space to move about for the necessity of sharing a single bedchamber with her son? How could this possibly be preferable? *He* had been enduring less-than-ideal housing, but hers had been comfortable. Surely she could have endured a little longer to find something better than this overly snug arrangement. Things had not been so miserable that she couldn't have waited.

The outside door opened once more. Aidan stepped inside, a hammer in one hand and a bag of what was probably nails in the other.

"Good to see you, Aidan. You've been put to work, I see."

Aidan smiled proudly. "I'm hanging a quilt from the ceiling beam."

"Dividing the room in two," Maura explained. "Aidan and I will each have a bit of privacy that way."

"You had plenty of privacy before."

She ignored him. Pointedly ignored him. She knew, then, that this was a worse situation for her and her son. Then why was she insisting on it?

"You don't have to do this, Maura," he said. "The soddie won't be uncomfortably cold for weeks yet. And with my harvest starting tomorrow, you'd have the house mostly to yourself for most of those weeks. You'll likely not see me for days on end. You can wait to find something better for you and Aidan than tucking yourselves into one small room."

Though Aidan didn't say anything or look at his mother, Ryan knew his attention was pricked. His posture held something hesitant but hopeful. The lad clearly didn't want to be pressed into so small a space after having the loft to himself.

"Come back," Ryan insisted. "There's time enough for finding something better. And who's to say you won't be the one chosen to keep the house in the end? You're being hasty here, lass."

"I am not being hasty." She turned and faced him directly. Heavens, he'd become well acquainted with that look of stubborn determination these past weeks. "This is for the best. It's necessary."

"It really isn't," he countered.

"It really, really is."

Aidan turned back to his task, but with a slump to his shoulders. Could she not see his disappointment? What could possibly make her eager enough to unnecessarily leave the house she'd lived in the past weeks despite her child's unhappiness?

"Were you so miserable?" He dreaded the answer but needed to know.

"I wasn't miserable at all." She stood with shoulders back, chin at a stubborn angle. "But this is for the best."

He stepped up beside her, his back to Aidan, and lowered his voice to just above a whisper. "Not long ago, you were so ill that you crumpled to the ground. Living here likely means longer work hours and never being away from your duties. Your health will deteriorate faster."

Her posture softened. Tenderness filled her eyes as she looked at him, and he felt the change in her wrap his heart in a blanket of warmth.

"I'll take care of myself," she said. "Katie and I have agreed that I will not do any work from after supper each night until after the children leave for school in the morning. I'll have time to rest."

"But *will* you rest?" He knew her stubbornness too well to trust that she would.

Her smile was a little too lacking in commitment for his peace of mind.

"You could come back," he said quietly, a little hesitantly. "I'd like you to."

She held his gaze, her brown eyes searching his. "Why?"

The question caught him unaware. Did she really need a reason beyond the many he'd already listed? "You'd be far more comfortable, Maura. Ma has enjoyed having you nearby. Though I've every confidence in Katie's commitment not to require you to work after hours, being away from here would guarantee you wouldn't. And Aidan would have space of his own again. 'Twould be for the best."

Her eyes shifted to the room, where Aidan had climbed onto a chair. "Can you reach, lad?"

He nodded. "It's not too high."

"Maura?" Ryan pressed. He'd answered her question but had received no reply.

She didn't look back at him. "This is for the best."

Her declaration held a finality he could not misunderstand. Nothing more was to be said on the matter.

He stepped backward and popped his hat on his head. "I wish you luck then, Miss Maura. Take care of yourself."

"And you." She spoke without turning toward him in the least.

He left. What else could he do? The walk back up the road toward home—which was really destined to be his now, if he could convince Tavish and Cecily to sell—felt longer than usual. His mind and heart were heavy. In all the years he'd thought about the possibility of his own home, he'd never imagined a weight on his chest when the moment arrived.

He'd won.

And he was miserable.

Chapter Thirty-two

Weekly supper with the O'Connors felt less uncomfortable than it had. Maura had begun to find her place among them. Knowing she was finding ways to help, however quiet and unnoticed, meant she worried less about being a burden. She could simply sit among them, seeing the joy in Aidan's face as he interacted with the family he was coming to love, and be grateful that he had a home in Hope Springs. Their current accommodations were less than ideal, but the benefit of being near family and the joy of having helped two families, Tavish and Cecily, as well as Ryan and his ma, outweighed all that.

She poked at the potatoes in her stew, thoughts of Ryan drowning out the others. How often that had happened in the days since he'd come to the Archer house. He'd been so put out with her upon learning she'd moved away. There'd been nothing overbearing in his objections. He'd seemed genuinely sad to see her leave.

Like a fool, she'd pressed him, wanting to know why where she made her home mattered to him. An utter fool. His answer? Convenience. That, and his ma having company. Not until that moment had she realized how desperately she'd wanted his answer to be something more personal.

"Thank you to everyone for being willing to come to dinner here," Tavish said to the room. "Maura was right. Cecily's been doing much better since deciding to stay home and off her feet."

Maura received a few nods, some hugs, a chorus of gratitude.

"We've something else to be grateful for as well." He had the entire room's attention. He nodded at her. "Again, thanks to Maura."

She had no idea what he was talking about, but immediately had countless eyes on her. She shrugged and shook her head, not understanding.

"Cecily and I had a visit today from Joseph Archer," he said, "and he told us of an idea Maura had that he thought would be of interest to us."

Ah.

Tavish hunched down beside Cecily, who sat in the rocking chair, and took her hand. "Granny owned her farm free of any notes or debts. Cecily inherited it that same way. *Our* home and land, though, we don't own outright. And while we've no objection to continuing to pay on it until we do, our crop's not been good the past few years. And this year, we've lost a lot."

The family was not shocked by the admission. They'd all worried over Tavish and Cecily's situation.

"Maura suggested to Joseph that, rather than leaving us to struggle to make our payments, he offer to make a trade."

Mr. O'Connor seemed to be piecing together the end of this tale. His eyes had grown wide, and his mouth hung the tiniest bit open.

"Joseph's offered to let us pay off all the notes on our land with Granny Claire's house and land. A trade. He'd own that property instead of ours."

The family erupted in excitement. Few people in the valley owned their land outright. Nearly all were paying for it on time. To be free of that debt would be a weight off their burdened minds.

"It gets better," Cecily said. "Joseph said that the Claire land is worth more than ours, it being larger, and he's offered to let us decide how we'd like to even that up."

"A good man," Mr. O'Connor said.

"Honest to his very soul," Mrs. O'Connor added.

"We've decided," Tavish pressed forward, "to have him divide the difference three ways and apply it to Ciara and Keefe's, Ian and Biddy's, and Mary and Thomas's land notes. Doing that will cut down what you owe. You can either make smaller payments every year, or keep paying what you are and repay your debt sooner."

Ciara and Keefe embraced enthusiastically. Thomas, standing near Tavish, thumped a grateful hand on his back, while Mary hugged her mother. Biddy put an arm across Ian's back, leaning her head against him, and mouthed a thank you to Maura.

Maura pushed back her emotions. She'd been happy to help Tavish and Cecily, but had helped the rest of the family far more than she'd expected to. Mr. and Mrs. O'Connor, she'd learned, owned their farm, having been amongst the first settlers in the valley. Their children had all struggled with the necessity of buying the land they needed.

"This calls for cake," Mrs. O'Connor declared. "Fortunately, I brought some along."

The family swept into action, gathering plates and forks and celebrating, exchanging hugs and grins.

Biddy sat beside Maura. She took Maura's hand in hers. "I cannot thank you enough. The family doesn't know it, but we weren't going to be able to make our full payment this year. Joseph would've been merciful; we know he would. But it hurt Ian's pride something terrible to think of needing that mercy, when this isn't the first time we've called on it. The burden has weighed on him."

"I am not the one who arranged it." Maura felt more than a touch uncomfortable receiving the credit.

"But you thought of the idea, and you proposed it. How none of us thought of it, I can't say. Exchanging land never entered anyone's mind."

"Sometimes you just need an outsider's viewpoint, I suppose."

She received a scolding look. "You've not ever been an outsider, Maura. You're one of us, whether you like it or not."

She pressed a hand to her heart. "I like it very much. And Aidan hasn't been this happy in years. He needed family; I simply didn't realize how much."

Biddy looked over at him sitting by Finbarr, the two lads deep in conversation. "He's been good for Finbarr. We don't know why Aidan doesn't make him uncomfortable the way the rest of us seem to, but we're so very happy to see him at ease with your lad."

Maura had given the same question some thought. "I think, in part, Finbarr appreciates that he has so much to offer Aidan. He knows things Aidan desperately needs to learn. Caring for animals. Farm chores. Things all the rest of you already know. He can't offer that to anyone else in the family."

Biddy nodded. "That was true even before the fire. Being the youngest can be hard."

"I do think it's more than that, though," Maura hadn't spoken her most recent thoughts on the matter.

"What else, then?"

"Finbarr grows instantly uncomfortable and withdrawn when anyone speaks of him 'before' his injuries, even if it's years before, like when I've mentioned knowing him in New York. Aidan has only ever known him since coming here, years after his injuries. For Aidan, there is no Finbarr 'before.' No mourning the change in his life. He has no expectation of Finbarr being who he used to be. There's something very freeing in not having to live to an expectation, especially if he feels himself unequal to it."

Mr. O'Connor, who sat in a chair nearby, inched closer, forming a little group with them. "I've been warning the children about that where Aidan is concerned, actually."

"I don't understand."

He balanced his plate with its slice of cake on his lap. "Aidan looks so very like his father. He has a similar sense of humor, even some of the same mannerisms. 'Twould be far too easy to expect him to be just like Grady rather than his own person. We don't want to put that burden on him."

A kindness, one Maura appreciated. And yet . . .

"He has no memory of Grady. Not a single one of his own." Saying that truth out loud hurt. Heavens, it hurt. "I've done my best to help him know his father, but—" Emotion clogged her throat for a moment, but she pushed on. "I knew Grady less than five years before he died, and not three of those were spent together before he left for war. There is so much about him I never had a chance to know. Aidan has many questions I cannot answer."

She pulled in a deep breath, hoping to dislodge the grief that seemed to settle in her throat every time she spoke of that painful part of her past. But the breath, as always, simply left her coughing. She quickly got her breath under control again, smiling in the hope of dispelling any worry the sound might have caused her family.

"We might be able to answer the lad's questions," Mrs. O'Connor offered, having come near them. "We would love to. We've not spoken of Grady enough in the years since we lost him. 'Twould do us all good to think back on him with joy instead of mourning."

Maura wanted to be able to do that as well. She would have to work at it. So much of her emotion connected to his passing was still difficult to endure. Guilt and regret filled all the cracks left in the part of her heart that had belonged solely to him. Yet she knew this family grieved for him as well. Easing that pain for them was part of the mission she'd given herself. That would be part of her legacy.

"I brought something with me that I think you will appreciate," Maura told them.

Her heart thudded and her hands were a little shaky. Very few people had ever been permitted even a glimpse at this, one of her dearest treasures. But they needed to see it. She knew they did. She'd brought her most treasured possession with her the past few weeks, trying to find the strength to share it with them.

"Aidan."

He looked up at her from his slice of cake.

"Will you fetch the tintypes from my coat pocket?"

He paled a little. He treasured them as well, and sharing them felt very personal. She understood that. But it was time. He crossed to the nail on which her coat hung and pulled two hinged leather frames from it, both fitting easily in his hand. He brought them to her. She squeezed his hand and smiled reassuringly. He knelt on the floor in front her as he'd so often done when he was tiny.

She set the frames on her lap and told her heart to stop its thudding. This was a good thing, certainly nothing to feel so nervous about.

"A photographer visited the Irish Brigade the week before Gettysburg," she said. "He wanted to document a little of the Union Army's experiences. His sister, who traveled with him as an assistant, was very taken with two particular soldiers, declaring them the handsomest men she'd ever seen. The way I was told it, she pleaded ceaselessly with her brother to take their pictures."

The whole room was silent, staring, hardly breathing.

"Saints above," Mrs. O'Connor whispered.

"The pictures came back to me after the battle," Maura said. "I have to agree with the photographer's sister. Two men handsomer than these brothers would be difficult to find."

Mr. O'Connor had moved to stand directly behind his wife's chair. Ian stood behind Biddy's.

Maura opened the first frame, the room's lantern light illuminating Grady's beloved face. She turned the hinged frame so the rest of the room could see the photograph inside. An audible gasp met the sight.

"Oh, my dear boy." The words shook from Mrs. O'Connor.

Maura placed the treasure in her mother-in-law's hands. Grady's parents bent over the frame, silent. Their tears flowed unchecked.

"My Grady," Mr. O'Connor whispered.

Maura turned to face Ian. He and Patrick, the brother immortalized in the other tintype, had been closer than anyone else in the family. Their bond had been obvious to anyone who'd spent even a moment with them. Ian and Patrick's connection had been special.

She didn't open the second frame, but she met Ian's hopeful, worried, cautious gaze. "Patrick," she whispered, and held it out to him.

His hand shook as he took it from her. Biddy hopped up and guided him to sit, then stood behind him, wrapping him in her arms. He carefully unhooked the frame, and opened it the tiniest bit at a time. Biddy pressed a kiss to her husband's temple as a tear fell from his eyes. Maura rose. The family needed time with these images, and the loneliness attached to them.

She crossed to where Aidan stood. Finbarr hadn't moved from his seat. He'd grown silent once more, his head lowered. Here was yet another thing he could not participate in. He couldn't see the photographs.

Ian closed the frame once more, openly sobbing. Biddy held him as he cried. How deeply he must have missed Patrick. Those two had been halves of a whole. Back in New York, one had seldom been seen without the other. Years of separation had stretched between them.

Mr. O'Connor took the frame from Ian. The rest of the family had gathered around, including the grandchildren, all studying the faces of these two sons, brothers, uncles. Mrs. O'Connor wept. Her husband swiped at his own tears.

"I should have shown you these sooner," Maura whispered.

"They loved Da, didn't they?" The confirmation seemed to comfort Aidan.

She pulled him into a one-armed embrace. "Your da and Patrick both. And they miss them fiercely, just as we do."

"Thank you for bringing these, Maura," Mary said. "To see their faces again—" Emotion cut off her words.

"I want all of you to be able to see them whenever you'd like. I would like to keep Grady's for myself, but I think Patrick's should remain with your parents, since he didn't want it."

"Since who didn't want it?" Mr. O'Connor asked.

"Patrick." She thought she'd been clear, but they were all a little overset. A more detailed explanation would likely help. "I told him he ought to keep the tintype because it was of him, but he said it didn't bring him any joy, and he'd rather not be reminded of it."

They were all watching her again, brows drawn. Mary and Tavish exchanged bewildered looks.

"These were taken before Gettysburg?" Mr. O'Connor pressed.

She nodded. "I imagine that is why he didn't want the picture. It reminded him of the battle, which he didn't care to relive. The battle and everything attached to it."

Dumbfounded silence followed. For a moment, she could only stare back. Why was this so confusing? In a flash of understanding, she pieced their thoughts together.

"By the saints," she said in a whoosh of breath. "You don't know."

"What don't we know?" Mrs. O'Connor's voice shook.

"Patrick," Maura said. "He's not dead."

Chapter Thirty-three

The room erupted in shock, denial and a myriad of questions. Maura couldn't begin to count the different responses bursting from the family. Curse that Patrick. If she'd had the first idea that he hadn't written to his family as he'd said he would, she'd have sent word to them herself. No matter that they hadn't wanted to maintain a connection with her during that difficult period of mourning, they deserved to know what had happened to their son.

Cecily whistled loudly, bringing silence to the group once more. The wide eyes that met the shrill sound told Maura her sister-in-law hadn't done that before.

"If we'd all keep quiet," Cecily said, "Maura could explain."

Mrs. O'Connor clasped her hands and pressed them to her lips. Emotion quivered in her brow. The family watched Maura, waiting.

"When the casualty list was posted for Gettysburg, both Grady and Patrick's names *were* on it." Maura swallowed against the lump that always formed when she thought back on those days. "I waited weeks to write to you because the lists sometimes changed. Battlefields are chaotic and mistakes get made. I checked the list every day, praying for a miracle, dreading having to tell you that your sons were dead." That had been a horrible, horrible time. "Some names were added, some were removed.

But after a few weeks, our lads' names were still there. So I wrote to you to tell you. I had no reason to believe that the report was anything but accurate, that we'd lost them both."

Even Aidan listened with rapt attention. Had she ever told him about the days and weeks after his father died? They were difficult to think about let alone speak of. But it was time. The family needed to know, so she needed to speak of it, at least a little.

"The war continued two more years. Aidan and I lived with my mother until she passed, and then my sister joined us, until she, too, passed. Then we moved to a flat in a building where we could afford the rent." The story was easier to tell if she skipped quickly over the loss after loss she'd endured in two short years. "The war ended, and soldiers began returning home. One day there was a knock at our door. I opened it and was, I swear to you, convinced I was seeing a ghost."

"Patrick?" Mr. O'Connor filled the name with heartbreaking hope.

Maura nodded. "He'd gone looking for us at the old flat. Not finding us, he began asking around. It took some doing, but he eventually found us. He hadn't been killed, obviously, but he had been wounded and spent time in an army hospital before rejoining the regiment. When the fighting ended, he was sent home. He brought the photographs." She motioned to the tintypes, Patrick's being held by Ian and Grady's in his mother's hands. "He told me that Grady was most decidedly dead. *That* had not been a mistake."

Mrs. O'Connor cried openly, not even attempting to brush away her tears. Maura had to look away. She could not allow herself to cry about this. Not with so much yet to tell.

"He stayed with us," she said. "He took up a farrier job and helped us tremendously. He was also the only grown man in our building, which made him incredibly popular." That was a memory she could smile at. Heavens, he'd been a flirt. In quiet moments, though, when no one was there but the three of them, he'd been withdrawn, pensive. She'd worried about him. "Aidan and I were very much alone when he arrived, and he— he was family to us when we needed it most: a brother, an uncle, and a friend."

Bless him, Aidan looked as confused as the rest of the O'Connor family. He'd only been five years old when Patrick had lived with them. She doubted he remembered much of anything about those short months.

"Why didn't you write and tell us?" Mr. O'Connor asked. He sounded far more baffled than angry.

"He insisted he would write to you, and I had no reason not to believe him. He was quieter than before the war, more contemplative, but nothing in his behavior led me to think he wouldn't tell his family that he was alive. I am, in fact, entirely unable to reconcile it."

"Where is he now?" Tavish asked.

"Canada. He moves a lot, though he answers my letters. I send them to the last location I have for him and somehow he always receives them. His responses often come from somewhere else, and that is where I send my next letter. Feels rather like chasing a rainbow, ever moving and always just out of reach."

Ian's foot tapped as he watched her. His brow furrowed. Tears still trickled down his face, though the sadness seemed to be giving way to frustration. "He writes to you?" He spoke through a tense jaw, lips pulled tight.

Maura wasn't the least bit offended. She understood what he must be feeling. The brother he'd been closest to, the one he'd believed dead for more than a decade, was not only alive, but had purposely not told him as much. Worse, he was corresponding with one member of the family—and not a blood relation—but not with him. He must be hurting horribly. He'd have to be. The two brothers had loved each other too deeply for this revelation to be anything but excruciating.

She didn't know what she could possibly say that would help. All she could offer them was the full and honest truth. "I don't know why he is so elusive, or why he didn't eagerly share word of his survival with you. But . . . he is different than he was before the war. I will admit that. Yet, I saw soldiers who returned broken—burdened and fractured—but he wasn't like that. I don't know the answer."

"Ten years." Ian stood with a jerk. "Ten years without a word. To any of us." He shoved the leather frame into his da's hands. He stepped back, nostrils flaring, jaw clenched. "He made us grieve for years. Knowingly. Purposely."

"Darling." Biddy reached for him, but he walked away, shaking his head, not looking back at any of them.

He walked right out of the house without closing the door behind him.

"I hadn't meant to cause him pain." A heaviness settled on Maura as she looked into the faces around her. "I'd not hurt any of you for the world."

Mrs. O'Connor reached over and patted her hand gently. "We know it, Maura."

"If I'd known, I would have told you years ago."

Mr. O'Connor nodded. "You didn't cause this pain, so don't you burden yourself with it."

How very like this caring and compassionate family to comfort her in their own distress. She'd needed this support and love and kindness over the past ten years. She would need a great deal of it over the months and, if she were lucky, years to come.

Joseph Archer stepped inside the open door, a frantic look on his face. "The weather is threatening to turn," he said. "And it looks to be a terrible storm."

Still reeling from all they'd just learned, the family could only stare at him, not understanding.

"The last of Ryan Callaghan's hay is still drying in the fields," Joseph said. "If it's out there when the storm breaks, he'll lose it all."

In a flash, the family was on their feet, rushing about, snatching up coats, even as they dried their tear-stained faces.

"Finbarr," Joseph called over the cacophony. "Come along. You're with me."

Maura stopped Mary with a hand on her arm. "Can I do anything?"

"We'll need all the hands we can get," Mary said. "Everyone who can will bring wagons and equipment and gather up the hay. If we can get it in barns or hay sheds, tucked away out of the rain, we might be able to salvage it."

"And we have only until the clouds burst?"

Mary nodded, worry in her expression. "It's a tall order, but we'll do all we can."

If everyone was saving Ryan's hay, what about theirs? "Does the family have hay to salvage as well?"

Mary pulled her coat on. "All of ours and a good bit of Ryan's is stored already. But he grew so much this year, it can't be brought in as quickly."

Maura looked over at Cecily as Mary slipped through the door. Mrs. O'Connor and Ciara hadn't left yet. Cecily sat with her hand resting on her rounded middle, a look of concern on her face.

Ciara met Maura's eye. "I don't imagine Cecily ought to even attempt to help."

She shook her head. "Simply walking about starts her labor pains. She would do best to stay exactly where she is."

Ciara hung her coat up once more. "I'll stay here."

"Send word if she needs me," Maura said. "There's no saying just when her labor will begin in earnest, and I'll not leave her to face it alone." Maura grabbed her own coat and slipped outside as well. With several people helping hitch Tavish's wagon, they'd have it ready to go soon enough.

Maura stepped up near Tavish. She spoke quickly, not wishing to distract him from his work. "Ciara is staying here with Cecily."

"Thank you," he said as he continued working.

"Hop in," Mary pointed to the wagon bed. She was helping with the hitching.

Maura climbed up, sitting beside Aidan.

"I wish I knew how to help hitch the team," Aidan said.

"So do I." She felt rather useless, sitting there, waiting.

Aidan leaned a bit closer and whispered, "What happens if Ryan loses his hay?"

"He'll be ruined," Maura said.

"We can save it though," Aidan said, but with the uncertainty she felt. What did they know of these things? Perhaps the efforts of Ryan's neighbors were little more than an exercise in futility.

The sky overhead was, indeed, threatening. Layer after layer of thick, gray clouds hung low, rumbling and shifting about. The air was heavy with moisture, though none fell. The light was growing dimmer with the approaching sunset. Without the clouds, they'd've had more light to work by.

After a time, Mary climbed into the wagon bed and sat by them. Tavish set the team in motion.

"How are we to gather the hay after it grows dark?" Maura asked.

"Lantern light," Mary said. "There'll be lanterns on the wagons and a few people standing about holding more aloft so we can see well enough to work."

That Mary didn't even have to ponder told Maura there'd been more than one frantic nighttime harvest in the thirteen years since the O'Connors came west.

This town looks after its own. Just as Maura'd hoped they did. Just as Ryan had insisted they must.

The wagon pulled to a stop outside the barn. Katie Archer met them there, lanterns hanging from her arms. "The remaining hay is all in the west fields." She handed up the lanterns. "Joseph's headed that way now."

"Da and Thomas'll be here in a flash," Tavish said. "They're fetching their wagons."

Katie nodded. "I'll send them your way when they arrive," she said, setting a box of striking matches in Mary's upturned hand. Her gaze fell on Maura. "I'm glad you came. Ennis Callaghan's in the house. Her baby's on the way."

Maura turned to Aidan. "Heed your aunt and uncle. They'll know what you can do to be of help."

"I will, Ma."

She gave his shoulders a squeeze. "You come back safe to me."

"I will, Ma."

As quickly as she could safely manage, Maura climbed down from the wagon.

"Are you clear of the wheels, Maura?" Tavish asked, his words tense and rushed.

"I am."

Tavish flicked the reins, and the horse obeyed with fervor. Even the animals seemed to recognize the urgency of the situation. The wagon took off like a rock from a slingshot.

"How's Ennis faring?" Maura asked Katie.

"Well enough." She made her way back toward the house, Maura following close behind "Having a midwife, though, will set everyone's mind at ease."

As they stepped inside the house, they found Mrs. Callaghan at the stove, likely boiling water. She looked up. "Oh, Maura. Thank the heavens. Ennis is in the room you used."

"And James?"

"I don't know. She was to visit without him, only with Nessa." Mrs. Callaghan motioned to the fireplace, where the little girl sat on Emma Archer's lap near the fireplace and Sean sat on Ivy's lap.

"Has he been sent for?" Maura asked.

Mrs. Callaghan nodded.

Maura turned to Katie. "Would you be willing to take Nessa to your home? It'd give us one less worry. And Nessa would not be distressed at hearing her mother in pain."

"Of course." Katie took Sean in her arms, instructing Emma and Ivy to each take one of Nessa's hands. She spoke cheerfully, likely not wishing to alarm them.

Maura went to the bedroom to find Ennis. The calmness of her expression was reassuring. She was likely between pains.

"It seems we're to pass an eventful night," Maura said.

"I hope the eventful bit doesn't last too long." Ennis said.

"For your sake, I hope so as well." Maura sat on the bed and laid her hand on Ennis's."Are you ready to meet your little one?"

A small smile touched her face. "Very much ready."

"Well, then. I look forward to making the introduction."

Chapter Thirty-four

Ryan stepped from his barn out into the downpour. By some miracle, all of his hay had found shelter before the skies tore open. Neighbors up and down the road had made room for his harvest in their barns and sheds. He'd be able to claim it in the days to come and deliver it to the ranches, as promised.

The rain pelting him was little bother. His hay was safe. His future was secure once more. Words were insufficient to express the relief he felt. He'd tried to express his gratitude to Mr. O'Connor for bringing his clan, but his thanks had been waved off.

"You've helped all of us reap our own hay with that mower of yours. Saved us time. Helping you finish up yours is the least we could do."

Some of those who'd helped lived far enough away that they likely hadn't reached home before the downpour. He felt bad about that. There'd be warm fires burning in homes throughout Hope Springs that night.

Joseph stepped onto the porch just as Ryan reached it.

"Are you for home?" Ryan asked. The roof of the porch protected him from the ongoing rain, but the wind cut into him something fierce.

"I am." Joseph buttoned his coat against the frigid weather. "Are you still interested in *buying* this house and land rather than paying rent?"

An unexpected topic. "I am. I don't know that Tavish and Cecily will sell to me, though. Maura and Aidan have moved out, but her family may yet give it to them in the end."

Joseph tucked his hands in his pockets. "I've made an exchange with them. They owned this land, and I owned theirs, so we traded. Why we didn't think to do so before, I can't say."

"*You* own the place now?" No matter that he was wet and shivering, Ryan stood rooted to the spot.

Joseph nodded. "But I'm not interested in being a landlord. I'd far prefer to *sell*."

A surge of excitement went through Ryan at being so close to a lifelong goal, but it ebbed quickly. Trading the land with Joseph meant Maura lost any hope of claiming it. "Maura wouldn't be able to make payments. Why would Tavish and Cecily keep her from owning the place?"

"*They* didn't." Joseph set his hat on his head. "It was Maura's idea."

Ryan couldn't find his voice. *Maura's idea?*

"She knew Tavish and Cecily needed the security," Joseph said. "And that you were the one best suited to this land, that yours was the stronger claim. She was quite firm. I've been married to a fiercely determined Irishwoman for more than two years now. I know better than to argue when I hear that tone."

Maura had arranged for him to have the land. She'd given up her claim on it. Mercy and grace, she'd given up her home as well as the future she'd meant to give Aidan. Saints above.

"Give some thought to the terms you'd prefer: how quickly you want to pay it off, what size of payment you can safely assume," Joseph said. "We'll discuss the details later this week or next."

After that, he was gone quickly, back into the continuing rain. Ryan stepped inside, his mind spinning.

He stopped in the middle of the room, dripping. His eyes took little note of his familiar surroundings. Too many thoughts seized his attention. Aidan was getting his farming education from Finbarr and Joseph. Maura had given up her claim on this land and house. She had no reason to stay. None Maura could see, anyway.

276

This is why she left.

The door to his bedroom opened. Ma shuffled out. Her gaze fell on Ryan. "What a night we've had," she said.

Ryan took a calming breath. "We got all the hay in."

"I'm very glad entirely to hear it. And you'll be pleased to hear your sister-in-law's had her baby."

He was pleased for Ennis indeed, and surprised. "Word's come of a safe delivery, I hope."

Ma smiled. "None needed to be sent. She's in the room just here, with James, and Maura as midwife. I never saw a soul so calmly assist a new baby into the world. She's a wonder."

"Maura's here?"

Ma moved toward her own room. "I'm fetching her something to change into. Delivering babies isn't a tidy business." She stopped short of her door and looked him over. "You're soaked, son. You'd best change as well." She peeked inside his bedroom. "James, fetch your brother a change of clothes and send them out with Maura." Ma closed the door and slipped into her room.

A moment later, Maura stepped into view. The sight of her bloodied clothes would have alarmed him if he'd not known how she'd passed the evening. He worried instead about her sagging posture and the slowness of her steps. Her eyelids were heavy and edged in the redness that came of exhaustion.

She brought him a shirt and trousers. He'd wager James had included some underthings as well, tucked in between less personal items.

With a feeble smile, she said, "If you're done playing in the rain, I think your brother would like to introduce you to your nephew."

He reached out and touched her pale face. "You look worn thin."

"I'm exhausted," she confessed. "But at least I'm not shivering. You really ought to change into dry clothes."

He took the pile from her. "You'll not run off?"

She shook her head. "I'm too tired." As if to emphasize her words, a cough seized her, shaking her entire frame with its intensity.

"Maura," Ma called from her doorway. "I've found you something to change into."

Maura slipped away and through the bedroom door, which Ma closed behind them.

Ryan climbed into the loft and made quick work of changing. Soon he was back in front of the fire, his wet clothes hanging to dry. Ma emerged from the bedroom, Maura's dress in her arms.

"She was heaven-sent tonight," Ma said. "But *m'anam*, she looks done in. And that cough of hers . . ." Ma shook her head, concern tugging at her mouth. "I don't know what's behind it, but it sounds worse than it has in weeks."

Ryan thought so too. "We'd best find a place for her here tonight. She'd only grow worse going back out in the wind and rain."

Maura stepped out of Ma's room wearing Ma's nightdress, which fit her rather enormously, yet was likely still quite comfortable.

"Over here, dear," Ma said, motioning to the fireplace. "You warm yourself. I'll see to the washing of your dress." She crossed to the sink, Maura's dress in her hands.

Maura crossed to where Ryan stood. She looked dead on her feet. A shiver shook her frame. Ryan pulled a quilt from the chair he often sat in at the end of the day. He slipped the blanket about her shoulders. She grabbed it with one hand, holding it closed in front of her. Ryan rubbed her arms, hoping to warm her.

Her gaze met his. "The quilt smells like you."

"Sorry about that."

"I wasn't complaining."

The woman liked that the blanket smelled like him. He couldn't have prevented the smile that answered that realization.

"Were you able to save your hay?" Maura asked.

"I was."

She looked utterly relieved. "Thank the heavens."

"And thank *you* for helping Ennis."

Joy tinged with weariness filled her expression. Without warning, she began coughing again. Deep, rattling, bone shaking coughs. She couldn't seem to fully catch her breath between bouts. The violence of them threw her off balance. She slowly lowered herself to sit on the floor in front of the fire.

Ryan sat beside her and put his arms around her, holding her as her lungs seized and her body shook with the effort to breathe.

"It sounds worse than it has," he said, once things had calmed down a bit.

"It feels worse too," she confessed. A few more coughs shook her as they sat there.

"What can I do?"

"There's nothing that can be done." She leaned into his embrace. "We haven't the right medicine here or a doctor."

"There's medicine for brown lung?"

"Medicine that helps," she said slowly. "No medicine cures it."

He kept her in his arms, though she was breathing better. "This medicine can be had in New York, I'd guess."

Again, she nodded. She'd grown a bit heavier against him.

"Why did you leave, then? You might've gotten the care that you needed."

"I needed Aidan to be happy more." She spoke slowly. "I chose what was best for him."

"Who's choosing what's best for you, Maura?"

When she didn't answer, he looked down and found her eyes closed. She felt limp against him.

Ma crossed to him. "Is she sleeping?"

"I think so."

"Let's lay her down," Ma said. "The floor isn't the softest place, but it'll be warm. Cold air makes coughs so much worse."

Maura wasn't fully asleep, but she did not object, vocally or otherwise, when Ryan moved and eased her to down to lie on the floor. She lay there without a word, eyes closed. He tucked the blanket more firmly around her. A short moment later, everything in her position and expression relaxed.

"I hope she sleeps well," Ma said. "While she was living here, I heard her cough all night long. I worried for her. I still do. She's said it's nothing but a cold, a little tickle in her throat, but it can't be that, not to have lasted as long as it has."

Ryan had vowed not to reveal what Maura had told him of her true situation. He simply nodded. "She'd likely be horrified if she knew she'd kept you awake at night."

"'Twasn't as bad as all that. She never woke me, but I heard it when I wasn't sleeping. It sounded better toward the end of their time here, but tonight reminds me of the sound early on. I don't like hearing it again."

"She ought not to have pushed herself so much tonight."

"You'd have had a difficult time convincing her not to," Ma said. "I know a stubborn Irishwoman when I see one."

A smile tugged at Ryan's mouth. "She is rather fierce, our Maura."

"*Our* Maura?" Ma pressed.

That was the wrong word. The only thing worse would have been "*My* Maura." Heat stole up his neck at the thought. *My Maura.* Heavens, he liked the way that sounded. Liked it far too much.

"She's rather stubborn, too." Ignoring Ma's curiosity seemed best. "I still can't fathom that she's living with her boy in a single room when she had so much space here. She could have at least waited until there was a better option."

"But there isn't. She is a woman alone, with a son to raise, and not a penny to her name. Has she ever talked to you about the building she lived in before, in New York?"

"Aidan mentioned it once. The Widow's Tower, I think he called it."

Ma nodded. "Filled to bursting with women, all alone, raising children with nothing to live on and an unreliable roof overhead. She learned there, no doubt, that life often snatches away opportunities, so it's best to grab at whatever chance she has. Her current arrangement isn't ideal, but it's welcome to one who is still trying to save people she fears she cannot help."

Ryan couldn't entirely make sense of his mother's words. "Who is she trying to save?"

"Who *isn't* she trying to save?" Ma countered. "She has a friend there she speaks of often who wishes to come west, but who doesn't dare until she knows if this place is survivable. She came west herself to save Aidan. She's looking after Cecily now that her pregnancy has grown a bit difficult. She's been caring for me. Giving you full claim to this land is her way of saving you. The one person she hasn't energy or resources enough to save is herself."

She was saving him? Did she truly feel she had to? He treasured her generous heart, but the thought of her sacrificing *for him* settled heavy on his mind. She deserved so much more than she was settling for, but life kept taking from her. She'd found a way to give Ryan the opportunity for which he'd been fighting for so long. He didn't doubt she'd give Aidan all he wanted and needed, might even find a means of saving her friend from the run-down tenement they'd lived in.

But who would help her? Who would care for Maura?

Chapter Thirty-five

Ryan suspected no one in the house slept particularly well that night. Despite their tiny size, infants had the ability to wake even the deepest of sleepers. Throughout the night, he'd found himself thinking of this house filled with the sounds of his own children.

In the midst of it all, Maura kept coughing. She'd confessed it had indeed grown worse of late. Only with effort did he prevent himself from climbing down the ladder to check on her. Coughing at night was normal for her, he reminded himself. Expected. And sleep would do her more good than anything.

By the time he rose to begin his day's chores, he was both exhausted and determined to find something he could do to ease her suffering. The Johnsons might have something in the mercantile that would soothe a cough. Mrs. O'Connor might know of a home remedy. Mrs. Talbert on the other side of town was nearing eighty and had likely come across stubborn coughs in her time; she might have an idea what would be helpful. What they needed was a doctor, but he couldn't get Maura that.

He climbed down from the loft, trying to be as quiet as possible, not wishing to wake the house.

Maura was no longer sleeping on the floor, but sitting in the rocker with the new little one in her arms.

"I thought you'd be sleeping." He kept his voice low.

"Your brother left, needing to tend to his animals. Poor Ennis was in desperate need of sleep."

"Are you not in need of sleep yourself?"

She smiled softly. "I don't often get to hold babies. Losing a bit of sleep is worth it."

He hunched low beside her rocker.

"Have you met your nephew yet?" Maura asked. "He's a dear little lad."

"I was introduced last night while you were sleeping. I suspect the two of us will be fast friends."

"I have seen how much your niece loves you, and the Archer girls. I've seen the kindness you show Aidan. I've not the least doubt this little bundle will love you every bit as much."

He felt the strongest urge to pull her into his arms, to hold the both of them, to spend his morning pretending he'd no chores, no worries or pressing responsibilities. For a man whose entire life revolved around plans, 'twas a shockingly haphazard inclination. The feeling upended and confused him.

"I likely should get to my work," he said. "The cow misses me when I'm late."

She smiled a little. He took the opportunity to slip out quickly without having to examine too closely his befuddled thoughts and the growing pull he felt to Maura.

A lantern glowed inside the barn when he arrived. Odd. "Is someone here?" he called. He stepped fully inside. The light was in the cow stall.

"Over here." Aidan. Had he trekked all the way from Archers' so early? Sure enough, he sat on the stool beside the cow, bucket in place, milking.

"You didn't need to do this." Ryan stepped inside the stall. "'Tisn't one of your chores now."

"Finbarr's going to do the milking at Mr. Archer's this morning because I wanted to show you."

"Show me what?"

With a grin of pure mischief, he sent a stream of milk not into the pail but directly onto the toe of Ryan's boot.

A laugh leapt from him. "Well done, lad." He shook the droplets off his boot. "You've mastered it."

Aidan's look of mischief turned to pride and glowed from him. He returned to milking, managing the task with great confidence, though without the ease of years of experience. "Finbarr says I'm a fast study. He's been helping me learn things, but there's some things he can't do. Because of his eyes."

That was understandable.

"But the way I look at it, Mr. Archer says Finbarr's worth his weight in gold, and if he can be that helpful even though there are things he can't do, then I can be helpful too while I'm still learning to do things."

Wanting to offer his support without interrupting Aidan's work, Ryan set a hand on the back of his shoulder. "An eagerness to help is a commendable trait. It'll serve you well."

"Ma says it's important to leave a place better for having lived in it. She says if you haven't helped someone, you've wasted your life."

That wasn't the first time Aidan had told him about this admonition of his mother's. The more he knew Maura, the more he saw that very philosophy behind the things she did. "She does, indeed, make the world better," Ryan said. "She makes the people around her better."

Aidan's milking slowed. His movements grew more distracted.

"Is something the matter?" Ryan asked.

"I was only thinking that she tries so hard to help other people, but it seems that no one helps her."

Ma had said much the same thing.

Ryan lowered himself beside the lad. "Is there something she's needing?"

"Rest." Aidan seemed reluctant to say as much. "She works so hard, but she's sick. She won't admit how much, but I know what her cough is. Almost everyone we lived near worked in the factory. I know the sound of brown lung. I *know* it."

"Oh, lad. I'm sorry."

Aidan focused on his milking, the pace picking up again. "It's not as bad as most I heard. But it's not going away, and who's to say it won't get worse?"

How he wished he could offer more comfort and reassurance. "And is rest what helped the people in the factory do better?"

Aidan didn't answer for a moment. "Nothing really helped them get better. Not working at the factory was the most important thing to keep the brown lung from getting bad so quickly."

"She's not there any longer," Ryan pointed out.

Thought pulled at the boy's dark brow. "True."

"And she's relatively new to working at Archers'. She's likely still sorting out the right balance of work and rest."

Aidan smiled a little. "Ma's never been good at resting."

"I can't say I have been either." Ryan could laugh a little at the truth of that realization. "Maybe if we had the two of you over for supper now then—supper my ma and I had prepared and had ready before you arrived so *your* ma couldn't possibly tax herself making it—she'd be forced to rest for an evening."

"She would like that," Aidan said.

"So she isn't good at resting, but she does like it."

"I didn't mean she'd like the rest." Aidan grinned up at him. "She'd like being here for an evening."

"Would she, now?" His heart bounced against his ribs at the thought.

Aidan nodded. "Don't tell her I told you, but she's missed you. She talks about you more than I think she realizes. And she liked being here with you."

That was more encouraging than Aidan probably realized. Ryan stood and ruffled the boy's hair. "Thank you, lad, for doing my milking."

"I like milking. I just wish the cow would be patient enough to wait until the sun's up."

Ryan chuckled. "You and me both."

He took his lantern, leaving the one Aidan had brought with him, and hung it on a peg in the middle of the small barn. He needed to fork some hay into the cow's stall. A few other quick chores would see him ready to begin the task of gathering up the hay he'd harvested first that was already dry and waiting. He'd take it out to the ranches now and deliver the rest once it was ready.

Before he could take up his pitchfork, the familiar sound of coughing met him from just outside the barn.

"Is that Ma?" Aidan asked from the cow stall.

"Sounds like it," Ryan said. "She was situated very cozily when I left the house. Why would she venture out into the cold?"

"She's not good at resting," Aidan repeated, keeping at his task.

"I'll see if I can convince her to try." Ryan stepped out of the barn.

Sure enough, there Maura stood in the chicken coop, lit by the earliest rays of dawn, tossing feed to the barely awake birds.

"You know, you and your lad are two regular peas in a pod."

She looked over at him as she tossed another handful of feed. "Is he feeding chickens as well?"

"Milking the cow." He pulled the coop gate open enough to slip inside without letting any birds out. "You both had the luxury of a warm house you could have stayed in, but here you both are."

"The baby is sleeping very deeply." She tossed a last handful and wiped her hands against each other. "He'll let his mother rest a bit longer before rousing her."

Ryan moved to her. "Aidan knows what your cough is. He said he recognizes it from watching it claim your neighbors who worked at the factory."

She paled a bit. "I'd hoped he wouldn't realize. He will worry, and that will weigh on him." She rubbed at her temple. "I want so badly to not be a burden to him, or anyone else. It is one of my greatest frustrations."

"You're not a burden," he insisted. "With all the people you help and the good you do . . . being ill doesn't negate all that."

Maura set her hand lightly on his arm. "You are a good man, Ryan Callaghan."

"You should come back here, Maura." He set his arms about her.

"Aidan would have room. You'd have someone to help you, and a chance to rest."

She shook her head without even pausing for thought. "This is your home. You deserve it to be yours. Aidan and I are making ours."

"A single room in someone else's house. Do you not think the two of you deserve something better?"

She was unmoved. "We've been in worse straits than this. Cramped quarters won't do us in."

Standing there, looking into those deep brown eyes, hearing her speak with such strength and determination about circumstances that would have broken nearly anyone else, he had to admit to himself that he was falling ever more in love with her.

"Please, come back, Maura."

She offered a sad sort of smile. Rising on her toes, she placed a kiss on his jaw. "You have a good heart, but distance is best."

"Distance?"

As if demonstrating, she stepped back, pulling from his arms. "The longer we're here, the more attached we'll grow."

"That isn't a bad thing."

She took another step away. "I know what it is to have thoughts and plans for a future, only to have death steal them away. That *is* a bad thing, Ryan. 'Tis a painful, difficult, soul-shattering thing. I won't do that to you."

She moved to the gate, pausing only long enough to tell him she would fetch Aidan and that they would head back to the Archers' together. Ryan remained behind, his spinning thoughts attempting to make sense of what she'd said.

As the sun peaked fully over the mountains, he had a moment of pure clarity. *Thoughts and plans for a future*, she'd said. *I won't do that to* you. To him. She understood that his invitation to return was more than an act of compassion for her health or worry about her circumstances. She understood that he wished her to return because he missed her, because he wanted her in his life. Because he loved her. And, he suspected, his feelings were not entirely one-sided.

She was dying, and meant to keep her distance to save him the pain of losing her.

He hadn't the first idea how to convince her that this grief would only be made worse by the regret of not having her in his life while he could, that reaching for love was worth the risk of losing it.

Chapter Thirty-six

For Maura, the next weeks moved at a crawl yet seemed to fly by as well. She had found a balance in her duties at the Archer home that didn't overtax her. Aidan split his time between Ryan's house and Joseph's fields and barn. The two men always had work for Aidan, and were patient as he learned the skills he hadn't yet acquired. The younger children continued attending school, but the older ones were home every day to help in the fields. Harvest had arrived fully, and every set of able hands was needed.

Maura saw Finbarr more during the busy harvest days than she did before, an unexpected turn she didn't know how to account for. He did work around the Archers' barn and house. He spent a lot of time sitting on the edge of the back porch, silent and still.

Not wishing him to withdraw further into himself—a real risk with the often-unreachable young man—she said nothing as the harvest continued. But day after day, she watched him and worried.

At last, when the crops were nearly all in, she took the risk of speaking to him. She stepped onto the back porch and sat beside him. "It's been a busy little while, hasn't it?"

He nodded. "Harvest time is always busy."

"I'm not overly familiar with the work," she admitted. "Aidan has tried explaining it. Seems there's a lot to be brought in all at the same time."

"There is."

'Twasn't the liveliest of conversations, but he was talking more than usual. She'd encourage that. "And next the crops are taken to the train depot to sell?"

"They keep what they can afford to keep. The rest gets sold. They make land payments and buy things they need. That's the cycle, every year."

There was a pattern to life here. She hoped she wasn't about to alienate him further, but she wanted to understand his situation. "Is sitting here waiting for them to bring in the harvest and return from the depot *your* cycle every year?"

Discouragement tugged at his features. "It is now."

Now. He missed being part of the effort. "You helped Ryan Callaghan with his hay this year."

He shrugged. "I only held a lantern while everyone else worked."

"Was the lantern needed?" she asked.

He nodded.

"Then you helped," she insisted.

He slumped forward a bit more. "I shouldn't grumble, I know. I just—I used to be able to do so much more. It gets . . ."

"Frustrating?" she guessed.

"Very."

How well she understood. Perhaps it would help if he knew that. "My lungs aren't healthy as they once were." This likely would never grow easy to talk about. "That's more than I've admitted to most anyone here."

"Really?"

"Really."

"Why would you tell me of all people?"

"Because I think you 'of all people' would understand." He knew this struggle, after all. "I can't work as long or as hard as I used to. Honestly, I hate the change. 'Tis difficult not to be bitter about."

"Cecily says trials can either make us better or bitter. I'm trying to be *better*." He pushed out a puff of air. "But I'm not doing so good at it lately."

Having nothing to keep his mind off his frustrations likely wasn't helping. "Is there nothing you can do in the fields during this part of the harvest?"

He shook his head. "I'd just get lost in them. Cecily hasn't figured out what I can do about that yet. I'm beginning to think there's no answer."

The lad needed a purpose of some kind. He needed work.

"Would you be willing to do something for me?" she asked.

He didn't answer verbally, but grew still leaning the tiniest bit toward her. He was listening.

"I've some tasks around the house I'm struggling to get done," she said. "My lungs fall to bits when I try carrying heavy things. There's a hole in the wall of my room that needs patching. Given a moment to think on it, I could make an entire list of things that need doing, but I'm either not strong enough to manage them or don't know how to do them."

"Joseph can see to the hole."

"I'm sure he could, but he's not ever available."

"And I always am," Finbarr mumbled. He needed a bit more encouragement.

Maura assumed a teasing tone. "Very convenient for me, don't you think?"

For a moment, he looked as if he might smile. "Were you always such a taskmaster, Maura?"

"Not with you. We used to be conspirators, you and I. Your ma would make scones, which were your favorite, and I would sneak one to you. And, because you knew I was fond of soda bread, you'd hide some for me every time your ma made some and save it for the next time I visited. Sometimes it was stale beyond eating, but you were so proud of having secreted it away."

An elusive look of amusement began peeking through his gloom. "Did I really?"

"You did. And you were so convinced that anyone who knocked on your family's flat door was a robber, so you and I developed a secret knock. I used it the last few months you were in New York so you'd know 'twas me and not someone with nefarious intentions."

His posture relaxed a bit, not the slouch and slump of discouragement he so often bore but a lessening of tension. "Did it ever occur to me that *you* might have nefarious intentions?"

She bumped his shoulder with hers. "I believe I had you fooled."

At last, he smiled, even laughed the tiniest bit. "I don't really remember New York, only a few snippets here and there. Ma says it's for the best. I don't think she was very happy there."

"None of them were," Maura said. "Except Patrick. He loved the city. None of us could understand it."

"Is he in a big city in Canada, then?"

"I can't say there are any big cities in Canada, none like New York, at least. As near as I've been able to sort out, he's keeping to smaller, more isolated towns."

Finbarr made a sound of pondering. "If he's happy in the wilderness, why didn't he just come here?"

"I don't know, Finbarr." So much about Patrick, who had once been so open and inviting, had become an utter mystery after the war. "I don't know."

They sat a moment, neither speaking. She'd intended to lighten Finbarr's load, not add to it. Perhaps she needed a different approach.

She coughed. It happened so often she hardly thought about it, except when they hurt deep inside. Finbarr, however, grew noticeably concerned.

"Ryan Callaghan worries about your cough," he said. "He asks about you all the time."

"I've told him not to fret over it," She wanted to be part of alleviating his troubles not adding to them. "He has enough of his own worries."

"There's more in his voice than just worry," Finbarr said. "I'm no expert, but I think he cares for you."

She knew he did. She'd seen the truth of it the night his nephew was born. And she'd felt the strength of her feelings for him the morning after. That was when she'd resolved to keep her distance; 'twas the only kind thing to do. But holding fast to her decision required that she keep reminding herself of the reasons for it.

"He's several years younger than I am," she said.

"Does that matter so much? Once you're—" Finbarr cut off as if searching for the right word.

"Old?" she supplied with a small laugh.

"I was trying to think of a kinder way to say it."

"I suppose age doesn't truly matter," she acknowledged. "But most eligible men his age aren't interested in an ailing woman with a thirteen-year-old boy."

Finbarr assumed an expression that was somehow both casual and pointed. "Maybe he's not 'most men.'"

Maura watched him through narrowed eyes. "Did Ryan ask you to say something to me about . . . this?" She didn't quite know how to put into words what she hoped they were discussing: that Ryan had a tenderness for her, that he cared, that he perhaps even loved her.

Finbarr smiled, the expression made crooked by his scars. "He didn't say anything."

"Then why are you taking up his cause so adamantly?"

"I'm taking up *your* cause, Maura. You have someone who loves you. Not everyone gets that chance."

His words held something very personal, and something heartbreakingly sad in his expression. Did he think that the future awaiting him meant being lonely and unloved? Underappreciated and overlooked? How much he was cherished *now*? Did he not see the good he was doing?

"Have I thanked you enough for helping my Aidan these past couple of months?" she asked. "He's learning so much so quickly, and I know that is in large part due to you."

One thing about gingers: they don't blush subtly. "He works hard," Finbarr said.

"He mentions you a lot," she said. "At the end of the day, he tells me over and over again whether you said he'd done particularly well. Your approval means a lot to the lad."

"He'll have plenty of time for listening to me once the men leave for the depot," Finbarr said. "It'll just be the two of us working in the barn each day."

"And mending the hole in my wall," Maura said. "Don't forget that."

"Mustn't forget the hole."

She leaned her back against a porch post, turning to sit facing him more directly. She didn't know if he was entirely blind, but even if he couldn't see her, facing him when she spoke to him felt more natural.

"Who is Lydia?" Finbarr asked suddenly.

"Lydia?"

He nodded. "Aidan has mentioned a 'Lydia' a few times. Near as I can tell, she's very young."

Maura let herself smile fully. Aidan remembered the wee one. "I've a particular friend back in the tenement building we used to live in. She has a little girl—she must be nearly a year old by now—whose name is Lydia. Aidan was very fond of that little baby."

"He misses her," Finbarr said. "He doesn't mention much about New York, but he does talk about her."

Maura missed Lydia—and Eliza—as well. She refused to believe they'd never be together again. She had to have some hope that life would reunite them one day.

Emma and Ivy Archer came skipping around the corner of the house, their schoolbooks and slates under their arms. The day was waxing on.

"We're to have a bit less peace now, it seems," he said, tipping his head in the direction of the girls.

Could he see them? "How did you know they'd returned?"

"Ivy is not particularly quiet." Finbarr grinned, a genuine show of happiness. The Archer girls were good for him. "You two are going to wake the spirits," he called out. "You'll have the banshee chasing you down, just you watch."

Ivy rushed to the porch and dropped onto her belly beside Finbarr. "You always say that, but nothing ever chases us down."

"Well, then you've been lucky so far. You'd best not press your luck, I'd say."

"*You* used to chase us," Ivy pointed out.

"Yes, but I also used to be able to see the ground. And see *you*. That makes chasing far easier."

Ivy flipped onto her back, her legs hanging off the edge of the porch. "You could still chase us, Finbarr. People chase with blindfolds on."

Maura watched Finbarr, but 'twas difficult to know what he was thinking. The scars pulled his features in unexpected ways. But Maura would wager that he'd been caught unprepared for Ivy's very rational argument.

"Aidan says you can do anything," Ivy continued. "He thinks you're smarter than everybody."

He blushed again, but his posture straightened a bit. "Well, that's very generous of Aidan."

Did the sweet little girl know how much Finbarr needed to hear these things? Emma had drawn near, but didn't speak. She was almost always quiet when Finbarr was nearby. Maura offered her a smile and received a tentative one in response.

"Pompah is going to the depot tomorrow," Ivy said, kicking her heels against the side of the porch, still gazing up at the underside of the porch roof. "Emma doesn't like when he goes."

Emma didn't respond aloud, but her shoulders stiffened and her jaw set. Apparently she was anticipating the need to defend her feelings on the matter. Maura pulled her in for a reassuring squeeze.

"Are you going to the depot, Finbarr?" Ivy asked. "You're big now. You could go."

He shrugged. "I'm big, but I'm not very useful."

"I suspect your brothers and Joseph would have plenty for you to do there," Maura said.

But he shook his head. "I doubt they'd want me."

"You should at least ask," she insisted.

He pulled his legs up onto the porch, wrapping his arms around his knees. No matter that he was nineteen; he looked about six years old just then, not terribly unlike the Finbarr she remembered from New York.

"They'd laugh," he said quietly.

"They would not." She knew for a fact they wouldn't.

"Annie Desmond did," he muttered.

Who was Annie Desmond?

"When did she laugh?" Ivy asked.

Finbarr rested his chin on his knees. "When I asked if she'd dance with me."

"She laughed?" Maura's heart ached for him.

"Cecily and Tavish were going to form a group with me so they could help me not run into anything or anyone," Finbarr said. "I wouldn't have been very good, but . . ." He took a tense breath. "I asked her, and she laughed at me."

Emma pulled away from Maura and set her books and slate down with a thud. With footfall so forceful that the sound echoed under the porch, she stormed off toward the side of the house.

"Emma?" Maura called after her.

The lass stopped and spun back, facing them. "Annie Desmond is a rat." An unexpectedly forceful declaration from the usually quiet and reserved girl.

"I know where she lives," Emma continued. "And I'm going to tell her she's a rat."

Finbarr stood abruptly. Deep color infused his face, highlighting the scars that marred it. "You don't need to do that, Miss Emma. You can hardly fault Annie for agreeing with your assessment of me."

"I've never laughed at you. I never would." Emotion shook the words. Actual, deep emotion. "No one ever should."

Maura looked from one of them to the other, feeling both confused and a little enlightened. She didn't know what had come between the young man and this little girl, but there was no mistaking the fact that they cared what happened to each other. Love was there, that of a brother for his tiny sister. The love of a sister for an older brother she admired, and, if Maura didn't miss the mark, missed having in her life.

"People will always laugh at me, Emma," he said. "Picking fights with everyone who does will keep you mighty busy."

"And mighty scuffed up," Ivy added. She received a narrowed-eyed look of reprimand from her sister. Ivy continued unscathed. "Will you dance with me at the *ceíli?* Aidan says I'm 'exhausting.' I think when he says that he means 'fun.'"

"I don't go to the *ceílís*," he reminded her, stepping a little further from the porch.

"You should," Ivy said.

"And you should also go to the depot," Maura tossed in.

Finbarr shoved his hands in his jacket pockets, kicking the toe of his boot in the dirt. "You ladies are exhausting." With that, he shuffled away, back toward the barn.

Emma watched him go, such sadness on her face. When she looked back at Maura, tears hung in her eyes. Without a word, she slipped into the house.

Once Emma's footsteps had faded, Maura turned to Ivy. "What happened with Emma and Finbarr?"

"She loved him," Ivy said. "But then there was the fire. Finbarr was mad about it, and then sad, and then he was mad and sad *at* Emma. That hurt her heart. So she doesn't love him anymore."

Oh, sweet girl. She still loves him. She most certainly loves him.

A moment later, Katie stepped onto the porch. "Come on inside, Ivy. I've not seen you yet today."

Ivy hopped up and eagerly threw herself into Katie's arms. "We had such a lovely day."

Hand in hand, they went inside once more, leaving Maura on the porch with far too much to ponder. She ached for so many people in Hope Springs. She saw pain and worry and weight in their eyes and felt helpless to do anything about it. She dreaded the day she would contribute to their burdens.

Mixed in with it all were Finbarr's words about Ryan, that Ryan had asked about her, not in a tone of worry, but in one of love.

An ache spread through her heart, searing the scars left from far too many losses, far too many sorrows. She loved Ryan Callaghan, there was no denying that. Neither could she deny that life had required him to adjust far too many of his plans for far too many people. She cared too much to be the next person to snatch away a future he'd worked for. That meant maintaining the distance she'd told him would be best. He could find someone else to build a life with, a life that wouldn't shatter. A future with her would bring him nothing but pain.

"Ma! Ma!" Aidan came running from around the house. He'd been at his grandparents' place, helping his uncles and Joseph bring in the last of the O'Connors' crops. "Grandfather and Uncle Thomas and Uncle Ian say I'm old enough to go to the depot, but only if you say I can, but I'm not supposed to tell you that you have to let me go with them or whine about it or anything. Michael and Colum are going, and I'm older than they are, so can I please go, Ma? Can I?"

"Slow down, *mo mhac.* You've said far too much in far too little time."

He sat beside her, eyes wide. Energy pulled at him in every direction. Bless him, the lad couldn't keep still. He explained again, only more slowly. "Michael and Colum are going to the depot this year because they're old enough. But I'm older than they are. Grandfather and my uncles said that lads my age make the journey every year. That's it good to learn the trick of it early on."

Aidan go to the depot? The journey took several days. She'd not been apart from Aidan at night ever in all his life. The idea of sending him far away, into the vast and unforgiving land . . .

Nervousness clawed at her heart, but she reminded herself that life was different here. He had so much to learn if he was to have any hope of building a future in Hope Springs. That included making the annual trip to the depot. She had the luxury of keeping them close in New York; she needed to learn to let go a little. "They wish you to go?"

He nodded. "I thought I'd be useless, since I don't know much yet, but they said there's always plenty to do, and that I'd learn."

She'd made the same argument to Finbarr, but he'd dismissed it. If Finbarr's family welcomed the help and company of someone as inexperienced as Aidan, they'd welcome Finbarr in a heartbeat. She knew they would.

"And Finbarr will help me," Aidan said. "He always does."

"Have you heard that he's going?" she asked.

Aidan looked at her as if she were daft. "Why wouldn't he?"

"Sometimes he leaves himself out of things because he thinks he's not wanted."

Aidan assumed an expression of stubborn determination. "I'll set him straight on that. All the men are going to depot. He should too."

His fierceness touched her heart. The two lads were good for each other, more than either likely knew.

Just then, Ryan rounded the house, moving casually toward them. As she watched his approach, an unexpected rise of emotion tugged at her. Relief surged through her at the mere sight of him, as if simply having him near lifted an invisible but crushing weight from her heart and mind.

But distance is best, she reminded herself, even as she silently begged him to sit beside her. He gave her strength when she felt weak, brought her joy when she was drowning in sorrow. She loved him, and she didn't know what to do about it.

"Has Aidan told you, then? About the depot?" Ryan asked, joining them on the porch edge.

"He has, but I don't know what to think of it." She was sorely tempted to reach out and slip her hand in his, offer herself the reassurance of that touch. She couldn't allow herself to indulge in the impulse, so she folded her hands on her lap.

"He's old enough to make the journey with the others," Ryan said, "and he's responsible enough to be an asset. If he means to make his life here, he'll need to know how this part of that life works. We can't survive without selling crops, and trips like this one are how they're sold."

"Except for you and Tavish," Aidan tossed in. "It's different for you."

He nodded. "I sell mine to the ranches, and Tavish, when he has enough yield, sells his from town to town."

"When does he leave to do that?" Maura asked.

"Usually about the same time we head to market," Ryan said. "But he lost too much this year. He'll be staying behind and tending animals on this side of town while so many are gone. I also imagine he doesn't wish to be far from Cecily as she's nearing her time."

Aidan watched her with almost heartbreaking anticipation. He clearly wanted to make the journey, but was it truly a good idea?

"Ian will have his own boy to look after, and Thomas will have his," she said, sorting the arrangements aloud. "Who will look after Aidan?"

Ryan scooted a little nearer. She liked that more than she ought. "Joseph is hoping to convince Finbarr to go. Keefe, Mr. O'Connor, and I, along with Finbarr and Joseph, will keep an eye on your lad, Maura. I swear to it."

"*You're* going?" Pure disappointment rushed over her. He was leaving. She pushed the unexpected pain of that aside, but the tendrils of it remained.

He nodded. "I need to build a couple of large hay sheds. Nowhere to get the supplies for them other than the depot. I'll help the men get their crop there, and, in exchange, they'll let me bring back supplies for the sheds in their wagons."

"The town will be very empty, won't it?"

He leaned closer. "Are you trying to say you'll miss me?" That was a flirtatious tone if ever she'd heard one.

She nudged him with her shoulder. "Don't flatter yourself."

"Can I go, Ma?" Aidan had not been distracted from his purpose.

She hesitated before finally answering. "If you go, you will work hard?"

"Of course."

"And you'll do as you're told and not wander away from the others?"

"Never."

She swore the boy was holding his breath. She looked to Ryan once more. "And you'll look out for him?"

He smiled tenderly. "As if he were my own lad."

The sincerity of his declaration echoed in the chambers of her heart. She met Aidan's eye. "I suppose I can let you go."

Aidan let forth a whoop so loud it had likely sent the cattle stampeding clear out on the ranches. He rushed toward the barn, no doubt meaning to tell Finbarr that he'd been permitted to join the men.

Maura watched him rush away. How tempting it was to call him back, to hold him close a moment longer. But he was growing up, moving away from her a little more every day.

"What supplies do I need to send with him?" she asked.

"Your brothers- and father-in-law mean to provide for him," Ryan said, "and we'll fetch food enough for the drive back while we're at the depot."

"Would you do me a favor while you're there?" she asked.

"Anything." That answer held something very comforting.

"Will you buy him a peppermint? I know it's a small thing, but he's not ever had a peppermint. I've been meaning to get him one, but I can't until I've bought the last things I need for his winter coat. It would mean so much to me to know he's enjoyed that treat."

"Of course, Maura. I'll make certain he has enough peppermint to truly enjoy himself."

"And you'll bring him back safe to me?" she whispered, tears clogging her throat. "He is all I have left."

"I will, Maura." He took her hand and raised it to his lips, pressing a soft kiss to her fingers. "And perhaps, in time, I will convince you that you have so much more than you realize."

There was no mistaking his meaning. How very easy it would be to toss away her determination to be wise where Ryan was concerned. She would not do that to either of them. "I will not tie you to a future of pain."

He cradled her hand in both of his, so gentle, so tender. "Being without you now is making *the present* painful." He kissed her fingertips. "I miss you."

The simple declaration, spoken with such tenderness and sincerity, tugged open the armor she'd worked so hard to keep securely in place. With the hand he wasn't holding, she gently touched his stubbled jaw. He leaned closer to her, the warmth of him filling the narrowing space between them. He slipped an arm slowly around her, shivers rippling in all directions from his touch.

"Do you really have to go to the depot?" she whispered.

"I really do." His breath tiptoed over her lips.

"But you will say goodbye before you leave?" Could he hear the desperation beneath her question? Grady had refused to bid her farewell the morning he'd left to join his regiment. He'd insisted that doing so would be bad luck. Ever since, she'd regretted not having that final goodbye. Over the years, the superstitious part of her mind had wondered if not saying goodbye had cursed his departure from the beginning.

"We leave early in the morning, dear. *This* will be goodbye."

She closed her eyes and tried to keep her heart still and calm. This was goodbye. "I hate goodbyes."

His lips brushed lightly over hers, a mere whisper of a touch. A kiss filled with uncertainty would only leave her more worried. In that moment, she needed strength from him, not questions. She leaned toward him, pressing her lips more fully to his.

He pulled her close, holding her firmly against him, and kissed her slowly and deeply. Maura simply melted into him. His embrace held such comfort, such warmth. With him, she found that elusive feel of home. This attachment, however, was unwise. Life would tear them apart; she knew it with certainty. She was inviting heartache.

After he left, she would steel her resolve once more, but in that moment, she let herself love him and indulge in thoughts of a plan that would require so much adjusting it would simply fall apart.

"Be safe," she whispered. "I've lost too many people."

"I will be," he said, "and I'll see to it Aidan is safe as well. We'll both return home to you."

Chapter Thirty-seven

Maura hadn't expected the entire town to grind to a halt while the men and older lads were gone, but she was caught off guard by just how bustling life continued to be. Tavish, as one of the few who had remained, kept almost shockingly busy milking and feeding cows and tending the horses that were left behind, addressing unforeseen problems in various barns and fields.

The women of Hope Springs set themselves to work as well. Katie insisted Maura leave her afternoons open to attend quilting bees and planning meetings. This, she explained, was the time each year when the women organized and prepared for the approach of winter. It was also when they unabashedly spent hours together every day, laughing and sharing stories, sometimes crying together, often celebrating. The men didn't discourage the gatherings nor prevent them—certainly not—but for these weeks when so many were gone, the list of chores needing to be done, and the number of mouths needing to be fed, were smaller, and their time was more their own.

For the sixth day in a row—six days since Aidan had joined the others on the long trip to the train station at the south end of the territory— Maura finished her work near lunchtime and headed up the road. Her sisters-in-law were having a quilting bee at Cecily's house. Katie would join them, but only after gathering the children still at school and walking with them up the road.

Maura arrived a little early, before any of the others. With Tavish gone so much looking after their neighbors' animals, Cecily was often alone. A bit of company would lift her spirits. And Maura wanted to assess Cecily's health, something more easily accomplished when the others weren't present.

Cecily welcomed Maura warmly.

"What can I do to be of help?" Maura asked, closing the door behind her. She set the bundle she'd brought with her on a chest near the door, then pulled off her threadbare coat, laid it overtop.

"There is not much to be done." Cecily made her way toward the gathering of chairs set out for the quilting bee. "Ciara and Mother O'Connor have both vehemently insisted on providing all the victuals today. Biddy is the one needing a quilt tied, but when I suggested everyone meet at her house so she wouldn't have to transport it, the whole lot of them banded together and insisted on meeting here so I could take part. They will arrive with everything firmly in hand."

"The O'Connor women seem to find a way of managing anything they put their minds to."

"*They?*" Cecily lowered herself into a chair. Maura took the one nearest it. "You're one of us, you'll remember, and every bit as stubborn."

She bit back a smile. "I like to think of myself as *determined.*"

"*Mysterious* might be another good word," Cecily said with a half-hidden smile of her own. "Speculation about the state of your health is rife. When you first arrived, you insisted that you simply had a little cold or a tickle in your lungs. None of us can reasonably believe that anymore. You've been here nearly four months and the cough hasn't gone away, neither has it improved. You grow tired easily. You're weary. A great many theories are being pondered."

Maura ought to have known she was being whispered about. Working for the Archers meant more people witnessing and hearing her coughs. Finbarr heard them every day, and he lived in this very house. The O'Connors heard her wheezing at every family gathering. Anyone sitting beside her at the *ceílís* or Sunday services would know that her struggles had not eased with time.

"I will not ask you to tell me exactly what is the cause of the trouble," Cecily said, "but I will ask you this: what can we do to help?"

Maura hadn't expected that question, yet it made perfect sense. The O'Connors were generous people, and Cecily was certainly no exception.

"There is not much that can be done," Maura admitted. "I'll likely always cough and get more easily out of breath than I'd prefer."

Cecily's mouth turned down. Still, she didn't press the matter. "When I first arrived in Hope Springs, the O'Connor family was not at all happy about my presence among them. More than *unhappy*, they were . . ." Beneath her green spectacles her brows tugged in thought. "I wouldn't say they hated me—that's too strong a word—but I was unwelcome, unwanted, and soundly rejected."

"Because you're English?" Maura posed it as a question but didn't doubt it was the right answer.

Cecily nodded. "I did not realize, not having been on the receiving end of the oppressive history our two peoples have with each other, what an enormous obstacle our differing backgrounds truly were. I quickly came to understand."

"I imagine."

"But, Maura, once they knew Tavish loved me—truly loved me— and that I loved him, that he was happier when we were together, and that he would be happier with me in his life, hatred built over centuries was no longer the impenetrable wall it once was. The grueling work of climbing that barrier became a calling to this family. When they love someone, when they wish for someone to be among them, they stop at nothing. And that labor is not a burden. It is a mission."

They had not veered far from the topic, as Maura had thought. "You're telling me that I should trust them with the details of my . . . cough."

"I am saying you should trust them enough to let them love you." Cecily reached for Maura's hand, though she did not find it quickly or easily. Maura, instead, grasped hers. Cecily held firm, squeezing her fingers. "I know what it is to desperately want to be part of this family but to feel like an outsider. The trick, Maura, isn't to wait for them to break the door down, but to simply unlock it yourself. They will step inside. They will love you and your son, no matter what difficulties have come along with you."

That was too pointed for Maura to misunderstand. "You know that my cough is not a simple thing, don't you?"

"I am not certain if it is tuberculosis or a lung disease brought on by the factories, but I know it is one of the two. I traveled this country for years before settling here. I've heard both, Maura. And I know that neither has a particularly good outcome."

Maura held fast to her hand. "Factory-damaged lungs don't have to deteriorate all the way. And even if they do, it is sometimes slow."

"But you don't believe either will be the case with you, do you?"

"I don't." She had to force out the admission. "I brought Aidan here so he would not be orphaned in a big city where he was already miserable. I wanted him to have family after—after I—" She couldn't finish. She suspected she didn't have to.

"I won't tell your secret," Cecily promised, "but I do think you should tell the family. I promise they won't buckle under the burden, neither will they resent it."

"Ryan has told me much the same thing, many times."

"He's a wise man."

Cecily suddenly stiffened. She even seemed to be holding her breath. Her hand pressed to her abdomen.

"Are you having pains?" Maura was very nearly certain of what she was seeing.

Cecily nodded, taking shallow breaths. "I've had—a few today." A few more short breaths. "I've kept still—but they keep—happening."

Her pains were intense enough that she was having difficulty talking through them. "How close together are they?"

"I can't say with certainty." She was breathing a little easier. "I haven't a way of timing them."

That was a complication. "If you had to guess?"

Cecily released a full breath. Her features eased into an expression of relief. "Two, maybe three in an hour."

"For how many hours?"

"Several." Cecily paused. "Should I be concerned?"

"You're still a little shy of your expected time, but much nearer than you were before."

"My time?" She sat up straighter. "You think this is—?"

Maura squeezed her fingers. "I suspect so. I'll stay until we know for certain, however long that might be."

'Twasn't long before the other O'Connor women began trickling in. They were all there when Cecily had her next labor pains. Looks of concern were exchanged all around, their eyes eventually settling on Maura.

Before she could say anything, Cecily did. "I may not be able to see any of you"—a quick breath—"but I know you've been staring at me." Another breath.

"It's been about twenty minutes since your last pains," Maura said. "That is near enough together that I think we can safely assume you, our dear sister, are soon to have a baby."

Cecily paled but nodded resolutely.

"What can we do?" Ciara asked.

Maura took full charge of the situation. "At the moment, I think our best course of action is to proceed with our sewing circle. If the pains get significantly closer, we'll focus on that then. Otherwise, we may have hours to go, and I've found most mothers-to-be can use a bit of distraction in the meantime."

Cecily nodded firmly.

"We have our task, ladies," Mrs. O'Connor said.

The women chatted as they set the quilt in the stretching frame. Cecily joined in the chat, her pains having passed for the moment. Topics ranged from what the children were studying in school to the expected price for grain at market, to a number of projects the women were looking forward to undertaking that winter.

All the while, they watched Cecily, though Maura watched her most of all. Her sister's labor had come too early and had proven very complicated. Neither mother nor child had survived. Early deliveries had made Maura nervous ever since.

"How are you getting along, Maura?" Mrs. O'Connor asked. "Must be odd having Aidan away."

She pulled her attention from Cecily and focused on the conversation at hand. "We've not ever been apart. I'm finding it difficult to remember that he's not a little boy anymore."

"Happens faster than expected," Mrs. Callaghan said. She was staying with Mrs. O'Connor while Ryan was away.

Maura coughed, something she'd managed to avoid for nearly an hour. Her lungs seemed intent on making up for lost time. One cough after another seized her. She stood and stepped away from the others, trying to regain control over the vital task of breathing. She had a child to deliver in likely only a few hours. Being able to breathe would make that far easier.

Mrs. O'Connor moved to stand beside Maura. She rubbed her on the back, speaking words of comfort and encouragement as Maura struggled for air.

"I worry for you, dear," she said as the fit died down. "This cough of yours doesn't seem to get any better."

Maura glanced at Cecily. She'd told Maura to trust her family. Maura was asking Cecily to trust *her* with the safe delivery of her child. She could instill confidence in Cecily by taking that leap of faith.

"My cough won't get better." She turned back to face the sewing circle. The time had come to be brave. "You remember the factories in New York, I'm certain."

"Unfortunately," Mrs. O'Connor said.

Biddy dropped her gaze, absentmindedly rubbing her arm. How well Maura remembered the horrible injury her then future-sister-in-law had suffered at the factory, where nearly all the family worked at the time. None of them had enjoyed working there.

"After Grady died," Maura continued, "I had to go back to work there."

"Oh, sweetheart." Mrs. O'Connor took Maura's hand and squeezed it. "I didn't know you'd gone back."

"I needed a more reliable income than I could get cleaning houses." She coughed once, then pressed on. "I worked there for nearly ten years. A decade in the spinner room takes a toll."

"Oh, dear." Mary pressed her hand over her mouth. "The cough."

Maura nodded. "Too many years breathing that heavy air."

"Brown lung," Mrs. O'Connor said, a catch in her voice.

Maura nodded.

"Is it certain?" Mrs. O'Connor asked.

"Yes," Maura said. "It is certainly brown lung."

"And do you know if your lungs are too far gone for at least some degree of recovery?"

She shook her head. "I won't know for some time, but my cough has not improved as the doctor hoped it would after I left the city. At times, it has actually been worse."

Mrs. Callaghan spoke into the silence that followed. "Why did you not tell us?"

"I've spent too many years looking after myself, I suppose. I didn't want to be a burden."

Mrs. O'Connor pulled her into a fierce hug. "We love you, Maura. Dearly. 'Tisn't a burden to stand with someone you love."

"Cecily told me as much," Maura said. "Defended you quite staunchly, I'll have you know. As did Ryan Callaghan."

Mrs. Callaghan looked somehow both surprised and not surprised in the least. Did she know how deeply Maura cared for her son? *Am I so transparent as that?*

She shook off the question. Another matter needed to be addressed in the moment.

"I've brought something with me," Maura said. "I had it in New York and have debated what precisely I ought to do with it. I thought perhaps Cecily and Tavish would appreciate having it for their little one."

She rose and crossed back toward the trunk near the door. She carefully laid aside her coat and took from beneath it an old, beautiful, and well-loved, infant-sized quilt. She held it carefully and turned back to face them.

Mrs. O'Connor pressed a hand to her heart.

"Grandmother's quilt," Mary said in breathless tones.

"It belonged to Tavish's grandmother," Maura said for Cecily's benefit. "She brought it from Scotland to Ireland and left it to our dear mother-in-law, who left it to me when the family came west. With her blessing, I would like to give it to you now."

Maura set the treasured blanket on Cecily's lap. Tenderly, Cecily ran her fingers over the top of it.

"Thank you," she said with tears in her voice.

Mrs. O'Connor gave Maura a hug. "Thank you, my dear girl. 'Tis the perfect newest journey for my mother's quilt to make."

"I've thought of it many times since we left New York," Mary said. "It was in our house in Ireland all my life, then in the New York tenement."

"It likely ought to have stayed with you," Maura acknowledged.

Mrs. O'Connor shook her head firmly. "I left it with you for a reason. I wanted you to bundle our Aidan in it. I could almost feel as if I were holding him again, knowing he was wrapped in my mother's quilt."

Maura blinked back a tear. "I treasured it. I was without family for so long. Sometimes the quilt felt like the only connection I had to anyone outside of Aidan. I needed it more than I can say."

She received another heartfelt hug from her mother-in-law, one she returned with earnestness.

"Maura." Cecily spoke her name with earnest anxiety.

One look told Maura that her sister-in-law was having more pains. This one came far closer to the last one than before.

Maura turned to Mary. "Help Cecily to her bedroom," she said. "Mrs. O'Connor and Mrs. Callaghan, gather some clean linens and rags. Biddy, set some water to boil."

Ciara stepped forward. "What should *I* do?"

Maura held her gaze. "Find Tavish. And tell him to hurry."

Chapter Thirty-eight

Ryan watched the spectacle of buying and selling play out in the enormous open field behind the train depot. He'd participated in the back-and-forth every year he'd worked the Claire land. Now his crop was safely sold, his income secured for the year. And, once they returned to Hope Springs, he and Joseph would draw up the papers that would make the Claire land *his* land. Life was looking up.

If only he could convince Maura to have faith in the future.

She'd kissed him. The memory of her lips pressed to his seared through him still, tempered by the words she'd spoken immediately after: "I've lost too many people." It had been a moment of fear and worry, not the toppling of her walls he'd been hoping for.

How could he show her that love was stronger than even the greatest of worries and could soothe the deepest pain? She needed to believe that. Not just for their futures together, but for her own peace of mind.

"Where do the crops go after those men buy them?" Aidan stood next to Ryan, leaning against the wood fence running the length of the selling field.

Ryan pulled himself back into the moment. "Depends on who buys them. Some send them to bigger towns along the rail lines where fewer people farm, so crops aren't as easily available. Some sell to ranchers and others needing them in this area of the territory."

"Like you sold your hay to the ranches around Hope Springs."

"Two of the ranches, anyway. But yes, it's quite the same. The men who buy crops here have to sell them for more than they paid; that's how they make their living. So the ranches buying from those men pay more than they would if they were buying directly from the farmer."

Ryan could practically hear the wheels spinning in Aidan's mind as he sorted through the explanation. "So the ranchers who buy from you save money?"

Ryan nodded.

"And *you* still make money too?"

"I do, but I save m'self the trouble of driving all that hay down to market. It'd take wagons and wagons, and I'd need to hire people to help drive them here, then return with the empty wagons."

"And you'd have to buy the wagons and horses in the first place."

The boy was quick.

"Yes, but the town makes the trip together so we can pool our resources—share wagons and trade drivers and such. And we've gained a bit of bargaining power coming as a group like we do. But my crop is needed right outside town, so it makes more sense to sell it there."

"And the ranches don't have to fetch it here, or pay more to the men who buy it first."

"Seems a good plan to me."

Aidan turned a bit, facing him instead of the ongoing bidding out in the field. "Why did you come, then, if you don't have a crop to sell?"

"To help drive," he said. "Also because we don't just sell while we're here. We purchase supplies we can't get in town—seed for the next year's crop if it's needed, equipment, building supplies."

"What supplies are you getting on this trip?"

"I need to build two hay barns so I'll not have to scramble to cover my hay if we get another ill-timed rain storm. This is the best place to get the wood planks, nails, shingles, and all the other things I'll need."

Aidan nodded. "And there'll be a lot of empty wagons making the trek back that you can put the wood and things inside."

"Sorted that quickly, lad."

Aidan smiled broadly. "Ma says I'm whip smart."

"Which shows she's whip smart, as well."

Aidan climbed onto the fence, sitting on the cross post. "You're fond of my ma, aren't you?"

"I'm a vast deal more than 'fond of her.' I think she's . . . rather wonderful."

"She is." Pride and tenderness filled the boy's eyes. "I'm glad she let me come along to the depot. I know it made her nervous."

"She's a brave soul, always trying to do what's right for you." 'Twas little wonder Ryan had lost his heart to her so completely. She never stopped amazing him.

"How much would a new coat cost?" Aidan asked suddenly. "For ma. Hers is worn, with holes in places."

"A coat is not a small thing," Ryan warned. "I doubt you've money enough to buy one, especially readymade."

Disappointment pulled at the lad's posture. "She spent her extra money to make me a coat. But she's going to be cold this winter." He turned his worried gaze on Ryan once more. "I don't know what to do."

A coat was not an optional thing during the bitter Wyoming winter months. Ryan would buy her one himself, but theirs was not an established enough connection for such a personal gift. The gesture would likely either feel like an overstep or an act of charity. Her boy could make the purchase, though. Except he likely hadn't a single penny to his name, and he didn't have a job to get any.

"You've become quite a good milker, and I've seen you fork hay to the animals," Ryan said. "What other jobs have you learned to do over at Archers'?"

"I've fed the chickens and pigs. Finbarr's showing me how to stack food in the root cellar. He says I'll learn to help mend fences once we're back from market."

"He's proving a good teacher, is he?"

Aidan nodded. "He gets frustrated sometimes, because he can't see things, and he doesn't always know how to explain or understand when I try to describe something. But we're sorting it, and it's going better than at first."

"Well, all those things you've been learning are things that need doing around my place." Saints, it felt good to call his land *his* place. He'd dreamed of having a place of his own nearly all his life. "I'll lend you the money to get your ma a coat if you're willing to put in some work for me to pay it off."

Hope shone almost painfully in his blue eyes. "I'll do it. Anything you want me to, as long as I know how. She needs a coat, Ryan. She's not strong like she used to be. If she's cold all winter, she'll get worse. I know she will. She'll—" He stopped midsentence, choking back the word he clearly didn't want to say.

Ryan set a hand on the boy's shoulder. "We'll not let her suffer, Aidan. Anything she needs, we'll see that she has it."

"Like a coat?"

He nodded. "A coat to begin with." He motioned toward the mercantile, not too far distant. "Run inside and see if they've any readymade coats. The clerk, Bart, will help us find the best price."

"Thank you." He hopped off the fence and ran across the dirt road.

Ryan followed at a slower pace. He meant to keep his promise to Aidan. Whatever role he was permitted to play in Maura's life, he'd embrace it, and he would find a way to ease her worries and suffering. He'd do everything he could to keep her healthy and strong, and, if she'd let him, he'd walk every step of her path—whatever it looked like—with her.

The mercantile was quiet; most everyone in town was at the crop auction. Other than Ryan and Aidan, only a single person was inside, the sales clerk. Ryan had come to the depot a couple times a year since moving to Hope Springs, and Bart had always been the sales clerk. But Bart was a short, stout ginger. This man was tall, lanky, with dark hair and a tan complexion no Irishman could hope to achieve.

Aidan had already found a display of clothing. One benefit of a larger town than the one they lived in was the broader assortment of merchandise. Among the dresses and men's shirts and trousers were several women's coats. Aidan looked them over with immense concentration. He cared for his mother, there was no denying that.

314

Ryan moved in the direction of a clerk. "Good afternoon. Ryan Callaghan." He held out his hand to shake.

The clerk accepted it. "Burke Jones."

"How much for a coat?" Ryan motioned toward the display.

He was quoted a not unreasonable price. "The lad there'll be choosing one for his ma. I've a few things to get m'self. Add the coat to my tally."

Burke nodded. "Is he your boy?"

Hearing the question asked so casually, Ryan realized he wished the answer were other than it was. He thought of Aidan in a fatherly way. He truly did. That longing he'd felt for so many years to have children of his own, to watch them learning and growing, had eased somewhat of late, though so slowly and subtly he'd not realized it. He'd been teaching and guiding Aidan, spending time with him in the way a father might.

"His ma is—" How did he describe his connection to Maura without growing too personal or belittling their connection? "I'm hopeful his ma'll marry me someday."

First, he'd been caught off-guard by the realization of his connection with Aidan. Now he was admitting *aloud* for the first time that he wanted a future with Maura. 'Twas quite a day for revelations.

Aidan looked back at him. "I like both the blue and the red one, but I don't know which would be better."

"She'd be stunning in red," Ryan answered.

The lad rolled his eyes. "You can't say things like that about her. She's a mother."

Ryan chuckled.

The clerk smiled as well. "What do you need besides the coat?"

"A full scoop of peppermints," Ryan said. That'd be enough to last the lad quite a while. Ryan hoped that seeing Aidan enjoy them would bring Maura a bit of joy. "And you don't happen to have a town chemist, do you? I could use some advice on medicines."

"So happens I could help you there."

"You're a chemist?" His laugh, one arising from his assumption that the man was jesting, died at the fully serious look on his face. "You are?"

"A doctor, actually. Graduated from Chicago Medical College a few years ago."

"And you're working as a mercantile clerk?" That seemed unlikely.

"I was meant to take a position in Laramie," he said. "It was no longer available by the time I arrived. I didn't find a lot of options for someone with no farming or ranching skills."

"But you have medical skills. Surely that gives you opportunities."

Burke motioned to his clerk's apron. "Obviously not."

A shame, really. "Life doesn't always follow the path we hope."

"No, it doesn't."

"I count myself lucky, though, that you're here," Ryan said. "I've two people in m'life who could use some medicine, but I haven't the first idea what would be best."

Burke motioned him over to the display of powders, teas, drops, and other medicinals. "Tell me what ails them."

He began with Ma, describing her rheumatism and how it bothered her. The clerk asked a few questions of his own, insightful queries that would've put to rest any lingering doubts Ryan had about the man's competency. In the end, he suggested two different powders, each efficacious for different symptoms. He even wrote out instructions for their best use. And he further recommended a flower-based tea that would, over time, likely provide some relief from her achiness.

Next came the subject of Maura's cough. Ryan hoped he was not breaking his word to her about not revealing the nature of her illness. He wasn't telling anyone she knew, and he wasn't naming her. And this was a rare opportunity for some expert advice. She'd given up the care of a doctor for the sake of her son. If Ryan could give her even a moment of knowledgeable help, he would.

"That case is trickier," Burke admitted. "Conditions contracted in the factories rarely clear up, though she may very well have left early enough for the disease to not progress quickly."

"That is her hope, as well."

"To calm the cough when it grows troublesome, I'd suggest this." He gave Ryan a bottle of tonic. "It can be diluted to stretch it further. The instructions are on the bottle. And this"—he selected a tin of powder— "might be helpful if she's been coughing enough to be in pain from the effort."

"What else?"

Burke shook his head. "It's almost impossible to say without actually observing the patient. Each time she grew worse would mean a new decision with new information. The disease likely can't be cured, and if it's actively progressing, it can't necessarily be slowed, either. But symptoms can sometimes be treated to offer some relief."

"You'd need to treat her in person?"

Burke nodded. "How far away is your town?"

"Two and a half days by wagon or stage. But we're fully isolated in the winter. It's not accessible then."

A look of true empathy filled his face. "I am sorry to hear that. These will help." He motioned to the tonic and powder he'd recommended. "I'd suggest bringing her down in the spring if you're able, but I don't know that I'll still be here. I know of another doctor in town who might be helpful, though he's only ever practiced out West, so he won't be very familiar with factory-caused illnesses."

"Thank you anyway," Ryan said.

Aidan approached the counter.

"Did you choose a coat, lad?"

"The red one." He turned sharp eyes on Ryan. "But not because she'd be 'stunning' in it. It has a flannel lining. Mrs. Johnson said having flannel lining is important."

Burke nodded and moved to fetch the coat. Ryan eyed the collection of powders and tonics in his hands, feeling the inadequacy of the offering. Ma and Maura needed more than his ignorant attempts at helping them.

Burke Jones—*Doctor* Burke Jones, knew about the ailments. He'd spoken expertly and competently. Ryan *could* bring both women back in the spring, but Burke wouldn't necessarily be there. There had to be a better answer.

In the next instant, his mind suggested something that just might work, and his heart simply froze at the thought.

Burke returned with the coat. Ryan set the bottles and tin on the countertop, but didn't pull out his billfold. Not yet.

"What are you doing this winter?" he asked the man. "Because I have a proposition."

Chapter Thirty-nine

Ryan was always eager to return to Hope Springs after the trip to the depot. This year, though, he felt an excitement he hadn't before. He'd be returning to his own land, to the promise of many good years to come. More than that, though, returning meant seeing Maura again. That she'd never left his thoughts in the two weeks he'd been gone spoke to the place of importance she'd claimed in his heart.

She was wary, and understandably so. She faced an uncertain future and had a son to consider. Yet he was not one to have his hopes and dreams undermined simply because seeing them fulfilled would be more difficult than he'd anticipated.

He, with Aidan up on the bench alongside him, drove the wagon they'd taken stewardship of, one belonging to Tavish but lent out for the harvest run. They headed first to the Archer house. Aidan wanted to see his mother; Ryan was no less eager. Tavish, he felt certain, wouldn't begrudge the delay.

They arrived ahead of Joseph and Finbarr, though likely by only a few minutes. He wrapped the horses' reins around a post, then joined Aidan as they walked toward the back door. Maura could usually be found in the kitchen—most of her duties were accomplished there.

He knocked on the kitchen door at the back of the house.

"Saints, why am I so nervous?"

Aidan laughed. Apparently Ryan had asked the question aloud.

"Ma'll be happy to see you," Aidan said.

"Do you think she'll be happy to see *you*?" Ryan countered.

He laughed again. The lad was happier, more open, than he'd been when he and Maura first arrived. Ryan hoped that he had contributed to that, at least a little.

Aidan eyed the door. "She doesn't usually take this long to answer."

"She might be somewhere else in the house."

The handle turned and the door opened. 'Twasn't Maura who stood just beyond, but Emma. And there was no mistaking the heaviness of her expression.

"Has something happened?" he asked, instantly alarmed. "Are you needing help, lass?"

She shook her head, looking from one of them to the other. Aidan grew instantly somber. Emma's gaze settled on her friend. "Your mother is very ill. We're all afraid for her."

The lad took a shaky breath. "Is she here?"

She motioned toward the bedroom just off the kitchen.

Ryan put an arm about the boy's shoulders. "Let's go see her, lad."

Together they made the short, yet painful, trek across the small kitchen. Ryan prepared himself for the worst, all the while trying to decide how he could possibly help Aidan through whatever they might find.

Mrs. O'Connor was inside, dabbing Maura's forehead with a damp cloth. Maura looked paler than she had in all the months Ryan had known her, yet deep, worrisome color splotched her face, a clear indication of fever. As far as he knew, she'd not been feverish since coming to town. That could not be a good sign.

Aidan pulled away, crossing directly to the bed where his mother lay. "Ma?"

Would she respond? Was she lucid enough to even know her son stood nearby?

Her eyes opened. A feeble smile touched her lips. "Welcome home, lad."

A sigh of relief rose in him. She was not so far gone as to be unaware of her surroundings.

Aidan sat on the edge of her bed. "Is this the brown lung getting worse?"

Mrs. O'Connor didn't appear the least surprised at hearing Aidan so casually identify his mother's illness. Had Maura told them at last? Had she done so before being laid low, or had her deterioration forced the confession?

"We knew I'd likely grow worse," Maura reminded her son.

"But I thought it'd take longer."

She smiled sadly, her heavy eyelids opening and closing slowly.

Emma stood in the doorway beside Ryan, watching the scene with pulled brow. He bent enough to talk to her in a low voice. "Have you something in the kitchen Aidan could eat? I'd wager he's hungry, and stepping away a minute would likely do him some good."

She nodded. "Katie made pasties this morning. There are a couple left."

"Lad," Ryan called.

Aidan looked over at him.

"Miss Emma has some lunch for you. Fill your belly. You can come visit your ma again after you've eaten."

The boy didn't argue. His shoulders slumped a bit as he drew nearer. He didn't meet Ryan's eye. Emma didn't immediately vacate the doorway to let him pass. Instead, she held her hand out to him. Aidan took it without a word. Emma led him away and into the kitchen; neither child spoke. Ryan knew enough of Emma's caring nature to know she'd be kind and tender with Aidan's heavy heart. He needn't worry about the lad while in the girl's care, allowing him to focus on Maura.

He moved to her bedside but addressed Mrs. O'Connor first. "How long has she been so ill?"

"A couple days is all, though it's grown far worse today."

He knelt beside the bed and took Maura's hand in his. She turned her head in his direction and opened her eyes.

"Hello there, love," he said.

She squeezed his hand; she had strength enough for that. "I've missed you, Ryan Callaghan."

"I've missed you, as well." He kissed her hand. "This isn't quite the welcome home I'd anticipated."

"I'd fully planned to greet you on my feet, I'll tell you that." She had her wits still. "And I meant to brag of my midwifery skills."

"You delivered another baby?"

"Cecily and Tavish have a new little boy. Tiny, but perfect."

Mrs. O'Connor dabbed Maura's forehead again, then her flushed cheeks. Maura coughed, a dry, rattling cough that shook her whole frame.

"That sounds different than before." But was *different* worse?

"Indeed," Mrs. O'Connor said. "I haven't the first idea what to do about it."

"And I ache," Maura said in the midst of her continued coughing. "Every joint. And my head hurts something terrible."

"Is that pain common with brown lung?" He didn't know enough about the ailment to say for sure.

"I don't know." Maura closed her eyes again, clearly exhausted. "When the disease got bad in New York, the sufferers quit coming to work. I didn't see them toward the end."

Toward the end.

The end.

He kissed her hand once more, willing himself not to let the enormity of those words settle fully on his mind. He refused to believe the heavens would be so cruel as to take her from him so soon. "I've some good news for you."

"You've brought me a new pair of lungs?" she asked with a tremulous smile.

"I'm not certain that's possible." He threaded his fingers through hers. "I've brought something else, though. A doctor."

Both Maura and Mrs. O'Connor eyed him with surprise.

"I met him at the depot. Dr. Jones is his name. He hasn't a practice of his own yet, and I suggested he might find work enough here to see him through the winter."

"Truly?" Mrs. O'Connor's mouth hung a bit agape.

"He's coming with Joseph and Finbarr."

"Oh, Ryan." Mrs. O'Connor clasped his arm. "He'll be here all winter?"

Ryan nodded. "There are enough of us, and enough in town with ailments, to keep him busy for the winter. I don't know that he'll stay beyond that."

"But we'll have a doctor for a time." A sigh of unmitigated relief escaped Mrs. O'Connor's lips. "We've needed one badly."

"I've thought so as well." He looked back to Maura, who watched him in silence, her expression unreadable. "Are you upset?" He couldn't imagine why she would be, but he worried. Maybe he'd overstepped himself.

"Did you have to pay him?" she asked in a strained whisper.

"Not exactly." He hadn't paid Burke directly, but he'd purchased the supplies the doctor would need to set up even a temporary practice in Hope Springs. They hadn't been cheap. He'd had enough left for only one hay barn, which wouldn't store anywhere near all of his hay next year should the timing prove unfortunate. But even if he lost half his crop, it'd be worth it if Burke could ease Maura's suffering, maybe grant her more time.

Ivy's shouts of "Pompah!" announced Joseph's arrival. Burke would be with him.

"I'll go send in the doctor," he told Maura.

"Thank you," she whispered.

He rose and moved swiftly from the room. If there was any chance Burke meant to make his way elsewhere, perhaps wander toward town, Ryan wanted to catch him before he got far.

Katie, with little Sean and her girls, greeted Joseph in an enormous family embrace. Finbarr was walking toward the house with the doctor. They stepped up onto the porch.

"Seems you're to start right away," Ryan said.

Burke's expression grew immediately earnest. "An injury or an illness?"

"Illness. The woman I told you about with lung disease from working in a factory."

Mrs. O'Connor had stepped out of the house as well. She gave Finbarr a quick hug before turning to Burke. "You're our new doctor?"

"I am." Burke spoke with conviction. "Where is the patient?"

"This way." Mrs. O'Connor waved him inside. He disappeared into the house.

"Maura's cough is from the factory?" Finbarr asked.

"It is, and she's grown more ill while we were away." He set a hand on Finbarr's shoulder, lightly urging him in the direction of the house. Ryan intended to look in on Maura again but didn't wish to be rude by leaving the boy standing on the porch, unsure where everyone had gone.

"Is that why you convinced Dr. Jones to come to Hope Springs?" Finbarr walked with him inside.

"Primarily, though he'll help plenty enough of others, including your new nephew."

"Cecily had her baby?" Finbarr spoke with excitement.

"Maura said so."

The Archers were on their way inside, so Ryan stepped into the kitchen and out of the way. Soon the room was filled with the sound of their cheerful voices. A reunited family was a beautiful thing to watch.

"Did you bring us presents, Pompah?" Ivy asked.

Joseph brushed a hand along one of her braids. "I did, but you'll have to wait until tonight."

She pouted rather adorably even as her eyes shifted to Finbarr. She skipped over to him. "Did you bring us something, Finbarr?"

"Ivy," Katie scolded, but was ignored.

Finbarr reached into his coat pocket and pulled out what looked like a wad of lace. He felt it a minute, then nodded. "These are for you, sweetie."

She took the offering eagerly and unwadded it. "Lace gloves!" She jumped up and down, clutching the gloves to her heart. "I've wanted lace gloves."

"I know," Finbarr laughed.

"Did you bring something for Emma?" Ivy asked.

Poor Emma blushed. "Hush, Ivy."

"Of course I did," Finbarr said.

"You didn't have to." Emma was watching him closely, though.

"I know." Finbarr stuck his hand in his other pocket, but didn't immediately pull out whatever resided there. "It's just something I thought you'd like."

Emma inched closer. "What is it?"

"A scarf pin." He shook his head. "I'm not certain what it looks like, but it feels very delicate, and the sales clerk said it's nice. He could have been lying to get me to buy it. You don't have to keep it if you don't want to."

"I could use a scarf pin," Emma said. "Especially when it's windy."

"That's what I guessed." He pulled his hand out, but kept it fisted. "If you really don't like it, though—"

"Just give it to her," Aidan said from the table. "Emma isn't fussy like that."

She sent the lad a smile of pure gratitude and, if Ryan didn't miss his mark, tender regard. Aidan returned his attention to his lunch, oblivious to the heart she wore on her sleeve. *Poor lass.*

Katie inched closer to Finbarr. "I'm dyin' to see this pin now. Let's have a look."

Finbarr held his hand out, palm up and fingers open. Katie leaned forward. Emma stepped directly to Finbarr, near enough to see the pin with little effort.

"Oh, Finbarr," Katie said. "That is lovely."

"It's very pretty," Emma said. She took it from his hand, then cradled it carefully in both of hers. "Thank you."

"You're quite welcome, Miss Emma." Finbarr buttoned his coat up. "I hear I have a nephew to go meet. I'll be back tomorrow, Joseph."

"I'll see you then."

After Finbarr slipped out, the Archer family made their way out of the kitchen toward the heart of the house, leaving Aidan and Ryan behind. Ivy had her gloves on already. Emma never took her eyes off her pin.

"Sometimes it's hard to know if those two are friends," Aidan said once the family had left.

"Emma and Finbarr?" Ryan asked.

Aidan nodded.

"They were once like brother and sister to each other. They've had a falling out, though."

"I figured." Aidan finished the last of his lunch. "I think they miss being brother and sister."

"I think you're right." He eyed the closed door to Maura's room.

What was Burke finding? Could the doctor help? Offer some hope, at least? Time couldn't run out this soon, before he and Maura had even begun to build a life together.

Across the table, Aidan was watching the door as well. "Ma's cough sounded bad."

"It did," Ryan said. "But she has a doctor now. He'll help her."

"We can't pay a doctor." Aidan met his eyes once more. "Maybe Dr. Jones has some work I could do for him."

"I've already made arrangements with him, lad. Anything your ma needs this whole winter he's already agreed to see to."

Aidan pushed out a puff of air, the sound of bone-deep relief. "We probably shouldn't tell Ma."

Ryan could smile at that. Maura was proud, in the best sense. She'd fret about being a burden if she had any idea the arrangement.

The door to Maura's room opened. Ryan rose. Aidan did as well.

"C'm'ere, lad." Ryan waved him over. The boy moved to stand beside him. Ryan set a hand on the back of Aidan's shoulder.

Burke looked at them as he stepped into the kitchen.

"How bad is the brown lung, Doctor?" Ryan asked.

"I'm not certain," he said. "I'll know better once this has passed."

Passed? Ryan looked to Aidan but saw the same drawn-browed confusion he felt. "Once *what* has passed?" he asked.

"Her current difficulties aren't from brown lung, though it is likely complicating her condition," Burke said. "She has valley fever."

Valley fever. That particular ailment had the potential to be serious, but generally resolved after a couple of weeks, sometimes a bit longer. More crucial still, 'twas hardly ever fatal. "Are you sure?" Ryan pressed.

"She has the tell-tale rash, and valley fever explains the achiness. Brown lung doesn't cause either."

Aidan moved closer to the doctor, Ryan's hand falling away as he did. "She doesn't have brown lung?"

"She likely does, but brown lung is not the reason for her worsened state."

Merciful heavens. "Then, she's not deteriorating?"

"I don't know." Burke moved to the back door. "As the fever clears, I'll have a chance to assess that."

He wasn't losing her, not immediately. "It *will* clear then—the valley fever, that is?"

Burke nodded. "I've given Mrs. O'Connor instructions, and I'll check on Maura a few times in the coming weeks—she'll likely fight this longer and struggle more than most, considering her lungs are already weakened—but I believe she'll be fine on this score."

Aidan rushed into his ma's room, not waiting for more reassurances.

Burke pulled the door open to leave. "Jeremiah Johnson suggested I check in at the mercantile to assess their medical supplies. I'll meet you at your place when I'm done. I assume he'll be able to tell me where to find you."

"He will. And thank you."

Burke paused in the doorway. "Thank you for convincing me to come. I'd begun to wonder if I'd ever have a chance to be a doctor again."

"You'll be needed here," Ryan promised him.

After a moment, Ryan was alone in the kitchen. He lowered himself into a chair at the table. He dropped his head into his upturned hands and just breathed.

Maura had valley fever. She wasn't dying. And she had a doctor.

Which all meant, they had a chance.

Chapter Forty

Maura remembered very little of the past few days. She hadn't been delirious or unconscious, simply asleep.

She stepped from her room, unsure of the day, and only vaguely aware that it was afternoon, already rehearsing the apology she meant to offer Katie. She'd not done a bit of work since growing ill, yet she'd been housed and fed, and, she assumed, so had Aidan. In that moment, she could smell stew simmering on the stove, meaning someone had done the cooking she usually saw to.

Mrs. O'Connor stepped into the kitchen just as Maura made her way toward the table. "Oh, Maura. You're up and about. Are you feeling better?"

"I am. Not perfect, but better."

Mrs. O'Connor led her to the table, urging her to sit. "Dr. Jones says you'll not be fully better for weeks yet. Valley fever can be very stubborn." Little about her words made sense.

"Dr. Jones?"

"You don't remember him? He's been here a few times."

Maura vaguely recalled someone unfamiliar being nearby now and then. "Black hair, with a deep, rumbling voice?"

Mrs. O'Connor nodded. "Very quiet when he's not doctoring. I suspect he may be a bit shy, which seems to me an odd thing in one who makes his living interacting with people. Still, quiet or not, he's an answer to our prayers."

"You've been wanting a doctor?"

"*Needing* one. We've lost so many to illnesses we didn't know how to treat, and to injuries we didn't know how to put right." A deep, remembered sadness filled her face. Finbarr likely still weighed on her. How many others did? Family members Maura had never met who'd not survived this often-cruel life in the West. "Dear Mrs. Claire was a midwife, but she was too frail to serve that way during her last few years. Having you here has eased a lot of worries. Having a doctor will ease a great many more."

Maura leaned her arms on the tabletop. How was it she was already devoid of energy? She'd only walked as far as the table. "I need to talk with Katie. She may need someone else to work as housekeeper for a while. I'm going to be rather useless."

"Katie's not worried, I promise you." Mrs. O'Connor poured steaming hot water from a kettle into a teacup. "Nothing's been neglected. But even if it had been, she'd be offended if any of us suggested she'd begrudge you the time you need to regain your strength."

"I hadn't meant for anyone to have to see to my work."

Mrs. O'Connor set the cup on the table in front of Maura. "All the O'Connor women have been dividing our time between Katie's and Cecily's—and our own homes, of course."

"How is Cecily? And the baby?"

"Both are doing as well as can be expected so soon after delivery," Mrs. O'Connor said. "Tavish, however, is just about more than any of us can take, so ridiculously in love with that little boy of his. Gushes endlessly, he does. Cecily just laughs and smiles at him the way she always does."

Maura set her hands on either side of the warm cup. "I know you've had your difficulties in Hope Springs, but the O'Connor family seems very happy here."

Mrs. O'Connor sat across from her, then reached out and patted her hand. "We're even happier now that you and Aidan are here with us."

Guilt swept over Maura at that. "If not for me, Grady would've come west with you. He'd've been here instead of fighting. He'd still be alive. I don't know how you can possibly want me here, knowing I'm the reason you don't have him anymore."

Mrs. O'Connor squeezed her hand. "My Grady was as kind and gentle a soul as I've ever known, but, *begor*, that lad had a mind of his own. If he'd not wanted to stay in New York, he'd have pushed back when you suggested it. I'd wager he didn't say any such thing."

"He didn't. Not at all."

She smiled softly. "You didn't force his hand, Maura. None of us believes you did. As you said, life hasn't been easy here. There's no saying how things might have been different. Patrick likely wouldn't have come either way."

Patrick. Heaviness settled in her stomach at the thought of him and the pain he'd caused the O'Connors. "I don't know what's in that man's head. To not even tell the family he's alive. I swear to you, if he were within arm's reach, I'd throttle him."

"Provided there was anything left of him after Ian had his say." Mrs. O'Connor shook her head. "Our poor Ian has been through so much these past years. And then to learn the brother he'd shared a special bond with has been lying to him, letting him grieve unnecessarily for a decade . . . I don't know how he'll make his peace with that."

"What of you and your husband? You must be a bit upended learning your son's alive and keeping his distance from you."

Mrs. O'Connor squared her shoulders. "If Patrick thinks he can hide in the wilds of Canada to avoid giving his parents an explanation, he'll soon discover he has sorely underestimated us."

They laughed at that. The O'Connors were nothing if not persistent. Maura could almost feel sorry for her prodigal brother-in-law.

The kitchen door opened. Maura turned in that direction in time to see Ryan step inside, carrying an empty laundry basket in his arms. "It's all hung on the line, though I cannot promise it's done as neatly as you'd prefer."

"Don't you fret over that," Mrs. O'Connor said. "Come greet our Maura. She's among the living again."

Ryan looked at her then. The warmth in his eyes sent an answering heat over her face. "Maura." He set the basket down and crossed to her, taking the seat beside hers. "Dr. Jones said you might be up today or tomorrow. Seems he knows what he's about."

"Which means you can stop hounding him," Mrs. O'Connor said to Ryan.

He smiled across the table. "If Burke would stop being so vague, I'd not need to press him to be certain he's paying enough heed. I'll not see our Maura neglected."

Our Maura. Mrs. O'Connor had referred to her that way as well. *Our.* They claimed her. She belonged among them, something she'd only dreamed of. Other than Eliza and Aidan, Maura'd not belonged in anyone's life for so long.

Our Maura.

She was immediately seized by a surge of emotion. "Pardon me." She stood as quickly as she could and moved back into her room. Crying would require far more energy than she had, so she closed her eyes, holding back the tears that threatened.

The sound of heavy boots signaled Ryan's arrival in the room behind her. She would have been embarrassed, but a small, quiet part of her had hoped he would follow her. Opening her eyes, turning and seeing him there, set the tears free.

He moved to her and wrapped her in his arms, holding her tenderly. "*Mo stór,*" he whispered. "What's upset you?"

She leaned into his embrace. *Mo stór.* My darling. Hearing those words sent a tremor through her chest, one that set her lungs seizing again. One cough after another shook her entire frame.

Ryan held her closer. He rested his cheek against hers. "Tell me what you need, dear."

She managed enough air to say, "Hold me."

"For as long as you'd like, whenever you'd like."

If she'd harbored any doubts that he cared for her, that his feelings were of a truly tender nature, that sentence, that promise, put them all to rest. How hard she'd tried to keep her distance from him. How firmly she'd tapped down her feelings for him. Yet, in that moment, pure gratitude filled her. Fate hadn't allowed her to push away the gift of his kindness, his affection, his strength . . . his love.

The comfort he offered soothed her. She found she could breathe a bit easier. Her cough calmed as well. It would return; she knew that well enough. But in the moment, her lungs were calm.

Out of the corner of her eye, she could see the bare floor. "Where's Aidan's blanket? It's usually right there."

"Mrs. O'Connor and Dr. Jones thought it best he slept elsewhere. He'd rest better, and tending to you would be simpler." Ryan rubbed her back, continuing to offer his support. "Ma would hear of nothing other than him staying with us in the loft where he slept before. He's been a great help around the place and hasn't missed school. He's begun calling Ma *Granny Callaghan*, which pleases her to no end. James hasn't brought his little one to see her as she'd assumed he would, which breaks her heart."

"He is causing pain to someone he loves, someone who loves him. He ought not do that."

"No, he ought not."

She leaned back a bit and looked up into his deep blue eyes. "You know that I am not going to get better. The valley fever will clear, but my lungs were not healthy before this. They won't ever be again."

He brushed a hand along her cheek. "And you are worried about causing me pain, and feeling that you 'ought not do that.'"

"I know what it is to lose someone you love," she said.

"I am fully aware of what you're facing, dear. And I am still here. I've *chosen* to be."

Those words offered more comfort than he likely realized. "You did promise to hold me."

"I stand by that promise, and every other one I will make to you."

She closed her eyes once more and rested in his embrace. She would accept the comfort he offered. Once Dr. Jones gave them a better understanding of the time she had left, they could address the matter of what Ryan could take on, how much she was willing to ask of him, and what that meant for their future together.

"Have you eaten?" he asked.

"I had a bit of tea."

"You need your strength. That'll require more than tea." He shifted so she was at his side, his arm still holding her close. "What sounds appetizing? I'll search it out."

He led her back into the kitchen. Mrs. O'Connor was at the stove, stirring the pot of stew. Her stomach rumbled a bit.

Ryan must have heard; he chuckled. "I believe that is a yes to whatever your mother-in-law is cooking up."

Mrs. O'Connor looked back at them. "Are you hungry, then, Maura? Biddy's dropping soda bread at Cecily's and bringing the rest here."

"That does sound nice." She sat at the table.

Ryan bent and kissed her cheek. "I've a bit of work to do back at the house. The O'Connor ladies'll look after you, I'm certain of it."

She sighed. "I so dislike being helpless like this."

"You'll be better soon enough."

"From *this*," she reminded him. "There will be many difficult days, many worse than what I'm passing through now."

"And I will be here for them, too," he said. "No matter that you try very hard to convince me that I don't want to be, I will always be here, Maura. Always."

Chapter Forty-one

How did one go about convincing a stubborn, independent woman that loving her, through every difficulty and obstacle, was an honor, not a burden? The tragedies of life had taught Maura to assume she hadn't the right to be anything but the giver in every relationship. Ryan didn't know how to show her otherwise.

"Telling her how I feel hasn't changed her view of things," Ryan said to his ma late Saturday afternoon. A fortnight had passed since he'd returned to Hope Springs, two weeks of worrying and hoping, of working and praying. The last few days of that had been spent attempting to convince Maura to trust his declarations of commitment. "Continually doing those things I am pleased to do for her hasn't convinced her either."

"She's afraid," Ma said. "Fear isn't washed away with words, and it doesn't succumb easily to proof, either."

"Then what do I do? I know she cares for me; I firmly suspect she loves me as much as I love her. But so long as she thinks she's a burden, she'll keep a distance between us. I can't build a future with someone who insists on staying far away."

"She's closer than you think, son. The hesitancy I've noticed in her recently is nothing compared to the rebuffings you received early on. She's learning to accept that she needs help; and she will have to learn to trust that her uncertain future is not a burden too heavy to be sustained by your love of her."

"It isn't."

Ma smiled. "I know that, and you know that. She will have to see it for herself."

"You are telling me to be patient?"

"A woman who has loved and lost will be cautious before opening herself up to the possibility of that sort of pain again."

That wasn't quite what they'd been talking over before. "She's hesitant because she doesn't want *me* to be hurt. That is the argument she always offers."

"Yes, but she's protecting her own heart as well. There is risk in loving a widow, and not only to the one who loves her."

"Is that why you never remarried or undertook a courtship after Da died?" He winced a bit. "That might be too personal a question."

"I relate to your Maura more than I would have admitted when she first arrived. I, too, was a young widow, with deteriorating health, an uncertain future, and children to raise. Though I was often painfully lonely, I could not bring myself to even think of opening my heart to someone new. Now, I often wish I had."

He took her hand, careful of her aching joints. "Have you been unhappy?"

"Not in the least," she said with full confidence. "But a heart longs for love. I never permitted mine to seek it again."

"Perhaps you could convince Maura not to tread that same path."

Ma smiled. "Oh, sweet boy, of the two of us, *I* am not the one most likely to turn her heart in that direction."

A quick knock sounded at the door. They weren't expecting anyone. Ryan stood and crossed the room. He pulled open the door. He'd have been shocked at seeing Maura there even if he hadn't just been talking about her.

"Good heavens, woman. Did you walk all this way? You'll put yourself on your death bed."

"Dr. Jones said I was well enough to go to the *ceílí* today, but I wasn't going to because I'm still a little tired. But then I started thinking about everyone there enjoying themselves, and I really wanted to go." Emotion began building behind her voice. "So I decided I would go after all, but everyone had already left. I started walking, but I am so tired." Her voice shook. "I can't go any farther."

"Darling." He pulled her inside and into his arms.

"I was afraid you would have left already." She didn't pull out of his embrace. "I was foolish to try to walk all that way."

He'd learned over the weeks that Maura grew more emotionally raw when she was tired. That she was crying in his arms again, so soon after having done so before, spoke volumes of the depth of her exhaustion.

"My brother is dropping his wife and children at the *ceílí* and then coming here to fetch Ma and me. If you're still feeling up to going, you're welcome to ride along."

She nodded. "I would like that." Her arms slid around him even as she tucked her head more tenderly against him. "Aidan went early with Ciara and Keefe. Seems his Granny O'Connor had hoped he'd help with a few things. He has certainly found his place among his family."

She made no move to pull away from him. He dared not release her enough to even close the door. He sensed she needed this embrace even more than she was letting on. Her one request upon fully wakening from her fever was for him to hold her, and he was determined to do so.

"Your lad has made his way into all our hearts," Ma said from her rocker near the fireplace. "He's a dear boy."

Outside, James pulled his wagon up to the front porch. He hopped down and tied the reins to a post. Ryan watched him approach, bracing himself against any words of censure he might receive for this current display of affection.

James eyed them, but didn't comment. He turned, instead, to Ma. "I'm ready when you are."

"We're taking Maura as well," Ma said. "There's room and plenty."

James nodded. "I've no objections." That was unexpected, but welcome.

Ryan slid his hands down Maura's arms and took her hands in his. "I'll just fetch m' coat and we'll be off."

She nodded.

He stepped away, moving swiftly to his room. Behind him, James spoke again, but not to Ma.

"We'd heard you were ill, Maura."

"I have been," she answered. "But the doctor says I am well on the mend."

Ryan could hear them still as he stepped into his room.

"I still can't believe Ryan Nothing-gets-in-the-way-of-my-planned-future Callaghan spent his wagon and hay barn money on bringing a doctor here. My brother never sacrifices his plans for anyone."

He'd not told Maura about that. She'd be shocked, maybe even upset. Ryan snatched his coat from its nail, fully intending to march back out and attempt to salvage the situation. He'd not taken a single step from his room before Maura answered James.

"How is it you are his brother and you understand him so little? 'Never sacrifices his plans for anyone.' Do you truly intend to accuse him of that, when he has sacrificed his worked-for future for *you*? He gave up his claim to a house he helped build, and a land he helped pay for, because *your* family needed them. He sacrificed them for you and *your* family."

Ryan stepped into the room, where Ma was watching Maura with wide eyes. James looked even more taken aback.

"He accepted the loss of all he had invested there. He adjusted all of his plans and made new ones, working for years to claim *this* house and land. And then my boy and I came and threatened them. But did he fight us tooth-and-nail, letting nothing get in the way of what he wanted, willing to tear *us* apart in pursuit of his goals? Of course not, because that is not who he is." She emphasized the last with such force she plunged herself into another coughing fit.

Ryan moved swiftly to her side as she struggled to settle her breathing. He gently rubbed her back. She pulled in one breath after another, each calmer than the last. But her glare never left James. Watching him, Ryan saw something he hadn't since they were boys: James looked humbled.

"And he took his hay mower up and down this road," Maura went on, "cutting hay for his neighbors *and* for you, saving you precious effort but costing him time to bring in his own. I've my doubts you ever thanked him, as I helped deliver your child and you never thanked me for that."

At that revelation, tension spread through Ryan. Maura had been done-in by her efforts as midwife for Ennis, and she'd not even been thanked?

"And now," Maura continued through wheezing breaths, "he's brought a doctor to Hope Springs, despite not needing one himself, and you belittle him for the act of generosity. Perhaps instead of disparaging his character, you should be grateful, and you shouldn't begrudge him the occasional use of your wagon no matter that he paid for half of it."

James dropped his gaze to the tip of his boot.

She coughed hard, her body shaking with it.

Ryan pressed a kiss to her temple and whispered, "Save your breath, *mo stór.*"

She raised her chin, mouth pulled in a straight line as she continued glaring James into an early grave. She, apparently, was not finished. "And your ma lives but a short drive down the road, yet when have you come to visit? How often do you bring her grandchildren 'round to see her? My lad lived years without his grandparents near enough for giving him the kind of love grandparents offer. I'd've given near anything to change that sooner. You speak of Ryan as turning his back on people in pursuit of his own selfish ends. Yet he's never forgotten about his ma. Or his neighbors. Or anyone else who needs his help."

Ma stood, her movements slow and painstaking. She moved to James's side and tapped his chin upward, making him meet her eye. "You look after your wife and your wee ones, and I'm proud of you for that."

"But I pushed you two off the land," he said quietly. "I could see it happening, but I didn't know what else to do."

That admission was one Ryan had never figured on hearing in all his life. Maura, with her unwavering firmness, had forced James to face the reality he had denied for five years.

"Life did that," Ma said. "But we've a chance now to move forward with things set right. You've a home and land. Ryan has a home and land,

and room enough for me. You two needn't come to scrapes over the way the past years played out any longer."

"I should've—" James's gaze dropped once more. "Ennis and I should've tried harder."

"Marriage is difficult enough early on without juggling a household so filled with people." Ma slipped her arm through James's. "Now that we've each a space of our own, we'll find that balance we've been chasing."

She walked out with James, leaving Maura and Ryan to linger a moment behind.

"A man couldn't ask for a fiercer defender than you," he said.

"Your brother oughtn't've said what he did about you. It isn't true."

Ryan lowered his arm so it rested about her waist. "His assessment used to be far closer to true. When you first arrived, and I realized you and Aidan might very well have claim to this land, I spent a lot of days pondering how to best you, how to push you out of the running."

"But you never did." She looked at him, a gentle smile on her face. "That is the point. You could have made a firm, and truthful, and *powerful* argument against our suitability, but you didn't. You're a good man, Ryan Callaghan."

"How do I convince *you* of that?"

"I'm the one who just said—"

"You said to James what I have been wishing you would believe yourself." How could he make her understand? "I don't turn my back on people, Maura, especially those I care about. Especially those I love. Not because I feel obligated or because I haven't sorted out how to shed myself of the 'burden' of them." He raised one of her hands to his lips and kissed it. "Because it is who I am, and it is how I love."

She held fast to his hand.

"When I tell you, Maura, that I mean to be at your side no matter what lies down the road, and when I tell you that walking that path with you is not a burden, I want you to—I *need* you to believe me."

Maura slipped her hand free of his and gently touched his face. "You will be required to give so much. What do I have to offer in return?"

He pulled her close. "You can hold me."

One corner of Maura's mouth tipped upward. "I've asked you for that a few times."

"And I rather like that you do." Ryan rested his forehead against hers. "Build a life with me, Maura, no matter what that looks like or how long we have. That is what I wish for most; that is what you have to offer me. It is the reason that purchasing a wagon and building the hay barns didn't matter one bit once I met Dr. Jones. He could give you better health and less suffering; he could give you time."

"He could give *us* time." She could not have responded in a way that brought him greater reassurance.

"Us," he repeated.

"*Us* ought to join your brother and ma at the wagon, or we're likely to be left behind."

He kissed the tip of her nose. "It's a very good thing I like headstrong women."

She smiled up at him. "A very good thing, indeed."

He felt a mere breath away from convincing her that their love and commitment to each other's happiness was reason enough to move forward, to plan a future even knowing they would have to adjust as life changed.

Chapter Forty-two

The musicians looked cold. Maura had heard this was likely to be the last *ceílí* of the year. Weather always determined when the parties ceased for the season, and it was already very nearly too cold for anyone to enjoy themselves. Yet, somehow everyone managed to find delight in the gathering. This was a happy town; she loved that about Hope Springs.

Maura sat flanked by Katie and Biddy on one side, Mrs. O'Connor and Mrs. Callaghan on the other. Little Sean Archer, bundled in a thick quilt, lay in his mother's arms.

"Well, we've reached the end of another harvest," Mrs. O'Connor said. "Astounding how fast the years fly."

"Indeed," Mrs. Callaghan agreed.

"I suspect everyone knows we're likely done with the *ceílis* this year," Katie said. "The dancing'll be quite enthusiastic, and the tales even taller than usual. Should be a fine evening."

"I brought Aidan here to give him a connection to his family, but I cannot tell you how grateful I am that he has also been given a connection to his heritage. And it's rather beautiful the way these weekly parties combine the sounds and tastes and tales of home with those from America."

Biddy nodded her agreement. "There is some comfort in knowing the young people will keep their connection to Ireland even if it will never be home to them."

Mrs. O'Connor took a slow, slightly shaky breath. "How I wish Finbarr would come back to the *ceilis*. I fear he's losing more than his connection to Ireland."

"We must have hope," Katie said. "He will find his way."

Maura turned to her mother-in-law. "And I believe Patrick will as well."

"I hope you're right," Mrs. O'Connor said. "Both of you. I dearly love those lads of mine, but life certainly has not been easy for any of them."

"And you have lost one," Maura acknowledged. "I would not wish you to lose another."

"I am determined not to."

The musicians being between tunes, Seamus Kelly called out over the crowd. "We have a special treat tonight, friends."

Someone shouted their guess. "A song for the doctor?"

Seamus shook his head. "He didn't come this evening."

"Wise man," was the cheeky response.

Seamus ignored that comment. "As you well know, we've sadly had but one piper these past years. For our unenlightened American friends, 'tis a tragedy, that. Having more than one piper means we never go without pipes, and if there's one thing a *ceili* should never be without, it's pipes."

The mention of pipes had Maura paying very close attention.

"My friends," Seamus said, "we've the beginnings of another piper among us. I'm told he's been studying the instrument only a couple of months, but he can play a tune or two and means to make his debut here tonight."

Applause and cheers accompanied the announcement. Maura held her breath. She'd not heard a word about Ryan teaching Aidan to play the pipes, though he'd said he would months earlier. She'd assumed they'd simply not found the time to do so.

Yet there the two of them stood, in the midst of the musicians, transferring the pastoral pipes from Ryan to Aidan, unheard words being exchanged between them. Ryan likely offered a few reminders and a good bit of encouragement. He chucked Aidan under the chin and gave him a quick nod.

"What do you mean to play, lad?" Seamus asked.

Aidan took a breath so deep his chest expanded with it, then collapsed as he pushed it forcefully out. His coloring had dropped off more than a bit. His mouth hung the tiniest bit slack. Maura clasped her hands together and raised them to her lips, uttering a silent prayer for her boy. Ryan set a hand on his shoulder but let Aidan speak for himself.

"I'm going to play 'The Road to Lisdoonvarna.' I'm going to try, anyway."

The musicians immediately began conferring. After a moment, Thomas Dempsey stepped out from among them.

"I'll play with you, Aidan. I know this one well."

Aidan pushed out a breath. "I'm not very good at it yet. And I'm not fast."

Thomas just smiled. "You begin playin'. I'll follow."

Ryan stepped back, letting Aidan have his moment. Aidan pumped the bellows beneath his right arm, the familiar drone emerging. He met Thomas's eye, but didn't begin playing yet.

"Get on with ya, lad," one of the musicians called out.

"Cain't be any worse than Ryan's playing," one of the American musicians added, earning a laugh from the others.

Maura hadn't thought of this benefit; not only was he learning to play an instrument, but he was also gaining a place in the town band, with support from the more experienced musicians, and kinship with the younger ones just now learning to take their place amongst the others.

"Whenever you're ready," Thomas said, his tone quiet and encouraging.

Aidan set his fingers on the holes in the chanter. He began pressing the air from the pipe bladder, and that oh-so-familiar sound of Irish pipes filled the gathering. His fingers moved about, and the tune, slower than usual, but well played, emerged. After a moment, Thomas joined in, not taking over the lead spot in the tune, but, with a few trills and flits, expanding the sound of the song in a way that gave Aidan's efforts a bit of polish.

Maura's gaze flicked to Ryan just as he looked over at her. She could not entirely keep back the tears of delight that sprang. Ryan smiled broadly, returning his gaze to Aidan. The song wasn't long; Aidan was, after all, not playing for dancers, nor participating in a number featuring all the musicians. But when he finished, enthusiastic cheers met his efforts.

Aidan blushed, but he also smiled. His attention turned immediately to Ryan, who stood mere steps away, applauding loudly. Unmistakable pride filled Ryan's expression.

"I think Ryan likes our Aidan," Mrs. O'Connor said.

Mrs. Callaghan corrected the observation. "He *loves* that boy. He truly does."

Maura turned to Ryan's mother. "I didn't realize they'd been undertaking lessons. 'Twas mentioned ages ago, but nothing seemed to have come of it."

"Ryan's enjoyed teaching the lad to play. The pipes have brought him a great deal of joy in his life. Watching him pass on the music he loves has done my heart a world of good, and I believe it's done his good, as well."

"And mine," Maura added. "I've a love for the pipes myself. And for that boy."

"What about Ryan?" Katie said. "Do you love him too?"

Maura turned wide eyes on her friend, who simply laughed.

"Everyone was thinking it," Katie insisted. "I am merely the one who said it."

"Our situation is not so straightforward as mere declarations of love," Maura said quietly.

"Love doesn't exist only in simplicity," Mrs. O'Connor said. "It's not meant to emerge only after life has calmed and settled. Love offers strength *through* life's chaos and upheavals."

"And through doubts," Katie said. "Doubts nearly kept Joseph and me apart, and that would have been an utter tragedy."

"Words left unspoken nearly kept Ian and me apart," Biddy said.

Mrs. O'Connor chimed in as well. "And the very real complications of life nearly divided our Tavish and his sweet Cecily. I am fully convinced we would have lost him if they'd been kept apart. Theirs is so deep and abiding a connection that without her, he simply would have drifted away." She took Maura's hand, holding her gaze with determination. "I see the same with you and Ryan. When the two of you are together, you both look lighter and less burdened. There's a support you receive from each other that no one else in this ol' world seems able to give. To lose that would be a tragedy, Maura. Do not wait for life to give you permission to love. Let love give you permission to live."

Maura blinked a few times. These past weeks, her emotions were so near the surface all the time. "I've spent so much of the past decade just trying to survive. I'm not certain I remember how to 'live.'"

Mrs. O'Connor motioned toward the musicians. "I see someone coming this way who can probably help you sort that out."

Ryan arrived in front of her only a moment later. He smiled, as he always did. "Our Aidan's quite a lad, isn't he? Took to the pipes like nothing I've ever seen."

"My da was a piper," she said.

"As are you," he said, "though I've yet to hear you play."

Survival hadn't allowed for such unnecessary pursuits. "Perhaps it's time I tried again."

"Truly?" He sounded genuinely excited.

"I doubt anything I played would be worth listening to," she warned him. "It's been many years."

"I guess that means you'd have to come by often to practice." His was a flirtatious smile. He offered his hand. She took it, and he helped her to her feet. He tucked her arm through his. "Pardon us, ladies," he said. "I'm going to take a turn about the *ceílí* with this lovely colleen."

She rested her head against his shoulder as they walked away.

"Do you really mean to play the pipes again?" Ryan asked.

"I've decided it's time to start *living* again, to start finding joy in the life I've been given."

His arm slipped free of hers and encircled her waist. "Do I get to be part of that life?"

She turned and pressed a kiss to his jaw. "If you'd like to be."

He tugged her closer. "With all my heart."

Chapter Forty-three

Ryan sat in his favorite spot out in the fields. The river ran slowly. A cold breeze blew. Winter had brought an end to the *ceílís*; two weeks had passed since the final one of the year. Not far distant, children rushed out of the schoolhouse for their daily lunch. Soon it'd be too cold for any of them to be out of doors for very long. He'd miss laughing at the games they played and witnessing the sheer joy they tossed into every moment.

Across the way, the older children were playing a game of rounders. Ryan hadn't played the game in ages. Aidan stood waiting his turn to bat. He looked away from the game for just a moment, spotting Ryan. He waved.

Warmth bubbled inside. This was a moment Ryan had imagined so many times. A child of his—for Aidan felt as much like a son as he could imagine—waving, connecting with him while they were apart.

Ryan raised his arm and waved back, smiling. Aidan smiled as well. His attention quickly returned to his game, but he'd seen Ryan there. He'd been happy to see him. He'd reached out.

The quick moment between them meant more than Ryan could say.

Footsteps pulled his gaze from the river. He knew the red coat on the instant. *Maura.* A smile pulled at his lips. Did this stubborn woman have the least idea how much he loved her? How much he missed her when

347

she was away? How much he would give to have her with him every day of the rest of her life?

"Ryan Callaghan," she said as she approached. "I thought I might find you here."

He rose from his rock and walked toward her. "You know my secret spot, do you?"

"I've seen you here many a lunch hour."

He'd never spotted her at the school.

She smiled. "You're visible from the spot near the Archer's barn where I do the laundry."

"Ah." He was near enough to hug her, and he didn't hesitate to do so. "You're breathing better, love. Sets m' heart at ease."

She set her open palm on his chest. "I have something for you, something that'll set *my* heart at ease."

"Have you?" He wove his fingers together behind her back. "Is it that you and Aidan are coming for supper tonight? Because that'd be a fine thing."

She shook her head.

"Is it that you mean to join us for the next piping lesson?"

She shook her head again.

"Why not, dear? You said you'd enjoy playing again."

She turned a little in his arms, managing to slip out of his embrace and take hold of his hand in one fluid motion. "I've a surprise for you, and you can't see it from here. So you'd best come along."

"Yes, ma'am." He followed willingly, happily. "Do you mean to give me a hint, at least?"

"It's something I've been working on, that's taken some doing, but I'm so pleased everything's finally coming together."

He chuckled. "That's not very revealing."

She tossed a smile over her shoulder at him. "I never said I'd give *good* hints."

They walked past the house toward the east fields. The soddie was visible in the distance, as were, when Ryan looked more closely, a great many people. Near half the town must have been there. Long planks of wood were stacked nearby. Most people held various tools. All were watching their approach.

"What is this?" Ryan asked Maura.

"You'd hoped to build two hay sheds with your profits this year, but you brought Dr. Jones here instead." She held his hand between both of hers, watching him almost anxiously. "I've been asking, and I found enough people with bits and pieces of lumber and nails and shingles and such, that, by combining all of those bits, we gathered enough supplies to build the second hay shed. It'll not be fancy, and it likely won't be as large as you'd have liked, but it can be done."

His mind struggled to accept the enormity of what she was saying. "They're here to build a hay shed, with bits they donated?"

She nodded. "And they're doing so happily. Your neighbors love you, Ryan. They really do."

He looked out over the familiar faces, touched by their willingness to help him. He knew enough of their individual struggles to know that for some, providing even a single nail would be a sacrifice. "I don't want to burden them."

"'Tisn't a burden. Some who hadn't anything to donate are here to give their time and labor, just as you've done for so many of them."

Amazement rushed over him. "I'm going to have two hay sheds."

She grinned. "And you'll not have to worry about losing your crop."

"And you made this happen." He raised her hand to his lips. "Wonderful, darling Maura."

"This is what I have to offer you, Ryan. I haven't the strength, or likely the longevity, I wish I did, but I'm headstrong and determined, and I very much care what happens to you."

He enveloped her hand in both of his. "You offer far more than that, *mo stór*."

"But you'll accept the shed?"

"Oh, I will accept it."

He laughed, and so did she.

"Go greet your neighbors, Ryan. They're waiting for your instructions."

"Thank you, my dear," he whispered. He pressed a kiss to her cheek, then, mind still spinning with disbelief, walked to his gathered neighbors.

Soon the project was underway. A shed was not so complicated as a house, or even a barn. They'd have it up by suppertime. Were the shed construction undertaken in less cold weather, they'd likely have ended the effort with a small *ceílí*.

Maura kept the workers supplied with tea and coffee, pausing now and then to give him a smile or brief hug. Heavens, a man could get used to that.

In the midst of the efforts, Burke emerged.

"You've joined us," Ryan said, rather shocked. The doctor was seldom seen outside of his official capacity.

"Maura can be very persuasive," was the explanation. Nothing in his tone or posture spoke of displeasure.

"Her breathing sounds better," Ryan said. "And she has more energy."

Burke nodded. "She'll grow tired quickly for a while, but I believe the valley fever is beginning to lose its grip."

"What about the brown lung?" Ryan asked.

"I'll need to have a listen now that she's closer to her usual state. That'll give me a better idea."

Nervousness mingled with hope in Ryan's heart. "Perhaps after we're done here this evening. She can just stay here. That'd save you both a bit of a walk."

Burke agreed. "I'll plan on it."

The last of his neighbors, bundled against the dropping temperatures, made their way up the road. Ryan set his sights on the house. Maura had gone inside a quarter of an hour earlier to warm up and wait for when Burke intended to check her lungs.

Lanterns burned inside. Burke was likely there already, making his assessment.

Ryan set his shoulders and solidified his determination. No matter what answers they would get that day, he'd be at Maura's side. He'd offer his strength and support. She'd done the same for him. They were stronger together. Happier.

As he walked toward the house, he eyed the dark skies and faltered a moment. *Please don't take her from me yet. I've only just found her.*

He received no answer beyond the continued wind and bite in the air. Apparently, the heavens meant to make him wait for an answer.

He pulled open the door to the house and stepped inside. No need to search out Maura; she sat in the middle of the room on a chair. Burke was listening to her lungs with some kind of instrument. Aidan sat with Ma, watching the examination from within the comforting circle of her grandmotherly embrace.

Maura met Ryan's eye. She looked concerned. Worried. Had Burke said something already?

Be her strength.

Ryan pulled a chair to hers and took her hand. He watched the doctor, waiting.

After a long moment, Burke stepped back, slipping his instrument into his leather bag. He didn't say anything. His expression gave away nothing of his findings.

Maura twisted enough in her chair to look at the doctor. She kept her hand in Ryan's, holding fast to him.

The doctor clasped his bag, then faced her once more. "I agree with Dr. Dahl. It is brown lung."

She nodded silently. Across the room, Aidan paled.

"How long did you keep working in the factory after your symptoms first began?"

"A few months," Maura said. "I'd've seen Dr. Dahl sooner, but it took that long to save the money to have a doctor in."

Burke nodded. "The disease is usually present for a time before symptoms appear. You've likely had brown lung longer than you think."

Maura's brows pulled. She watched the doctor closely.

"Having said that, I'd place you in the earliest stages of the disease."

"That seems like good news," Ryan said hesitantly.

"Certainly better than the alternative." Burke was a difficult man to decipher. Ryan never could tell if he was worried or unconcerned, pleased or unhappy. "This is far from the terminal stage."

"What does that mean?" Aidan asked.

"*Terminal* means that death cannot be avoided," Burke said.

"Then she's not dying?" The poor lad looked desperate for, but terrified of, the answer.

Everyone watched the doctor with as much intensity as Aidan did.

"I cannot promise there'll be no deterioration," Burke said. "Brown lung is caused by the accumulation of bits of cotton or other milled material inside the lungs. That material can't come back out. It remains, irritating and inflaming the lungs. There's the possibility of more damage to come. Every cold you contract, every lung-related illness, will take a toll." He was looking at Maura again. "Yours are lungs that will age faster than they ought."

"How fast?" Her voice didn't shake. She faced this diagnosis with the fortitude Ryan had come to associate with her.

"Provided you don't contract any illness that, itself, damages the lungs—tuberculosis, whooping cough, something of that nature—you have every reason to anticipate many years yet. I wouldn't be at all surprised if you have another two decades remaining before the brown lung truly takes its full toll."

Maura's grip turned almost painful. Ryan hardly noted it, shocked as he was by Burke's pronouncement.

"Twenty years?" Maura pressed.

"I cannot *guarantee* that long, but I do not think it overly optimistic to plan for it."

Her breaths came sharper and quicker. "Why did Dr. Dahl make so dire a pronouncement?"

"It's nearly impossible to tell what is permanent and what is irritation from the heavy air being breathed from day to day while you were still at the factory. But you've been here a few months, free of that bombardment. What is left, aside from any lingering valley fever, is the permanent damage. I can likely hear it more clearly than he could."

Maura closed her eyes. She whispered, "We left in time."

Aidan pulled away from Ma and rushed to Maura, tossing himself into her embrace. Ryan put his arms around both of them. Ma watched, a tear in her eye.

Burke took up his bag and gave a quick nod. "Let me know if you need anything else." With nothing more than that, not a word of parting or happiness at Maura's positive diagnosis, he stepped outside, pulling the door shut behind him.

Ryan didn't think the doctor was uncaring. He kept very much to himself, closed off. But he could have been the gruffest man on the face of the earth, and Ryan would still have been unspeakably grateful that he was in Hope Springs. He'd brought them reason to look ahead with optimism. He'd given Maura back her life.

After a time, Ma called Aidan over, insisting he help her set out supper.

Ryan and Maura remained near the fireplace. She stood in his embrace.

He hardly had words to describe all he felt in that moment: gratitude, hope, relief. "Thank the heavens I met Burke Jones at the depot mercantile. Bringing him here was a gift straight from above."

Maura hooked a finger over a button on his shirt, fiddling with it a bit absentmindedly. Her expression, however, was anything but casual. She met his gaze. Heavens, she was crying.

"Oh, Maura."

"We have time, Ryan. Years. Perhaps decades."

He brushed a tear away with the pad of his thumb. "Even if he had told you that you had mere days, *mo stór*, I'd have asked you to marry me tomorrow and spend those days together. What he said doesn't change what I want from the future; it simply changes the length of that future."

"You are braver than I," Maura said quietly.

"I know for a fact that is not true. *This* in particular worries and burdens you. Let me carry this burden. Then come next harvest, when worry over my hay weighs on me, you can help me carry that burden. And we'll both worry over Aidan and Ma and our neighbors."

"And we'll worry over each other?"

He shook his head. "We will *love* each other. That is my plan."

"That is one plan I hope you never adjust," she said.

He kissed her forehead tenderly. "Do you remember not long after you first came, when you asked if I believed in the old ways—fairies and superstitions and such?"

"You said you had a healthy respect for the possibility."

"There's one bit of the old ways I believe in entirely," he said. "Flickering moments of the second-sight."

She looked up at him, head tilted to the side, eyes wide and brows arched. "Do you have premonitions, Ryan?"

"I have, a few times in my life—nothing specific, no fortunetelling—simply an unshakable knowledge that m' life was about to change. The most recent was only a few months ago, just before you arrived. I couldn't say what was coming, only that it was important. I couldn't shake the feeling, couldn't explain it away. It grew and grew until that day in the barn when I first saw you."

"Truly?" she asked quietly.

"I knew in that moment that the change I'd been sensing . . . was you. And I knew that everything was going to be different. I just didn't know how."

A hint of guilt tugged at her features. "I brought such upheaval to your life."

"I feel that you brought me my life," he said. "You brought me depth and purpose I didn't realize I'd been missing. It was change, sure enough, but change of the very best kind."

"Have you any premonitions just now?" she asked.

"I don't need the second sight to sort out this next part," he answered. "It's clear enough." He took her hands and held them, looking deep into her eyes. "Maura O'Connor, will you build a home and a family with me? Will you let me be part of your life? Will you let me love you? And marry you?"

"Every year I have left is yours," she said.

"Ours," he answered.

"*Ours*," she repeated in a whisper.

She raised herself on her toes a bit. She set her hands on either side of his face and kissed him, softly and lingeringly. He held her close to him.

"I love you," she said against his lips.

"And I love you."

Life had given them a new start and a second chance.

He didn't mean to waste a single moment.

Chapter Forty-four

The ceremony was a brief one but well attended and universally celebrated. Maura knew much of the delight was for Ryan, who had quietly done so much for his neighbors, but she felt certain a good deal of the happiness was on her account as well. She'd come to Hope Springs utterly unsure of her place or her welcome. She'd found the family she'd missed these past ten years, who loved her and accepted her. She'd found home.

The weather had turned too cold for a large celebration, there being no building in town large enough to hold everyone. Instead, she and Ryan made their way to Mr. and Mrs. O'Connor's house for a small family lunch and celebration.

James had offered Ryan the use of his wagon for the occasion, something he did with increasing frequency. He also interacted with his brother with far less resentment than in previous months—or, Maura suspected, *years*. Indeed, the two brothers had even enjoyed a pleasant couple of visits. Maura held out some hope that they would, in time, be reconciled.

She and Ryan had been the last to leave the chapel, having remained behind, receiving particular well-wishes from the preacher and his wife.

Now, as they rolled down the road, Maura rested her head against his shoulder.

"Are you happy then, love?" Ryan asked.

"Blissfully."

He smiled at her briefly before retuning his gaze to the road. "I do like that answer."

"And you are happy as well?"

He leaned his head toward her. "Beyond words."

Minutes later they stepped into the senior O'Connors' home to a warm family welcome. Music filled the room. The aroma of a dozen different dishes set Maura's stomach rumbling. She held to Ryan's hand as they wove though the gathering, receiving embraces and well-wishes.

They were soon situated in adjacent chairs, plates of food balanced on their laps.

Mr. O'Connor called the family to attention. "What a blessed day this has been." He turned to her. Beneath his smile was a tenderness that touched her deeply. "And Maura, we're so very happy for you. Having you among us again—you and Aidan—is a joy we never thought we'd know. We thank you for trusting us enough to take the chance on coming and starting a new life here. We don't take that trust lightly."

"And we're right pleased to welcome Ryan to the family," Mrs. O'Connor said. "You're most welcome, lad. Most welcome."

"I'm pleased to be considered one of you," he said. "I've not yet met an O'Connor I didn't like."

"Except Tavish," Ian tossed in.

"You can't talk that way about me anymore," Tavish said. "I'm a father now."

"I've been a father for years, but that didn't change the way you talked about me."

Tavish shrugged. "Turns out, you're not worth talking about."

Ian laughed and gave his brother a shove.

"Speaking of things unsaid," Mary jumped in, "have you decided on a name for the wee one? It's been weeks."

Cecily sat in the rocker, her son in her arms. "We have. Matthew, after my father. And Grady, after his uncle."

Ryan squeezed Maura's shoulders and pressed a kiss to her temple.

"Matthew Grady O'Connor," Mary said. "A fine name, that."

"Fine, indeed," Mrs. O'Connor declared.

Embraces were exchanged along with quite a bit of teasing. The O'Connors were an inarguably happy family.

Ryan set his plate on a small table nearby, then tucked her up against him.

She rested her head on his shoulder. "This is quite a family to have joined, isn't it?"

"It is, at that."

She adjusted, so she sat more comfortably in his arms. "And it is further a fine thing that your ma was already a grandmother to Aidan. He'll be surrounded by family."

"*You* will be surrounded by family as well, my dear," he said. "You won't ever have to face this life alone again."

She twisted enough to brush a kiss to his cheek. A corner of his mouth quirked upward, an endearing sight, one that set her heart pattering a bit.

Aidan slipped over to them. "Is it time for your surprise, Ma? I can bring it over."

"You've a surprise?" Ryan eyed her with curiosity.

"For you, in fact." She'd been looking forward to this.

A smile twinkled in his eyes. "Your last surprise was a hay shed. I'm full dying of curiosity to see how our Aidan's meaning to bring a hay shed over."

Our Aidan. What a heaven-sent blessing this man was.

She nodded to Aidan, who slipped out of sight. "He's been my partner in crime for weeks now. I'm a little alarmed at how much he has enjoyed stealing things from you."

Ryan's eyes opened wide, pulling a laugh from her. Aidan returned in the next moment, Ryan's canvas bag in his hands.

"My pipes?" His brows pulled low. An instant later, they shot upward. He'd solved the mystery.

She pulled the pipes from the bag and carefully positioned the instrument. Smiles touched faces all around the room. She pumped the bellows and set her fingers on the chanter, beginning the slow strains of "The Minstrel Boy." Her ability didn't come close to Ryan's, but she'd found over the previous weeks that she'd regained much of her skill despite the passage of so many years. She'd practiced again and again over the past weeks, wanting this moment to be special, He had so often said he wished to hear her play. He didn't look the least disappointed.

The O'Connors cheered when her song came to an end. Ryan kissed her. Aidan grinned.

"Seems we've *three* pipers in town," Mr. O'Connor said. "Three in one family."

"*Family*," Ryan said. "I do like the sound of that."

"As do I," Maura answered.

Aidan returned the pipes to their bag, apologizing with a smile for stealing them.

"Any time your ma wants the pipes, you go get them for her," Ryan insisted.

"I must not have been too terrible," Maura said.

"You never cease to amaze me, my Maura."

She sat in his embrace as the afternoon wore on, watching the family, enjoying their tales and their music and the love they exuded. Coming to Hope Springs had been the right decision. Aidan was joyous. Her health was improved.

Most of all, she had Ryan.

She closed her eyes and let the sound of happiness sweep over her. The warmth of his embrace offered comfort and reassurance and affection she had longed for these past ten years. There had been moments when she'd wondered if the heavens even remembered her. They had, it seemed, simply been waiting for the right moment to bring her and Ryan into each other's lives.

His beloved voice whispered in her ear. "Do you need to go rest, love? It has been a very busy day."

Between the disease in her lungs and the remaining impact of her bout with valley fever, she did grow worn more easily than she'd like. Today was no exception. "I likely should."

Without hesitation, embarrassment, or apology, Ryan simply stood, announced to the room that Maura was asleep on her feet and needed to rest before her health was affected. The family grew immediately felicitous. Her coat was fetched, along with a quilt, for good measure. Ryan was sternly charged with looking after her. They were given a basket of food to take home, instructions to send word if anything was needed, and ushered out of the house to a chorus of well-wishes.

Ryan handed her up onto the wagon bench and tucked the quilt across her legs, the food basket set securely in the wagon bed. They waved farewell to the family—Aidan included, as he and Mrs. Callaghan had been invited to stay with Mr. and Mrs. O'Connor for a few days— and Ryan led the team to the road.

She tucked herself against him. Heavens, she loved having him near, unfailing in his support and love. "You executed an expert departure just now."

His body shook with a chuckle. "I knew nothing short of a firm declaration would see us out of there with any degree of haste. I needed only tell them your health depended on it."

"Which nearly sent them into a panic," she pointed out.

"If they ever grow suffocating in their solicitousness, you let me know, *mo stór*," Ryan said.

"I will," she said. "But, to be perfectly honest, there's something comforting in knowing they love me enough to worry."

They rumbled down the road, reaching the edge of their—*their*— east fields. The hay shed that the town had built was visible from the road. A heartwarming testament to their place among the people in this tiny corner of the world.

"I've been giving thought to my work at Archers," she said.

"I meant it when I said I'll support you in whatever you choose to do on that score."

She stretched enough to press a kiss to his cheek. "I know, love. I don't doubt you."

"Have you made a decision, then?"

She nodded. "I'd like to stay on. If we put the money I'm paid aside,

I'd soon have enough to send for Eliza and her little girl. And I'm hopeful I can convince Katie and Joseph to let Eliza take my place. She's a good worker and a dear person. They'd be happy to have her."

"And *you* would be happy to have her here," Ryan said.

"Very happy," Maura said. "She's like a sister to me. I've missed her dearly."

Ryan nodded firmly. "We'll do all we can to get our sister Eliza here."

Our sister. How readily and fully he cared for the people who mattered to her.

"I love you, Ryan Callaghan. I love your good heart."

"That is a very good thing; otherwise this new arrangement of ours would be terribly awkward."

She laughed and slipped her arm through his. "And you've not had any worrisome premonitions about this new journey of ours?"

"None whatsoever. Indeed, I've come to realize my last bit of second-sight wasn't a warning of bad things to come but a promise of the very best sort of change."

She set her head on his shoulder. "Are you glad, then, that we came and disrupted all your plans?"

"More than I have words to say."

They pulled off the road and up the drive. Ryan brought the wagon to a stop but didn't hop down immediately. His eyes were on the house. He didn't say anything, but his smile had turned . . . not sad, but something like nostalgic or wistful.

"What is it?"

"I was only thinking of all the times these past months that I stood at the barn, looking up at this house, and racking my brain, trying to decide what to do about you."

"About me?"

He smiled at her. "You'd a claim on the house I couldn't deny. I couldn't bear the thought of trying to toss you out, yet—" He shook his head, as if unsure what words came next.

"Yet you loved this house and land, and couldn't simply give up your claim, either."

He nodded. "The answer to our difficulties then seems so obvious now."

"We had to find our way there, though," she said. "We had to make that journey."

"'Twas a long journey home, wasn't it?"

"Long and lovely and worth every twist and turn in the road."

"And now we get to journey together." He spoke with real pleasure and happiness.

He stepped down from the wagon and crossed to her side. She took the hand he offered and stepped down herself. He tucked the quilt around her shoulders, making certain it was secure.

She kept nearby as he unhitched the horse. Though the air was cold, she wanted to be with him. He looked over at her a few times, his smile soft, his gaze warm.

"You could've gone inside," he said as he led the horse to its stall. "You'd not be out here freezing."

"I'd also not be out here with you. I'd not like that one bit."

He closed the stall door, then held out his hand to her. She took it, grateful for the reassurance she always found in his touch and the strength she felt in his company. They walked together out of the barn and to the front porch.

They paused at the door. He turned and faced her, locking his arms behind her back. "I love you, Maura."

She leaned into his embrace and stretched on her toes. She kissed him quickly, gently. "I love you," she said against his lips.

His lips pressed to hers fervently even as his arms pulled her flush with him. He rained kisses along her jaw to the sensitive spot beneath her ear. "My darling, darling Maura."

"My wonderful Ryan."

He kept her in his arms on the front porch, his forehead pressed to hers. "Welcome home, sweetheart. Our home."

"Our home," she repeated. "Our lives. Our future."

Acknowledgments

- The Bradford Industrial Museum, for valuable information regarding the textile mills of the 19th Century
- Dr Solis Cohen's 1872 book on the diseases of the throat and lungs
- Pam Victorio, for encouraging me to continue this series that I love so deeply & celebrating with me its continuation
- Heather Moore, for making this book possible
- Annette Lyon, for making this book worlds better than I could ever have made it on my own
- Nancy Peterson, for lending her voice, her talent, and her expertise to the beautiful audio version of this tale
- My family, for supporting me and encouraging me

About the Author

Photograph © Annalisa Rosenvall

SARAH M. EDEN is the *USA Today* bestselling author of multiple historical romances, including the "IndieFab Book of the Year" and Whitney Award winning *Hope Springs* series. Combining her obsession with history and affinity for tender love stories, Sarah loves crafting witty characters and heartfelt stories set against rich historical backdrops. Sarah is represented by Pam Victorio at D4EO Literary Agency.

Visit Sarah at www.sarahmeden.com

CPSIA information can be obtained
at www.ICGtesting.com
Printed in the USA
LVHW01s2338190918
590748LV00001B/95/P